Journal

of an

Unknown Opera Singer

SUSANNA JAMES

Note for Librarians: A cataloguing record for this book is available from Library and Archives Canada at www.collectionscanada.ca/amicus/index-e.html
ISBN 1-4120-5560-1

Printed in Victoria, BC, Canada. Printed on paper with minimum 30% recycled fibre. Trafford's print shop runs on "green energy" from solar, wind and other environmentally-friendly power sources.

TRAFFORD™
PUBLISHING

Offices in Canada, USA, Ireland and UK
This book was published *on-demand* in cooperation with Trafford Publishing. On-demand publishing is a unique process and service of making a book available for retail sale to the public taking advantage of on-demand manufacturing and Internet marketing. On-demand publishing includes promotions, retail sales, manufacturing, order fulfilment, accounting and collecting royalties on behalf of the author.

Book sales for North America and international:
Trafford Publishing, 6E–2333 Government St.,
Victoria, BC v8t 4p4 CANADA
phone 250 383 6864 (toll-free 1 888 232 4444)
fax 250 383 6804; email to orders@trafford.com
Book sales in Europe:
Trafford Publishing (uk) Limited, 9 Park End Street, 2nd Floor
Oxford, UK oxi 1hh UNITED KINGDOM
phone 44 (0)1865 722 113 (local rate 0845 230 9601)
facsimile 44 (0)1865 722 868; info.uk@trafford.com
Order online at:
trafford.com/05-0458

10 9 8 7 6 5 4 3

The most important function of art and science is to awaken the cosmic religious feeling, and keep it alive.

ALBERT EINSTEIN

So music sprung a bridge between the worlds,
Controlled his ruby harmony like a horse.
Too wild and fast without the sapphire spurs.
Cascading rhythm pulsed and shone through space,
Appeared and disappeared to leave its sacred trace.

TAMARISK

For all my musical friends, who have dedicated their lives to our wonderful art, and who have inspired me more than they could possibly know.

Preface

The story of Matilda is from the heart and pen of a singer. No one knows why singers need to sing, least of all singers, and one cannot pin-point the exact second that sound seduces the consciousness and sets about moulding the child. It certainly does not ask your permission! All you know is that well before puberty your heart, mind and soul have been apprenticed to the hardest Taskmaster in the world. Whether he responded to inborn inspiration or if he planted it himself, who can say? But strong, pitiless and very beguiling, he creates many beggars and some rich men. A few become famous but many more remain unknown and yet they all tread the same path.

We live in a vision-orientated world, and very beautiful it is too. But do we limit ourselves? Most people hear but do not listen. Also, the music gets lost in the search for theatrical effect. But beware the Taskmaster, he is more powerful than you think. (If indeed you think of him at all.)

Matilda, Carlo and Lothus are the same sliver of consciousness viewing the world through a different focus. This focus affording everything to be created there, including the time frame.

Other lives are surely not meant to set our paths in stone, and in some strange way their times live side by side because they are illuminated by music. The author has drawn on her own experiences and if anybody reading the following story recognises the company that provides the 'format' for the company which Matilda joins, as having been one of the greatest in the world, I will say just this. That it is out of great love and affection for a musical force that has invoked the Taskmaster and played the tune.

THE AUTHOR

ACT ONE

An End

TIME: 36,000 YEARS BC. PLACE: ATLANTIS

FROM THE JOURNAL OF ANTHORUS,
MASTER MUSICIAN AND PRIEST SCIENTIST

I had asked that they bring me another, younger this time and not yet bearded and they did. My trusted guards of the Temple, who do my bidding without question and who speak of my actions to no one. They rode out into the hills and found Lothus, and they tempted him to the town with a promise of lessons with the High Priestess of the Temple of Aum, the great Osiria. They hinted to him of glory and wealth that was only just out of his reach. The sort of wealth that such a shepherd boy might well dream of in the hills outside our city as he watched over his flock. Of course he could not resist, this shepherd boy, this peasant with voice. He could not wait to pull his tiny harp from his meagre belongings and accompany his rich singing that echoed and fell around one of our great halls that soft evening that they brought him to me.

But it was not for singing lessons that I had summoned him, but for another far greater purpose. I have long been searching for the combination that I now beheld. Such a sound as his, rising from a heart that has not been educated. And so many times before I had thought to have found it and I had begun in excited anticipation. But they all died. One after another in various attitudes of discomfort, one might even say, agony. The balance, do you see, was not right. They were insensitive, clod-like. Too much like the earth they worked, incapable of aligning themselves to the finer vibrations. And when I tried to achieve such an alignment, they could not survive. There is no loss from the deaths of such miserable creatures. No morbid songs need rise from our temples, for they are nothing and go unmourned.

But as my research continues I become alarmed. I believed that I heard something in the sound that first evening, but put it to one side as fancy, a whim, such as the light sometimes plays with the eyes. I can however, no longer ignore what is becoming so clear to me and now my whole work is challenged. I have, for some time, been attempting to plant in these simple people some small awakening, only to now discover that it already exists. It only awaits the right time for its blossoming.

In Lothus I can even measure the extent of the growth. And if it exists in him where else does it also reside? It is too much! I had planned, on completion of my research, and when all was safe, to allow only a slow introduction in a few chosen members of society, where I decided and where I knew I would always have some control. And now I find that my own work has been sabotaged by Nature herself. Whatever I decide later, I must immediately remove this arrogance of spirit from the shepherd boy.

Pray the gods that he is not aware of it, that he does not feel the strength it gives him. The inner voice that must shout at him in exhilarated passion of its own truth. That when he sings in his prison, as I know he does, he does not catch the glint in the harmonic. I must act quickly and instead of instilling, I must extract. Like a rotten tooth from its gum, I will pull the new pulsation and prevent a cancerous spread:

From the journal of Caperus,
assistant to the great master Anthorus

I have asked him before and now will I beg him. The tremors are coming more often and always stronger like a child demanding to be born. It is cruel beyond belief that the boy be caged beneath the Temple and alone at any time, but with the earth beneath us shuddering it is nothing short of inhuman. How must he suffer? And, it is not as if he would make immediately for the hills and his sheep if he had more liberty. I would be amazed were he to find the tiny village from which he was taken, never mind his long lost herd. No, he will remain without bars to ensure it. And so, I will take him to my own house. Julias I am certain will have no objection.

Anthorus is brilliant but so intent on his work that he seems to forget that he deals with human beings, that they belong to the same race as we do. I will persuade him to allow me to make a house guest of the shepherd boy. Lothus must be treated especially well before the final experiment. (May it please the gods that he will survive it.)

Meanwhile we make our secret plans for escape by sea when

the time comes as it surely will, and soon! Our ship will be large enough for all my household and I intend for there to be cabin space for Lothus.

LOTHUS THE SHEPHERD BOY AND PRISONER OF ANTHORUS

If only I could write! Never before have I wished such a thing. I mean, if man has a good brain what need has he for parchment and pen? But now, for the first time I admit to wishing that I could translate these thoughts to a scroll and leave it, to be found dusty and faded, so that some future race will know and understand what is happening to us, for something surely is!

Caperus and his wife have taken me to their home, a very large airy Villa close to the Temple and Halls of Knowledge. My room is so fine that I could never have dreamt of such a place. With its golden inlaid bed big enough for three people, or six lambs were they motherless some cold spring night, and the walls painted with pictures and strange symbols. Also, stretching along one side of the room, a window which lays the world at my feet with the gossiping and bartering beneath it, and the hills pulling away from the busy town. Up and away from the port and reminding me once more of my sheep and causing me to wonder how they fare without me.

Anthorus promises me lessons with Osiria! Lessons with the great High Priestess of Aum. But I still have not as yet either met or sung to her. Every day in my precious and scarce free time I take my harp and practise, and every day passes without any further comment on the subject. Meanwhile Anthorus has asked me to help him in some private work that he is engaged on . At first I was only too pleased to agree, but today we began and it was not pleasant. I do not understand what he wants of me. My mind races, I become unsure of where I am. Caperus assures me this will pass. He is with me in the workplace of Anthorus. But so are the Guards of the Temple and it is at them that I spit and curse as they hold me, against my will, on the slab while their Master works with the light. I do not like that light, it makes my head feel as if it will surely burst!

Today I kicked one guard so hard that he cried out. Anthorus shouted in frustration that he 'all but had me' whatever that may mean. And Caperus appeared to bite his lip and suggest that I had endured enough for one day. He then brought me home and himself laid me to bed.

People are becoming anxious of the tremors. Late this evening they were so bad that some small busts of heroes past, placed on plinths and lining the marble roads leading to the centre of the town, were thrown to the ground and crashed to pieces. Caperus has told me not to concern myself. He will, he promises, look after me.

FROM THE JOURNAL OF THANIUS: STUDENT AND STONE CUTTER TO ANTHORUS

Caperus is a fool. He accuses Anthorus of causing the earth tremors through some of his experiments. No, not those involving the boy and the other miserable ones before him, rotting in their cages in unspeakable filth, but those experiments he has worked over a long time. Using the sacred words of the gods he can cause the mountains to vibrate and to scatter their loose rocks and to pour boiling lava down their burning sides. It is a powerful sight!

And Caperus should be proud that he assists such greatness. But the idiot tries to convince Anthorus that what he does is wrong, and that this form of work is a misuse of the power that has been given to him.

Mind you, Anthorus's judgement sometimes leaves much to be desired. I have long held the hope that once his experiments are completed and the procedure safe I might benefit from the knowledge for use in the Temple. That he might endow me with something that even the great Osiria will not ignore. Oh how I tire of stone cutting! I would join the company of the Sacred Singers. Of this I dream at night and think of by day, almost to the exclusion of anything else. Of course as our student rank allows, Pheorus and I along with the others are allotted a few hours each week in the company of Osiria and her chosen Singers. But this is nothing, what can I prove to her here? To witness the pure fullness of her sound and try to emulate it? This too is denied me, for I cannot ask her questions I am treated as one of the chorus backing the Sacred Singers and am graced with little more than a brief greeting, and a nod when the scant, magical time is gone. I have no chance to prove myself to her.

It was hard enough that she has recently favoured Pheorus over me. I suspect some intrigue for in truth he is not that good! But worse followed, for now the old man has fallen in love, it seems, with the sound of a shepherd boy. It is rumoured that he is the chosen one, although of late I sense a change in Anthorus, as if he has paused in mid-air and quite suddenly changed direction. The procedure too is different but exactly how I cannot say. I questioned him on it and asked once more to be considered, actually offering myself up to his hideous experiments! I would indeed risk all for even a brief glimpse of knowledge that Anthorus's work might bring me.

His reply was strange, and only half a reply at that. I wonder if he loses his wits? For he muttered to himself as if he had forgotten that I was there. Then, glaring snapped at me. "I will not risk you or any of the others in this work. If it were that easy I would not need to raid the countryside for my peasants. But you still worry at me with your requests Thanius, so I will give you something. You will come to curse me for it, but if you so passionately desire a taste of this power I will give it to you. First however, you must assist me in the cutting of the emerald crystal I have shown you. It is by far the most important cutting of any stone you have ever produced for me. Now leave me."

And I left him, withdrawing quickly to some quiet place where I could consider what this gift he has offered me could be, and why, in spite of his promise, which I have no doubt he will honour, I feel a vague sense of disappointment and some trepidation.

Weeks passed. The earth continued to terrify the people of that land. Every few days, new and more violent eruptions were occurring. The atmosphere reflected itself in everyday lives, as in fear man turned on his fellow man. But it was not fear that caused Thanius to fight with Pheorus, accusing him of an illegal liaison with Osiria. Pheorus was angered enough to make it quite clear to Thanius that he was indeed correct. He had held the knife-wielding student at arms length and laughed, chiding him for losing his temper with a friend over a mere woman. High Priestess or no, no doubt she was as all the rest beneath her robes of office. "Or not!" He had shouted, still laughing but speeding as fast as he could away from an intense Phoerus down a long golden corridor that joined the Temple to one of the large Halls. When they had both calmed down, Thanius pointed out as innocently as possible that it seemed that neither of them would be awarded the knowledge since Anthorus had fallen for the shepherd boy's sound and no doubt Osiria would do the same. Along this track he managed to lure Phoerus away from the seduction of the Temple and into the more practical world of Anthorus.

But Phoerus never recovered from his heartbreak. He had loved Osiria in every way that it is possible to love another, and without her he was bereft. Worse, there was no one that he felt he could confide in. Both for Osiria's sake and his own sense of privacy, he had made no mention of the affair and even now spoke to no one about it. Such a natural act may well have helped him.

The destruction continued to rumble up from the earth and one unusually fine and calm morning, that filled the citizens with hope, he was no longer to be found in the Temple, the Halls of Learning, nor even the town itself. Phoerus was not seen again. Osiria was mystified by her young lover's disappearance. But with so many other things on her mind she didn't have time to dwell on it. She had been making her own plans for escape. Laria, her most prized hand-maiden had a place already procured with her under the generous patronage of Caperus. They were good friends, her and Caperus. Like him, Osiria was not happy with the many deaths that had occurred as a result of Anthorus's experiments. Her own rather revolutionary thoughts on many issues were carefully secreted beneath the high altar and Laria was under instructions to make sure that when the time came for escape, those papers went with them.

Osiria's long and rigorous training was responsible for many abilities that she possessed. But it was only the gods themselves who could have endowed her with the gift of prophecy. Osiria read the future well although not completely. When she fell sick and died along the way as they fled, she took with her a fierce passion for the sound that she had worked with in the Great Temple. What she lost was the memory of that which Anthorus was trying to accomplish. It was all too close to the cries and moans of the men that sometimes reached her private apartments and chilled her caring blood.

Three days before the end, and the final destruction, the worst tremors hit their land. It was a signal to Caperus to wait no longer. They must make their departure, and soon. The sea, usually calm had become increasingly tempestuous, and even the tides could no longer be depended upon. He was on his way to Anthorus's work place. For the last few days he had been barred from it. Anthorus claiming that his presence made Lothus fight him more, and that it interfered with his work. This only served to strengthen Caperus's resolve to leave as soon as possible and with Lothus.

An unwanted picture of the boy flooded into his mind, in spite of his attempts to prevent it. Oh but Lothus had courage! Again and again he refused Anthorus as he worked with the bright and confusing light, allowing it to pass between the boy's eyes. As he worked, the emerald amulet sparkled, hanging from his neck. The guards sweated in their attempts to still Lothus. He writhed and shouted, refusing to give his mind to the priest.

"You have no right!" He screamed, as the light moved closer and ever brighter.

"Right or not, I will have it!" Scowled Anthorus.

"What will you have? What do you want?"

And in desperation Lothus began to hum and then to sing. Anthorus stood back with a cry of frustration, but shook his head as one of the guards produced a vile looking gag, and he dismissed them. After the great door had swung closed he moved to a small table and picked up a decanter that stood there, and which, every morning, was filled with fresh fruit juice by one or other of the maids. Anthorus's reputation in matters of the flesh was no less remarkable than his reputation in the abilities concerning his work as Musician/Scientist. The proof of that great understanding had long ago been acknowledged by the conferring on him of sacred title of 'Priest.' In more fleshy matters it had been quietly noticed that all those who worked in his household were always of a gracious beauty, that indeed Anthorus was always surrounded by loveliness to such a degree that it was suspected that some form of enhancement was likely. What or how it was accomplished was left in the dark shadow of ignorance.

Anthorus turned back from the table and handed the boy a crystal glass of sweet grenadine juice and tried to persuade him to sit down. Lothus refused.

"For a shepherd boy you have amazing fortitude and courage Lothus. Can we not be friends? I have no wish to hurt you. If only you would not struggle, the pain is caused by the guards as they try to keep you still. For I cannot work if you are not.

Close your eyes and be calm. I only want a little stray part of you, something that you do not need, cannot use, and indeed something that left unimpeded could destroy the structure of our life as we know it. It is rather like a plague you see? And I must stamp it out "

Lothus was silent, mutinous. The only attraction in that room for him was the beautiful green amulet around his torturer's neck. He had backed away and was against the wall. He smelt the stale sweat and his own fear, and he longed for the sweet fresh air, he glowered at Anthorus.

"What I have the gods have given to me. It is not for you to touch it."

"You know what you have?" The priest looked surprised, not to say concerned. Lothus avoided his gaze, without even a glance at the glass dome above them he was aware of the sudden darkening of the sky. Finally he replied and it hissed like a challenge across the space between them.

"Yes! And I know it is important." It was a bluff, he had no idea but he wished to strike back at his tormenter.

"How? How do you know this?" Anthorus had risen and stood in the middle of the room, leaning forward onto the table that still gleamed with sweat as he spoke.

"I know mad Priest because otherwise I would not be so important to you were it not the case." And he laughed, a high hoarse sound. Anthorus's patience broke. He had not wanted to force the boy into sleep, unsure of the affect it would have on the whole procedure, but enough! He had tried to treat him almost as one of his students. Talking, even explaining to him in a way he had never done before to any of the peasants that had passed through his hands. No more, and he screamed for the guards and rummaged through a draw in his desk for the bottle containing an instant anaesthetic. He had filled a small syringe with some and held it up for the boy to see. Lothus went ashen, sensing quite rightly that here was something he couldn't fight.

"Coward!" He screamed. While Anthorus approached him and he was held more firmly than ever on the table by the guards. Then as panic took control only one thought lived.

"Caperus!" He called out suddenly feeling his strength fail him and seeing himself finally helpless. At that exact moment, Caperus was striding through the outer courtyard. Anthorus raised his eyebrows but said nothing and held the syringe close to the boy's arm letting loose the mixture with a soft whispering hiss. Lothus felt his arm deaden instantly. The rest of his body followed and then his mind threatened to black out. He fought it, but it had him in its foggy grip. This was good because a few moments later, when the worst tremor yet wrecked the work place of Anthorus the Great, Lothus did not know or feel a thing!

As the building crashed around them, the guards let go of their charge and fled, only to be crushed in the corridor outside. Anthorus, his hand flying instinctively to his throat, fell with the precious Emerald crystal amulet in his death grip. As the great tremor finally abated, Caperus hurried from his place of shelter and sped to the work place. He knelt by the body of Lothus and gently lifted him from the rubble. Tears rose to his eyes and made their salty way through the dust that was caked on his grief stricken face. Lothus was dead. Caperus had no understanding of why he felt so affected by the death of one he had known so short a time. His eyes scanned the room for any other signs of life and he caught sight of the green glimmer of the amulet. He bent down, retrieved it quickly and placed it around his neck for safety feeling an uncontrollable fury with Anthorus, and a heavy sense that he had failed this young and innocent shepherd boy.

Those who were destined to escape left that day. Had they not done so it would have been too late. They buried Lothus at sea. By the time Osiria sickened and died they were travelling due North, and had said farewell to Thanius some time before when he and a small party had turned East. Caperus and Julias with most of their household, set up home on the shores of a large warm country that one day would give birth to the Roman Empire. But Laria, Osiria's papers well hidden within her belongings walked on through many miles of the place that would become Europe, and one morning, there being, at that time, no stretch of water to prevent it, exhausted and still badly shocked from all that had happened, she and the few remaining travellers who had joined them along the way, settled in a deep moist and cool valley on the Western part of a more Northern land. A valley that would one day ring famously with the very sound that Laria had pledged her life and service to through the High Priestess of Aum. That sound being the human voice.

Venice: at the turn of the 17ᵀᴴ.& 18ᵀᴴ. centuries

Angelo took me to his home for a short holiday. This is something he offers to many of his students and more especially, apparently, to those to whom he feels close. We travelled some way inland until we came to a large rambling house which stood outside a small town. We were alone there except for a few servants.

I have not known Angelo so very long as yet. My training as a Castrato having only been in evidence for a few months. Some students are a little afraid of our Maestro, mainly on account of his amazing eyes. Their shade seems to change as he looks at you. I have no fear of him, but he had some strange questions for me as we sat with our wine by the fire one evening after supper. I felt my scalp tingle as I realised very soon into his discourse that he was travelling along a familiar road, one down which my own mind often takes me, when I am daydreaming or involved in some trivial pursuit. He began to speak of a place where there was fantastic knowledge, far in excess of our own. Of long golden corridors in some ancient setting. Somewhere where there was great beauty, but also where there hovered a great fear as if of some impending disaster.

"I do not know what to make of it all. For just as I am at the point of understanding and remembering something, it all slips away like snow in the sun." He mused.

I found that I had no wish to think on these things, but couldn't give good reason why, even in the secret places of my own heart. Angelo simply smiled at my obvious discomfiture and refilling our glasses, asked me suddenly about sound.

"Sound?" I asked.

"Yes. Sound, music. Opera, the voice. Our sound!" And he laughed at my blank face as he laid his hand over the place where his heart was beating as I often note singers do at certain times during their discourse. But I, felt suddenly, very inadequate. I did not understand what he was asking of me and I became a little sulky. This made him laugh all the more.

"Do you tease me Maestro?" At which he turned immediately serious and assured me not. The night wore on and the rain began to lash against the windows. I stood up and walked over to one, and stood staring out across the grounds that surrounded the Villa, catching from time to time, flickering lights from the village as the wind whipped the branches brutally across my vision. The wind sent smoke from the fire back down the chimney whence it had come as if to scorn the arrogance of it billowing out into the fresh night air. There was silence for so long that I felt bound to speak. Still staring out into the night I began. My voice sounded strange in the silence of the library where we were. Somewhat haltingly I said.

"On our way here Maestro, we skirted a village. A village which suffers from the pox." Here my voice failed me and copious tears thickened my throat and assailed my cheeks. I put up my hand in silent apology, but Angelo shook his head. He better than anyone understood. After such a dark and bloody passage as we suffered, it was always the way that we took on, for a while, the quick and mercurial emotional fluctuations of women. Patience would see that it passed. As yet mine had not, and I own that I hated it most violently. Is it not enough that we become deprived of so much? But my own wounded nature apart, the experience had upset me for although our way was barred from passing through the place, nothing could shield us from the mounds of unmentionable heaps still smoking from their purgative burnings, and from the terrible stench from which we covered our mouths with our lace kerchiefs. The very richness of which seemed only to highlight the horror of the scene before us. Anyway, somewhat recovered I continued, and Angelo lent forward, his mouth resting on hands in an attitude of prayer. I glanced over at him and felt my confidence growing.

"I sometimes feel that somewhere in music is such a power, such magic that it could not fail to be used in some wonderful way outside the Theatres and Concert Halls. Providing of course we could discover how to release this power!" I had returned to my chair and ended this little speech by sitting down on the seat and leaning forward towards Angelo suddenly convinced of my belief, wild and unformed as it was, and also convinced that Angelo must feel it also.

"You mean, sing the pox away!" He mused. I feared that he laughed at me until I realised that he had not asked a question, but made a statement. I stared at him in amazement.

"Can this be possible? Do you think......I mean. How? How would we do such a thing?" But he put up his hand to me rather like a conductor interrupting a rehearsal. He stood up from his chair and stared at me thoughtfully. After a silence he sighed and replied.

"Something is missing. Something so vast and important that we could never find words to launch even the beginning of whatever it is we speak I am afraid that this is simply not the time. But I am sure of one thing."

"Yes Maestro?" I asked, a little disappointed that he had appeared to discontinue our discussion so easily without anymore thought. He leaned over the back of my chair and rested his hands on my shoulders in a manner that was almost protective.

"I know it is you who walks beside me along the golden corridors in the ancient place of which I so often dream. Where knowledge and terror walk hand in hand, and where music is of some great import. We were together there as we are here. I know that this was so." We left for Venice the next morning and have not spoken of it again.

A Beginning

PLACE, ENGLAND. TIME, LATE 20TH. CENTURY

Far, far into the future there lived a little girl who one day fell in love. Not with a prince or a pop star, but with music. Yes, with old-fashioned classical music. She became so entranced that she lived it every day, diving into the velvet depths and sparkling heights. She spent happy hours exploring the fabulous architecture that changed with every bar, while offering security in the truest form.

Later she discovered opera and she moved from being in love to worshiping with a lust hardly suited to one so young and innocent. However this great unstoppable energy appears to have no conscience. Nothing is spared the open ear. In fact the more open the ear, mind and heart, the harder it hits, and the harder it hits the more the ear, mind and heart open. It became the focal point of every day. The main experience second to none. It was a life saver. And when the world growled and shook (which it often did) it beckoned smiling from a safe planet bathed in light and warmth. This faithful follower arrived breathless and in great anticipation one day at the very door of opportunity. She knocked. It opened. Oh how well it started, bursting with possibility!

JOURNAL: SEPTEMBER 8ᵀᴴ 2010

Today was the first full chorus call of the season. I arrived early, extremely anxious not to enter late, or even last, into a room full of sixty-odd strangers. I don't want to give the wrong impression so I found an empty studio (which I've discovered to my relief is not difficult to do at 9;30 in the morning) After eating breakfast in the canteen, I still had 20 minutes in hand and I stood by the notice board staring unseeing at it, while hoards of strangers filed past me, most tanned by some foreign sun, fresh from their 5 week break, their voices settling with intimacy into the walls, as if the Opera House were welcoming them back having had enough silence. My knees were water and my stomach knotted with hot cotton wool. But I needn't have worried, a nicer group of people I have yet to encounter. There was a warm greeting on my introduction and a kindly and joking (I hope) reference to my age from one of the tenor section and we plunged straight into rehearsal.

Well I have been, as you might imagine, anticipating many things of that first musical entrance on that beautiful September day. Since the phone call back in July inviting me in for an interview, I had imagined just what it might be like to be part of such a high profile musical experience. But nothing had prepared me for the power of that sound. I found myself totally engulfed as if I were drowning in voices. My mind seemed to fizz with electricity while individual sounds assailed my ears. A deep mezzo there, a bass…..tenor, that baritone and a glorious glint of a true dramatic soprano the owner of which was to become a good friend. It was beyond beautiful and very moving. There was however just one small problem! I couldn't sing! From the first collective Verdian chord (we are rehearsing Aida) an emotional rocket fired its way through me leaving no chance of executing the functions normal to a singer. It was a good ten minutes, during which I obediently opened and closed my mouth at the appropriate places, before anything came out at all.

Dear God, if I'm dreaming. Please don't wake me up.

JOURNAL

My first week has finished. The 'House' is still closed, opening night three weeks away. Also we have not, as yet, ventured onto the stage itself. I scan the rehearsal schedule with anticipation, secretly I can't wait. Having watched that space enviously during my three years at college with such an intensity, it has become almost a living thing. I was in fact at the stage door, glued to next week's rehearsal times and places for that very reason earlier today, when I was pulled from my concentration by a familiar voice.

"Well, what are you doing here Tilly?"

"I've joined the Company." I replied, trying desperately not to sound too proud about it. Not easy to do, and there was a short silence followed by heavy sarcasm.

"How did you manage that?"

"I auditioned." This with clipped irritation. I mean how did he imagine I had got there? He laughed at that, the old ironically-pitched effect that I had known only too well. But please let me introduce you. This is Martin Roberts. He is an 'ex.' Ex lover, ex friend, ex life, since at one time not so long ago the sun and planets appeared to rotate around him. It was to him I yielded up that which is no longer considered important in our society, and it was from him I tasted my first inkling of my own sexual being and the bitterness of abandonment. (That is actually rather a dramatic word to use but bear with me, this did not happen so long ago!) He disappeared suddenly without warning from my life and returned as one close college friend explained with difficulty, very married.

"So…" He continued in the same drawl. "Well done Tilly. I didn't know you had it in you!"

"Maybe that's because you didn't take my singing seriously." I retorted.

"Aye, maybe." Still laughing. "See you around next week, we'll have a coffee, talk about old times. I'm rehearsing here at the moment."

Apparently the Opera House is gracious enough to allow some small professional companies access to rehearsal facilities from time to time. Martin turned to go with his usual jaunty dismissal in spite of which I realised, with a sharp jolt, that he was very distinctly jealous.

"If you don't mind my saying Matilda, you need to watch him." One of the tenors from the chorus had been standing close enough to hear the conversation.

"Oh?" I replied.

"Yes, from all accounts he's a nasty piece of work, especially where the ladies are concerned. Oh it's not simply that he likes the fairer sex, we all do!" He grinned. I was suddenly curious just what these other rather dubious characteristics could be that Martin apparently possessed. I certainly had not been aware of them during the two years that I had known him. I didn't quite know what to say and strange as it may seem I felt an absurd rush of loyalty.

"But he's married now." I ventured as mad Mike, who is one of the Irish tenors, grinned again and came closer, sitting down next to me on the faded pale green velvet seat.

"How long have you been out in the big bad world? A week? Give it another month when the season's in full swing, You'll soon lose that delightful naiveté, you will see things, to quote dear old Gilbert, that will astonish you. It's the innocence that that type like. We like you Matilda, be careful!"

"Thank you, and it's Tilly to my friends." He grinned again, wished me a good weekend and left, the stage door slowly swung closed behind him. I stayed for a moment where I was. I rather wish that Martin didn't know that I am here. Not likely since the Operatic world is exceedingly small. Oh dear, a tiny cloud in heaven?

Dear God, please don't let it rain!

JOURNAL

I know, I know! I don't write every day, but sometimes there's just not time, and anyway I can always catch up. I mean I'm not likely to forget anything! Last night we opened. How to describe that sort of excitement both personal and general? I suppose the opening to a new season must always hold a certain amount of tension and drama, after all there's been a 'break.' What if things simply don't 'gel'? Do people get rusty over the summer? But no, the orchestra played, the stage exuded and the singers sang. And what singing! Such sounds! As if the universe had interrupted this technological age in order to remind everyone that it still holds natural sway and that it could snuff out every mechanical device on the planet if it so desired. But this sound, this music was in part its own child given glorious birth by man, and this it would never destroy. This speaks without words and its meaning is mysterious, vital and everlasting. Nothing can stop it. It is buried deep in the rhythm of the blood and bursts forth to engulf an unsuspecting world with its primordial sophistication. When God created music, he'd had a really good day!

JOURNAL: AUTUMN 2010

Today I reached the Opera House at my normal time of around 9:30am. Autumn is clearly on the way, not that I care, but it's definitely rehearsing the 'icy' bits. I was heading towards the studios to do a little warm up before the rehearsal started, and there he was. Arms folded, leaning against the door almost as if he knew I would be arriving and was waiting for me. I was very surprised to see him. No one arrives that early, and it's only my insecurity of singing when I haven't warmed up, that ensures that I do. The words of my concerned colleague were dancing around the edge of my thoughts seeking attention, but Martin cut across them.

"Well, fancy seeing you here at this time of the day. Bit keen aren't you Tilly?" He was as sardonic as ever but I managed to stand firm.

"I come in early to warm up."

"Oh come on. No one's going to hear you amongst that lot!" With a detrimental nod in the direction of the chorus room. I swallowed defensively at his words, but remembering his obvious jealousy of a few days before I decided not to rise to this particular barb.

"It doesn't matter if anyone can hear me or not, it's for my own vocal health."

"Ooh…..Vocal health is it? Come on have a cup of coffee with me. You've got 'till 10:30. Haven't you?"

"11:00. o'clock actually." I said regretting it instantly.

"Well there you are then, to hell with 'vocal health' for one day. Live dangerously Tilly. Come on let's go down to the canteen."

I looked at him thinking that I had already tried living dangerously as he should well know, but he misunderstood my hesitation.

"What's the matter? Ashamed to be seen with a member of a small and insignificant company since you've joined the international ranks Tilly? Or, and much more juicy, got a new boyfriend already have you?"

"No to both as you well know Martin. I was just thinking that well……people notice and then they assume…… and then they talk…..and you are married aren't you?" I ended with some difficulty, and feeling myself blush. He nodded as if I had enquired about his impending execution. I was not going to feel sorry for him. Suddenly he grabbed my elbow, just a little too hard and veered me in the direction of the canteen.

"Come on Tilly. I'll let you buy me a cappuccino out of your fat wage packet." Short of creating a ridiculous scene I felt I had little choice, and after all it was only an invitation for coffee with an old friend. Was it not? Something deep inside me nudged me, cleared its throat to speak, but it was at a loss for real reason and became quiet.

The canteen was quite full. Some of the ballet were there sweating from morning class which was still taking place in the large studio. I can't as yet work out the politics of ballet class, certain members seem to slip out as and when they feel like it. But what do I know? Anyway I love ballet and find dancers at a level such as this, fascinating, wouldn't it be nice if we could all have such physiques? Martin demanded a jam doughnut with his coffee. I dutifully purchased the items and sat down opposite him. I didn't like the way he was looking at me, it made me feel uncomfortable, so I said the first thing that came into my head.

"Are you rehearsing this morning?"

"Later." He dismissed the subject with the tone of his voice. I shuffled in my seat, the ballet pianist changed pulse and tune, new exercise obviously, and someone closed the studio door. Martin was stirring his coffee, his lips pursed, and still staring at me enquiringly. I resisted the temptation to say "What?" and finally he asked.

"So darling, how are you getting on here. Bored yet?" And he picked up his cup and sipped through the froth, still staring.

"Bored? You must be nuts. No, it's fantastic. I wouldn't want to be anywhere else."

"Oh now you disappoint me Tilly. You mean you wouldn't rather be on a desert island with me than around this lot? I can't believe that."

So this was the way the conversation was going! Well mad Mike might have a point. Martin it seems has another side to him, and not one that I have seen before! He threw back his head and laughed at my silence.

"You look as if you've been stuck with a pin, Tilly. Be honest now, you miss me surely?" I was becoming more and more on edge by now and wished vehemently for our call to stage. The canteen was filling up rapidly with company members grabbing a drink before the rehearsal started. Frankly I was amazed at his question, but I realised that if I didn't reply with a bit of a punch he might well assume a certain acquiescence. I glanced at the next table and caught a nod and smile from Maria the owner of the superb dramatic soprano voice. I returned her greeting and lowering my voice, we were far too close to other people for such a conversation, I half whispered.

"What's this Martin? Early seven year itch?"

"Oh, not forgiven me Tilly?" He replied smiling at me as if I might be a second jam doughnut. I picked up my bag, surely it was nearly 11:00 o'clock by now? And replied.

"I don't know Martin. I don't know what I feel. I suppose I was numbed by your behaviour and as far as you're concerned I haven't really come back to life yet."

"Well. Please let me know when you do." And he looked at me lecherously. There was a crackle over the tanhoy and the now familiar voice of our stage manager filled the room.

" GOOD MORNING LADIES AND GENTLEMN THIS IS YOUR CALL FOR ACT ONE. ALL BEGINNERS PLEASE, THANK YOU." Thank God for that I made my escape. Martin watched as I put my purse back in my bag and was pushed against the table as there was a mass exodus for the stage. He made no attempt to move and I half fell against him. I glanced down and apologised, at which he shook his head.

"Think nothing of it darling. Off you run. See you later no doubt." I caught up with Maria.

"Trouble?" She asked as we hurried along the corridor.

"Long story." I replied. I felt a mixture of confusion and anger. I had worked very hard at getting him out of my system when I finally learned about his marriage, and I was quite sure that I had completely eradicated any attraction or feelings. Suddenly I was uncertain. By the time I reached the side of the stage my heart was thumping. I just wish he'd leave me alone, or then again, do I? I found my place and melted into the beautiful prelude to La Traviata. Soon the agony of the descending strings transcended everything else and blissfully blotted out my problems, until just before the end of Act One that is. I happened to glance across at the prompt corner, and there he was, staring out of the darkness. How he managed to be there I don't know. The stage staff appeared to ignore him, I tried my best to do the same and pulled my full concentration back to the 19th. Century salon in Paris and joined in the chorus 'goodbyes' to Violetta. She was about to launch into her famous and taxing aria once we had left. She smiled at us and muttered under her breath.

"It's too bloody early for this!"

I have already learned that on the continent, rehearsals involving the orchestra, which necessitate the soloists giving their all, or at least something that is only one stop below a real performance, do not take place in the mornings! I suddenly realised how dreadfully exposed one must be as a soloist. I'm glad I'm in the chorus, I can't see me ever being seduced to 'centre stage' as it were!

There is a whole act before our next entrance. I stood in the dressing room trying to decide what to do for the best. The bags and outdoor clothes were spread around like exhausted guests. The other ladies who shared this small room were downstairs chatting over tea and coffee, This was ridiculous! If Martin was there all I had to do was stand up to him. I wouldn't allow a negative situation to develop, I mean I was acting as if I were the 'guilty' party. If the word 'guilty' could even be applied here. I gave myself a mental shake, picked up my purse, and headed for the canteen. Only members of the Company were scattered at various tables. I joined Maria and two friends. They were in the middle of an intense discussion about the forth coming trip to Italy as I sat down, and the pros and cons were flying back and forth about what we should accept, what we ought not to let ourselves be talked into, and what we would and wouldn't do. It seems such a long way off, March next year in fact, to be concerning ourselves with these sort of details just yet. But this was not appreciated when I said as much. By this time Dai one of our Welsh tenors had joined us. They were all rather shocked at my innocent remarks. I mumbled my apologies and was immediately forgiven, after all I was still only a baby, For some reason this irritated me, it seemed to highlight my 'Martin problem.' Then like a sudden shower of rain I remembered something. Just before I awoke this morning, I was dreaming of an old man. It was a very lucid dream. I could only see his face and from his head sprouted thick white hair that stood up by itself as if powered by human electricity. He shook his finger firmly in my face. As I awoke with a start I tried to distinguish if it were a warning or something else he was trying to communicate to me. I soon had to own that I had no idea, and promptly completely forgot about it until that moment. Maria laid her hand on my arm.

"Are you alright?" She asked, presumably thinking I was upset by my chastisement.

"Oh…..Yes thank you , fine….." At which point Act Three beginners were called.

As we were performing tonight in the double bill traditionally known as Cav&Pag. there was no afternoon call. I decided to stay in the theatre and was musing over the day's events when Martin plonked himself down in the chair opposite me. He was scowling and did not appear to be in a very good mood.

"Stupid bastards!" He growled throwing sugar in his tea and stirring it as if the unfortunate 'bastards' were hiding in the depths of his drink. I supposed it was my cue to inquire how is morning had gone.

"What's up Martin?" I asked, but he didn't answer at all for several seconds and then changed track completely.

"I suppose you've finished for the day? La Dolce Vita eh?" He said brightening up a little, no doubt due to the fact that he could use his ridiculous sarcasm on someone. I was not best pleased, I'm only just beginning to feel that I have gained enough stamina not to feel tired out when I drop into bed at night. Not that you'd find me complaining mind you! But this is a hard job and it takes a little while to adjust.

"Well we are back tonight." I pointed out.

"Oh sorry!" He pleaded, hand on brow in mock exhaustion. "I don't know how you do it, I really don't!"

"And where will you be this evening?" I retorted. "Sprawled out in front of the tele?"

"Tilly! I'm pierced to the heart, I really am. Cut to the quick, faint and bleeding." It was impossible not to smile. It was also a big mistake, he grabbed my hand across the table before I had time to withdraw it. (The canteen, thank goodness was nearly empty.)

"I really hurt you didn't I?" He lowered his voice and lost his devil-may-care look.

"What do you think?" I replied. He removed his hand, sat back in the chair and sighed. After all the months of wanting, in fact needing to scream at him, and not being able to. I found strangely, that I did not even wish to discuss it. Martin, however, for reasons that were soon to become only too clear, most definitely did want to do so.

"I'm sorry Tilly. What can I say? I'd promised Con, you see? She'd have been so disappointed, you know?" I wondered how 'disappointed' she'd be if she could see him now, but I remained silent, I had the mistaken idea that he would soon run out of steam, finish his drink and go. How wrong was I? He brightened slightly and leaned across the table again, I slipped both my hands beneath it.

"It doesn't have to make any difference to us does it?" Oh do be careful what you wish for because you'll surely get it. I thought. How many times over the last few months had I fantasised about Martin begging me to forgive him, to 'take him back'? If you can do that with another woman's husband. And now that it was happening, the text almost word for word, I wished fervently that it wasn't.

"What do you mean Martin?"

"I mean we can carry on as before. Why not?" He added as I raised my eyebrows. "It isn't wrong. Look, I've made a mistake, I don't intend to pay for the rest of my life. And I don't believe you're not interested Tilly. Come on make my day. That bloody lot have pissed me off, stupid buggers........." He trailed off. I was desperate to change the subject if only long enough to allow me time to get my thoughts together. So I asked him about the rehearsal again. He shrugged and as I gently pushed by suggesting that it was better out than in, he admitted to having done something really stupid. Standing on the rehearsal floor that morning, within earshot of the tenor soloist he had given vent to his frustration at being a chorister to such a group of 'piss' artists, and had, understandably upset the whole company, and ended his day with a severe reprimand by the company manager. I couldn't quite take in what I had heard, This was really stupid. For the first time I recognised the huge insecurity that lurked just beneath the surface. But this was no way to deal with it.

"That silly fat little plonker he sounds like a woman Tilly. I could sing him off the stage and on again."

"I'm sure you could." I began carefully, stepping as delicately as possible over the bruised ego. "But the point is that at the

41

moment he's the soloist, and it won't do you any good to upset him." Martin didn't reply but he screwed his face up in a distortion of disgust.

"As to the other Martin. I'm sorry, but I can't do that. You've only been married five minutes." Martin interrupted me.

"That's all it took. Five minutes for me to realise I had made a ghastly mistake. I spent most of my honeymoon bloody thinking about you." This I had great trouble believing. Even had I wanted to it just didn't ring true. Also, I was having difficulty dealing with my own feelings. I wasn't sure that I even felt attracted to him any more. But where does forgiveness begin and vengeance end? I really don't need this just now. I was so happy and content with my life. Why does something always seem to come along and spoil it? Is there a rule that we can't achieve happiness for any length of time? Oh I don't know. I'm tired now, Cav&Pag is a long night for us. Martin told me he won't give up. That was bad enough, but when I left him sitting over his empty cup in the canteen, the mirrored wall offered me a reflection. He was muttering to himself with a surprisingly malevolent expression on his face. A cold shock engulfed my solar plexus. Surely I was mistaken? Maybe it was the angle, or the light. I can't give into emotional blackmail I just can't. Now I really must sleep.

Dear God, please keep me strong.

The Old Man

Deep in the vibrant quiet of Matilda's inner being were many magical places that were utterly dependant on her. They did not exist inside her physicality of course, but in her mind, and in that forever expanding commodity they were in happy profusion given birth by the familiar thought patterns, given growth by her shining energy. Each pursued its own destiny but was entirely vulnerable to her inner expression, and she was in her turn vulnerable to their echo of herself as they responded to it. The 'Old Man' wasn't actually old at all, or indeed any age in our reckoning, and appeared 'old' to Matilda because his wisdom and quiet self-possession automatically projected to her the idea of age. He had slipped into her sleeping consciousness, and using the strong paternal urge to protect and guide her, he drew closer and closer to her dream world until he had managed to penetrate and establish himself in her memory.

He knew it was not going to be easy, dealing with that part projected into three-dimensional reality, that part called Matilda. He understood the driving need to work with sound, the all-consuming passion that was called 'being an artist.' After all it was his own great passion for sound that had led him into the dark valley that had blinded him to the full measure if what he was doing, and numbed him to the suffering he was causing.

Even now, in the self-imposed prison where his consciousness for the time being resided, he would shudder when he considered the ghastly final arrogance that he had been intent on committing. It had taken enormous determination and will to catch Matilda's attention, so intent and happy was she with her daily life. But now that he had managed it, he must carefully consider the best course of action. It was not without frustration, he felt rather like a lawyer forced to allow his client to run their own case while he can only guide their course.

At the moment however, Matilda was experiencing strength and her dream landscape echoed this as a gorgeous mountain shimmered as if in a heat haze and took form in the distance. The 'old' man smiled and allowed himself to float into the violet mist, soaking up the vibration from the beautiful tone thoughts emitting from the depths of the turquoise water.

JOURNAL

Sir Clive Anderson is our personal Maestro, Musical Director of the Opera House, and only one step away from God. Weeks of anticipation for all of us culminated today in the much feared 're-auditions.' Sir Clive, of course was not in attendance at one's first audition and had no part in saying who was or who was not offered a contract, being far too busy leaping around the world from Opera House to Concert Hall at the very top of the profession. However once a singer became a member of his Company he had the power to say pretty much anything he felt like saying.

This causes great concern and nervousness as the chorus prepares for its yearly horrors. And horrors they truly seem anticipated to be, for more small brandies poured into tea or coffee or sipped with honey, I have never seen!

Over the last few weeks, being moderately able at the piano (It having been my first instrument at college I jolly well should be) I have played for many colleagues in order that they can rehearse their chosen piece in some privacy. Paranoia seems rife at the moment and very few are willing to expose themselves to any of the music staff.

"They all talk you know!" One second mezzo assured me before launching into a rich rendition of an aria from La Gioconda. "They'll make up their minds before you get to the audition if you're not careful." She continued over a cup of tea, which is the only payment I feel I can take. I don't think this is true, but nerves are a terrible thing.

I have been amazed at the vocal wealth hidden behind the chorister label.

Some are quite outstanding. It set me wondering why they hadn't left in order to allow solo careers to blossom. I have heard various reasons and excuses for this state of affairs from inconsistent health or inconsistent singing, to laziness or simply born at the wrong time in the wrong country! This I find generally depressing and negative so I have no wish to inquire about it anymore! I would rather contemplate the darker side of life through the dark crystal of music.

I heard one or two stories about other people's auditions, including that fact that Mad Mike will have to sing again later in the season because he took the powers that be at their word when they asked for us not to sing pieces that are too long, and presented Othello's entrance during which he sings precisely 34 notes and is finished in less than one minute. As I waited nervously to be called into the room to sing he disappeared in a cloud of furious Celtic temperament muttering to anyone prepared to listen:

"Bloody hell! What DO they fucking want?"

When I was called in I could not help but notice that the panel were still grinning broadly. It was, perhaps, not the best preparation for me, but I can't blame my singing on Mad Mike! Not that it was that bad. But I was aware of a rather notable deviance in the sound between the upper middle and the top of the voice. The lower middle (just above the chest) was slightly sharp. For some reason the space between oneself and the audience is what brings one's attention to such things, and try as I might I couldn't put them right. Naturally I felt rather depressed, but after I had finished on a hefty if healthy cadenza, Sir Clive spoke to me.

"I don't think you are doing yourself any favours by singing as a mezzo. I think you are a soprano." Now I've been told this on several occasions before and indeed have always thought it to be the case. I've even been told that I look like a soprano (Whatever that may mean.) However his words stung the air like a thousand icy bee-stings.

"What." I wondered "Did that mean in connection with the job I am so much in love with?"

My fears were ill-founded. All I have to do is present myself next year at the auditions with a soprano aria. I won't be taken to the stage door and escorted into a snowbound street clutching my vocal identity to me like an illegitimate baby. Now that I have calmed down about it, it is becoming rather exciting. It's like having a whole new range of colours added to your palate. All sorts of possibilities open up as many people are quick to point out. A large range of music and characters to die for. After all, friends insist, it's bound to be a 'big' soprano of one sort or another.

Dear God, does size matter?

Giorgio

Martin closed the door to the flat. Silence swept gently towards him from every quarter. His wife, thank goodness, was out. He poured himself a drink and sat down on the settee, remembering as he did so Matilda's words of some weeks before.

"Sprawled in front of the tele………."

He swallowed the gin and gripped the glass tightly. He would dearly love to throw it clear across the room. He resisted the urge, Connie would be in at any moment, and how would he explain such an act to her? Recently he felt that he should explain everything to her and have done with it. But he was not sure of Matilda, and his own feelings were in a turmoil. Matilda's link to her past was (at least many people would think) rather tenuous and uncertain. Martin's then was much more so. His remembrance was lodged purely in the depth of his emotion with no intellectual explanation as to the reason for the volcanic eruptions he felt tear through his heart from time to time. And no understanding of why he behaved in the way he felt compelled to behave, especially when it came to women. From their first meeting, Matilda had always had a powerful effect on him and unfortunately for both of them, he made no attempt to rein in his masochistic response to almost everything about her. And because he didn't question himself, he scarcely recognised the root of jealousy and fear that held him upright. Overlaid was his hatred of the way he had handled the situation with Matilda when he disappeared from her life so suddenly to marry Connie.

Guilt had bitten deep when he left, and now jealousy bit even deeper. The idea of her with anyone else made him gasp, and the Opera House was an extremely seductive place. Famous, and he had to admit, talented singers came and went on an almost weekly basis, not to mention conductors. Charm, charisma and sexual energy oozed through every bar of music and beckoned to many, especially the uninitiated, those too young to realise the bigger picture. Usually the passing flings only served to furnish pleasure to both parties, but there were occasions when such situations offered a little more. There were stories of quite famous singers who had taken a quantum leap by springing off the mattress and thus advancing in the queue to an enviable position as it were. A young singer might be forgiven for thinking that this was an easy road to take, since it had happened enough times before. He didn't really think that Matilda had any interest in this particular path and also realised that for the moment anyway, all that held her was the music and being part of it. He was as sure as he could be that she did not think of herself as a potential soloist, at least not yet.

Anyway, his thoughts continued. If the silly little cow wanted to hop into bed (she'd be lucky if there was one, more likely the dressing room floor or handy table top) with every Lothario who stayed in town only long enough to earn many thousands of pounds very quickly, let her!

The anger curled up from his diaphragm as if she had already done just that. Again he realised he was the stealthy purloiner of Matilda's innocence. Miserably he acknowledged that he was powerless. He also knew that she possessed a fucking fine voice. He had heard her once, had slipped into the college theatre when she had been rehearsing on the stage, and slipped out again without ever telling her. He had been momentarily knocked for six. Not so much by what she was producing at that moment, but by the fabulous potential he could hear. Every note and execution of musical phrase promised it. A sound which was dark and bright at the same time, a superb awareness of pitch. A sound that seemed to speak from her soul. He had tortured himself for hours rerunning the tape in his mind's ear until he convinced himself that he had been exaggerating and laughed it off. Still he had not been surprised when he came across her at the stage door and learnt that she had joined such an illustrious Company, no he hadn't been surprised at all. He had, of course, done his best, using his finely honed technique, to keep her 'in her place.' But his velvet-clad knife stabs glanced off Matilda long before they hit their target. She was not interested in comparisons, and if his exaggerated descriptions of some of the female singers he happened to be working with did ever cause her to wonder why she was being regaled with them, she was far too polite and intelligent to rise to the bait. So having played all his cards, more than once, without receiving any response that he could work with further to control her, he had given up.

Now however he was inspired again. He was in a perfect position, armed with knowledge and instinct. But maybe, considering what he had put her through in the past, this was wrong? He heard the key in the front door and his wife calling out.

"Martin, you home?" Intense irritation tightened his jaw. The hell it was wrong!

JOURNAL

I shall go home tomorrow for the weekend. Well I have to go sometime, play 'happy families' and pretend that it is real.

Heard some news that's not so good. Martin, having finished his present contract with the company he's been working with (I bet they heaved a sigh of relief) has joined the 'extra' chorus. This is a body of singers employed by the Opera House to swell our ranks in the bigger works both vocally and regarding bodies on stage. I really don't know where to put him in my mind and I can only suppose that is the problem with unfinished business. I did have a talk to Maria about it though. She is very forthright and not afraid of saying exactly what she thinks, as one might imagine a good Scot to be.

"If you really want my opinion Tilly. I don't think you need that sort of complication. When I look at him I see a control freak before me. Oh very charming no doubt, but I get the feeling he'd take over completely in a very short time before you even realised what was happening. And it's the devil's own job to get out of that one! I think he's a total plonker!" She stopped and looked a little embarrassed.

"Sorry! Maybe I've said too much. Do you still have feelings for him?"

I said I didn't know. And I don't, I just wish it would all go away. All I want to do is work hard and enjoy my wonderful new life, but I've a sneaking suspicion that Martin isn't going to go away, and, that there is something running much deeper that is holding us, if not romantically, then in some other way that for the moment I can't fathom.

"I think he likes you." I told her. "He always refers to you as that 'sexy Scottish piece!'"

"That does not mean he likes me." She laughed. "It means he wants me on his side."

Such wisdom! I suppose I'll acquire some in time. But she also pointed something else out that no doubt needed to be said.

"The real point Tilly is that you should be concentrating on your voice. Remember that you need to find a teacher to retrain you. Don't leave it any longer than you have to. Before you know it, it'll be reaudition time again. Go to bed with him if you must and you think you can handle it, but don't waste yourself. You'll never have this chance again you know."

Something strange filtered through my mind at Maria's last statement, almost as if some knowledge shook its head and laughed, and reminded me of the old man.

Dear God. Where do dreams end?

JOURNAL

I'm on the train. It's quite early Monday morning but I have until this evening to get back, not that it will take that long even from the depths of Devon. The depths of Devon! That sounds like peace and relaxation in an eye watering life, and to be honest the countryside is exactly that for me. I managed several walks off on my own to all my favourite haunts. Not far from the village is an area of wild land known as 'Fairies Ferry.' Through a small copse of trees and off the side of a well worn horse track are meadows through which flows a full fast-flowing stream. Lower down in the second and third meadows the stream becomes a small waterfall. In spring the area is a mass of wild flowers and the air is delicious. The large group of trees off to the south known as Baby-Devil's wood, becomes so full of bluebells that it is impossible to walk there without stepping on them. The villagers, have, by tacit agreement avoided the wood when it is in full bloom, and leave the intense beauty largely to itself. It is still too early for any of this as yet, but wading through the mud yesterday reminded me of it all and how much like another world it is. Unchanged by all human drama. Strong and independent of any interference from man. Anyone observing this part of the countryside under a full moon, could be forgiven for believing that they had been transported body and soul to another planet, in a universe bent only on harmony and peace.

Local people have, over some centuries now, nurtured the belief that at certain times of the year, hordes of 'little people' on 'little horses' swarm over the undergrowth and are ferried across the stream to the woods where they perform magic and keep a secret but firm rein on man's insanity. It's a comforting thought that some super intelligence is keeping a watchful eye on the ghastly games we sometime play. I don't, of course, believe in fairies, but there is a calming effect in this local legend. And whether they live in some tiny corporeal form, or only in the imagination, their strength appears to exist. I arrived home fully aware of something extra around me, vibrating like an aura.

My Father is a doctor and a senior partner in a Health Centre which serves four villages including our own. He works with three younger doctors, one of them not so much older than myself. And here we come up against problem number one. My Mother, would I know, like me to marry this particular young man, settle down 'properly' and get this 'silly singing thing' out of my system. Sometimes I wonder why she thinks I've worked so hard to achieve even as much as I have so far. But my relationship with my Mother has always been a little fraught. I'm an only child and that hasn't helped.

Anyway, Doctor William Shaw, the youngest of my Father's partners is a handsome man in a nineteenth century sort of way. He kissed me once, after a pub lunch at 'The Mocking Lady' which faces the square in the centre of Kingsley Woods, a village only a few miles from our own. I remember it was a beautiful day, the very essence of the English countryside.

In the warmth of the quiet air, anticipation was delightful if not lustful, and the kiss, pleasant if not passionate, gave me no desire to repeat it. I was embarrassed by my lack of interest, but William was not. He appeared to take it as a sign of the commencement of something. I felt trapped and was infinitely thankful for my imminent departure to college.

"Will you have time to see William, Matilda?" My Mother's voice cut across my thoughts and I jumped, her choice of subject at that precise moment was bizarre. I parried. I had to be back for Monday evening.....there really wasn't time......maybe next time? But she was not to be put off. She wished I would find time.....He always asked after me...It wouldn't do any harm now would it?

Short of initiating the opening battle to World War Three, I had little choice but to agree hoping that I would still avoid a situation which I was sure would be awkward. William, I sincerely hope, had long ago lost interest in me. It seemed a pointless exercise, but my Mother was not about to give up. She invited him for Sunday lunch. It was nice to see him but I felt very on edge until both my Mother and Dad disappeared to make coffee, which seemed to take an interminable amount of time and needed to be watched by two people.

William, I then realised had a bright twinkle in his eyes that suggested he was quietly laughing at all of us. He leant back in his chair and said, smiling.

"Your Mother's a very determined lady isn't she Tilly?"

"I'm sorry William this is really rather embarrassing!" At which William's twinkle deepened.

"No no not at all! But I do think I ought to explain something to her."

"What's that?" I asked.

"That I'm recently engaged to be married." He finished triumphantly. It's amazing how quickly an atmosphere can change. To me, the very room seemed to relax!

"William that's great I'm so happy for you!"

"So am I." He grinned. "Very happy for me!"

We were deep in discussion about his fiancé, who happened to be someone I had been at school with, I was racking my brains to remember as much about her as I could, when coffee finally arrived.

Later I made my parents 'au fait' with William's situation. Dad was delighted for him and sang his praises as long as my

Mother allowed. Then she told him to shut up, which he did! I've never been able to understand why he does as she tells him so complacently. Then she became irritable and finally rude about the clothes I was wearing, what I'd done (or hadn't done) to my hair, even the expression on my face came in for considerable criticism. I suppose I'm used to it but it was still nice to catch Dad's eye as he winked at me and escaped to his room to 'work' as he put it. I only had twelve hours left to put up with such snide comments. I wish they were happy, maybe I'm wrong but I don't see how they can be. I almost feel guilty leaving Dad to his 'fate.' But he has his work as I have mine.

Thank you God, and do we choose our parents?

Journal

Yes, yes it's been a while, well I don't want you to get bored. At the moment I'm trying to dispel some guilt. No, I haven't done anything, not yet anyway. But Martin has been ever present at rehearsals. We're shortly to be presenting 'Tannhauser' in a couple of weeks in fact. Wagner has never been a particular favourite. In fact I must admit to falling (momentarily) asleep during a performance of Parsifal once when I was at college. But we were way up in the 'gods' and I'd had a heavy and long day! Anyway I'm in love with Italy and totally faithful. However I must be clear that it is impossible not to feel something while participating in this great music, and pointless to deny it. So, I greet it as a new experience and allow this profound creation to sweep over me without resistance. And I find my psyche presented with phantoms of inexplicable brooding. And encountering a terrible nostalgia that appears to believe it is a memory even when it is 'being' At every rehearsal, and much, much more so when the orchestra is present, we set off into the Black Forest to hunt for the philosopher's stone with a passing nod to Italy in the Venusberg. I love it but I do not hanker after singing it. (Probably just as well!) I have no desire to repair instantly to a studio after the rehearsal with the Prima Donna's voice still ringing in my head, searching for my own identity inside it, as I do with every Italian role that falls anywhere near my range and present ability. No, Wagner is delicious but slightly too heavy for my musical palate. But do I understand those people who fairly salivate at the mere mention of his name? I do indeed.

This settled, there is Martin. And here is Martin and over there and well just about every where really. I'm not sure where women are supposed to stand on sexual appetite. I mean no one tells you, Well, they've never told me anyway! Oh they all seemed to understand about men. The level of understanding there is remarkable! In my short time here I have heard graphic stories of how many girls this baritone required before a performance or how many this tenor required after one. Basses it seems can require such entertainment before and after the show (lucky them) something to do with keeping the voice down apparently. Funny, I thought we all had diaphragm and abdominal muscles for that purpose, but then what do I know? Anyway, none of the singers of today, however athletic their reputations are, come even close to the stories repeated down the years of the great bass Chaliaplin. His exploits were so remarkable one wonders if time has embellished them? I have also been advised that it is extremely unwise to enter a soloist's dressing room during a quiet afternoon in view of what just might be going on in there.

The best place to pick up on the latest scandal is at one of the canteen tables. I find it quite hard to keep up with which dancer or chorister which soloist has fallen on now, how long the last one lasted. And what, if anything the 'chosen one' had to say about him This, it seems, is what people want to know. They seem to live an extra sexual existence through these people without placing themselves in any moral dilemma. I can't say I marshal up any shock horror regarding all this. It's hard for me to come to any real decision on it all, so I don't bother! However, given all this and the music, the air is positively charged with sexual energy that is close to magical. Thus Martin's most sophisticated and seductive approaches (he's really trying) is close to exquisite torture. But there is something else. Martin has found a new singing teacher about whom he positively raves. I've never heard Martin rave before, it's quite an experience. I need to start afresh with someone other than Julia Fordham of whom I'm very fond, but with whom I've worked since I was 18. With all respect, however clever a teacher may be, there comes a point when familiarity of the sound can work against progress. More important she doesn't feel happy about retraining me as a soprano. Something to do with a bad experience she had in her youth when the same thing was attempted with her. It didn't work and she had to stop singing for 6 months to allow her instrument to recover. Martin, on the other hand assures me enthusiastically and often, that Giorgio (who apparently walks on water) is the answer to this maiden's prayer. I see him next Friday.

Dear God where do you stand on sex?

Martin was waiting, staring into space as he registered the ringing tone at the other end of the line fast approaching interruption by the answer machine. At what seemed like the last moment the receiver was picked up.

"Si. Giorgio here."

"Hi Giorgio, it's Martin. I was wondering if I can book myself in after Matilda on Friday and maybe sit in on her lesson first? I'm rather curious how she will respond to you."

"Don't you trust me Martin?"

"Of course Giorgio, otherwise I wouldn't have suggested she get in touch with you. I'm just interested."

There was a short pause then Giorgio said.

"Of course my boy! Happy to see you. Bye now!" Martin hung up. He could sense Giorgio's attitude, and he was quite sure that he was expecting some sweet little soubrette to tip-toe into his studio the following Friday. He didn't want to miss the look on Giorgio's face when she delivered her first phrase across the piano at him. He knew, or felt pretty certain that he knew Giorgio's hang ups. He recognised the river from which his bitterness flowed, after all he was drinking there himself. And he was quite certain that Matilda, dear little lucky, talented, absurdly young and bloody tight-arsed Tilly was exactly what Giorgio didn't need.

JOURNAL

Giorgio Smith, unlikely I know, but I think it's probably true that he is half English and half Italian. He hates to be called George because he likes permanent recognition of his Italian blood. He speaks with only a very slight accent, and has lived here for many years. He's had three wives and is recently divorced from the last of them, is quite tall, sort of compelling rather than good looking, if one wants to be compelled, and seems to be in his mid-forties. There's something else that I cannot place. Anyway he thinks I have talent and potential and am definitely a soprano. All in all a good day! We begin in earnest next week. And I do hope Martin doesn't come. It was very difficult afterwards. Giorgio invited me to stay and listen to Martin's lesson, not something that ever appeals to me, I always feel that a singing lesson is rather a private affair. However I did not want to appear to be rude, so I accepted.

Giorgio had played, unwittingly I presume, right into Martin's hands and afterwards he sidetracked me into a pub and then proceeded to pressure me unashamedly. I'm afraid I gave in, well to a point. It's just that suddenly it all became too much. The apprehension, the lesson which was like an audition in some ways, a glass of wine on an empty stomach, and Martin in top gear and full throttle. I finally stopped struggling. You know when you've had just a touch too much alcohol? Not so much as to be obvious, but enough that you can convince yourself that you're not really doing what you plainly are doing. Enough to turn your body treacherously against your mind?

"So Tilly, you've finally forgiven me ?" No doubt he imagined that the next stop was the bedroom.

"No Martin I haven't forgiven you." My head began to spin slightly.

"Well, remind me to kiss you again when you have!" He grinned at me and stroked my cheek as if he had just recovered some lost property. Now let's get this straight. I am not, repeat NOT flattered! I have no intention of allowing things to proceed any further. It was a pretty good kiss, but he seemed strangely uninvolved. Passion by proxy, as if he were sitting back from the scene and assessing his performance as seen by some invisible audience.

"Well, must be off, the little woman will be waiting." Unbelievable, but not exactly unexpected! I rose from the table on super human reflexes before he had finished the sentence. The speed of the movement prevented any possibility of being hurt by him again. Even he was surprised at the rapid rate of travel and uttered a sound which was a cross between surprise and a groan.

I realise we are at war, a rather erotic war. Every tiny surrender followed by instant withdrawal. We walked to the bus stop making singer's conversation, or at least Martin made conversation.

"I'm not one to be taken in by bloody singing teachers darling, most of them out there are charlatans of the worst kind. Dangerous bastards. But Giorgio knows what he's talking about. I mean I know he's made a difference to my sound already. You can hear it can't you?" I nodded, but in all honesty it's a bit hard for me to tell.

"I'm not kidding myself am I?" I shook my head.

"What he says makes obvious sense. You must do exactly as he says Tilly."

Why? I wondered would one go to a teacher of any sort and not do as they said? Something lent hard into my ribs from inside. I acknowledged it, but missed the point. Something wasn't quite right about all of this. Martin was hyper, desperate for me to go along with Giorgio, his teachings and lessons. I don't understand. After all I've committed myself to studying with the man and frankly it will work or it won't! We'll have to see. I was tired, nervously exhausted. So called 'consultation lessons' can be very taxing. I mean Giorgio could have said anything based on his experience and opinion. I was hungry, and still reeling from Martin's kiss (I haven't been kissed for some time!) Anyway I need a good teacher, a capable, knowledgeable, even caring person. I don't see the need to look further, at least not at the moment. The bus passed the stop for the Opera House. I stayed where I was.

Thank God for the ballet!

Matilda was dreaming. A strong lucid dream of great beauty. She was standing by an incredible lake of shimmering turquoise near to the old man of former acquaintance. His head was surrounded by violet mist and he leant against a weeping willow tree staring towards a mountain in the distance.

Matilda felt wonderfully safe standing there. Her body was full of colour and light. Her conversations with the old man were purely telepathic, except he didn't always answer straight away, and sometimes he didn't answer at all, forcing her to find the answer herself. He gave the strong impression that she could call on him whenever she needed to, and that in some strange way he had always been there which was why she recognised him.

"Whom do I trust?" She asked of him, as small clouds descended from the mountain.

"Now, at this moment? No one. Do not open yourself up. You will be asking for difficulties if you do."

The clouds sank lower. She wished he would look at her, it

made everything so serious when he didn't.

"Such low clouds." She whispered.

"They'll go." He replied looking deep into the water.

"When?"

He didn't answer.

JOURNAL

Giorgio's house is in a cul-de-sac not far from Dulwich station. Walking down the hill to the quiet road today I found myself more than a little apprehensive. Music, all in new keys to fit my 'new' voice jumped about in my shoulder bag. I had no idea, in spite of sitting through Martin's lesson last week, just what to expect. I have worked with only two teachers so far. Some of my friends have tried so many different teachers that it seems like a career in itself, and reminds me of someone constantly experimenting with new hair colour because they can't resist the name on the box.

The house is quite large, I pushed the door bell and waited. Giorgio's Mother opened the door she speaks only Italian, but whether by calculation or necessity I can't tell. Tentatively I tried out my 'singer's Italian' in other words phrases from various operas that probably made me sound like a 19th.Century mad woman. I'd just about run out of them when Giorgio appeared at the music room door.

"Ah! There you are cara. Come in, come in."

He threw open the door and I walked passed him into the same room where I had auditioned for him last week. French windows show a lovely old garden looking as if it had prepared itself for an artist. Everything in it, even the first aggressive approach of spring has a softness which only comes with age. It is a delightful place with steps that lead nowhere in particular and beautiful statues that stare endlessly into the future. I have always been unsure of watching statues for any length of time. I feel they may well move.

"You should see it when the roses are in bloom." Giorgio had come up behind me.

"I shall look forward to that!" And I laughed although he had made me jump. It was no good trying to hide the fact. He had noticed, (I get the impression that very little escapes his notice) but I was annoyed with myself. The last thing I wanted to do was to give the impression of an elderly schoolgirl nervous as a kitten when faced with a new situation. Not very professional!

The lesson began. Twice, during it, the old man appeared clearly and definitely in my mind. It was difficult for me to discern any specific reaction from him. He seemed to be in a different place than when I had seen him in my dreams. It was a place that, although I couldn't picture it clearly, made me feel very uncomfortable. I ignored him and he disappeared.

Giorgio is one of those teachers who demonstrates freely both technically and musically. This can make things much clearer of course, but in this case it does make something else rather apparent, and I must admit it concerns me a little. He has an alarmingly slow vibrato, what we at college use to call a 'thwack' in the voice, as if it is some weighty object that can't move itself fast enough for the pitch, as if it is always running behind its own breath. Still, none of this seems to bother him, neither does it prevent him from explaining exactly what he wants. He also plays the piano (he owns a beautiful grand) rather well, a boon for any singing teacher, not all of them play at all. I did my best to provide what he asked of me.

"The sound must be clearer, more focused. It's too 'thick' and anyway it's not your sound. It's something you have gradually developed over the years because you've been told you are a mezzo. You are not a mezzo, most definitely not."

I find the exercises alien, and it bothers me a little that he never once mentions the God-almighty diaphragm, which we used to laughingly refer to as the reason for anything not being quite right at college, including being late for class. Most of us were indoctrinated about it, and my own teacher was an absolute stickler who had been known to send students out of her studio before the end of their time for consistently refusing to make the considerable mental and physical effort required. I argued with myself that Giorgio must know what he's doing. Apart from anything else he's half Italian, and probably had all his own training in Italy. Maybe he feels all that side of things is well enough established. But I still worry over it. For singers the body is as important as the vocal chords. Ultimately there must be a perfect marriage or the latter may suffer hideously. I felt new pulling sensations and awareness in my throat where none had been before, dry patches, and quite violent coughing, verging, rather embarrassingly on retching. But all these things Giorgio explained easily away, making me feel stupid for mentioning them. I accepted what he said, after all I heard new clarity coming into the sound. The beginning of a finer focus. Then he dropped a bombshell.

"You are trying to make a beautiful sound. Don't! Be happy with an ugly sound first."

This I find impossible to accept. All singers desire beauty in their sound. No one wants to listen to a voice if the sound is unlovely. Tiny areas of lesser quality may be forgiven or overlooked in a great artist, but the reasons that the problem exists in such cases, are not the reasons that I was being given.

So, this evening at the theatre I listened avidly to the soloists. From the side of the stage I concentrated until I became disorientated and nearly missed a cue.

"What's wrong with you?" Ruth Shortland hissed from behind me. "Move! We should be on!"

I catapulted myself forward. Throughout the performance I continued to question in my mind Giorgio's worrying comment to me. Whichever way I turned it the outcome was the same. Every instinct screamed at me, but so did Martin when, just before the final scene I questioned him on it.

"My instinct......" I began.

"It's not instinct, it's bloody ego." He replied. We were making our way to the stage.

"Who do you think you are?"

That was unfair I think and at the time really upset me. I needed to discuss this seriously and surely I'm not expected to ignore my inner sensing on the subject? Martin continued.

"You've never been trained properly before." He whispered as we picked up our props from the prompt corner.

"You've been allowed to sing on raw talent like most people do, and then a few years down the line they wonder why they can no longer contain the 'beast' in such a flimsy cage, and why they are into trouble. For goodness sake it's your first lesson, give the man a chance!"

"Ladies and gentlemen please be quiet." The stage manager hissed at us. "Tilly, I don't usually have to remind you!"

"Sorry." I mouthed and tried to align myself with the music if nothing else in order to calm me down. But it didn't work. That's the first time I ever remember that happening! I can't think what it all means because, not surprisingly, I'm exhausted now. I must sleep and I hope I don't have a problem. Night time, as we know, is when all the little gremlins just love to get on their party gear and dance the night away in your head. At least I have tomorrow off until the evening. As I was coming home tonight I found myself wishing that Martin was on the other side of the planet, and that I had never laid eyes or ears on Giorgio and his mystifying directions. That's a lot of wishing. If wishes were horses then beggars could ride.

Dear God. Where's the cavalry?

The old man sighed. He had levitated to the top of the mountain and reached up to pluck a star from the velvet darkness. Once it was in his hand he didn't study it, but flung it behind him in a graceful arc. It shimmered and sparkled as it fell towards some earth unknown to him. It had in its glorious pointed lights some memories which he knew Matilda needed to become aware of. Something from the past time long ago and highly concentrated in singing. A place where life itself (or the prospect of it) was sacrificed to the art. She didn't need the whole life, just enough to render a tonic to her instinct, so cruelly railed against by these antagonists. He could only hope that she would be receptive.

JOURNAL

It's been nearly 2 months since my first lesson. I was working with Maria today and she became very thoughtful after I finished the aria we were looking at.

"It doesn't sound like you Till. I know it's bound to change considerably in some ways, but it just isn't you."

"I've only had a few lessons." I began defensively, not wanting to face the prospect of having to question everything again, and quietly irritated at myself for assuming that 'different' must equal better. It obviously doesn't!

"Exactly. A few lessons and so much change so quickly? Well that's one thing, but not when it removes some of that lovely quality that everyone likes when they hear you! No, I'm sorry luv, but you asked me. There's something bothering me. Look I know you hate to do it, (don't we all?) But pluck up the courage and record it. You're by far the best judge of your own sound. You'll know immediately with the very first phrase whether it's right or not."

I'm not sure if I agree with all of that, but I did as she suggested and I have just this second turned off the tape. People are kind when they like what they hear. And even if your technique is threadbare in places and resembling badly darned holes elsewhere, they'll find something nice to say.

To have quality, colour, and natural expression over the phrase, all these are more than necessary simply to start with, and are, at least to some extent, still there. I recognise a turn of the phrase where the individuality of the instrument shows through in spite of what its stupid owner is doing. But the colour is white-washed, and the warmth is gone. If this is me being a soprano, forget it. I will not lose what I had by nature in order to attain mediocrity, because that is what it sounds like. It could be anyone singing. Doubts as big as black crows crowd me. I'm completely unsure and quite desperate.

Gear God. What shall I do?

"Dream." Breathed the old man.........."Dream."

Carlo

Matilda had always been a natural dreamer with the ability to be fully conscious in her dreams. Her experiences in this realm are too numerous to list. She had even dreamt within a dream, convinced that the second dream was her waking state, until some familiar sound had worried at her like a sheepdog at a rebel sheep and dragged her back to everyday life. She had awoken dazed, but fascinated by the incredible ability of the human mind.

What she was experiencing now, however, was new to her. She had begun in pitch blackness, first perceiving herself as a 'sliver' of extremely energised consciousness and aware that she, as this 'silver snake,' was travelling over humps and shapes that she could only feel. The shape and size of the bumps expressed themselves to her as feelings, deeply buried and all but forgotten, and she had the strangest awareness. She experienced the feelings, but she did not 'feel' them in the normal energy consuming way.

Suddenly there was a burst of colour, and wonderful, wonderful sound. Notes held beyond human endurance. Part of her crawled in exquisite agony, and inextinguishable lust that threatened to relieve her of consciousness. It terrified and mesmerised. 'Who was that?' She wondered.

Then a greater truth dawned. It was her, she was singing and she was controlling everyone around her by her art. Except she wasn't a 'her' she wasn't a 'him' either, she realised instinctively. She was a strange mixture, and it was this 'mixture' that gave birth to the unparalleled brilliance that poured into the air. And the name of the exquisite creature who engineered the brilliance was Carlo, and the place was Venice and centuries ago. This rich artistic life was overshadowed by a painful truth, its origination in the past with the erotic cut. Its continuation into the future until God released him, hopefully (Carlo often prayed) not to plunge him into something even more horrendous. Softly Matilda spoke to him.

"Don't be afraid Carlo, it's not like that." Carlo turned from the brilliant sun and peered into the shadows.

"Che cosa? What was that?"

"What?" Asked Raimondo, placing his arm around Carlo's slender body. Tall, slender and very beautiful, Carlo was a lover of both men and women. Neither eclipsed the other because of their gender, only because of themselves. With Carlo, there was, in his excesses, an innocence. Strange bed fellows, but neverthe-less true. He simply lived. There was no deceit or deviousness. It was his way of expressing his appreciation of the beauty around him, and he was very susceptible to beauty, often seeing it where others did not. Often finding it in obscure, or unlovely places. Raimondo on the other hand, loved only Carlo, at least this year, and he was very, very jealous.

"I heard a whisper like silk on skin." Said Carlo.

"Silk on skin!" Sang Raimondo, using a bell that was sounding to curtail their siesta, as a base pitch and extemporising with 'silken skin' and 'skinned silk' using every musical cadence within his knowledge and throughout his entire vocal range, until the rest of the group of students who were lolling around in the alcove swilling wine, were helpless with laughter.

"I heard it!" Carlo grinned. "I did. Look goose bumps!" At which Raimondo grabbed his arm in mock concern. Carlo's green silken tunic was loosened in the afternoon heat and the sleeve of his shift revealed the slender limb. .

"Dio………Gran Dio…….He has the, my God I dare not say it…….The goose bumps!"

Raimondo, if the truth be told was more actor than singer and dealt with his 'grand tragedy' by playing the 'court jester' at every available opportunity. One rarely saw the Raimondo who was hiding in the shadows cast by his own self loathing. Except that is, when passion fired its way through all his pretence and made him forget to hide from himself. Then Carlo would hold him like a baby to his breast, while Raimondo sobbed as if his body would break in two.

"Gooses bumps, heat, fever? There is only one place for you Signor, and that's bed!" And he ran on ahead, continuing his extemporisation and now putting himself in danger of severe punishment since the content had strayed from both silk and skin into a land punishable by a whipping across the long muscular back. Lucciano drew close to Carlo.

"Caro mio, why must it always be Raimondo?"

"It is not Lucci. You know how jealous and vain he is. He'll soon find another peacock and be off! You and I understand each other, and we'll be together again." Actually, he wished they would all shut up and leave him alone for a while, he wanted to concentrate on that whisper, but he drew closer to the trembling Lucciano, and traced the young man's exquisite cheekbone with his finger.

"We can wait......No!" As Lucciano attempted to control his trembles. "For they are as lovely as you!" He turned and watched Raimondo as he disappeared into the darkness of the palazzo.

"Keep an eye on the wretched fellow, caro, he will bring trouble to himself in this mood, and he has completely forgotten that I have a fitting."

Lucciano swallowed hard and stared at the ground, looked up into Carlo's glorious green eyes for the loving eternity of some seconds, nodded, and fled down the path.

Carlo did not have a fitting. Carlo was enamoured with his secret. He felt that without losing any of his prodigious talent, he had opened a shutter long enough to allow someone else to share his view of his beloved art. No, not his view, his understanding. But who was she, this sweet voice who had so easily calmed his fears of eternal damnation? Suddenly as he sat, alone at last, in a dark cool inner hall of the palazzo, he knew beyond any doubt that just as the sweet voice had assured him. "It's not like that."

That evening Carlo joined another group of friends. Whenever the rarified atmosphere of his training and the seemingly endless bickering of his well loved friends became too much to bear, he would escape with a band of street singers.

"Like a Prince in a farmyard!" Raimondo had jibed at him when he first learnt of his regular sojourns around Venice. Carlo laughed it off and replied gently that if only Raimondo would get off his high horse long enough he might find that 'the farm-yard' was in fact a magical place. Needless to say Raimondo, nor any of the others ever considered joining him, a fact which Carlo was not at all certain that he minded. He needed space from the other castrati in order to remember how to breathe again.

Tonight, however he had another reason for wanting some space from the Academy. He found himself drawn like a magnet to the soprano. Not to her exactly, for they had long since run that voluptuous course, but to her sound. For the first time, he mapped the rise and fall of the velvet voice, not just with his ear, but in his heart, and suddenly he knew beyond any doubt that he and his 'kind' had only a short time left to them. Those standing around him in the dark beside the lapping canals, these voices, sopranos, mezzos and the pitch of tenors and basses that Carlo often found himself thirsty for. They that wove their ways between the cries of the gondoliers, and thanked their patrons for a glass of wine. They were the future of Opera. He bad them goodnight and made his way home. The city was as it always had been and he loved it more than ever. But in his mind a whole new world was opening up. In a tiny moment he felt, rather than heard a future of sound that threatened to engulf him with its power. In spite of himself, Carlo was content. Somehow it seemed right.

JOURNAL

I had the strangest dream last night. My awareness kept flipping between myself now and some other self in a past time and some other place. And yet that place was as present as the morning when I awoke. In some ways it was much more alive and shimmering with colours. I also have the weirdest feeling that my presence in that dream, helped someone, or eased some worry or suffering in some way. Whether that's true or not I have woken resolved. I will be myself. Total surrender is not an option.

Thanks God!

The 'old man' counted the stars. His chosen one had returned, and sparkled brighter than ever. He smiled and curled himself into the violet of the mist.

Fairies Ferry

JOURNAL

A whole year and a half has elapsed since I joined the company. Also, a while since I wrote here so I must bring you up to date. Next week we leave for Italy to perform at La Scala for a fortnight, this is an unbelievable accomplishment for me even as a chorister, and I feel the enormity of it. I'm so excited that I have to deliberately play it cool. A few of my college friends joined this season. In particular, Pixie, ridiculously named but it's better than Priscilla. She lives quite close to the Opera House. I'm extremely fond of Pixie, we have always got on well since our very first day at college. Well, we were having a lovely evening gossiping and giggling about nothing when suddenly she mentioned Martin.

"Just what goes on with you two?"

"Nothing." I replied.

"Oh come on Tilly, everyone's talking about it."

"What?" I was genuinely horrified, and hurried on to explain. "Look, I can't say I haven't been a smidgen tempted…….."

At which point she grinned at me wickedly.

"But…." I continued. "There's nothing 'going on' as you put it. Apart from anything else like he's married, I don't want to get involved again. Also, to put it bluntly, he's not really a very nice person you know?"

"So who is? All the time anyway. We all have our little foibles."

"No, you don't understand." I was frustrated, must I go into old history? But Pixie was off on another track and it took me a while to see where she was heading.

"Maybe not." She answered me. "But I think life's a bit tough for him at the moment. So maybe when he's a bit 'off' it's nothing personal. After all, here you are a single girl in regular steady work, and he has a wife to support, and well, you know what singers are like when they can't find work. They get suicidal some of them, it's understandable you know. I was desperate before I joined the chorus. I won't tell you some of the jobs I had to do to make ends almost meet."

"I have no intention of tailoring my career to him or his bloody wife." I growled.

"O.K. Till! Sorry, of course I didn't mean that. It's just that I think he's rather sweet."

"SWEET!" I thought, but I had no intention of arguing with Pixie over Martin. So I added more gently.

"Look. O.K. He's very attractive and he can be charming and amusing. Truth to tell he doesn't know when to stop. But the bottom line is, I don't trust him. I won't go into why now, it's too…well fresh in my mind if you understand."

"Hmm….." Pixie mused. "It's a shame though."

"A shame?" I didn't understand what she meant. She proceeded to enlighten me. Pixie has been seeing a rather gorgeous stage hand the stage staff are also coming to Milan with us. Light was dawning, also a slight feeling of guilt.

"If we shared a room in Milan, and Martin and Mike also shared we could just swap around. No one would be any the wiser, no gossip and no recriminations from anyone who might suddenly feel the need to get brownie points with God. I can't be doing with all that rubbish."

"Oh I see. I'm really sorry. I just can't........."

"No problem Tilly. But I would have thought he'd asked you."

To tell the truth he never stops, but that was not something I was about to admit to anyone. I don't take it as a compliment. He's just like a dog worrying at a bone. I muttered something to the effect that he was making jokes about it, and returned my attention to the sausages, chips and baked beans piled up on my plate. This was followed by apple pie and it was all washed down with Chablis.

"Pixie, that was great, really delicious!"

"Well, you can see what I spent the money on." She laughed as she emptied the bottle into our glasses. Not much later we said goodnight, after all we are working girls! I have to admit that I felt a bit bad that I couldn't oblige over the room in Milan, and briefly as I hailed a taxi, which I had promised myself, it occurred to me that it wasn't exactly 'wrong' to indulge in a couple of weeks of intense passion, was it? As long as everyone knows exactly were they stand after the event. After all people did it all the time these days and especially in this profession. I leaned back in the taxi, I was nearly home. In front of me on the back of the driver's partition was an advert. I stared at it without really seeing it.

"Right 'ere love?" Asked the driver pulling me out of my reverie.

"Great, thanks!" And I held onto the strap as the taxi swung into Cross Street as only a London taxi can, full of speed and grace. A few minutes later, as I put the kettle on I was still turning the possibility of accepting Martin's seductive offer over in my mind. I must admit the actual idea of that sort of sexual freedom is hugely delicious and I was smiling to myself when suddenly, the advert in the cab flashed into my mind, registering very much more than it had a few minutes before. It was an advert for pensions, and it made up my mind for me.

PLAY SAFE, INVEST IN MARTIN PENSION SCHEMES.

Well that's that then. Sorry Pixie, sorry Mike, but the message couldn't really be clearer! Play safe, and Martin aren't really words that go easily together. There goes my career as a libertine if one can apply that word to a female!

Journal

I performed my soprano aria at the re-auditions this year, not long before we left for Italy. I felt good about it and had not entertained the possibility of any problem until later the same day. The lady who had been on the audition list to sing after me, a great character known to us all as 'Flower' for reasons buried in the past and best left there, bounced up and asked me what had I done to the panel?

"Done to them?" I was mystified.

"Yes. I had to wait over 5 minutes before they called me in to sing."

"Well I'm sorry, but I can't imagine why that was." I could feel the worry beginning to spread from my face into my heart which started to sink like a stone. Flower, as sensitive as most singers would be in such a situation to a colleague, waved her hand in the air and grinned.

"Probably nothing to do with us at all." Adding wickedly. "Maybe they needed a drink. A quick glass of something to keep them going bless them!" And she bounced off again. So when Adrian, another friend from college came across me in the canteen, looking as he said…."As if the sky had fallen and most of it on to me…." I told him what Flower had said.

"Ah!" He placed his coffee on the table and sat down. "Well it's nothing to worry about. If I assure you of that, and say that in fact it is the opposite, will you let it rest?"

I looked at him as only a singer could in those circumstances and he grinned.

"Obviously not! Well, I'm not supposed to say anything." I kept looking at him until finally, with a sigh, he gave in.

"The pianist, you know Richard, told me. But of course he shouldn't have repeated it to me or anyone else for that matter. But he knows that you and I are friends."

I still hadn't said a word, but my eyes were boring into the poor chap, and I knew he was going to tell me. Well honestly, I mean who could walk away from something like that without hearing the whole story. Not me for one! He took a sip of his coffee, a deep breath and said.

"They like you Matilda. In fact they were very impressed. They were discussing possible steps to help you on your way as it were."

"You mean they're thinking of giving me a tiny part or something?" I was incredulous. And Adrian kept glancing about as if he were divulging state secrets.

"No, something more substantial than that. Sometimes they send young singers off abroad, to Italy or Germany, somewhere like that. I didn't know that, Richard told me. You get sent on a scholarship, which is quite generous, well it would be from here I suppose. And you are expected to return in 6 months, reasonably capable in the language and trained to the utmost in one or two well chosen roles that you would be capable of singing now. Not things that we all hope we can cope with in the future, but actual workable roles."

I was having a hard job believing what I was hearing, but sent many blessings to Carlo during the next few moments. I could feel my eyes growing huge as I stared at Adrian across the table, but he averted his gaze and stared into his coffee. Finally he said.

"I hate to be a wet blanket Tilly, but I wouldn't hold your breath, and please don't let on that I've told you. Well not for a long time anyway, promise?"

"Of course Adrian, I won't say a word." I assured him. I expect they'll forget, or change their minds or something. But it's very comforting to know what they think. My compromise must be working in spite of what I sense as Giorgio's rapidly gathering boredom with me. Adrian glanced sideways at a pretty ballet boy who nodded at him. Then he said.

"Don't you sometimes feel that it's all going a bit 'pear shaped'?"

"What do you mean?" I asked through all the 'sugar plum fairies' that were dancing in my head.

"The art form. Our art form. All this." He gestured towards the tanhoy through which we could hear our fabulous orchestra rehearsing. "I feel it's being pushed into something it isn't, and being denied something that it is, which is surely timeless and incorruptible. When you really think about it, music is one of the few things that isn't corruptible. We leave it as we find it. It forms us, or it hones and focuses our talent. But we can't actually touch it." I had no idea Adrian felt so deeply. I found myself suddenly very interested. He continued.

"Look at all this 'status' business for a start."

"That's bound to happen, and to be fair I think it always did." I said, thinking of Carlo again.

"Of course." Adrian nodded. "But it's getting out of balance somehow. I can't put my finger on it, but did you know that the ancients believed......."The ballet boy finally bit the bullet and came over.

"May I join you?" This was my cue to leave. As the Greek god sat down, I rose.

"We must talk more about this Adrian. I'm really interested in what you've said, and thanks so much for the other." I flashed a smile at the Greek god, who had relaxed considerably, and left.

JOURNAL

The Opera Manager stopped me in the corridor today.

"I guess you're the lucky one." She said.

"The what?" I replied.

"I decided I'd offer it to the first member of the company that I saw today, and you're the first. There's a spare single room going in Milan. You want it?" Did I ever!

"Oh yes please Pauline. That'd be great, thanks!"

"O.K. It's yours."

Later I bumped into Martin.

"So." He began. "Who are you going to be sharing with on our Grand Tour? Got some little lesbian scene going, have you?"

"Don't be stupid Martin. You should know whether I'm gay or not!"

"Well darling, I know you certainly didn't used to be. I thought the wind may have changed direction."

"No, the wind hasn't, and it so happens I have a single room."

"Lucky you. I can come and see you then, no one else to worry about, clever girl!"

"No Martin, you can't come and see me." I replied, the irritation obvious in my voice. He turned away, appeared to stare down the corridor, then suddenly spun back to me and almost spat in my face.

"You know Tilly, you really are the most stuck up little bitch I've ever fucked. You lead me on, but you're nothing but a prick teaser. Who do you think you are anyway?"

I was shocked and mortified the last thing I had expected was such an outburst.

"I thought we were friends Martin. I certainly never intended to tease your….I mean tease you, you know me better than that!" (The whole idea is ridiculous.) "Maybe we should terminate our friendship, now!" He lifted his head from its too-close proximity to mine and looked at me down his aquiline nose.

"Do you have ANY feelings?" He thundered.

"I don't know what you mean, that's a stupid thing to say." My heart was thumping and my stomach danced 'flamenco,' fairly good indications of feeling. I glanced down the corridor hoping that somebody, anybody, would appear from somewhere. It was deserted, wouldn't you know it? Martin hadn't finished.

"You think you're too good to live don't you? With your precious so called lirico-spinto voice. Do you have any idea how many sopranos there are in the world? Bloody thousands!"

"No Martin, there are thousands of women with soprano timbre to their voice. That, however, does not necessarily constitute an operatic soprano of any sort. He was momentarily taken aback.

"Well, the voice has a brain!"

"Let me pass Martin."

"Oh going to practise are we? Keeping up our, what did you call it?……..Vocal health? Do you know how much of a stuck up little prig you sound, talking like that?"

I didn't want to hear any more of this.

"Martin, I really don't know what your problem is, but…….."

"I'll tell you." He hissed, stabbing me with his finger. "You! You are my problem, and one day I intend to be yours!" And he strode away.

The 'old man' sighed contentedly. He was sipping a silver wine beneath the shade of his beautiful tree. He didn't need the shade of course, he didn't need the wine either, but it helped him to relax. It was hard work dealing with this third dimension projection. The glorious tone thoughts continually surging up from the very centre of the 'being' were beautiful, pure, untouchable and guiltless, like a tiger's rage.

He stood his crystal glass down, amused with himself for needing to camouflage his energy in this way. But he loved, and greatly missed the sensual side of humanity. There was such energy, often wasted in his opinion, but the potential was beyond imagination.

Lothus, Carlo and Matilda. One and the same and yet so different, and all linked by a part of a secret. A secret so powerful and wonderful that he knew he must overcome all opposition and bring it altogether with the necessary precision. If he failed, it would mean the passing of another huge chunk of time before the chance would offer itself again.

But he was concerned for Matilda. She was like a deer in a valley of wolves. A courageous little deer, but a deer, and at risk nevertheless. Her love of the music was there, this was not debatable, but she was swimming dangerously close to the sharks, one of which was knowing, and the other not aware of anything outside his own difficult emotional world.

She was too easily influenced, far too ready to please everybody. Also she showed little or no real ambition, and one day she would have to ride that particular energy at full gallop. He was not able to reveal these things to her directly. He could only watch and be there if she needed him. Flash into her mind when her concentration was totally absorbed elsewhere, or involved in dream experience. He could change nothing, for she must do that. He could point out nothing, for she must do things for herself. He picked up the golden crystal, and over its sparkling rim, surveyed the mountain. A sudden memory of a young shepherd boy struggling against the light on his work table flashed unbidden into his mind. He shuddered.

"Matilda, keep the mountain strong." He whispered. All this the old man felt, he did not need words in his domain.

JOURNAL

I went home this weekend, it will be the last time before we leave for Milan. And much to my delight I managed to spend some time with Lucy. Aunt Lucy actually, although she insisted that I drop the 'Aunt' years ago when I was still a teenager.

"Come with me to Fairies Ferry, there's a full moon tonight."

"Oh full moon is it?" Lucy's Mother had been Welsh, and that lovely Celtic lilt often perfumes her speech.

"Well it's supposed to be the best time." I insisted.

"The best time for Fairies' Ferry is when you feel it to be the best time Tilly. Oh it's very magical with a full moon I grant you. O.K. I'll walk you to the great oak and wait for you there. Beyond that you're on your own."

"Why are you going to wait there?" I asked her a little puzzled. "Why 'wait' anywhere? Come with me."

"I can't." She smiled at me. I knew she would have what to her would be a good reason, but I couldn't imagine what it was. She was giving me one of knowing psychic looks, I had to ask her.

"Why can't you Lucy? I don't understand. Don't tell me you've become skittish about being out in the dark."

"Of course not." She laughed. "The point is you're the one being called, not me."

"Called? No I just want to go."

"Well how would you feel if you didn't go?" She kept probing at me. I was taken aback.

"Oh I must go." I replied without thinking and she sat back, nodding and smiling at me.

"Then you've been called." There was nothing more to say. Two hours later, wrapped up against the chill we set off for the edge of the village and picked our way carefully along the track. There had been no rain for a while and the hardened ground with its high ridges was hurtful to the feet if one was careless. We stopped by the oak.

"I'll be here, off you go." And Lucy made herself as comfortable as she could while I continued into the open meadow. It didn't occur to me to be frightened. Apart from anything else there was a strange almost warm feeling overriding the cold air, and it intensified the nearer I drew to the waterfall. There was a pinkish glow over the entire area. I found myself humming the opening bars of 'Casta Diva' from Bellini's 'Norma.' Quite suddenly however I felt so drowsy that it was impossible to believe that I had been walking through the night air. I knew that I had to sit down on the bank. I could hear music by now. Unrecognisable, beautiful and played superbly, as if some Symphony Orchestra had secreted itself in our countryside. The music became louder and louder drawing me like a magnet until my head was spinning and I seemed to lose consciousness. When I awoke it was bright day light and sitting not far from me was a strange Being. The only thought moving around somewhere in my head was that I wondered why Lucy had not come to collect me and had apparently left me here all night. Although it didn't seemed to matter so removed from everything else was the thought. The 'Being' is difficult to describe as it appeared to be composed of light and the form and features undulated with the pulse of the music that I could still hear. It seemed to be concentrating very hard on me, staring at all of me at once. I felt as if I were being scanned. But I didn't even entertain the idea that I ought to perhaps be feeling a little concerned.

"It is prodigious that you hear our music." He finally spoke. (I guessed by the octave of the voice that he was male.) "Our music is ever present. We spin it into space for you."

I was mesmorised. His voice was like a flute and 'cello combined. It echoed and sustained as if he were singing in some great Cathedral. I realised he was expecting me to answer him, and the words came to my mouth without any conscious thought.

"And we?" I ventured, my voice sounding dull and flat after his.

"You." He continued sounding like a silken roar. "You all take from it what you can. In direct relationship to your talents, abilities and musical intelligence. You draw from it and soak up what you are able." I nodded briefly, full of questions suddenly, but also wondering if I was dreaming. The 'Being' sighed a sound like a thousand sleepy snakes and waves of pink flicked across the space between us.

"You should know that this is not a dream, since you know dreams." I felt I had disappointed, and was deeply ashamed, as if

I had trashed the moment by such a consideration. But the 'Being' I realised was not interested in my apologies. It was extraordinary for as I lent towards a feeling, long before it was a verbal thought, the 'Being' had sent back to me his reply. He continued speaking and I concentrated on not forming any opinion about the content of his speech. At that moment I endeavoured only to soak it all up. I knew I would always remember what was happening and any human need to analyse could, and indeed must, wait.

"We are the Guardians. You may consider yourself privileged but not limited. The limits lay outside the music. There is something that you must do. You must go into the sound. Allow it to open into a universe as great inside, as you see here in the sky above. Whatever happens you are not to stop. Do you understand?"

I was confused. I felt as if he were speaking in riddles, he and the music were beginning to fade, and with them both, the light. It was in fact, quite dark. But just before it all faded completely, the 'Being' threw something towards me in a graceful arc, something sparkling. I waited to feel it strike me, but I felt nothing. I tried to hold on to the experience, but it was as if I were standing at a station, watching an express train pulling away at the speed of light, and powerless to board. Then quite suddenly, it had all gone. An owl called from Baby-Devil's wood and the water resumed its silvery quality beneath the moon. I felt energised and relaxed at the same time. I stood up quickly and headed back to the oak. Lucy was still there humming to herself.

"That was quick!" She said looking at me intently. We started back to the village.

"What were you humming?" I asked. I felt quite dazed and I couldn't put my finger on the familiar phrases.

"You should know. " She chided me. "Norma! I picked up where you left off." I stopped in my tracks so suddenly, that Lucy took a few steps before she stopped and turned around.

"But….I mean….Why did you leave it so long?" She came back to me looking even more closely into my face then a few moments before. She slipped her arm around my shoulders and said softly.

"I didn't love, I carried on immediately. I do have some musical sense you know. Come on let's go it's cold." But I found it hard to move. "Tilly? Come let's go to the pub."

"Lucy, something strange happened in there." I turned and gazed back from the way we had come.

"Are you alright? What happened? You were only there a few minutes."

"I can't have been. Lucy, it was day time, and I thought you'd left me there all night, and then there was the music, and I had stopped singing that Norma phrase ages ago……I don't understand."

Lucy waved her hand up and down in front of my face. I was magnetised to the spot, and she shook me gently saying.

"The pub Tilly you need a brandy, then you can tell me all about this, because I think you need to."

Milano

Lucy ushered me firmly to the old fashioned pub in the middle of the village. 'The Hangman's Noose' is a doubtful tribute to the spot on which it stood. But inside it's fabulous. I've always loved it, and no other pub, for me, has ever come up to this one. A fire roared in the corner and luckily the table close to it was unoccupied. Lucy sat me down literally by applying firm but gentle pressure to my shoulders, and then went off to by us something to drink. I felt like a doll sitting there. A few people nodded in recognition, I had grown up in this village of course, and I managed to reply in the like, but I had to think about it. My body was acting as if it had been left out on the cold wastes of Antarctica for too long, and yet in the centre of my being I felt warmth. The clink of glasses in front of me sounded a hundred miles away.

"Come on sweetheart, come back." Lucy leaned across the table and performed a rather strange little ritual. She picked up my glass and made me take it. I found myself staring into her familiar face, so at peace with everything, that each second seemed like an hour and the whole world had gone into slow motion.

"Drink!" She commanded. And as I took a sip she said quite curtly. What's your name?"

"My name?" Even in my distant state I registered the absurdity of her asking me. She stared at me with such intensity however that I swallowed the warm brandy and peppermint and told her. At which point she insisted that I drink again. Then she asked me my address both in the village and in London. I gave them both and she leaned back and relaxed a little. Picking up her own drink she said thoughtfully.

"I never realised that you were psychic." She bit her lower lip before adding. "Does this sort of thing happen often?"

It seemed as if the air had been held up. As if some unseen hand had pulled a cord and rolled it up like a blind. Now, with an audible sigh it sank gratefully back to its accustomed place and I felt normal again. I told Lucy everything. My dreams from as far back as I could remember, my experience with Carlo, the 'old man' and the strange Being. Then I burst into tears.

"I'm sorry!" I chocked. Silently she handed me a handkerchief saying. "No apologies."

(That made the second time that night that my apology was not required.)

"I wish I had realised, I could have been helping you with all this Tilly. But you've never said a word."

"I assumed that these things happen to everyone, that it's normal but a bit private, not to be openly discussed." At which Lucy smiled broadly.

"As to the point of it being 'normal' for everyone don't we wish! Of course I believe it should be that way."

"But Lucy, don't you have things like this happen? I mean,

you must be psychic." Lucy has a bit of a reputation in the village (not least with my parents) she stared into the depths of her brandy glass. "You mean my Celtic blood?" She mused.

"I thought people of that lineage have strong leanings in that way. But Lucy, I don't feel psychic. I mean I can't predict things, or heal people, you know?"

"Telling the future is only one, often very abused, part of the psychic world. As for the other, I wouldn't be too sure." For a moment she looked as far away as I had felt when we first sat down. Then she sighed gently and continued. "This is very different from the things you've mentioned, and far, far rarer. This is an expansion of the mind, the consciousness. Some people train all their lives for just one experience like the ones you've been describing to me."

"Sorry ladies…….." Barry the landlord was standing by the table picking up my empty glass and looking hopefully at the one Lucy still held in her hand……..""I must ask you to drink up."

"Jeeze." Said Lucy. "I didn't realise the time. Come on Tilly."

And I got up, feeling completely myself again. We walked back to Lucy's cottage where I usually stayed over night when I visited her, my parents having encouraged it from when I was quite young, indeed they would have been very surprised had I returned home that night. We were both unusually quiet all the way back, and when Lucy offered me more brandy by the kitchen fire, I shook my head, excused myself and went up to bed.

I lay there in the comfort and warmth fighting sleep, wanting to drink in the wonderful silence. The owl called from the wood again and I saw the 'Being' in my mind undulating to the music its energy caught up in sounds beyond belief. A vibration like a bass drum rumbled at the base of my spine and without warning roared up into my head spreading sensations like fairy dust to every part of my body. Lights and colours filled the room. I didn't know if I slept or woke. Every nerve became alive, even the skin on my face seemed to dance like cobwebs in a breeze. The last thing I remember was the 'old man' his head flung back in the violet mist and laughing so hard that tears poured down his cheeks and splashed into the turquoise water. I realised while my fast-drifting consciousness allowed me that he is not 'old' at all. His hair was as black as night. Behind him the mountain had become a long fabulous range which rivalled the alps themselves.

Goodnight God.

Lucy sat staring into the fire, thinking. How could she have missed all the signs? Of course it would be this way with Tilly! Her own sweet Matilda. She felt privileged, for as she saw it, she was the obvious guide, for Tilly trusted her and Lucy knew better than to interfere in any way. This was a brilliant gift and as far as she was concerned an obvious off shoot of her musical ability. Then with something of a jolt she remembered something else. Something she had read in the old yellowed papers that had always, according to her Great-Grandmother, been part of the family's history, and now resided among her books. What did it say now? And why should it come into her mind tonight?

Lucy had once asked an old Welshman to translate the writing for her when she had been only a little older than Matilda was now. He had taken the papers off to his cottage for a few days. The language was indeed Welsh, but an ancient version of it and it took him many hours to work out an English translation. Even then the meaning was very unclear, full of poetic and mystic phrases, it made little sense. Only one of these phrases sprung to her mind as she sat by the fire late that night: ONE SHALL COME AND BE UNKNOWN. Or, as the old Welshman had pointed out, UNKNOWING. It was impossible to decide on the grammar he had explained, there was no modern equivalent. Either way it sounded like a rather pompous credit to a Hollywood movie. Lucy giggled but she went to her bookcase and pulled out the old papers, another book, refilled her glass and tip-toed up the stairs.

Miles away, however many it may be, in London, Martin filled his glass. Connie had gone to bed long ago, exhausted she had claimed. But why? Exhausted by what? It was the weekend for Christ's sake. She hadn't been to work, in fact she'd done bugger all, all day. Which brought him back to their situation. They hadn't been married five minutes and already they behaved with the grinding familiarity of an old married couple who don't like each other very much. He shuddered and moved over to the phone. Picking up the receiver he pressed in Tilly's number....... No reply.......So where was she? He knew that he had no right to phone her under any pretext whatsoever, given his behaviour at the Opera House earlier in the week. But he just couldn't let go, he was bent on destruction and his hatred for Matilda was growing apace. Why? He didn't know, and the force of his emotion was so strong that it didn't occur to him to question himself, or his behaviour. All he knew was that his hate held equal sway with his unquenchable lust. The power of the later surprised him, usually such a wave was easily abated in the normal way. Either a quick seduction or, were he on occasion refused by some little tart, a shrug which indicated boredom, and you-have-no-idea-what-you-are-missing, in equal parts. But with Matilda he was at a loss to know how to proceed. He rang the number again, and this time he left a message.

"Tilly, it's Martin. I need to speak to you. Please!" Contrite and uncharacteristically low key. That should get her! He replaced the receiver and stared down into his whisky. He felt powerless, and he didn't like to feel powerless. He lay back down on the settee and felt himself beginning to drift off. As he did so a curious picture formed in his mind. It was of Matilda sitting on top of a mountain.

JOURNAL

We've arrived! I've checked into my single room. I didn't really believe that I would have it. I was convinced that some mistake would be discovered, But here I am all by myself. You may ask why it is so important for me to be in a single room by myself. Well, actually I don't know, it's just a feeling. O.K. it's more than that. It's Carlo! I am in his country now remember, I just want my own space while I'm here, no reflection on the lovely ladies of the chorus.

I'm meeting Martin for tea. I spoke to him briefly earlier, during the flight. He looks terrible, it seems churlish not to speak to the man. I know, I know he doesn't deserve it, but conversation over tea can't hurt can it? More later.....

We are invited to dinner tonight. The entire company plus soloists, to a restaurant near to the hotel. A wonderful show of welcome, I only hope that the Italian company are receiving the same first class treatment in London. Martin wants me to go with him, that is to sit at the same table so we can 'talk.' I sort of expected an apology for you know what, but all he really said, amongst a lot of 'nothingness' was, 'Let's talk over dinner.' Well he obviously has something to say! The meal was delicious, well this is Italy, what did we expect? And Martin? Martin wanted to talk about Giorgio. For once he kept his hands and his sexual innuendos to himself. I'm going to save the content of the evening for later. I'm exhausted, it's been a long day.

The starter had been eaten and the dishes cleared away. We were waiting for the main course to arrive. One of the choices just happened to be my favourite. Fettucine Alfredo, green salad and garlic bread.

"Garlic bread? " Martin exclaimed. "Just as well you do have a single room Tilly!" I hoped we weren't going down that well worn path again, but he said no more, drank his wine and refilled his glass. He offered me more, but I had scarcely made a difference to the burgundy level.

"I won't take advantage." He promised. "In fact I'm meeting someone later." As he glanced at his watch, I smiled at him a little ruefully.

"You know drink and me Martin, a little goes a long way." I replied wondering who the 'someone' was. What poor deluded and unsuspecting creature would find herself used for a few hours then dropped unceremoniously without a second thought.

"Doesn't your wife..........?" I began, but Martin jumped in.

"Connie doesn't give a f-er doesn't care what I do." He corrected himself, he was really trying to behave, in fact it was almost funny, so used am I, to the Martin of old.

"She's not interested anymore anyway, doesn't want to know. That's what happens when you tie the knot Tilly. Still, imagine anyone not fancying me, beggars belief doesn't it darling?"

I ignored his last comment as best I could while he surveyed me intently over his third glass of wine. I studied him as subtly as possible and whatever else you might want to say about him I have to admit that I found his wife's attitude hard to understand. Even if she no longer loves him, a feeling that might be difficult in the light of all that he gets up to when he's on the loose. There is no denying his looks and what is perhaps even more evident, his sexual energy. He leaned back in his chair and like a panther appeared relaxed, in total control, and charged up like a race horse impatient to leave the starting line, at the same time.

My inner mental musings threw a question into my mind. What exactly are my feelings for this man? Am I capable of simply being a friend, or do I kid myself? I remembered my unexpected behaviour after my first lesson with Giorgio. Or is all this just a normal reaction to a build up of sexual appetite that has nowhere much to go at the moment? Martin sat there with his arms crossed, staring at me with a slight and cynical smile on his lips. How would you ever know if he were for real or acting? He has the makings of being a superb actor, at least in real life, and there is a familiarity to that thought, but I can't think why.

The main course arrived and for a while we simply ate. In

fact there was a low hum throughout the restaurant. Everyone was obviously hungry. I think that conversation would have suffered anyway, the food was so good. While we were waiting for dessert, Martin finally broached the subject.

"It's Giorgio." He began. "I had a lesson last week and he mentioned you. He's……"

"Bored. Yes, I realise that." I interrupted.

"I was going to say concerned." That surprised me and it took me a few seconds to respond.

"Concerned? What do you mean?"

Martin's spoon cut easily through the crisp outer layer of his dessert. He slowly lifted it to his mouth and raised his eyebrows as he tasted it, moaning in exaggerated pleasure. It was a little embarrassing. Our Chorus Master and some of the soloists happened to be sitting at a table near to us, and they glanced sideways.

"Martin!" I hissed. "For goodness sake stop it. What do you mean concerned?"

"Well, he's worried that this job is too tiring for you. You're still young and you're also changing over to soprano. He doesn't think you are giving yourself a fair chance, and he thinks you should leave."

"What? No way. I never feel tired, well no more than anyone does sometimes. I'm not leaving. I couldn't, it's fantastic. I'm lucky to be at the Opera House as well you both know. And anyway how does he suggest I live? Work at some awful little job that barely covers the rent while trying to find the time and energy to work on my voice, fit in lessons, and coaching, then perform with what's left of me, like some of my friends have to? No absolutely not!"

"I told him you wouldn't go for it."

"Well for once you were right." I was furious. I was paying this man a fat fee to retrain and guide me, not to suggest a fast track to financial ruin. It was with great fortitude that I did not blurt out what had transpired at my audition, indeed I might well have done had I not happen to glance to one side and catch Adrian's eye across the restaurant, he lifted his glass to me, I smiled and remembered my promise. Martin turned to see who I was acknowledging, turned back and said.

"He's thinking of moving."

"Oh? Not too far off the planet I hope!" At which Martin grinned. I think he was enjoying this.

"Not far away. But listen Tilly before you get too much on your high horse. Giorgio's loaded you know, he has a lot of money at his disposable. Most of it in a Swiss bank."

"In spite of three ex-wives?" I was still fuming, and Martin was still grinning, yes. He was definitely enjoying this!

"He has a superb lawyer, or solicitor, whatever the word is."

"The word 'bent' comes to mind. Anyway how do you know about the Swiss bank accounts?"

"He told me." Martin replied.

"It seems he tells you everything." I growled. "So where is this leading?"

"His plan is to take on a large property south of London in Surrey, I think he said. The place he's interested in has one spectacular feature, a beautiful amphitheatre, and a ready made theatre inside the house as well. It's unbelievably good luck."

"Hmm……..unbelievably. So what's he going to do with all these theatres? Sing in them?"

"He wants to start a resident company and put on full scale performances. He thinks he might even rival Glyndebourne. The grounds are apparently terrific, everything is there just begging for it"

I doubt he could rival Glyndebourne, dream on Giorgio, I thought, but I said.

"Well that sounds very exciting, but I'm not leaving the Opera House."

"O.K. darling, obviously no one can force you to, except the Opera House of course! I just thought you might be interested. You see, you're not likely to be offered roles at 'Villa Giorgio' if you don't leave the chorus."

"I don't see why not. But what roles am I going to be 'ready' for in the near future anyway? You just said yourself that changing from 'mezzo to soprano is not without its stresses."

"Tilly! You do yourself an injustice!" (Praise from Martin? My instincts began screaming at me.)

"Exactly what has Giorgio in mind?" I didn't really want to know, but I felt compelled to ask. Martin leaned across the table. His eyes were slightly full of drink, but he was far from tipsy, in fact he was deadly earnest it seemed.

"Giorgio has in mind an unheard of (as far as I know) concept. A company living and working under the same roof. No restrictions on rehearsal, plenty of time to prepare your work, loads of studio space. You could look after your 'vocal health' to your heart's content." At which point I glared at him, but he just grinned, shrugged his shoulders and raised his eyebrows. I probably should have just smiled and agreed with him, but I'm afraid I found that impossible to do.

"Sounds like an operatic commune to me, and I can't think of anything worse. I mean.." I added, lowering my voice. "I'm very fond of everyone in this company, but I don't think I'd want to live with them!"

"It won't happen immediately Tilly, it'll take ages to arrange everything. Maybe you'll change your mind by the time it's sorted." Then he quickly drained his coffee cup (coffee had arrived during my outburst, making the waiter smile) and glanced at his watch.

"I must be off, Sorry Tilly but duty calls! Will you be alright getting back to the Hotel on your own?" I assured him that I would. I walked back to the Hotel with Maria and relayed some of my conversation with Martin to her. I had imagined her to laugh it off immediately but she became thoughtful.

"Maybe you should start to think a little about your future Tilly. After all you don't want to stay here for ever do you?"

And how do you explain to a more mature experienced singer who you respect, that actually, as far as you can say at the moment, yes you do. You do want to stay where you are for ever. Especially when you haven't been where you are for more than five minutes! The answer is you can't, so I didn't. I did what I should have done with Martin, I nodded and smiled but said nothing beyond a…."Oh. I'm not interested." She stopped in the quiet Milan street and looked at me seriously for a few seconds. I realised suddenly how different each city 'smells' How the whole feeling that wound its way around us couldn't be London, or anywhere else probably. I breathed it in not wanting to forget a second of my short time here. Maria spoke again.

"On the other hand Tilly, I don't trust Giorgio any more

than the other one." Maria has not changed her mind about Martin. I decided to put all this on hold until it raises its head again. We had arrived at the Hotel by now.

"Want to go down to the Piano Bar?"

"O.K!" She replied. I finally crawled into bed at 1.30 a.m.

Martin found a phone. It took a lot of change to call London. He spoke briefly to Connie (very briefly) And then he spoke to Giorgio. The young student hanging around, waiting for his girl-friend, passed the time practising his English by translating the one-sided conversation that he could hear. He was quite pleased with himself, but of course it made no real sense to him at all.

"Hi, it's me Giorgio.".........."I have.".............. "No!"........."Well, I warned you!....... "What? Oh come on Giorgio!"........."Yes, yes.".........."O.K........" "I'll do my best, but I do have a life you know!"........."Yes."... .."No."........Right! See you!"

JOURNAL

That was yesterday. Today rehearsals began. Everything has been prepared to within an inch of its life before we left London. In fact, I'm quite sure that any one of us could have been dragged from our beds in the middle of the night, stood upright, be given a cue and respond perfectly.

It was as exciting to walk out on to that stage as it had been for me, my very first night at the Opera House. Everyone feigns nonchalance (myself included) But I would bet a very large sum of money that at least some of them feel as overawed as I do.

Once the stage was ready we launched into glorious Britten,

with 'Peter Grimes.' We were told before we left that this work is a particular favourite with the Milanese audience. A Suffolk village appeared like Brigadoon, in the middle of Italy. And in spite of it being only a rehearsal, the electricity generated by our phenomenal 'Grimes' would have kept many companies going for several performances. The power and understanding of the man is amazing. All thoughts of Giorgio's company flew from my head with his heroic tones. If one can experience art of this richness, why change anything? Anyway that's how I feel at the moment, I don't see it changing either!

We have, amongst the rehearsals and performance schedule, a day and an evening off, which will give us plenty of time to be whisked off to Venice. I hear the word and strange but wonderful sounds assail me again, which I certainly will not here there. And I see hot, bright sun bouncing off the palazzo walls. Which I doubt I will see there, not at this time of the year anyway. Carlo! Why have I not transcended the barriers between us for so long? But I'm looking forward to Venice. The very word is magical and timeless.

Dear God. In Venice I would love to see Carlo. Can one see one's own ghost?

Venice

We were to travel there and back in one day. On our arrival there was a watery sun, but by lunch time it was conquered, and dark slate leaned into the water. We explored anyway, following paths over countless bridges each one a work of art, or so it seemed to me. We discovered cafés , restaurants and enchanting shops at every turn. They were however quite expensive and it didn't take me long to exceed the monetary limit that I had put on myself before we left Milan. But I quickly decided that it didn't matter. We were like a small swarm of bees suddenly introduced to new and exotic blossoms and busily trying each new nectar as it came in our view.

A group of about seven of us spilled into a restaurant around lunch time, very hungry with parcels and packages everywhere. Everyone, it seems has overspent, it's not logical that that should make me feel better, but it does! Anyway, most of the things I have bought are presents for Lucy, Mum and Dad. Venetian glass and beautiful little statues. I don't suppose my Mother will like hers, but I'll never get that one right.

And did I see Carlo? Yes, later that afternoon when I had

drifted off on my own, and had found a quiet little café off the Gran San Marco Square. Deep in my cappuccino I saw him, and I rather wished that I hadn't. Maybe I should have listened to Martin (who hates all organised trips on principal) for once, I mean there must be a few brain cells working occasionally.

As I sat staring, the noise of modern Italy receded. It was suddenly late one hot evening and I appeared to be in front of a door……..

Carlo hesitated before he knocked on the door. There was no answer. He pushed it open and called. "Angelo!" The room belonged to Angelo Fernandi. It was his private studio, his teaching sanctuary where as a younger man Carlo had come to accept his share of the stupendous knowledge. He called again and the beautiful acoustic of the place, lifted the word like a leaf in the wind and levitated it to the centre of its glory, then let it descend throughout the room like warm snow.

"Son qui Carlo, I'm here." Angelo appeared, carrying an open book from an alcove which served as a small library. He stopped, eyeing Carlo carefully. He knew every plane and dimension of that beautiful face. Every indigo highlight of his hair and the glorious green of his eyes. And there was something wrong, he sensed it instantly long before the young singer had managed to speak.

"Maestro…….." Carlo could get no further than that. His face contorted, and he burst into tears and violent sobs. Passion of the Castrati, Angelo named such an outburst, secretly to himself. He had experienced it, occasionally still did, and seen it so many times in others that it begged to be named. As if the body, perceiving a chance to rid itself from some of the agony of the mind, opened up flood gates and exorcised some of the demons. Angelo laid his hands gently on the shaking shoulders while the sobs continued to tear through him, and only as they abated did he lead him gently to a chair and sit him down. He poured them both some wine, and Carlo, somewhat fortified, began to explain.

"Something is missing.......Or wrong. When I sing.....Non e posso......I cannot....."

He stared into his teacher's brown eyes that seemed to oscillate within their own colour and almost change shade. Some people were frightened of it, Carlo had always been fascinated. Angelo stood his glass down and leaned back in his chair not taking his eyes from the younger man.

"I know." He said. "I have heard, Carlo." Carlo gasped, he was all to well aware of the competition that held sway in their lives, and which never seemed to let go its strangle hold, even when one was set for the kind of fame that everyone else was convinced lay in his immediate potential.

"Heard? My enemies are at my throat already?" Angelo smiled gently and shook his head.

"No one else is aware caro. You're far too good for it to be obvious so quickly. You see, I often attend performances. I like to hear my students, to see where they are going with what I have taught them, especially you Carlo. You are very special."

"Then, since you have heard. What is wrong?" Carlo ended on a cry as if facing some terrible monster, a demon of his nightmares. Angelo picked up his glass again.

"You tell me. It will help you to sort it out." At which words

Carlo's spirits lifted. At least Angelo believed it to be salvageable. In that second he knew exactly what he had been trying to avoid looking at. He had counted on being able to ignore it while Angelo waved a magic wand, or mixed one of his famous potions he gave to his singers for fevers and such like, and hey presto no more problem, back to his glorious life. But it was Carlo himself who must do it. He must grab the serpent by the neck, look into its beguiling eye and dispense with it. He hung his head, then, almost whispering.

"It's life Angelo. It takes my breath." Angelo's laugh was low and gentle.

"A trifle dramatic, caro. But what do we expect from a singer of opera? But it is not 'life' is it my son? We know to whom we refer, si?"

"Si, Maestro."

Raimondo had discovered Carlo and Lucciano one hot afternoon beneath the silken shades of Carlo's bed. His agony of jealousy was almost too much for Carlo to bear. He felt trapped, and threw himself into the arms of the superb Contessa Domenica, which enraged Raimondo even more. Worse however, was to follow. Fond as he was of all his amours, Carlo now promptly feel deeply in love with the beautiful Contessa, causing a veritable war with Raimondo. Dark, furious looks, and scalding sarcasm rained down upon Carlo at every opportunity. He tried to shoulder it. After all, he felt responsible if not actually guilty. But it became too destructive and all-consuming.

Then he began to notice small things in his singing. A slight shortening of his prodigious breath, an almost imperceptible tightening of the god-like flexibility. Tiny flaws, but they were there. Carlo was just 26 and so, far too young to consider a natural decline the culprit. He had stared into his mirror, the sweat of fear on his youthful brow. And he had prayed in a whisper.

"Not yet! Per favor Gran Dio, not yet!"

Now, he turned back to Angelo. "It is as if he has reached into my body with a cold hand and destroyed my breath, my very inspiration. The muscles here…" He clasped his abdomen. "They refuse to obey me. They flutter, or they overwork. Maestro, I am desperate."

"Calma Carlo, calma." Angelo got up and moved to the table where his crystal decanters stood in quartet, each winking a different colour into the sinking, evening light. He refilled Carlo's glass, then his own and sat down again. The twilight and the reflection form the deep-red liquid turned his amazing eyes into hypnotic lights. Carlo caught his breath. The Maestro settled himself more comfortably. There was silence for a few moments, he appeared to be choosing his words carefully. Carlo waited, calmer now.

"Raimondo does not wear his tragedy easily. It is, of course, not easy for any of us. But he has found no way to contain it. It overwhelms him, Oh not just sometimes, but always. Every long second of every day. It has in effect driven him mad. Not insane, but mad. I make a difference, you understand?"

Carlo nodded slowly. Angelo leaned forward and continued.

"He does not have your talent, you know this. He cannot drown his sorrow in the music because his voice will not permit, indeed cannot provide. This poison overflows and it is only a matter of time before someone like you becomes infected."

Carlo looked quickly away.

"Infections my dear Carlo, can be cured. You are young and resilient. You have not suffered any lasting damage. The physical effects that you experience are purely transient. You know what you will do?

Carlo nodded. His mind raced ahead. He would go to London. He had already been invited several times, but had always found some reason not to accept, telling himself that half the audience would turn out from morbid curiosity. Creatures such as himself were not made there, in fact he understood that it was illegal. But no matter why they came to hear him, once he had them in front of him he would torture them with his sound. He would use his art and have them writhing in exquisite agony. He smiled and his confidence roared up from his belly like a tiger. Angelo was lighting the candles, Carlo walked over to him.

"Maestro, grazi. Grazi tanti."

Angelo laid down the smoking taper, and clasped Carlo's shoulders, holding him at arms length.

"You are most welcome Carlo. I am always here for you. But, please be careful. God has given you everything. And even that which man has taken from you has magnified and focused God's given talent. You take what you have for granted because you don't know what it is to be without it. Once I was very much like you. My career was cut short by such a jealousy." And he pulled open the ornate dressing gown which covered his hose and revealed, in a livid curve right across the diaphragm, an old deep scar like a dead snake, still laughing at its own impotent poison. Carlo was overcome. Gently he placed his hands over the scar as if by so doing he could eradicate it and turn back time. All he could say was. "Maestro……Angelo, e terribile!"

Angelo allowed his dressing gown to fall back and cover his body saying.

"No matter, not any more. But you mio bello, take care."

The door opened and a tall youth with deep golden hair which flirted outrageously with the lighted candles, entered the room.

"Ah, Riccardo, come in." Said Angelo and turning back to Carlo he said.

"You excuse me? Riccardo has a lesson. A very fine voice this, perhaps even another Carlo Ferruci."

Carlo smiled at the young student. "Buona sera." He said, and left.

He stood in the corridor leaning against the cool wall and listened to the rich young voice as Riccardo began to sing. He stayed in the shadows for a long while. He stayed until the servants brought flames and the deep yellow and orange lights flickered from every bracket in the rising breeze, as another velvet Venetian night crept across the water. Suddenly he pushed himself away from the wall and strode towards the gondoliers that had been collecting all evening near to the Palazzo. He must see Domenica!

In fact it was all much easier than he thought it would be. In the end it was Lucciano who was inconsolable. So much so that Carlo had to promise to take him with them when he left for London. Only then did he become quieted and his normal sweet self. Raimondo merely took a deep breath and said. "Va bene caro mio, if that is how it must be. Va bene!"

After Carlo's last performance in Venice, he came to the dressing room carrying a stirrup cup.

"Here, for your magnificent throat." He said, handing it to a smiling Carlo. He had recaptured his voice and was the weaver of musical spells again. All was set for the journey. Carlo smelt adventure, excitement and freedom. The next chapter of his life stretched before him painted in glowing colours. The golden liquid was a perfect meld of sweet and sour, just as he liked it. His muscles relaxed and his heart opened even further with soft contentment and love for everyone around him. He handed back the empty cup to Raimondo who kissed him on both cheeks as a brother.

"Addio Carlo."

"Addio." Carlo replied softly.

At the door, Raimondo turned back one last time. Carlo was still smiling. The candles seduced his eyes, their green became overwhelming. He stood there as close to perfection and as vivid with life as a man could be. By the morning he was dead.........

"Matilda!" Matilda jumped. "Grief Tilly, where were you? That's the third time! Come on, we have to go."

Without thinking Matilda looked out across the ever present water.

"Good." She said softly.

JOURNAL

Martin didn't come to Venice, he said he hated the idea. I can't make him out, I don't understand how anyone would miss out on the chance to visit one of the most beautiful and exotic cities in the world!

"In summertime." He informed me. "Do you know that it stinks?"

"No, I didn't know, anyway this isn't summer, and even if it were it wouldn't matter."

"Oh! Regular little romantic aren't you?" He taunted.

Dear God, I asked to see and I saw. Not the happiest time in Carlo's life. Thank you anyway.

Beyond Death, Beyond Time

Giorgio was a haunted man. Sometimes he wondered if he were not sick in both mind and body. Always he laughed off such thoughts, however. In his estimation it was all a bizarre joke. And 'sick' was not a word that the greedy modern world would apply to his, shall we say 'condition.' For a start, he was, if the tiny amount of knowledge which history revealed, can be believed, far too young for it. Facts concerning this strange malady (which had generally disappeared with the commencement of the Industrial Revolution) had filtered through to him over the times he had spent incarnate, and the usual age and condition for the onset, was extremely rich older men, at least in their late seventies. A nice little trick that, he had always thought. Mother Nature laughing at man's planned doctrine of youth and excess, and knocking it neatly into a top hat.

No, the age he didn't have, the wealth he did. But it didn't

114

matter, all this fact finding. He was sure that he knew where it came from, if not how or why. The blind sexual energy was 'bleeding through' from another time and place. It had tortured him before. He had memories, real sensed memories, and the 'monster' was always there.

Sometimes he could believe himself cursed, for when these sensed memories were upon him he saw France, Italy, England, rolling by, century after century. But clearer by far than any details from these times, was Venice. He remembered Carlo so well, as sharp and clear as a spring morning. His eyes, the great peaceful inner strength, but most of all his voice. His sound which still caused exquisite snaking through the very centre of one's being. Carlo was beyond both man and woman. He remembered the death, and after it Lucciano. His devastation, and finally his suicide by a knife to the throat, across the lovely pearls of wisdom which, if not possessing the ability to cause quite the furore in the senses that Carlo had caused, nevertheless always captured a breathless beauty and a limpid sadness.

Raimondo had not intended this death, and it drove him to hate Carlo beyond death, Venice and time. It urged him to extend his consciousness and memory until now, when in the blinking of an eye, or so it seemed, there he, or in this century, she, was. Positive, free, and as in love with the music as ever.

'But this time, my proud little peacock.' Giorgio thought. 'Death is too easy by far. Now was the time of the brotherhood of the tenors, and damn her to hell, she would not survive!' Giorgio did not accept the usual understanding of 'time' since as far as he was concerned, the present was formed by the past and the future, whatever that may hold. And to say that all this was in the past and should be left there was, to him anyway, totally absurd. Added to this he felt that he was being constantly 'nagged' at by some unknown awareness. There was definitely something that he was being pressed to do. And destroying sweet little Matilda was a big part of it.

The doorbell pierced through his thoughts. Giorgio was expecting a new student. A soprano, so he understood, yet another! He had so many, there were so many out there in the world, and most of them very ordinary. Oh he could train them! After all, anyone capable of repeating a pitch accurately could be trained, and indeed improved, and helped to grow. But real quality, highly individual sound? That was God-given, or a blessing by Nature anyway. Giorgio didn't believe in God. For the rest, Giorgio enjoyed the power he felt as he watched them vie amongst themselves for his attention. He didn't tell them that certain aspects of being a singer couldn't actually be taught. He never explained that the mysterious communion between brain and organ could not be captured, traced and served up to just anyone. And so they believed in the existence of a talent which he had never actually acknowledged. Matilda, however was a thorn in his side. He flung open the front door.

"Come in cara, come in!" He exuded his considerable charm, sighing however, to himself at the same time, as he took in the woman's physique. Not a ribcage in sight! What did she think he was going to teach her, how to slink down a cat walk? Opera demanded body and incredible stamina. There was no way around these facts, these things simply had to be there.

The young woman had finished her rendition of Puccini's 'Un bel di.' And it was as Giorgio had suspected it would be.

Not one note of it was 'on the breath.' The 'chest' was non-existent, the middle weak almost to the point of breathy, and the final top Bflat sounded like a sick cat (very sick!) But he smiled at her over the piano.

"Very nice my dear. I hope you are prepared to work very hard." Oh yes he would teach her, no question. He would let her think she was destined to take the Operatic world by storm. She didn't stand a chance out there. Another £60 an hour for his overflowing coffers then. She should pay him double for having to listen to her. How could she possibly imagine she was even acceptable, never mind talented?

She left, falling over herself to thank him. He had to clench his teeth hard together to prevent himself from saying what in all honesty should have been said. Matilda flew into his thoughts. The unconscious awareness of her own worth was as untouchable as ever. That of course, made her quite a challenge. He smiled at the excitement that thought fired in him, and the insipid little woman smiled back.

"Ciao." She said offering him her hand.

"Ciao." He replied thinking, 'God, surely she doesn't expect me to kiss it!'

He glowered at her from under his eyebrows as she headed up the path. There was actually a spring in her stride. No doubt she felt that she had accomplished the first step towards operatic fame. His 'glower' intensified and he dropped his chin further, narrowing his eyes. Then he brightened slightly, nice little arse though!

Meeting

JOURNAL

There are only a few days before we return to London. This visit is not something I'll ever forget, even Martin has behaved and actually been quite pleasant on the occasions that I have been around him. Rumours about him abound of course, but that is really not my concern. It's quite nice to have him as a friend. I don't like to lose touch with people I've known, it seems unnecessarily careless. So everything was calm and peaceful and I was not even aware that I was missing anything. I felt that I could float on for ever. Then, this morning, something happened, something totally unexpected.

"Scusatemi Signorina, you wid de Opera, si?"

I was sitting by myself in the covered arcade near to the Opera House drinking hot chocolate this morning, and was as usual, miles away. It took me a moment to get mind in to focus.

"I am, Signor." To which reply he held out his hand and said. "Dante Vittoria. Please to excuse, may I sit for one quick moment."

"Just for one quick moment." I grinned wickedly.

He sat down and hailed the waiter in a single easy movement. He ordered coffee and invited me to more chocolate. Obviously the moment would not be that quick then! And you could not, at least, I could not, take offence. I imagine he charmed the birds out of the trees easily when he wanted to, and I felt the full force of sincere desire to please. It was irresistible, as of course it was meant to be.

He settled down and by the time our drinks had arrived, he had told me he was a writer. It seems he is working for a large publishing house. They are sending him all over Europe, and later to the States and other places yet to be decided upon, to write about life back stage in the main Opera Houses of each country. He has recently completed Italy and soon he will be heading for London.

"That sounds like an interesting project." I squirmed inside before I had even finished the sentence, after all he probably has some great novel or film script cramming every brain cell and desperate for release. So I added quickly and I fear a little lamely.

"While you're not writing your own work of course."

He hadn't taken offence. He simply caressed me with his beautiful eyes and said.

"I musta come to your Opera House in 'ow you say? A fortnight? Two weeks yes, is right?"

"Yes." I assured him. "That's right." He smiled and leaned into the table, placing his elbows on the glass top, he flooded me with his charismatic, Italian charm without pity.

"Perhaps I aska for you when I come dere. Perhaps we 'ave anoder chocolata?"

Any intention that I might have had to fob him off fled in the light of his smile. It was perfectly wonderful. So I found myself replying.

"Yes I would like that!" There was a silence, during which he looked at me quizzically. It occurred to me that he appeared to be waiting for something. Then I realised that I had not introduced myself, how can he ask for me if he doesn't have a name. I could just imagine the tanhoy message.

"Will the member of the chorus who allowed herself to be picked up in the Arcade in Milan, please contact the stage door."

I wrote down my name for him. Well, he isn't English he may find it hard to remember. He might even forget it, we can't have that! Anyway I had a real desire to see Dante again and it was laced with something else. A yearning familiarity, and a slight feeling of being face to face with a very important situation which I must not ignore. I've never experienced anything like it before. For a while I saw his face everywhere. Eyes to die for and a mouth to kill for.

Dear God. Am I turning into a lustful lady?

And On Our Return

Martin dropped his suitcase with a sigh and pushed the front door to his flat, shut.

"Con, you in?" Hoping that she wasn't. He was exhausted. He couldn't even remember how many ladies he had divested of their honour, but he really didn't care. He felt, in spite of his success, rather depressed. There was a note by the phone from Connie.

'Trouble with our 'save messages.' So in case it hasn't survived, please phone Giorgio when you get back. A.S.A.P. was his request!'

Martin groaned, he needed time to recover. Giorgio was becoming a little bit of a pain. He enjoyed working with him, enjoyed the tenor camaraderie and the regular assurances that they were indeed the only voice type on the planet, but he could do without all that, or indeed anything else, tonight. He made for the whisky bottle, swigged back a healthy amount, and only then did he return Giorgio's call. Giorgio sounded a bit 'odd.' His speech was almost 'staccato,' the tension in it palpable even over the phone. He admitted to Martin that he had a 'touch of his trouble.' what exactly that was, Martin had no idea, but he did know that when it abounded, Giorgio could neither eat, sleep nor stay in one place for more than a few seconds. He looked like a soul possessed and often resorted to strong tranquillisers. Martin felt as sorry for him as he was capable of feeling for anyone, but much more, he felt relieved. Giorgio was obviously in no fit state to meet at the moment. They made a date for the next weekend.

"Bring the lovely Connie, she'll be quite safe by then, I'll have recovered." Said Giorgio. Martin laughed dutifully, but raised his eyes to the ceiling. Obviously an older man's fancy regarding his sexual power. He should have been with him in Milan, that would have shown him a thing or two!

What Martin did not realise or understand was that Giorgio's concern was very real. When he was stricken with his 'fever' Giorgio was not a pretty sight, and quite incapable of being able to concentrate on conversation, eating, or anything else except any females in the vicinity. Giorgio had no desire to be seen as the dishevelled roué he became on such occasions. Long ago he had disciplined himself for such times, and he proceeded like a man who, knowing that he is a werewolf, makes sure that he is locked up every full moon, or a vampire desperately avoiding the faintest aroma of blood. For Giorgio, out of time and in the region of 25 years too young, suffered from 'satyriasis' and knew too well the anguish of desire, impossible to slake. Indeed, any attempt to do so only inflamed the condition. In the 17th. and 18th.centuries it was understood with a grudging respect. This century, for all it's sophistication, would probably see it as a good reason to hold him in some mental institution and study him like a laboratory rat.

When Connie put her head round the sitting room door Martin had been asleep for hours.

"You're back then!".... 'Obviously.' He thought......."Yes." He said. "Have a good time?" She continued........'Bloody fantastic'.....Screamed his memory....."O.K.: He said. "Bloody hard work though. Hardly had a minute to do anything except sing. I'm exhausted!"

Connie kissed him quickly on the forehead, then disappearing into the kitchen she said.

"I missed you darling!"

"Me too Con. I phoned Giorgio and he's invited us out on Saturday for dinner. He especially asked for you to come."

"Don't you have a show Mart?"

"Not Saturday, no. You will come won't you?"

"You know I don't like Giorgio." Martin got up and followed her into the kitchen feeling a sudden flame of impatience.

"Oh come on Con. Why the hell not? He's a great guy." He moved closer to her. "I've been away for a bloody fortnight, surely you can tear yourself away from your rich friends for one Saturday night to come with me?" He got close enough to put his arm around her. She looked at him for a long second, straight between the eyes. Martin felt uncomfortable.

"It's got nothing to do with my friends, rich or otherwise, Martin. I don't trust him. I'll come if you really want me to but......There's something about him that's almost inhuman."

"Don't be daft luv!" Martin thought about kissing her, after all she was his wife, beside which she smelt nice. The nap had revived him, and he felt a slight delectable tingle. But Connie had turned back to the dinner. Martin returned to the settee and turned on the television, he wasn't however really concentrating. Connie's look had chilled him, she wasn't given to dramatic responses. He supposed it was possible that certain elements of his life style in general, and Milan in particular, had seeped back home. Well if that was the case he'd seen the movie, 'Divorce American Style.' And learnt the lesson therein. 'Deny.....Deny......Deny!'

JOURNAL

We've settled back in to normal (if there is such a thing) operatic routine. A college friend of mine has asked me to do a concert with her next season, probably in November. I feel much more secure singing as a soprano and discussing and working out a programme will take my mind off other things. We are running a Mozart season at the moment and that makes life a bit easier for the chorus. The weather is moving fast towards spring and it's time I went home again. Also I must book a session with Giorgio and discuss the concert with him. He will, I'm sure, have some good ideas. But this evening (Saturday) the ballet has everything in hand with 'Swan Lake' I believe, and I intend to relax in front of the T.V. and be very, very, lazy.

When Martin and Connie arrived at the Italian restaurant, Giorgio was already seated at one of the best tables. He stood up with a delighted smile when he saw them.

"So you persuaded your charming wife. How lovely to see you my dear." He took her hand and kissed it. Connie had a hard job to control the shudder which expanded in her stomach. Martin sent her a quick withering look and pulled back a chair for her. They had ordered wine and their meals when Giorgio launched into what promised to be an evening of 'singing talk.'

"You will excuse us my dear, for a short while? This is all rather important." Giorgio smiled at her. Connie had heard that before on similar occasions. The 'short while' usually lasted half the night. She switched off into a world of her own.

"Who's Tilly?" Connie asked sleepily late that same night. Martin was still padding around the bedroom thinking that Giorgio always looked slightly different after one of his so called attacks. He was sure it wasn't his imagination. Connie's unexpected question shocked him back to present time. He thought quickly. She knew nothing about Matilda and he didn't want her exploring that particular avenue at the moment. He was glad that the bedroom itself was in darkness, and that he was only illuminated spasmodically by the bathroom light. He couldn't for the life of him remember through the wine and brandy haze, how much Tilly had been mentioned. Giorgio could be a real idiot sometimes. He had been attempting to have a conversation by numbers, as Martin put it to himself. Saying one thing and meaning another, and only Martin was supposed to understand. Did he think that Connie was stupid?

"Hmm?....." Connie was sitting up in bed suddenly wide awake apparently. The penetrating look she had given him the evening of his return from Italy unfolded in his mind. Oh boy this was probably it, big explosion any minute!

"Sorry?" He said, padding quickly into the darkest shadow he could find and doing precisely nothing when he got there.

"What are you doing Martin? I asked you who is Matilda?"

"I'm looking for something. Matilda is.......just one of.... Ah here it is......just one of Giorgio's students. She's at the Opera House." He added, hoping that by offering a little information Connie might back off from the big jealousy act that he sensed was raising it's ugly little green head. But Connie wasn't jealous.

"Is she? Why does he mention her so much? Got the hots for her has he? It just sounded a bit odd to me. From where I was sitting, I'd say he's up to something. I may not know anything about the world of opera. But people are people, and I've come up against men like him before."

"Men like what exactly Con? Giorgio is concerned for a young student who has got herself a job that can be very taxing and who he considers might be in real danger of spoiling a very nice little soprano voice. We only get one you know and if it goes, that's it. Bye, bye career."

"What does her career have to do with you Martin? And why do you all act as if he has some golden key that no one else possess, but if you are really good boys and girls he might just let you borrow it to unlock the door to success. No, there's something very fishy about that man. I wish you wouldn't have any more to do with him."

"Oh come on Con. Don't go all dramatic on me, I'm supposed to be the thespian around here, remember?" And he laughed hoping to lighten things up a bit, adding. "You know Giorgio!"

"Well no, actually I don't. But in spite of that, I've told you. I think he's a very dangerous man."

"You're nuts." He growled, sensing a night in the guest room, this was tuning into an argument. Connie was quiet for a moment and Martin held his breath, maybe the storm had passed. Then she said quietly.

"How old is she?"

"How should I know? She's about 23, 24 maybe." And he shrugged and tried very hard to look bored. Connie was staring at her hands that were folded on her bent knees, a soft pale green mound of duvet in the moonlight. Her face was in total shadow he couldn't see her expression at all.

"She's too young Martin. Far too young." Martin's stomach lurched, not a pleasant feeling when it contained so much alcohol. This was definitely it! All the chat about Giorgio was a hidden path to confronting him about Tilly. Some bastard must have told her! There was nothing he could do to put her off the scent now, so he stood still and prepared for battle. From somewhere he found his voice, slightly husky from the wine.

"Too young for what Connie?"

"For bloody Giorgio..........." Stand down. Martin's heart thumped a relief signal to the rest of his system.

"He'll eat her alive Martin"…….Disengage weapons…… "He'll eat her up, spit her out and destroy her. I know his type. I think you should talk to her. If you know her well enough that is." The guest door swung closed. Guilt had encased Martin's limbs in concrete, with a great effort he managed to walk to the bed. He sat on the edge and smiled at his wife.

"I can't do that Con. I don't know her that well. Anyway

we don't know anything for sure, do we? You're guessing and you're tired. It's all presumption." He took off his dressing gown and got into bed. As he laid back Connie snuggled up to him. His response was purely that, just a response. It could have been anyone, there had been so many. But it filled a need if stopping short of the ecstatic, although he suspected somewhere in the blackness of his mind that that was his fault. He was far too selfish, but he didn't care, anyway he hated women. His eyes flew open in the darkness. Well, that was a nasty little truth that popped up uninvited. Pity he wasn't gay really. But no, he'd tried that once, didn't do at all. Anyway he didn't actually 'hate' women, they just made him feel inferior and he knew that that wasn't their intention. He could hear Connie's gentle breathing as she sank deeper into sleep. He turned to look at her, just making out the still slight form under the duvet. His hand stretched out and gently he touched her bare shoulder. The bottom line was, (and he almost laughed out loud it was such old hat) He simply didn't understand them, and Matilda he understood least of all.

$\mathcal{D}$ante

"Will Matilda Gasgoine please contact the stage door." Well, unless My parents or Lucy had suddenly descended on to London, it could only be one person. I felt as if I had taken a breath in the canteen (Where I was when I heard the message) and didn't release it until speaking made it necessary.

"Dante!" He was sitting on the only seat at the stage door looking so Italian as to be outrageous. But mainly he looked gorgeous. Two ballet girls were hovering, glancing at him with studied flirtation, they're so good at it damn it! But to my intense relief he seemed not to have noticed them. He stood up as he saw me and walked straight passed them without a second glance.

"Matilda, cara. I ama so glad you 'ere!" His accent was even more exotic in England. The ballet girls looked amazed. Well this would all be around the company by tonight's performance! I'm pretty sure that it's a safe bet to assume that I have been labelled 'nice but frigid.' The second part frankly doesn't bother

129

me (I know I'm not, I also know you can get into unhappy situations trying to prove it, so frankly they can think what they like) The first isn't an arrogant assumption, it's just that everyone has continued to be extremely nice to me. Dante kissed me on both cheeks which promptly turned scarlet, and pulled me onto the seat.

"So, when are you free? I 'ave only little timea today."

"I'm free until the half this evening." He looked at me closely and frowned slightly.

"De 'alf ofa what?"

"The half hour call. Half an hour before the performance starts." I laughed.

"Anda so we 'ave coffee and chocolata?" He raised his eyebrows in a attitude of hope which was flattering to say the least, betraying as it did an impatience. I stood up and said.

"Would you like to have it here?" He didn't miss a beat. Standing up and encircling my waist with his arm he replied.

"No I woulda not. Please you come wida me." At which Stan the stage door man grinned and winked at me and found a sudden huge interest in some piece of paper on the desk in front of him.

"O.K." I smiled. "Good afternoon Miss." Stan said from the depths of the paper before we had even moved.

"Bye Stan, see you later." The door swung closed behind us and Dante led me off saying.

"Youra stage man 'e very joie de vivre si?" I smiled, nodding and said. "I imagine he sees a lot of human drama sitting at the stage door in an International Opera House day after day." Then there was a maze of back streets, which I have never been along. There was coffee and chocolate, yes. But I will admit to you (and to you only) that we had very much more than that. This is not my normal mode of behaviour. Oh that sounds rather superior doesn't it? The point is I don't know what my mode of behaviour is really. I'd only had one lover to date, and I suspect that the overture is always different. But whatever, by the famous 'half' I learnt that there is most certainly such a thing as love at first sight, and that a deep unswerving trust can spring from nowhere. Dante and I could have known each other forever and the safety I felt in his arms (amongst a lot of other things) was totally unexpected, and as welcome as something familiar and forgotten.

Dante returned me to the Opera House and I made my way to the dressing room feeling as if the air itself was sizzling around me. I must be very see through, because as I came through the door, Maria looked up from a book she was reading.

"Well, hello!" She said with heavy emphasis on each word. "You obviously had a good afternoon." I smiled at her but said nothing. I need to keep this secret to myself, just a little longer.

Dear God. What now?

As Matilda and Dante made their way back to the Opera House and embraced one last time in the darkening evening by the stage door, and looking as if they felt that the whole world had receded from them for the moment, someone else was also hurrying towards the Opera House for the 'half'. Confronted by this little scene and completely unobserved by them, he froze. He had been ruminating on many things since last Saturday. He had even begun to question himself, but in an instant it all vanished. Jealousy whinnied and tossed her green mane. Revenge strode after her and flung himself into the saddle. Oh but it was good to be back! The familiar energy coursed relentlessly consuming every thought. No more pretence, no more listening to the tiny voice of conscience. Matilda had really bought it this time. She was nothing but a little whore, she deserved all she was going to get. Martin was back in Giorgio's court ready to fight to the death!

The 'old man' slipped back to the inner landscape and surveyed the immense growth since his last awareness. It was breathtaking. He found himself several yards from the sea shore in clear warm water. Behind him flowers of every colour and perfume grew down to the shore line. In front of him and to each side of him, a crystal surf thundered. He had never felt more exhilarated and relaxed. Matilda was blossoming and so therefore was he.

Of course he remembered Dante. He recognised him immediately as his rather more humane assistant from another time. As a man of moral fibre and who, to his shame, he had treated with less than respect. Well that was his crime, this was his punishment, and his self-imposed prison was, at times like these, not only beautiful but beginning to allow him to sense freedom. They were not there yet, not by a long way. And yet the arrival of Dante did much to lift the 'old man's' spirits.

He understood that there would be problems. He could only hope fervently that Matilda would not allow the world to have too much of an influence on her when it came to certain situations. He must tear himself away from this glorious creation, he would repair to his library where there was always work to do.

After all this is what he 'did.' This 'old man' one time Musician, Priest and Scientist of Atlantis. He decoded the beautiful blue messages as they leapt from one nerve ending to another, catching them in a particle of a second that was impossible to record it was so fast. And then he decided how much of it to redistribute into Matilda's dreams. That was his 'job' as humans called one's occupation.

He laughed a great joyous roar that wouldn't stop and threatened to render him unconscious, if that was possible. He didn't know, and that made him laugh all the harder! Whereas Matilda opened her throat in the Opera House that evening feeling so happy that she could burst, and causing two or three people in close proximity to her to say later, amongst themselves.

"God, you know that girl can sing when she puts her mind to it!"

What they did not know was that the 'mind' in the way they understood it, had absolutely nothing to do with it.

Anne Gasgoine

Anne replaced the receiver. Doctor Gasgoine was preparing to leave for morning surgery.

"Who was that Anne?" He asked as he fastened his bag and made for the front door.

"Oh, just an old friend. I may pop up to London and visit next week."

"Uh, uh…..Well I'm off. See you later." And he was gone. The door slammed behind him and a few seconds later his car burst into life. Anne watched as it pulled out of the front gate. She left the dishes to Mrs Hunter and went upstairs to her room. She needed to think somewhere quiet. Anne had always had her own room since Matilda…..Matilda! There was before Matilda, and after Matilda. Anne never called her Tilly, stupid little girl's name! Mrs Gasgoine liked her privacy, and Duncan? Well as far as she was concerned, Duncan could do whatever men in his position do, she couldn't care less.

She called down to Mrs Hunter for coffee and biscuits and sat down on the window seat. It was raining again, great sheets of West country wetness slashed against the pane. Anne's gaze followed the grey horizon across to Baby Devils' wood. There was promise of some break in the clouds there, not that it really mattered to Anne. She had no intention of leaving the house today, she had it totally to herself for some time since Duncan would be late tonight. Duncan was always late on Wednesdays.

Mrs Hunter tapped on the door and came in carrying a tray with coffee, biscuits and a small vase of fresh spring flowers still wet with the rain. She must have picked them on her way over. She was a treasure and completely loyal to Anne. Duncan often remarked that he felt a little like a man whose wife was guarded by a pet Rot Weiler that barely tolerated his presence. This had amused him, but irritated Anne, it wasn't something that he often mentioned therefore. Mrs Hunter was giving her an 'old fashioned' look.

"You alright Mrs Gasgoine?"

"Yes thank you Poppy. I'm fine, just a little tired today. I think I'm going to take it easy."

"You do that my dear. I'll see that everything is sorted downstairs, now don't you give it another thought." And she bustled out. She needn't have worried, Anne had no intention of giving it another thought. She had other mental fish to fry. The phone call that she had received was not from an old friend. It was from someone who knew Matilda, in London. In fact it was Matilda's singing teacher. He had quite a nerve ringing like that out of the blue, and then announcing that he would, as he put it.

"Very much like to meet you dear lady. If that's at all possible. I need to have a word about Matilda. I don't think a phone call is quite the right place for it."

Anne's back bristled. She had managed all these years to

contain intense secrets and feelings that were far better buried, but it only took a phone call from a stranger to pull everything back into focus again.

Nearly 25 years ago Anne had had to chose between Matilda and Duncan. She had only been 22 herself at the time, and recently married to this handsome young doctor. The evening that he broke the news to her, had been a large crossroad in her life she realised later.

Anne didn't often consider herself to be wrong about anything. And so gradually she began to wear her martyrdom rather like a piece of costume jewellery. People were very aware of it without being sure if it was genuine. The result was that they either liked Anne, playing openly to her silent game of 'poor me,' or they considered her a cold, silly little woman who deserved neither her respected husband (and who could blame him for what the gossips rattled on about, if it were true) nor her bright, warm and talented daughter, who, incidentally they found it very hard to believe that she had produced. And the truth was of course that she hadn't. Matilda was Lucy's daughter, a fact that only she Duncan and Lucy knew. They had decided to keep it from Matilda for now.

Pouring herself another coffee she bit into a digestive biscuit and tried very hard to keep her rage in check.

Duncan had betrayed her with this woman, the 'witch' as Anne had privately named her. She was quite convinced that in Lucy's dreary little cottage (where of course she had never been) there were herbs and books of incantations to raise the very devil. She prayed vehemently for protection from such evil. Once, when the pressures all became too much to bear, she had approached the vicar about her concerns, but she had not got very far.

'Well he was a man wasn't he?' She had thought to herself with self-righteous disgust. And even in his calling he probably felt a casual sexual thrill when he saw Lucy, most men did. It seemed they just couldn't help themselves. What was with these men anyway? They didn't seem to be able to function without some great sex scene going on at home or away from home, whichever. Well she wanted nothing to do with it. She had never wanted anything to do with it. Even her honey moon had been a disaster. Duncan had finally booked himself into a separate room at the beautiful hotel in Rome. This was, no doubt, something that he must have found excruciatingly embarrassing, since they had checked into the honeymoon suite on arrival. She was not moved by such a possibility and still found the eternal fuss about the subject contemptible. As a friend had once crudely suggested to her, it was just a question of 'in out, in out...Repeat as necessary!' After a difficult few weeks during which Duncan had tried with considerable gentleness (she had to admit) to win her over. He finally exploded.

"Why the hell did you marry me? This isn't exactly Victorian England. Anyone would think that you've never heard about the physical side of relationships. Please Anne, consider seeing someone and talking this through, if not for us then for yourself. I mean what is it, were you abused as a child?"

Anne told him not to be disgusting. Did one have to have been abused before forming such an opinion about sex? And no, she wouldn't 'see someone.' The idea of some counsellor or psychiatrist rummaging through her most personal and private thoughts was not just absurd, it was completely unnecessary. There were no dark secrets, no suppressed emotions keeping the lid on some unspeakable horror. Actually the truth was that Anne Gasgoine was that rare and infuriating bird, a person of total selfishness. It was the way she saw survival. Any surrender to another person of anything, especially involving the physical side of things. Her reptilian line of defence brooked no understanding. You stand on her head, you get yourself bitten. She began to see Duncan as a man typically incapable of any sort of control over his nasty little habits. And gradually, even a passing caress or quick domestic kiss became less and less part of their day-to-day routine, finally stopping altogether.

Then there was Matilda. They had been married only a few short months when in spite of the fact that she really would rather not have to be aware of it, Anne noticed a change in Duncan. His confidence, so shattered by their disastrous marriage, seemed to be returning and he was suddenly much more relaxed. The terrible tension in him had abated. He now spent longer over his personal appearance than she considered any man should, and she actually heard him humming to himself, on more than one occasion. During the year's social calendar of the four villages several events were held, one of these being a party to which she and Duncan had been invited. It was at this party that she overheard some gossip which at the time she ignored. Apparently, at the other end of their village lived a 'bewitching creature.' Anne had laughed to herself when she heard this ridiculous phrase being bandied about the masculine element. Try as she might though she couldn't raise any support from the other wives. On making the point to Tabitha Welbeck she was informed immediately that it was quite true, a young woman of extraordinary beauty and a rather special 'quality' (Tabitha hadn't enlarged on exactly what that was) had indeed moved into the cottage known as The Retreat for some reason, which stood on the edge of the opposite end of the village. Shortly after this, and in circumstances that had never been quite clear to Anne, the inevitable happened. Duncan and the 'witch' apparently named Lucy, met, fell deeply in love, and quickly into bed. Although Duncan had assured her (and she suspected that it was true) that they had taken as much care and precautions as possible, Matilda soon resulted. And she was forced to have to make a choice that no woman of her sensibilities should have to trouble herself with. There ensued a veritable pantomime. She and Lucy both left the village. Lucy's condition was far from obvious, and her absence didn't raise much interest. Of Anne's however, the story was that she needed a change, she was run down, not feeling too well, etc,etc... The cure for which she sought up North with her parents.

In fact Anne could not go to her parents exactly since they were dead, but she still owned the family house which she adored. Indeed, at one time she had hoped to persuade Duncan to move up there and go into private practice by himself. The property was certainly big enough. It stood in its own quite impressive grounds. All that of course had gone by the wayside, since the arrival of the 'creature' into their lives.

Within two months of the birth, the baby having been weaned, was to return to Kings Grantham with Anne as her own. Or, and what a choice she was given. She and Duncan must divorce. In spite of her strange preferences regarding relationships, Anne did not want this to happen. She had her pride, and she desperately needed security. She had made some friends in the village, and one or two of them were even in her 'class.' So she decided that living a rather huge lie was the better choice. It didn't matter to Duncan of course. He was the Father whoever he was with! On the day she told him of her decision she had her list of requirements ready. Her own room. No consorting of any kind and no pressure so to do. (Duncan agreed to all this with maddening ease and lightness) A nurse for the baby (She had no intention of looking after it, not on a day to day basis anyway) And Lucy, out of their lives for ever. Over this last requirement Duncan dug his heels in and refused to comply. This had caused considerable stress between them. Then, quite suddenly, (Anne suspected the witch again) he relented.

So Matilda was born, Duncan brought the little baggage to her, and the three of them returned to Kings Grantham to play happy families. It wasn't so bad, Mrs Hunter adored babies. Except for appearance sake on certain occasions she took over completely. Anne was very grateful, and slowly they settled down to what seemed to the outside world as ordinary family life.

A few years on and Lucy returned to a village close by, and then only months later and by some unbelievable fate to the actual cottage that she had inhabited in Kings Grantham, before she left. Anne had attacked Duncan in her crisp, self-satisfied tones.

"We had an agreement Duncan. I'm not prepared to put with this. I intend to do something about it."

"There's nothing to do Anne. If you make any waves, it will all come out and everyone will know. Is that what you want? But you can still leave if you want to. Mrs Hunter is wonderful with Tilly, there's no problem. She won't pine for your maternal hand in her life, will she?"

"Don't discuss my maternal qualities with such flippancy Duncan. How dare you? You blackmailed me into this. Matilda is not my child and you can't expect me to be mooning over her."

"Why not? Mrs Hunter finds it quite easy." Duncan snapped. Anne's voice began to take on the pitch hated by all men as with marked sarcasm she replied.

"Oh, I see this little plan was hatched from the beginning. Just give her time she'll get fed up and agree to a divorce. The two of you have had it all worked out from the first disgusting little encounter, haven't you? Haven't you Duncan!"

Duncan had given her such a look of studied boredom and said quietly.

"Don't play the hysterical victim with me Anne. This is largely your doing, at least at the very root of it, it is, and you know it. Now which is it to be?"

Anne had no intention of leaving her house. The idea of being without such security terrified her and she couldn't even begin to think beyond it. Anyway she had poured all her energy into it and as Duncan had had to admit to himself more than once, she had made a very nice job of it. No it was hers! She would not leave it whatever the cost! But she wasn't going to be completely taken for granted either.

"I trust you're not still seeing her." She said more quietly but her jaw still rigid with fury. Duncan looked at her intently before he replied, then he said.

"With your beliefs and unwifely behaviour, you have no right my dear Anne to even ask me."

Anne's rage fired up once more and before she could stop herself she spat out at him.

"Well for God's sake don't get her pregnant again." At which Duncan had turned pale and left the room.

After that Lucy had become Auntie Lucy, or Lulu as the little Matilda called her. She adored Lulu. Well, she would wouldn't she? The stupid woman bent over backwards to make her feel special, giving birth wasn't enough it seemed. But Anne found an up side to all of this, and it was quite a blessing. She needed time to herself and wanted Matilda around as little as possible, even if it meant her spending a considerable amount of time with Lucy which as she got older, she did.

Then Matilda's talent was discovered. What rejoicing! You'd think that a young child had never expressed musicality before. Duncan, of course, had insisted on the best training which meant that one of them (usually her, since Mrs Hunter didn't drive) had to drive her miles every week to take her to piano lessons. Then later, when she was 14, for singing lessons as well, if you please! Her hate and resentment deepened. Matilda was, she realised quite insecure in some ways. But deep down she possessed an overwhelming positive force that wouldn't lay down and die. God knew where it came from and Anne found it very, very irritating. She often longed to slap the smug little face, but she didn't dare, and anyway Matilda gave her no cause. She was so sweet, so good and so bloody naturally charming, everybody loved her. Anne had begun to feel more and more alienated.

And now, she'd agreed to meet this man, what was his name?

Giorgio? She supposed that meant he was foreign, although he hadn't sounded it on the phone. Again she was trapped. She may not be the loving Mother, but it seemed she still had to act like one. Just how long did this parenting go on? She wondered. Oh well, at least she'd have a trip up to town. She hadn't been to London for ages. She could spend lots of money. Anne had her own private income from invested stocks, another little perk from Duncan's carelessness, how expensive a few seconds of mind blowing pleasure could prove she often thought to herself, men could be so stupid. Also she had sold her family home, and since she wasn't hoping from foot to foot desperate for a quick buyer, she had been able to wait. When the cheque from the sale finally hit her bank account, it was almost obscene.

Anne was to meet Giorgio at the Ritz for tea. London, she decided was becoming less and less the London she remembered, and much less likeable. Dreadfully crowded, you could hardly walk in a straight line along the pavement, and full of beggars. It all appeared to have slipped a millennium. After spending until her credit cards were wilting she took a taxi and was soon standing in the warmth of the tea room.

Giorgio was sitting in a winged armchair, reading an Evening Standard. Somehow she knew that it must be him, but sat down by herself in case she was mistaken. She arranged her many packages around her chair and picked up the menu from the table in front of her. She would order a full cream tea, Why not? It would be ages before she was home, and she didn't care about her figure, neither did anyone else and she preferred it that way. It meant she could eat exactly what she wanted.

A shadow fell across the menu. She looked up expecting

to see a waiter. Giorgio stood there. Now Giorgio, when he so wished could be amazingly charming. Some women saw through him of course, or were suspicious without knowing why, but Anne was not one of them. From the first instant she played straight into his manipulating hands. She was completely taken with his sophistication, his ease of manner, and the incredible inner power which she sensed in him. As if he would be in total control in any situation.

Anne liked that, she liked it very much especially when, on top of it all he had a way of making her feel as if she were the only woman in London that afternoon. But never once did he say or appear to do anything which made her feel uncomfortable, or ill at ease. She came to the conclusion that he probably had the same sensible attitudes to life as she herself had, and even entertained the idea that they might become friends.

Poor, deluded Anne. Giorgio, on the other side of the charm mask, couldn't believe that such a hard-faced bitch had given birth to the lovely and talented Matilda. He sensed that what he was setting out to do would be much easier than it might have been. After the scones and sandwiches had disappeared, he'd never seen another human being eat like Anne just had. He ordered more tea, and clearing his throat pulled out an Oscar-winning performance of sensitive concern.

Lies

"My dear Mrs Gasgoine."

"Oh Anne please!"

"How kind. Anne. Now the reason for my visit… Where to start? I'm sure you realise how talented your lovely daughter is?"

Giorgio could see that just behind that stilted smile, Anne was bleeding with envy.

"So we've been told." She managed. Surely he hadn't dragged her all the way from Devon to tell her that?

"The problem is…..Oh dear this is not easy………" He was sensing, feeling around the edge of Anne's energy field. His instincts, as usual, were incredibly accurate especially with someone as easy to read as Anne. Someone who had many hooks of attitude to attach to. Not like her daughter, so bland in that way one was likely to slide off. He pushed the thought of Matilda roughly to one side, it had caused him to lose the connection with the woman in front of him.

"It's difficult to say, I don't want to upset you my dear." He oozed a deep charm and his eyes bore into Anne with machiavellian darkness. As she stared into the handsome face, she felt the room swing slightly, as if she had drunk too much. When she spoke, her voice was suddenly hoarse and her throat felt dry.

"Oh you won't upset me Giorgio, please go on."

'Ah!' Thought Giorgio. 'The beautiful kingdom of the throat. The place of purity.'

During his travels in Tibet and India he had learnt much, including that the voice was the place of sincerity and truth. Denial was pointless and the words meant nothing since that truth was always in the sound. One simply had to be sensitive and discriminating enough to hear it. This was child's play for Giorgio. He spent many hours a week concentrating on singer's gymnastics. Anne was a knock over, and what he heard in her reply was stark rage and jealousy, tinged with bitterness. He didn't know why of course, but that didn't matter. She was a link with Matilda and another potential way through to her destruction. He leant back in his chair and caressed her with his eyes in a way that began to ignite parts that neither Duncan nor anyone else had ever reached. She was briefly reminded of the occasional dream of long ago. He was extremely subtle. The instant she registered anything, he released the pressure and watched as she became completely confused as to what had happened. At the same time, Anne noticed that with Giorgio there was none of the body language that men sometimes employ in order to say something without actually wording it. There was no exaggerated facial contortions, he was totally still, and the strength which came from inside him was nothing short of hypnotic. Anne flushed, suddenly she felt very unlike herself. She tried to extinguish the heat she felt rising, the feelings, but she was too confused to concentrate. Besides he wasn't doing anything was he? The man was sitting in a public place, he didn't even lean towards her across the tea table. He certainly hadn't attempted to touch her, not even in the most innocent of ways, and therefore she felt her sensibilities were not offended. At the same time she could allow herself to wallow in the deliciousness. It was her secret, no one knew.

It never occurred to her that Giorgio knew, that he was totally responsible for everything that she was feeling, and that she sat right across from a man who was much closer to her concept of the 'devil' than poor Lucy could ever be.

Giorgio noted the flush, the dilation of the pupils, slightly parted lips and the increased respiration as his maverick energy did its work. He let Anne approach feeling uncomfortable, then he began to speak.

"Our Matilda, my dear, is, as I have already said very talented. But with talent so often comes other, much less desirable characteristics. And I'm very much afraid to say that it seems to be the case with her."

He sighed, and allowed a few seconds of silence to descend. The murmur of conversation and clinking of china became louder. Giorgio was enjoying himself. This was like composing an orchestral score, and then conducting it. He certainly had Anne's attention. It was obvious that she couldn't wait to hear negative things about her daughter.

The fresh tea arrived. Such an interruption may have irritated some people, but Giorgio used it like the Master he was. Every pause intensified Anne's black curiosity. He deliberately watched the waiter walk away. She was on the edge of her seat by the time he turned back to her.

"Of course it's not for me to say what is actually happening with Matilda, but someone in my position you can understand, becomes very aware of shall we say…variances in the personality,"

"Variances?" Asked Anne.

"Well yes. I suppose that's the right word. I see her quite often you see. Also another pupil of mine a tenor, Martin by name, have you heard her speak of him? No? Oh well, I believe that they were an 'item' if that's the correct phrase, at one time. And although she assures me that now they are only good friends, since he's recently married you understand, he does know her very well……and he also is rather concerned…."

"*Married!*" Anne exclaimed. "You mean Matilda is involved with a married man?"

Giorgio took full advantage again of the interruption, then he raised his shoulders, his hands upturned and his mouth corners turned down, but he didn't say a word. Anne, meantime, was having considerable trouble not to smile. 'Blood will out' She thought joyfully. But Giorgio was not giving any more information on that subject. Giorgio was moving on.

"I'm more concerned with her physical condition. I believe your husband is a doctor?" Anne nodded, her eyes as bright as brittle glass.

"Then he may be able to put your mind at rest without even mentioning anything to Matilda. But personally I feel that she is under some considerable strain. It shows almost immediately in the breath you know with us singers. Any little glitch in the emotion, and there it is magnified a dozen times."

"There's a problem with her voice?" Anne was totally still. The shadow of triumph unmistakeably evident.

"Well......" Giorgio replied. "Let's put it this way. There certainly will be if she doesn't get back on line. What we always say is. First the breath: Then the sound: Then, if allowed to continue, the actual organ. After all that's the way we approach the voice positively, it's the same door you see? I'm quite sure it won't come to that. But I just wondered if she was taking something. Perhaps some sort of medication? Singers are very paranoid you know, some of us will try anything if we believe it might improve our performance." He made as if to laugh gently. Anne ignored him. She didn't wish to be placated.

"What exactly do you mean by 'taking'? She gasped trying to appear concerned but giving Giorgio the unmistakeable impression that she felt as if all her Christmases had arrived at once.

"You mean drugs? Matilda is taking drugs?" At which Giorgio feigned amazement.

"Oh surely not....I didn't mean hard drugs......Well she is your daughter of course. You and your husband know her better than anyone. Do you think it's possible?"

"I don't know." Replied Anne, knowing full well that Matilda would do no such thing. She felt such a surge of vindication for years of suffering that she remained totally unaware that Giorgio had turned the balance between them around. He remained silent and she continued, picking up so beautifully on cue, that he would have liked to have been able to congratulate her.

"What exactly are her symptoms? I can explain to Duncan, my husband you understand."

Giorgio played for time again. The more on edge she became the more likely she was to embellish what he was telling her.

"Well....Let me think. Sometimes she seems to have vast

mood swings, not just from week to week but within a single lesson. At such time her eyes seem strange to me. I'm not a medical man of course, so I could well be completely mistaken. But I can see you're worried. Look, have a word with your husband Anne. Then, here........"

He reached into his inner pocket and handed her a card, aware that her eyes followed his hand there, and lingered longer than one might expect. He smiled to himself and added.

"Give me a call and I'll keep an eye on her, and keep you both up to date. That is, of course as long as you agree, I have no wish to intrude."

"She doesn't deserve your kind consideration Giorgio. She is the most ungrateful girl, most ungrateful. If you knew the sacrifices that have been made for her, so that she can persue her dream."

"We must do what we can to keep the young lady on the straight and narrow, must we not?"

"My husband will be absolutely horrified."

"I'm sure he will." Giorgio paused then added quietly. "He's a lucky man."

"Excuse me? " Said Anne. Giorgio smiled at her. "Married to you my dear."

'If only you knew.' She thought, and the sensations began again. She felt herself drawn into Giorgio's eyes, his look was so intense.

"Would you like a drink? Alcoholic this time. Then I'll put you into a taxi. You are going home are you?" The question was gentle. Anne felt as if she were drowning in something that she would be quite happy to melt into, if she were given half a chance. But was she being given the chance? She couldn't believe where her mind was taking her and the rate at which her treacherous body rushed after it.

"Th-thank you." She managed. "A drink will be nice." She turned to look at his unreadable face and added. "It will give me time to decide whether I'm going home tonight or nor. It's such a long journey down to Devon."

Giorgio flung himself into his armchair and allowed the silence of the house to wash away the day. He had done all he could for now. Sown a little poison and discovered Anne was an easy ally in his plans should he ever need her again. But it had all taken a lot of energy, he was a bit out of practice with the 'energy probing' bit! And beyond pouring himself one last brandy, all he could do was sleep.

Anne herself, of course, was not important. But Giorgio knew from vast experience that you can never tell how far the poison would seep once you let it start to run. The more contact he could maintain regarding Matilda, the more he was likely to discover about her. And the more he discovered, the more easily he believed that he could twist her fate. His need to crush her registered in his mind as a pure line from Venice. But Giorgio, for all his knowledge and abilities had some huge blanks in his memories of his incarnations, and at this point in time, of Atlantis, he remembered nothing.

Frustration

Martin was frustrated. He slammed the door of the building from which he had just emerged and started down Holborn's Kings way in what at one time would have been aptly described as a 'high dudgeon.' Or in other words, completely pissed off. He had been invited to audition for a quite prestigious, if rather small company. And he had arrived that morning as full of positive intention as it was possible for him to be, assuring himself that this was the one to make the difference.

The company was not capable of paying even medium fees, but then outside the obvious Houses, who did have the funding in this country? No one seemed to have money for operatic productions. Nevertheless it was a place to be heard and many singers had found it had led to bigger and better opportunities.

Now Martin knew that he had a voice, looks, and a certain amount of experience, but he also knew that when it came to actually standing in front of an audition panel, or an audience for that matter, something was missing. He had to have a serious discussion with Giorgio. After all he was paying him enough, and he wasn't some amateur trying to break into the profession for God's sake. He had no other training to fall back on like some lucky sods he knew. No, he had remained true to what he did, and had plugged away for well, years now, and that ought to mean something. Right, he'd phone Giorgio that evening, make him shape up a bit!

That settled, he felt calmer and made for the nearest pub. There was, after all, time for a pint before the afternoon call. Soon he was musing over his beer and trying not to allow those mental wanderings to latch onto Matilda. Secretly he was mystified by Giorgio's teaching he had to admit that, but only to himself. It never occurred to him to discuss his fears with anyone else.

He allowed himself to travel the well worn path which described Giorgio's technique. The instruction made sense in some ways. At least the science behind it did. If you talked about it there was a veritable Aladdin's cave containing gems of knowledge. Giorgio would make frequent and tantalising reference to techniques of the past, long forgotten by the world. Some ancient knowledge which somehow he had access to. He would constantly quote fabulous singers (also from the past) of whom Martin had never heard, but who gradually became as familiar to him as the tenors who sang the big roles in the Opera House now, and he found their names slipping easily from his lips. It gave him a feeling of superiority to mention these singers and watch seasoned members of the company quietly racking their brains as they wondered who the hell he was talking about. Despite all this, however, Giorgio's so called 'real McCoy' technique, raised gloriously from the depths of operatic history, simply did not work in performance. At least it didn't at the moment. Maybe there were still some basic keys that he had not, as yet, been given. Perhaps he must work in sections. Martin did not want to explore that possibility, since every instinct told him that you needed to work with the whole sound at the outset. It was not possible to work one area separate from all the rest of the spectrum, and expect the voice to integrate smoothly and successfully. Giorgio had better have some good explanation and…….. Martin was jolted out of his reverie by Mike, Pixie's boyfriend, who sat down opposite him nursing his own favourite brew.

"Want another?" He asked indicating Martin's now three-quarters empty glass.

"Better not." Martin replied. "Must keep on the right side of the management!"

Mike laughed and nodded, then he said. "So, how are you? Haven't had a chance to speak to you since Milan. And were you oh so busy there, m'lad! You er…………recovered?"

Martin returned Mike's good natured grin and assumed sham-modesty.

"What can I tell you Mike?" He said. "One does one's bit!" At which, Mike punched him playfully on the arm and congratulated him on being a 'dog.' Then took a long gulp of his drink, and said, as he wiped the froth from his mouth with the back of his hand.

"And how's the lovely Tilly?"

Martin froze. But as he happened to be looking into his beer at that moment, Mike didn't notice, and he continued.

"Quite a little lady, that one. She looks as if she owns the place, you know what I mean?"

Martin managed a nod……..."Walking about as if……Oh

I don't know. But then you get talking to her, get to know her a bit and she's so natural and down to earth. Bit of a mystery our Tilly. If it wasn't for my magnificent Pixie, you might find you had a rival my man! Although I suppose we'd both have to stand in line in deference to the Italian boyfriend. I guess you know all about him?"

"No." Growled Martin. "Not really." He did of course. That touching little scene by the stage door was still so bright in his memory. He had been trying to forget it. He grabbed his glass and swung it back, draining it. He would have another, damn it!

"Changed my mind." He said getting up. And he slapped a five pound note on to the counter. The barmaid surveyed him nervously and served him quickly. Martin sat down again and hoped that Mike would shut up about Matilda, but he didn't. He kept on and on until Martin's head was swimming. He felt sick at the idea of her with anyone else. Suddenly he picked up on his friend's uninterruptible flow...... "What did you say?"

"I said that according to Pixie, she spends every weekend that she's not working, with Alitalia backwards and forwards to Milan to spend a few hours with lover boy. Now ain't love grand? What do these Iti's have anyway, can you tell me that? I mean......."

"It won't last!" If Mike had known Martin a little better, he would have been warned by the sudden quiet tone of his voice. But he didn't, so he just kept going.

"Well! That's not for us to say is it?"

"It won't. She'll soon come running back to good ol' Martin when she's had enough of the Italian crap. Or when he's had enough if her, which is much more fucking likely mate. Do you know how long I've known her? Bloody years. I mean what does she think she's playing at?"

Mike stared at him in amazement, realising that he had hit a raw nerve, he tried reasoning.

"Come on man. You're talking as if you have a right to her. Think again mate. First, you're married, which as far we know this Italian isn't. Second you lay anything that moves and will stay still long enough, or should I say STAND still long enough. From what I've heard you don't even allow the poor cows time to undress. Why would a girl like Tilly put up with that? You're a degenerate man. I mean I know we all joke about it, but when it comes down to it, you can't treat people like you do….."

Martin cut loudly across him, his words spilling out.

"I don't need your judgement Mike. And you can talk. Last time I looked you were well and truly married. And don't compare us with you and Madam Pixie! She needs to be taken down a step or two that one, think you might have bitten off more than you can chew there mate! But Tilly's just a misguided little bitch! How dare she? Who does she think she is?" The pub had suddenly quietened, Mike glanced over his shoulder and lowering his voice, said.

"Come on Martin, you're wasting you're time. This thing with this bloody guy is obviously important to her. I mean who spends time and money, not to mention energy flying backwards and forwards all the time?"

Martin turned his face directly to Mike. The look was indescribable. His eyes were focused somewhere else entirely. His features were contorted in a paroxysm of agony that knocked the next words from Mike's mind. The whole reaction seemed hugely extreme. Mike did not understand, he just knew he felt very uncomfortable.

"Fuck off!" Martin screamed at him……….. The pub went even quieter and the manager moved towards the phone…… "Just fuck off!"

Mike picked up his beer, glad of a reason to go. Out of the corner of his eye he noticed some fellow stage hands staring in their direction. He started towards them, but as a parting shot he said, dropping his voice.

"You've got it bad man, REAL bad."

Deception

I come here full of apology. I know that I have been extremely lax. You see I've never been affected by anything quite so completely as my relationship with Dante. I'm not going to go on and on, and I do intend to catch up with everything else, but this is the first time in my life that anything other than music has consumed me so completely, so you must bear with me. Maria asked me.

"Well, was it worth the wait? You know, are you glad that you didn't succumb to becoming the 'other' woman?"

"Yes." I smiled at her. "Very glad!"

"Good!" But she couldn't resist adding, in mock amazement. "Of course, I don't know how you managed it. To deny yourself Martin and all that charm and er....everything!"

You'd think that I'd get tired popping over to Milan so often, but I hardly notice the journey, it's no different from boarding an inter-city train really. Anyway, Dante comes here as often as he can arrange it. Singing and Dante, what more could I possibly need? I have discovered a little more about him. He is 30 and very much more successful with his writing than he originally led me to believe. He already has two books of his own published. One a novel, the other a history of opera as viewed from the singers' point of view. An ingenious idea (even if I am just a little prejudice.) I'm eagerly awaiting the English translation in spite of the fact that my Italian is naturally improving in leaps and bounds because of Dante. I'm sure I wouldn't be up to reading a full novel in the language, it would take too long, I'd become far too impatient.

I have tried on more than one occasion now, to discuss my programme with Giorgio, and I am no closer to understanding him. He doesn't seem to be really interested. I mean he has no real enthusiasm. I suggest pieces that I know are for me, that are the repertoire that I should be looking at, but he doesn't pick up on anything. Basically he just isn't giving me very much help or guidance. Also, I will be performing alone, which makes it a recital, I suppose, since my friend Hannah Guild, is off to Europe with a solo contract for an Opera House in Germany clasped to her excited bosom!

The venue for the concert is a reasonable size. A hall in a big house, at one time probably used for balls and such like, just off Kensington High Street, not Verona Arena! The music which Giorgio suggests is not appropriate for the hall, but more, it is unsuitable for my voice. This is worrying. I cannot imagine why he would deliberately subject me to potential problems in this way.

I've tried to speak to Martin about it, but he's turned cold and vicious again. I can't get near him. So for the time being

I've put it to one side. I do have another project pending. Pixie was asked to sing 'Susuki' in a one off performance of Puccini's 'Madama Butterfly.' The company had not cast Cio Cio San and asked her if she knew of a soprano suited to the role. She does of course, bless her. I accepted without delay and was very excited about it. I carried all this excitement into my last singing lesson. I was positively bursting with it, however, after I told Giorgio he said nothing straightaway. He lent back in his chair, and those eyes of his bore into me, after a few seconds he finally said.

"So, you think you can sing this, do you?" Of course that made me immediately unsure. I searched for the right words.

"I.....Well...er...It is for my type of voice, isn't it?"

He raised his eyebrows, pursed his lips and sighed, then he replied.

"For your voice? Your type of voice, maybe. Whether it's suitable for you right now, remains to be seen."

I was perplexed, considering what he had been suggesting I sing at my recital, this was completely absurd. He continued. "Do you have the score with you?" Of course I had the score with me. In fact I had two, one for him in case he didn't have his to hand. He waved his hand in the air while I was fumbling in my bag. "Well, let's see."

He let out a huge sigh, as if the task before him was really asking too much. And took several minutes trying to find Butterfly's first off stage line.. Impatiently, he slammed the score shut. This was not going as I had anticipated.

"What edition is this? I can't find anything in here."

I took that copy from him and silently handed my own, already open at 'Butterfly's Entrance.' I found the corresponding place in the offending copy very easily. Boy did he get out of bed the wrong side this morning! As if all this were not enough, he then made me feel as if I were on trial. He stopped every few bars. Now this in itself, is quite normal when working any role in depth, it is what one would expect. But it is the way he did it that was upsetting. But worse, I had the sneaky suspicion that he enjoyed it. I could have sworn it was all an act. There were more exaggerated sighs, and bemused shakings of the head, and well, act or not, it began to get to me. We really do find ourselves in extremely vulnerable positions sometimes. No wonder, as a relative newcomer to the profession, I am acutely aware of levels of stress and tension around those who may not be as established as they would like to be. Giorgio was acting as if I had never opened my mouth before. I was unable to accept that it was quite as bad as he intimidated. Voices do not deteriorate in the space of a few phrases. I tried to lighten things up a little.

"Oh Giorgio. It can't be that bad!" There was a silence during which the atmosphere in the room seemed to crackle, and my heart began to thud in my chest. I could see the heavy rhythm just above the rim of my top.

"Oh can't it cara? Can't it indeed? Well now, what makes you think that?"

Suddenly it was as if someone had thrown a switch. The world seemed ever so slightly different. Even the sunlight dappling the lovely garden outside, was altered. My stomach sank into a bottomless pit and the next phrase was extremely unsteady.

"Matilda! What are you doing?"

"I don't know. I don't understand. This has never happened before, I mean......."

Giorgio released yet another long sigh. "Oh spare me Matilda, please!" He looked at me as if I were tone deaf, and leant back from the piano, folding his arms.

"What is happening to you Matilda? I mean you sound as if you've never had a lesson in your life. How long have you been training? You're surrounded by the best in the world every day, and you can't come up with something better than that which you have just produced. Or is the job the problem? You can't be serious about attempting this role young lady surely!"

My knees were by now, so weak that I thought I would cease to be able to stand upright. This was terrible. Whatever I still had to learn (and that may be a considerable amount) I have always been able to rely on basic vocal behaviour. A healthy response to breath, heart and mind. Giorgio continued, his voice like smooth ice.

"You girls! You think you can have it all, don't you? I suggest young lady that you curtail your extra activities, that you stop jetting off to Europe at every opportunity, and start behaving like the professional singer that you purport to be!"

"Yes, Giorgio." It was almost a whisper. "Now take your scores, and go." At which I started to fumble in my purse.

"No, I don't want your money. And do not waste my time like this again!"

There was someone waiting in the hall for a lesson. No doubt some lucky person who sings solely for pleasure, and has a well paid, uncomplicated job. Suddenly that seemed almost desirable. I managed to nod in her direction. Then I opened the door and fled. All I could think was that, tomorrow. Dante will be here. It went round and round in my head like a litany, and it seemed as if it were the only thing that supported me during the long journey back to the Opera House.

After Matilda had left, Giorgio's next student followed him into his studio.

"What a beautiful voice she has. Who is she Giorgio?"

"That my dear, was Matilda Gasgoine. She also has a big problem."

"Oh, what's that?"

'Me.' Thought Giorgio. He turned to the attractive woman who had little vocal ability, but a bank account which he could appreciate.

"Now, now cara. I can't divulge private particulars about other students, that's very naughty. And 'naughty' as you well know comes later, after the lesson. Anyway it's not very interesting. Now. Let's work."

This one paid more than money for the privilege of being taught by the 'great' Giorgio.

JOURNAL

I have never cried on front of Dante, rarely in front of anyone actually. But this weekend, after my traumatic lesson, I found myself sobbing uncontrollably in his arms. Great searing sobs that completely took over my body, rendering it incapable of anything for some moments, except supporting this onslaught from the solar plexus.

"Ssh..Cara." He whispered. "I am here for you. I am always here for you."

When I had calmed down a little, we talked about our lifestyle. There's not much we can do about it at the moment. I assured him that the travelling was not the cause of any problem that I may or may not be experiencing. I'm so confused at the moment that I still can't work out what it was all about yesterday with Giorgio. It has left me feeling exhausted. Dante suggested that I call in sick on Monday and take a rest. At first I was horrified, but the idea is beginning to appeal to me. I feel completely devoid of energy. I don't think that I could sing to save my life. Dante also had a few things to say about Giorgio.

"You needa gentle 'andling cara. I notice when youa singing….."

"What?" I snapped at the object of my desire and adoration, and Dante looked tortured.

"Well…….De tension she is coming 'ere." He ran his finger seductively along my jaw. "An' sometimes you not even breathing proper."

"Ly." I said with unnecessary venom." "Che?" He said. "Ly……..Properly!" I snapped.

"Darling, when youa correcting my English, I know you tink I ama right."

"You're not a singer Dante. What do you know about breathing?"

"I see de whole pictures. De details, I not know to put dem right! I 'ave whata we call istinto."

"God save me from people with 'instinct' Dante!" I had moved away from him during this because I basically didn't want to hear it. Somewhere I question that he may be right, but I can't look at it now, I simply can't. Dante caught my hand and turned me back to him.

"Leave 'im, cara. For you, for me! I know isa something bad 'ere."

Is this all Italian drama? Maybe also, a little Italian jealousy? I don't think so. Dante is after all very intelligent, not given to flights of fancy. He even listens to the accounts of my dreams with patient, healthy scepticism, perfectly understandable in one who has not experienced for himself this phenomena. But it only illuminates his obvious concern regarding Giorgio. And why do I feel that I can't leave him? It's ridiculous when I think about it. I'm in a position to discover the best teachers in London, and yet I hesitate. No it's something deeper than hesitation. I can't go into the feeling just now. It's too thick and grey and unwelcoming.

My mother rang this evening. She wants me to go home. She and Dad apparently have something that they need to talk to me about. Sounds intriguing, mystery is not her style.

Dear God, I really don't want to go, and I don't know why. Any suggestions?

Just as she was falling asleep Dante said.

"You are still a little baby in dis world ofa opera, you know dis. You 'avea de time. Why you so reluctant to take my advice? You not even considered it."

The Matilda laying in Dante's arms had no answer. But somewhere in the vast regions of her unconscious memory she knew. Because the last time she had listened to Dante (or rather Angelo) about something important, she died.

Giorgio and Martin were having a drink. Connie had refuse to go, but Martin hadn't exactly encouraged her. He wanted Giorgio to himself with no excuse for distraction. He had lost no time in challenging his teacher about his lack of success, but so far the older man had side stepped him completely. Martin sulked, Giorgio was a devious bugger. Why did he find it so hard to walk away? He just couldn't shake the idea that there was no one else out here who could help him. He knew it was stupid, but nevertheless it was a very strong feeling and so far he had come nowhere near to breaking it. Giorgio was off on another tangent.

"You know the only real problem you have is Matilda, don't you?" Martin's stomach lurched.

"Matilda? Bloody hell Giorgio. That was over ages ago, before I was married. I don't give a monkey's anymore, if I ever did."

"Liar!" Replied Giorgio. "I don't mean that you're in love with her, Martin. I mean you're still hung up on her." He paused, and then, as Martin said nothing, he continued more quietly.

"She's dangerous. In my opinion women like her are the worst type."

"Why?" Growled Martin, still sulking from the insinuation, and furious to discover that Giorgio was right, and that his 'hang up' was neatly embroidered through his hate.

"Because she doesn't realise it." Giorgio continued. "Innocence, or ignorance if you prefer the word is as deadly as snake bite."

Martin shuffled in his seat. This conversation was not going the way he had intended. But Giorgio hadn't finished.

"She's affecting you. You can't open up when you sing, especially in auditions and performances. Most people can put these sort of things to one side at such times. But you don't Martin. And why don't you? Because you can't. Don't you see how strong this is, how completely destructive she is to your career? Listen Martin, this is important. Get her out of here......" He tapped his head. "And out of here........." He patted his trousers. "She's just another soprano after all my boy, they're ten a penny!"

Martin nodded, but he knew that wasn't quite true. Matilda had something a little more than average. Why did Giorgio deny it all the time? What was he afraid of? He glanced at his teacher across the table.

"Is that the case Giorgio? I mean many people seem to be of the opinion that Matilda could have quite a future if she's handled properly."

"Not if I have anything to do with it." Giorgio said softly his eyes seeming to glaze over. He felt a strong burst of energy soar upwards from his lower limbs as if his words had opened a further door in his mind. For a second he caught a glimpse of a long, golden corridor, and the awareness of heat and danger.

'That wasn't Venice!' He thought. A deep sound filled his head, it was accompanied by a yearning so strong, that he paled. He wanted to be part of that sound and merge with it, but he couldn't. He needed something, something that would allow him to take his place, to be involved in the very height of musical brilliance. He breathed out the experience and Martin shook his head, was it the booze? He felt light headed and there seemed to be a strange glint in Giorgio's eyes. He didn't like it, but he couldn't turn his head away, he felt as if it were in a vice.

He had every intention of getting up now, of leaving and never seeing Giorgio again. He wasn't going to put up with this! He tried to push his chair back from the table, but nothing moved. His body refused to obey him. Giorgio appeared to be staring straight in front of him as if he were completely oblivious of Martin, never mind his predicament. He didn't move, but those eyes of his! It was as if all his awareness and energy were focused through them.

Then there was a vibration in Martin's head. It was in sympathy with his pain, the anger and anguish. It was becoming a sound at the very pitch of his agony, now he could actually hear it. Christ! what was happening? Then Giorgio was grabbing him by the arm. "Hey! What's up my boy? You look as if you're about to pass out. I'm an old man remember, don't do this to me!"

"You're hardly old Giorgio." Martin replied, suddenly aware of Giorgio's amazing strength, but not being able to pin point its exact source. He shook himself, maybe he'd imagined it. He felt as if he'd come out of a dream.

"I'm O.K. thanks." He said impatiently as he tried to remember what it was that he had been talking about. It was something important.......What the hell was it? But all he could bring into his mind was that his hate for Matilda had grown ten fold.

Giorgio went to the bar and ordered brandies. He needed Martin to have some success. He obviously wasn't going to be content with chorus work. If it had been anyone else he would have told them they were bloody lucky to have the job they had, and to stop moaning. But he needed Martin on his side, he couldn't have him slipping away. After all he told himself, as he picked up the drinks from the counter, they belonged together the three of them, but this time things would be different. Oh yes, this time he intended for them to be very different indeed.

And anyway there was no reason why Martin couldn't have a modicum of success. He had a good tenor voice, a real tenor, that wasn't exactly rare, but not so common either. He couldn't understand why Martin had so much disappointment. That little company he had auditioned for the other day, they should have grabbed him, but they didn't. He placed the drinks on the table and watched as the younger man picked his up immediately.

Giorgio mulled over the problem for the rest of the evening, pushing the unexplained vision from his mind. It occurred to him that he had, in fact, never seen Martin perform. What didn't occur to him, however, was that in this present time and place, his teaching technique was wanting, that his knowledge even in Venice had been less than brilliant, and that his arrogant attitude prevented the sympathetic link necessary for developing potential artists. No, none of this occurred to him.

Mother Mine

Journal

My mother picked me up from the station. This is unusual. It's always my Dad who picks me up. She was very quiet all the way back to the house, which was empty when we arrived. I, of course, asked her where he was. She informed me that he was at an International Conference in Sweden. I couldn't suppress my surprise, and she muttered something about it being at the last moment, he was covering for someone, and it couldn't be helped.

I don't believe her. When I asked her what it was they wanted to talk to me about, she cut me short. She was tired, she said. We would talk in the morning. I asked her if Dad would get back before I had to return to London. She became quite irritated.

"I've told you Matilda. He's at a Conference and I have no idea when he'll be back, now goodnight!"

Needless to say, I did not sleep very well at all. I have for some time now, had a vague unease rather like a slight indigestion. I find it hard to relax mentally, also I have not dreamt spectacularly for what seems like ages. This I really miss, because it always has such a rejuvenating effect on the whole psyche, and helps to keep everything in beautiful perspective. Finally I got out of bed and stared out of the window. Summer was gathering pace. Early morning mist hung quietly over the garden, and the day promised to be hot. Fairies' Ferry must be wonderful and I suddenly felt a strong urge to dress quickly, slip silently from the house and go there. After all, I would be back long before my mother was likely to wake. But I have not been there since the night with Lucy. I wasn't afraid to go because something similar might happen again, rather because something might not. That is no frame of mind to be visiting such a magical place, and to look for, or expect an experience of that nature again was asking a lot. I must content myself with the memory. Eventually I did manage to sleep for a couple of hours and heard my mother's impatient knock on the door through a thick mist. I did not relish a day on my own with her, but little did I know what that day would bring, or how my life would change in a few hours, for ever.

Breakfast was laboured. Polite enquiries as to what I'd like to eat. Solemn requests for various items to be passed. Just her and me. I never realised how much Dad's presence enhances the situation and keeps a semblance of the 'norm' alive. I watched her as she piled the dishes into the dish-washer, feeling as uncomfortable as on many other such occasions. I have never known whether to offer to help her or not. So many times I have been cut short before the offer was even finished, that it seemed sensible to let her continue alone, although I'm never sure when that will be criticised, either. But as I was feeling so wretchedly tired, I opted for the easy version. She didn't comment, just asked me to go and open the French windows since it was such a lovely day. She would make some more coffee and join me shortly, she said.

I did as I was bid. I was leaning against the open windows breathing in the warmth of the day and beginning to feel very much better, when the rattle of cups pulled me out of my peace.

"You're always dreaming Matilda, What exactly do you think about?"

"I don't know really." I replied, then as she looked at me with an expression of exasperation on her face, I continued. "What I mean is I can't explain. It's a non-state. As soon as I catch myself in it, and become consciously aware of what I'm thinking, the mood vanishes."

I probably sounded a little irritated, because I was. I could have sworn that just before she arrived I saw Carlo leaning against our apple tree, smiling his beguiling smile. Was I ever like that?......... I had begun to unload the tray, and my Mother moved the coffee pot... Had I experienced Carlo in glorious Venice? My mind snapped back to the present, there were three cups.

"Dad's back!" It wasn't a question and I felt a little guilty at the sudden lightness in my voice.

"Why do you suppose that Matilda?"

"Well you've brought three cups in." My Mother laid some mats on the table and placed one cup on each of them in silence, leaving me to champ at the bit. "So, is Dad back?"

"No Matilda, we have a visitor. I've asked the vicar to pop in after the morning service. He has agreed, which is very nice of him, considering that it's Sunday."

All this was said as if it had been my personal request. Feeling even more irritated I asked her.

"Why would he do that?" For a moment she didn't answer, then she turned to me and replied.

"I would have thought that you might have some idea why I've asked him to come. Just a little inkling maybe?" I looked at her blankly. "No? Well he obviously thinks it's important enough to make the time, since you are so busy and, no doubt, will be running back to London first thing in the morning, if not later today."

This was all delivered in an extremely sarcastic tone. I was baffled and felt the 'unease' return swiftly and with a vengeance. Instinct clothed itself in respectability, and tried to aid me.

"Well, before he arrives, I'm going to phone Lucy"...... Silence!…"O.K. Mum?" …..Silence… Now this was a 'game' she has always played. And I end up feeling as if my throat, head and solar plexus, are nailed to the wall in three different places. I said.

"I won't be long." And I made for the door to the hall. As I picked up the receiver, the front door bell rang. I pressed in Lucy's number. Mum passed on her way to the door and glanced at me over her shoulder, saying.

"I wish you had worn something else Matilda. You don't look very respectable for a Sunday you know."

A few seconds later, the vicar strode down the hall looking very grave. Lucy's phone was ringing, but I acknowledged him.

"Good morning Vicar." He nodded, and replied simply. "Matilda."

I didn't like the tone of his voice. For one terrible moment I wondered if something had happened to Dad, and she couldn't bring herself to tell me. The sitting room door was open. I could see the vicar sitting down, and my Mother offering him coffee. Lucy, please pick up. Suddenly it was dreadfully important for me to hear her voice. My Mother positioned herself between the vicar and me, and made impatient signals for me to join them, while saying with hypocritical sweetness in her voice.

"I don't think Lucy can be there Matilda. Can you come in now?"

I had to give up. I replaced the receiver noticing the Vicar's irritated body language at the mention of Lucy's name, took a deep breath and joined my Mother and her guest. He, the very Reverend Philip Bartholomew is quite new to the village. I don't really know him, his arrival having coincided with my leaving for college. And he knows nothing about me at all, at least I thought he didn't. Anyway I liked our last vicar, he was much more human.

My Mother handed me a cup of coffee, and then stepped out into the garden, leaving me and the Very Reverend alone. I followed her exit in amazement, realising too late that this was something of a set up. But as suspicion jumped through my body to logical awareness, I couldn't begin to understand why. The vicar sipped his coffee and surveyed me over the rim of the cup, was gracious enough to invite me, in my own parents' house, to sit, and said.

"Now Matilda, how are you feeling?" How bizarre a question was that? I glanced at my Mother positioned close to the French window, she appeared not to be listening, but of course she was. Then I turned back to our guest. Immediately I registered a strong impression of imprisonment, of a soul forced to live out a lie, and energy for the task fuelled by resentment of anybody who loves what they do, or who loves life. He is from an old school, a dying school, and death throes can be terrible.

"I'm feeling very well, thank you." I replied.

"You look a little tired, rather strained around the eyes in fact." He said. 'And you'….. I thought, while I forced myself to smile at him……. 'You look sucked dry of your own essence, and very, very, angry.' "I didn't sleep too well, last night." I tried to pass it off, after all it was the truth anyway.

"Does that often happen?" He seemed to leap on what I had said. I paused. My twenty four and a half years, and being at the Opera House have given me some confidence. Besides which, Carlo was in front of me. He was as clear as when I had seen him in my cappuccino in Venice, the room, the vicar and my Mother receded somehow. Who knows how these things work? He was talking to a young student priest in the palazzo. It was winter and he had a fur cloak pulled tightly around his slender body. The logical side of my mind began to protest. 'But Carlo is dead!' The other side told it to shut up since this scene in Carlo's life was obviously earlier. Our lives don't run entirely parallel, otherwise I would have already copped it, dropping dead in Venice from poisoned cappuccino, I suppose!

Carlo was being led to apartments deep in the palazzo. Apartments that belonged to Cardinal D'Oro. He knew why he was summoned, and it angered him. I watched Carlo, but answered the vicar.

"Oh, everyone has a bad night sometimes, don't they?" He was looking at me strangely, almost as if he could see what I was seeing. He placed his coffee cup on the table mat in front of him and said quietly.

"Well you know what they say Matilda, about a clear conscience and sleeping well?"

"No, I'm afraid I don't know what you mean. In fact with respect vicar, why are you here? I mean why are we having this conversation?"

At which point my Mother hurried back into the room. (I told you she was listening) It had become so warm outside that you could smell the heat swirling around her. "Matilda! I never thought you'd be so rude. I didn't bring you up to speak to people, especially the vicar like that. I'm so sorry Reverend Bartholomew!"

I had a little trouble not smiling at this remark, it was so transparent. But, at the same time I felt strongly that I should be concerning myself with what was going on. The vicar had raised his hand and shaking his head solemnly, said to my Mother.

"Oh please Anne, it's quite alright."

I was becoming impatient. I had in fact, said nothing that could be considered remotely rude. I opened my mouth to speak, but the vicar forestalled me.

"Now Matilda. Your Mother and I are rather concerned about you." 'And my Father?' I thought. 'Exactly where does he fit into all this?' And where was he? Not in Sweden I'd bet. The vicar continued......"I'll come to the point........" (Oh goody.......)

Carlo and his guide had reached the Cardinal's apartments. In the inner sanctum a huge, welcome fire crackled on the hearth.

"Aspetta Signor per favor. The Cardinal will join you shortly." And with that the young man left and Carlo moved closer to the fire where a red velvet cushion lay on the beautiful carpet before it. His lovely green eyes travelled slowly around the room. A great dark-wood table full of books and papers stood beneath the huge window overlooking one of the prettiest quadrangles in the palazzo. In the summer it must give such pleasure to the owner of these apartments simply to stand here and look out at the fountains and graceful statues. Carlo loved statues, he felt that they looked as if they were about to speak to you.

He pulled himself back to his present situation. If the old man thought....... Carlo gritted his teeth. How dare he subject him to this humiliation now? He thought that was all over. It was bad enough to catch the attention of some person in authority when one was a young student. After all one lived and studied under their patronage. Everyone knew what happened, and everyone turned a blind eye to it. After all what higher authority could there be to whom the students could appeal? No, it became, as Raimondo, while laughing it of as best he could, christened it.....'The Necessary!'

"I have to perform 'the necessary' this afternoon." And he would turn up his aristocratic little nose and make his eyes bulge in expression of his disgust.

"If you go in looking like that Raimondo, you won't have to perform anything. You should try it!" Giggled Lucciano.

Then of course, everything would get out of hand, They were young enough to allow themselves some release in 'pantomime' and anyone observing the next minutes would have considered them all totally mad. That is how they dealt with things then.

Now, was different. Apart from anything else, Carlo wasn't sure where he stood. He was financially independent and fast becoming one of the most famous castrati in Venice if not Europe. What, therefore, he still owed the Cardinal he couldn't fathom. He had made large donations to both the poor of the city, and the Academy itself. He helped anyone who needed help when he could. But as far as his old patrons and certain other 'activities' were concerned it was all a very 'grey' area. There were no rules concerning this sort of thing, he laughed ironically. No, of course not. The scribes would have a very hard job writing that sort of thing down on paper, it was unthinkable. He took a deep breath and reiterated to himself what he had decided from the first moment he had been summoned. Whatever the consequence, he was not going to drop his hose for that old fart. The door opened and the Cardinal entered carrying two thick volumes in a firm embrace across his chest.

"Carlo, come sta?" He said. Carlo's long training had indoctrinated him with an automatic respect for the priesthood. "Well thank you Monsignor. I trust I find you the same my lord?"

The Cardinal paused in his hurried pace to the table, glanced at Carlo and nodded with a brief smile that transported Carlo back to his childhood. In spite of his fury at being summoned like a student, he couldn't help but remember this man's kindness to him. There had been pain of course, even the Cardinal couldn't do much about that. But he had been as gentle as he knew how to be. Carlo had known even then, that he could have fared so very much worse. He watched the priest as he leaned over the table and released his burden from its ecclesiastical embrace. Carlo had to admit it, he had felt very loved by this man, and that he couldn't dismiss with honour.

The Cardinal was avoiding his eyes. It had been some time since they had been alone together. A passing nod, or a brief snatch of conversation after a performance was about the only contact between them, and he seemed very uncertain of how to proceed. Perhaps he sensed Carlo's resolve. Carlo waited, the fire crackled and the Cardinal said quickly.

"Sing for me Carlo, per favor…..Canti!"

Carlo was taken aback, but he obliged. His glorious sound filled the room with light, as the grey afternoon turned darker and darker. Cardinal D'Oro, still staring out into the quadrangle, sighed.

"Bellissimo Carlo. There is no one in the world of opera to come near you. No one else can cause such a fire in the heart." He turned back into the room, and Carlo noted his breathing. Was it age and carrying the heavy volumes, or was it passion? In which case it appeared his singing ignited fire in other parts besides the heart. The Cardinal walked passed him closer to the fire and continued.

"God has been so good to you Carlo. Please, can you still be good to me?" His voice broke slightly, but whether from embarrassment or excitement, Carlo could not tell. He allowed himself to be pulled gently towards the velvet cushion waiting by the fire, his mind working overtime as to exactly when he should make a stand. But he felt the Cardinal's unease, registered the look of fear in his eyes, he also smelt the bergamot and lavender that wafted around the priestly robes. The latter he appreciated, the rest caused him to feel compassion for the older man. He determined not to make a scene, and sank gracefully to his knees, the very act itself intensifying the priest's obvious passion. Some seconds of relative silence followed until the Cardinal, uttering his first groan, raised his eyes to heaven and started to recite the 'Libera Me.'

At first Carlo was horrified. He had great regard for God, even if he did secretly consider that his army on earth was severely wanting. But then he felt such a great desire to laugh, that his erotic act became extremely difficult. He was shaking with mirth at the ridiculous situation, and truly concerned that he might be overcome by his laughter, and roll onto the floor in convulsions. Then, briefly, he raised his eyes and caught a glimpse of the priest's face. A contortion of fear, need and ecstasy ignited in Carlo's soul, a terrible searing pity, and an understandable contempt for the whole hypocritical charade.

He felt a supreme need to distance himself, to take his friends to some warm place, somewhere virginal of their pasts. Where no reminders lurked, where they would find the closest thing possible to wholeness. Sea, fresh air and rest, that was it! He might even persuade Angelo to go with them. What a time they would have! It would be perfect.

The chanting, which had become breathless, caught on an indistinguishable word and stopped suddenly. Carlo breathed a sigh of relief. It was over. As a student he had slept in the Cardinal's arms for a while. His pains eased by the older man's tender administrations and ointments, and his confused little heart healed by the whispers in his ear.

"You are the son I have not been granted Carlo. Io t'amo. No harm will I allow to come to you. God forgive me, but I love you."

Carlo had no doubt that God would forgive them both. That he understood much more than this tortured priest could imagine. Now the Cardinal offered him wine. Carlo expected nothing more, his heart was confused no longer, but it still desired some gentleness, and at that moment positively ached in his breast to hear the right words. He drained his glass, and took his leave. At the great door the Cardinal spoke to him one last time.

"Carlo, you are still my dearest love. Wherever my body sins, you hold my heart. But take care lest people use you for your pity."

The door closed behind him and he was in the cold corridor where he paused for a few moments musing over the Cardinal's words. They made little sense. He pulled his heavy cloak around him and hurried back through the maze of passageways and little squares that were deserted at this time of the year. But they reminded one that soon the fountains and shade offered by the trees would draw any member of the palazzo's vast household there on the slightest excuse. And they would pass their free hours again in happy comradeship, bathed in the perfume of jasmine, honeysuckle and the very best of wines. And would he hear the sweet voice again? It was strange but he feared for her, although he knew it was foolish. The alien world from which he sensed she came had no doubt learnt much. Things far beyond his understanding, but he sensed that it also had lost much, and it was in that losing that Carlo feared for his 'little sister' as he had come to think of her. "God keep you safe cara." He said quietly as the great gate of the entrance to the palazzo came into sight. Ahead of him he could see the watchman's fire and some of his friends rolling dice and letting the old man win over and over again. He could hear Raimondo's voice carrying on the cold night air.

"But no. No Signor you do yourself ill. It was a double six, most definitely. Was it not Lucci?"

"Oh certain." Laughed Lucciano, as Umberto and Tonio pushed large amounts of coins into every available place about the old man's person. In the deep pockets inside his cloak, and under his hat. There was enough gold there already to change his life. He was so bemused by it all that he laughed and cried alternately, sliding from one emotion to the other and back again, with true Latin ease.

Carlo stood back in the shadows and watched, smiling. Their humanity lifted his spirits and the recent tacky little scene with the Cardinal was relegated to the dark place in his mind where all such scenes lay. As an icy blast of air caught him he hurried from the shadows and towards his friends. Oh they deserved a holiday, he felt a deep sweet love for them all.........

"Matilda, are you listening?" I nodded and the vicar continued. "I understand that you have a boyfriend?"

So, this is a crime now? I nodded again and glanced over at my Mother who had assumed the position of umpire, at least I thought she had. She was wearing one of her worst masks. Her, why can't the world be as pure as me? Mask.

"I also understand that he is married." I was too stunned to answer. "Now......" The very Reverend continued. " I know that this sort of thing is accepted as normal nowadays, especially so I understand in your chosen profession, but your parents are very concerned for your welfare, and your future. And if you are also using drugs...." I found my voice.

"Oh but he isn't my married." There was a silence. "My boy-friend, he definitely isn't married."

"Are you certain Matilda?" Asked my Mother. "Because I have it on good authority that he most definitely is." At this I went cold. She sounded so certain, so utterly sure. I saw Dante in my mind's eye smiling at a young Italian wife, with a flock of children around them. While my heart was denying the possibility, suspicion was offering me evidence for examination. Dante had said so little of his family, or his background. The future was never an issue in our conversations and meeting his family had never even been mentioned.

"How do you know this?" I asked my Mother.

"Never mind who told me Matilda, I'm afraid that it is quite true. Now, your Father is most upset by all this."

"So why isn't he here? What's the point of this discussion when he isn't around to discuss it as well? Not that 'discuss' is the right word, I mean......."

"I told you Matilda, he's at a conference." My Mother inter-rupted.

"I don't believe you." I said. "Now Matilda.........." The vicar began. Sometimes, being a singer has other advantages outside singing glorious music. Because it was fuelled by true emotion, my vocal crescendo completely obliterated the rest of his words. I felt a fantastic power momentarily as the two faces before me registered disbelief. I had stood up and I took a couple of steps towards them. I could hear my words echoing around the room.

"I don't, I don't believe a word of it and I'm going back to London now."

I had not bargained with the vicar who also stood up, and as I got within range on my way to the door, he struck me hard across the face. As I gasped, he struck me again. My face burned. Out of the corner of my eye I could see my Mother. She had not moved, indeed she sat as composed as if nothing in particular was occurring. She said absolutely nothing. So much for the umpire!

"How dare you speak to your Mother like that? You're nothing but a drug-swilling little slut. God forgive me, but it has to be said".

That had the absurd ring of 'This has hurt us much more than it has hurt you,' about it. I hoped that he wouldn't come near me again, because if he had done I was afraid that I would kill him. I would strike at him with all my strength. I can't begin to describe my anger, as huge tidal waves of fury at the injustice of it all swept through me, threatening to overcome me completely. I couldn't believe my ears.

"I want my Father. I want to speak to him. You must have a number for him in Sweden. I want to speak to him now." There was silence. The room felt heavy with all that had just transpired, then my Mother spoke, she delivered the final death blow quietly and without any emotion whatsoever.

"I'm afraid he doesn't wish to speak to you Matilda. Not just at the moment anyway."

"But why? I've done nothing wrong. I've done nothing."

The vicar shook his head in exasperation. My throat contracted violently and tears poured down my face.

"That may be the way that your generation see it Matilda, but to us I'm afraid you're everything I've said." I felt exhausted suddenly, my energy ebbed as quickly as my anger had risen. I said quietly. "But I didn't know. I had no idea that Dante is married…….." My mother glanced quickly at the vicar…."As for the drugs, did you say? It's ridiculous. I don't even take an aspirin unless I really have to. Singers don't do drugs, we'd never be able to sing. We expect too much of our bodies, we wouldn't take the risk of what chemical abuse might cause. Anyway I don't need drugs I'm much to……..I was much too happy. This is my livelihood!"

I turned from my mother to the vicar. He had relaxed his look of fury and there was a flicker of a question across his face. I saw a glimmer of hope, but so it seemed did my Mother, and before I could say anything more, she snapped.

"Shut up!" She stood up and I saw by the vicar's face that my 'moment' had passed. "I think it would best if you leave. Call yourself a taxi, and leave."

I did so. My mind is in the most terrible, grey swirling turmoil. I can't believe that I will ever be happy again. It is as if I've slipped into an alternative dimension, a parallel universe, where everything that supported me has collapsed, and I am adrift in an alien ocean.

Dear God. Where are you?

Father Mine

Duncan was indeed not in Sweden. He was at that moment sitting in a hotel in Edinburgh, waiting for Lucy. Anne had told him nothing of the conversation with Giorgio, and he had no idea that his daughter was at home that weekend. The lovely daughter of whom he was so proud. He smiled to himself, fancy at the Opera House! Even after nearly two seasons he felt something of the thrill that had coursed through him when an excited Matilda, in tears of joy had rung to tell him and (of course) Anne. He didn't want to think about Anne, he was waiting impatiently for Lucy.

Twenty five years had not diminished their passion one little bit. He would listen to disillusioned friends and colleagues talk about the honeymoon period being over. How the first flush lasted for only a year, if you were lucky.

"You're magic!" He used to whisper to her. She would laugh and make some comment about her reputation in the village.

"Don't you mean, I'm a witch?" She would answer. But then he would shake his head and tell her to be serious, because he meant it. And he did. There was something a little mysterious about Lucy. For a start she seemed to play with time. She had hardly changed since the first day he had met her. Well maybe he was prejudice and hadn't noticed the tell tale signs. But no, there she was striding through the great hallway to join him. Her huge energy unabated, if anything greater than ever. And there was the appreciation. Half the room turned to watch her. Dour, correct Scotsmen, following her with their eyes directly, or if they weren't alone, (Duncan couldn't help but smile at the deviousness of his own sex) more subtly in the mirror behind the bar. All downing their beloved Scotch and chatting to their neighbours as if nothing was rippling over the surface.

He was immensely proud of her, of them in fact. They had kept their relationship in tact against all the odds. And one day they would tell Matilda. One day soon, when she was just a little more settled in her career, and the lovely confidence that he had lately sensed in her had blossomed, they would sit her down and quietly tell her everything.

He had no doubt that she would be delighted, and also, it would clear up many things about Anne's treatment of her. Anne had never actually crossed the line physically. He wouldn't have stood for that. And as Matilda had grown he had become very attentive for any sign whatsoever. He had realised, too late, that they had not dealt with the situation in the best way. Divorce would have been much preferable, and actually more responsible, or so it seemed to him now. Matilda, he knew, had hungered for some maternal love and attention, and had often been bemused by Anne's coldness. And so he had encouraged a relationship with a delighted Lucy. She in turn had found it extremely hard at times, but had valiantly struggled with her emotions for everyone's sake. And now they were nearly there. Soon they could explain to Matilda. This was one of the things he wanted to discuss with Lucy that day.

"Ready darling?" She stood in front of him, and she was breathtaking. He took her hand and they made their way to his car. They had a trip planned, and it was a glorious day.

The old man experienced a rude awakening from his meditation. He was sitting in his library, a high white tower in the green forests, and had been in the act of tracing the deepest past to join up with the immediate future. Dealing with such tiny windows of time within the 36,000 years which yawned before him, was not easy.

He had constructed a 'Timerthron' something which he had been working on in Atlantis before his death. But there, he had had the powerful mantra's of the gods to work with. Now, he had to rely on the power (or otherwise) of his own mind. The enormity of the task before him had caused him to lose concentration, and he had fallen into a meditative state over one of his particularly ancient books which he was using to help him. And all he could remember were vast golden empires and pyramids, while single seconds of intense corporeal awareness erupted. Seconds blossoming like a rose which gave up a life-time's perfume at once, filling him with haunting memory of the time before he had lost his humanity and compassion.

When suddenly everything lurched violently, and the book slid off the desk on to the wooden floor. He glanced instinctively at the mountain, and stared horrified at the red lava coursing down its side. Matilda! He must contact her.

JOURNAL

Finally, when I could hold it all in no longer, I poured my heart out to Pixie. She was very understanding and made all the right noises. To begin with it all felt comfortable and desirable to be telling everything to someone else. But by four o'clock in the afternoon (we had met for lunch) with my head throbbing painfully, and the tension in my throat at bursting point, I began to feel the need for something more than consolation. I wanted to do something. If my world really was falling apart, I needed to prop it up for now and then set about rebuilding it.

"This isn't doing your voice any good." Pixie pointed out. "I know!" I wailed. "I feel trapped in some nightmare. The way out is to release it all by singing, but I can't sing, so I can't get out."

" You need to look at each horror separately Tilly. What about Dante? Have you spoken to him?" She asked.

"He's in the States. I can't reach him there, anyway I've dumped on him enough recently. You too Pixie I'm sorry! I've taken you're whole afternoon."

"Oh and I had so much planned! Er....sleep probably. I can do without that! Don't be silly. This is not a small thing. But what I actually had in mind regarding Dante.....please don't get any more upset, but is there any possibility that he is married?"

"I just don't know Pixie. I don't think so......But there is something....."

"You must ask him outright. No, don't look at me like that Tilly, you have a right to know. Get that cleared up as soon as possible, that will ease one big thing on your mind. God! It must be like Piccadilly Circus in there!"

I managed a smile. "Yes, that describes it very well."

Pixie was rummaging in her bag. "Here, some aspirin. Take them." And, as I hesitated she added. "Oh stuff the Very Reverend what's his name. It's an aspirin, it's not a class 'A' drug. You buy it in the shops remember? Take some, lay down in the Green Room. I'll make sure you're awake for the half."

"Thanks Pixie I think I will."

I allowed the sounds of the Opera house to filter further and further away. Although I could still hear them, they did not disturb me and I floated in and out of dozing. On one of the downward spirals from the every day world. I saw the old man. He was descending slowly in a ray of golden light. I willed myself closer to him and instantly we were standing in the violet mist near the turquoise water. Communication was more difficult than usual, I did not seem to be able to slow down. I kept finding myself on the opposite side of the water, and also I found it increasingly difficult to pull myself back to him. Severely I told myself to relax, but the very verbalisation pulled me away from the inner world. And I became aware of a conversation that was going on in the next alcove, but the harder I tried to ignore it, the more insistent it became.

"They haven't got a chance man…."

"Sure they have." Came the reply. "They've got a bloody good defence for a start."

"You are joking…….."

My last glimpse of the old man gave me the impression that he was trying to contact me. I sat up and sighed. My head was still very heavy, but the ache had passed. I decided to get myself a cup of tea. Pixie was in the canteen. "Oh you look much better."

She said. She was sitting with Mike, well almost in his lap actually. I didn't like to intrude, so I took my tea up to the dressing room. I was early but I decided I might as well make up for the evening's performance. It would keep me occupied, the last thing I wanted was to have time or space to think!

I was huddled over my locker picking out what I needed to turn myself into a lady from ancient time, (We were doing Nabucco.) when I thought that someone had come into the room. I could have sworn the door opened. As I looked up something caught my attention in the mirror. I stared in disbelief, it was the old man. I still think of him as 'old' although of course, he had changed radically after 'Fairies Ferry' all those months ago. I leaned forward and tried to contact him with my mind. He undulated and was not so clear as he is in my dreams.

"What is it?" I tried to impress on him. "Please speak to me." All I could detect was his emotional state. He was disturbed, worried even. What am I supposed to do with this realisation? At that moment, as I was moving even closer to the mirror, the door suddenly burst open and the other ladies who share the dressing room rushed in. Ann Jarvis, took one look at me and grinned and said.

"What's the matter Tilly, can't you believe what you see?" I got the giggles, her innocent remark was too near to the truth. Close on everyone's heels came our dresser.

"That was the five minute call you know." She said, grabbing the first freshly pressed costume from the rail, and holding it out to the owner. The small room turned into frantic activity. Everyone was late tonight it seemed but strangely, the familiar backstage banter and panic which ensued as a result, made me begin to feel better. Nabucco did the rest. And by the time the curtain came down for the last time that evening, I realised that I felt like my own self again. The face under my hastily applied make-up was much less tense than the one I had owned a few hours earlier.

This has helped me to come to a decision. In spite of what my Mother told me, I will ring my Dad and find out exactly what is going on, and specifically why he doesn't wish to speak to me. I live on the top floor of a Georgian house. I suppose it used to be the attics, but it has been brilliantly adapted, and I love it. As I let myself in at the main front door, I could hear my phone ringing. I wasn't quick enough up the stairs to catch whoever was calling, and they didn't leave a message. Oh well, if it's important they'll call back. I was too tired to bother with 1471. Having finally relaxed, all I wanted to do was fall into a bath followed as closely as possible by bed. I trust that tomorrow, the mists that have gathered will have cleared some more, and I can find a fresh start out of all this greyness.

O.K with you God?

All One Summer's Eve

Duncan was puzzled. He had not spoken to Matilda in weeks, and he hadn't seen her for months. Anne, on the other hand had seemed so different for a short while, that against all experiences with her, he had come to entertain the idea that she might have a man in her life. She had actually lost some weight, not as much as she should, for her health's sake, but certainly enough for him to notice. But then it all changed again, she reverted to old form. Mentally he shrugged, maybe the boyfriend had dropped her, if indeed there had ever been one. Poor Anne! She was even more uncommunicative than usual, but he must speak to her this evening about Matilda, whether she wanted to talk or not.

He buzzed for his next patient and clicked the notes up on to his computer screen. Inwardly he groaned, a well known hypochondriac burst through the door, looking about as sick as an

Olympic athlete. Duncan surveyed him over his glasses. Damn it the man was bursting with health. He really didn't have time for this, especially since he was expecting a patient of his who was rather ill sometime during surgery today. He laid bets with himself as to which part of the wretched man's anatomy was up for scrutiny. Then he adjusted his glasses and his professional smile.

"Well Mr Turner, we haven't seen you for a while have we? Goodness nearly a month!"

The sarcasm was lost on Mr Turner, who launched immediately into a description of his ailments. Duncan (to all intents and purposes) switched off. He suddenly realised how much he needed to hear his daughter's voice.

"What?"

"I said." Anne replied. "That the last time she was here, when you were away. She made it quite clear that she doesn't want to speak to you."

"Don't be ridiculous. Why ever would she say a thing like that?" Duncan replied. Anne avoided his eyes and shrugged. "It's probably just a phase that she's going through, Duncan. You know what these girls are like. I'm sure she'll come around."

"She's hardly a girl any longer Anne. She's a young woman and not one given to that sort of behaviour, as well you know. Why was she here that particular weekend anyway? She usually waits until we're both around."

"Because she can't stand being alone with me you mean?" Anne snapped.

"Oh Anne for God's sake. This isn't about us. It's about

Matilda." He had never known such a self-centred person. He walked to the window and stared out into the garden. It was a beautiful evening and he ached for Lucy. A nasty, fretful little worry niggled at the back of his mind regarding Matilda. He thought, no, he was certain that he knew her well enough to be convinced that she would never treat him this way. He traced the pane of glass in the window and stared out into the garden, much as Matilda had been doing that Sunday when Anne had come in with the coffee. She shuddered. If Duncan should ever discover what had happened here that day, his rage would be something which she would not wish to witness, and the consequences unthinkable. He must not find out, even if his precious Tilly had deserved the Vicar's anger, which of course she most definitely had. But remembering that scene, and Matilda's reaction there was some doubt in her own mind regarding Giorgio's information. But why would he lie? He had no reason which she could fathom. No, there must be some truth in what he had told her, somewhere. Suddenly Duncan turned back into the room, Anne jumped, but he didn't notice. He was still deep in thought, but he said.

"Did she know I wouldn't be here?" Anne swallowed and tried to keep calm, and decided to try to change the subject, at the same time to gauge a little more about Giorgio.

"I really don't know Duncan. She doesn't confide in me, never has done. Hmm…..Do you have a few moments?"

Duncan had already decided to drive through the village and see Lucy. It wasn't just the beauty of the fast approaching dusk, he also needed to talk to her about all this.

"What is it? I'm going out soon." Anne's mouth tightened.

'Why am I not surprised?' She thought, turning away before she continued.

"It's a little awkward. It's er……Well. You remember the friend of mine I went up to town to see a while ago?"

Duncan curbed his impatience and nodded, resisting the urge to glance at his watch.

"Well. She told me something, something rather strange. I though you might be able to shed some light on it. I said that I'd ask you. In fact I think you might even be interested."

Duncan doubted that and he sighed, folded his arms and leaned back against the window. "What do you mean by awkward?"

"It's just……Well, considering our arrangements regarding our personal life…" Duncan interrupted.

"We don't have a personal life Anne, at least not with each other." Anne clenched her fists and replied quickly. "Well, exactly Duncan. And in spite of the impossible situation you have always placed me in, I have no wish to embarrass you."

Duncan repressed a laugh, how in the world could this ridiculous little woman embarrass him? His impatience was becoming more difficult to control. For heaven's sake what was she about to tell him?

"Just out with it Anne. I promise you, you won't embarrass me." Anne walked further into the room and sat down on the settee, where, through a certain amount of hesitation, she blurted out something of her experience with Giorgio, keeping firmly, of course to the idea that this had all happened to a 'friend.' Duncan was, in spite of his impatience to be off, slightly intrigued. Anne finished her little 'recital' and looked expectantly at her husband. He pushed himself away from the window, his arms still crossed, and gave what she had said some thought. He sniffed, rubbed his finger across his top lip as he often did when thinking and said.

"Well, first of all Anne, this is not really my subject, given that it sounds as if it could be some form of hypnosis that is. But what I can tell you for a fact, that the 'subject', or in this case we might use the word 'victim,' since she hadn't agreed to whatever was going on, has to be willing. What I mean is no one can make you do anything that you don't want to do. That's the theory anyway. Whether anyone has been able to counteract that, I just don't know. Neither, in all likelihood does anyone else. Although if you bring sex into the equation it immediately becomes more complicated."

"Why?" Anne asked, rather too quickly. She was really intent on his every word Duncan noticed, he looked at her in the same way as he had observed the hypochondriac earlier.

"Well." He continued, still watching her. "Everyone, well most people anyway, want some form of sexual gratification. Even if it is only the idea that they have some power of attraction. Sometimes people become completely besotted with the idea, it is arguably the largest form of addiction on the planet. So, given that, how far can you label them, 'victim'? It really is a hugely complicated subject, the human mind, Anne. We still know so little about it, except that we have hardly begun to use it in the ways that some people believe we are potentially capable of. Look. If you are worried about this friend of yours, I wouldn't be. I suspect that once this man got her to the bedroom…" Anne sat up straight.

"Oh but they didn't go to bed Duncan. Oh no! All this happened......." Duncan interrupted. "Where? Where did it happen Anne? Across a table in some restaurant? Come on, use your head! She's having you on for her own reasons, I can't imagine what they could be, but she's your friend, go figure. The only other explanation is that the little lady's nuts. Now, I'm sorry but I must go."

"Of course." Anne replied. She waited until the front door clicked shut, then she went into the kitchen and turned on the kettle, picked up a cup and dropped a tea bag into it. She wasn't sure if that brief conversation had helped at all. But she did know one thing for certain. She was not nuts. She had been there, and all that she had explained to Duncan had really happened. Mystery spread like a patch of scented rain through her being and she actually felt excited. She vowed that she would think of an excuse, any excuse to phone Giorgio. She needed to hear his voice.......

"Lucy, I'm worried about Tilly." Duncan had arrived at Lucy's cottage and hadn't even bothered with the usual lip service he paid to 'being careful.' His well known car was parked right outside for all to see. But his concern had grown considerably on the short drive, and he couldn't bother with such things at the moment. Lucy caught her breath. "Why? Nothing's happened has it? I mean, what are you saying?"

"No. Nothing's actually happened." Duncan assured her pulling her close, worry and desire flowing through him like a potent drug. Lucy relaxed and smiled at him.

"Well if nothing's actually happened, maybe we should talk

later, say an hour or so? You can share my supper if you're good!" She was already half way up the stairs. Duncan followed her two stairs at a time, first things first......

"Hello Giorgio? This is Anne Gasgoine, Matilda's Mother."

Giorgio stiffened. 'What the hell did she want?' "My dear Anne, what can I do for you?"

That would take some explaining, thought Anne. "I've had a word with my husband regarding what we spoke about the other week and…"

Giorgio focused on the ceiling. He had guests waiting. An important agent with whom he was trying to set up something for Martin. Ann was mumbling on and on, and in light of the lack of any encouragement from Giorgio, she ended a little lamely…" So I just thought I'd let you know my husband's views on the subject."

Giorgio recognised the need for some form of contact, He guessed that Anne had been gearing herself up to ring him for some time, hoping that he might suggest another meeting, or even (heaven forbid) thinking of inviting him down to glorious Devon. The scent of brandy caught his awareness. Louise, his lady of the moment, was pouring some into his superb brandy glasses. Giorgio had a phenomenal sense of smell. He had noticed how all his senses magnified in strength at each corporeal existence. Something to do with the overlapping of consciousness he supposed.

"Anne, it is very kind of you to phone me, and we must talk more at length soon. Look I will contact you. But just at the moment I'm rather busy. I have guests you see."

"I see." Anne was slightly cool. Giorgio heard the latent jealousy there, and grinned to himself. Normally he would have told her to bugger off and hung up. But, he might just need her again. He wasn't sure of his next step regarding Matilda yet. Mum might come in handy.

"Do, please forgive me. This has been planned for some-time now." He said, and he leaned into her energy. Anne's spine tingled and her whole attitude changed instantly.

"Oh Giorgio, do please forgive me for keeping you from your guests." And after the usual 'farewells,' they both hung up. Giorgio laughed quietly to himself and shook his head slowly. He was sure he had Anne's measure. She would, no doubt, lay down at the first little scratch and moan. Whereas Tilly would fight with her last breath and stand defiant until the last drop of blood left her veins. Which was precisely why, of course, she was such a delectable challenge. He had to find something very worthy of her strength, something special for her destruction. He realised that it would have to happen in steps, but the final blow, her final realisation must be in glorious Technicolor and stereophonic sound as some American Musical once said.

He had been visited by the same vision now a few times since his drink with Martin. And an overwhelming feeling of danger surrounded it. A feeling that seemed to emanate from the place itself (wherever that was) and from the deepest part of himself at the same time. In fact the one appeared to mirror the other. He settled himself back onto his settee and pulled Louise close to him. She took it for affection naturally. But Giorgio had no real affection, his feelings were purely sexual and fired at that moment violently by the power he had just wielded over

Anne, and the delicious thoughts about Matilda's fall from… Well what exactly? And why? He was momentarily confused, Tony London cut across his thoughts.

"So, this young tenor of yours Giorgio. You think he's ready for my concerts, do you?"

Giorgio bristled, he rested his chin on Louise's soft blond hair and breathed in the herbal smell. His senses twitched violently so sensitive was he. And he found himself spiralling down on the wave of perfume to some distant point in his psyche. He was a panther emerging from the undergrowth of some beautiful tropic. He felt the deep alert relaxation of the beast. He was dark and gloriously powerful. His eyes glittered across the space between him and the waiting agent. Kissing the top of Louise's head, he replied.

"No Tony, I don't think that Martin is ready. I know that he is."

Tony London made a mock bowing of his head and avoiding the glittering eyes said. "Then as soon as I have some detail I'll be in touch Maestro. O.K?"

"Perfect Tony, as always." Giorgio replied. Then Tony added. "Oh, by the way, while we're discussing work. I'm on the look out for a soprano. I want a new name, won't cost me so much, any ideas?"

"What type ?" Giorgio asked, the tension that suddenly invaded his body causing Louise to pull away and look up at him. He smiled at her, whispered something that even she didn't hear, and pulled her back to rest against his shoulder. She melted instantly and completely. One of Giorgio's finer talents was a gentle dominance in public situations that gave the impression of a sexual impatience which was intoxicating for almost everyone concerned. Tony had seen this happen many time before, but he never failed to be affected by it. He had had to admit to himself over the years that Giorgio was something of a positive genius with women. Of course they didn't last long. He pulled himself up quickly. "Oh, mid-range, Italianate. Lirico-spinto you'd call it I guess. Any ideas?"

Green eyes swam in front of Giorgio. The thorn in his side stung. Always she pulled him back to the same place in Venice. To the very second that he dropped the poison into Carlo's drink. "Maybe." He replied. "I'll give it some thought Tony." And he smiled. There was more than one way of killing the cat!

"So what's all this about Tilly, my love?" Lucy placed a plate of apple cobbler in front of Duncan and threatened it with cream from a jug which she held poised above it.

"No." He laughed. "Grief girl, I shouldn't have the pie, never mind the cream!"

"Cobbler." Said Lucy. "Excuse me?" Duncan raised his eyebrows.

"No darling, not cobblers. Apple cobbler. And you worry too much."

"Whatever it is it's gorgeous." And Duncan set about demolishing it, until about half way through he laid his spoon down and began to explain to Lucy. His conversation with Anne, the fact that Matilda had not been in touch for some time, everything.

"She's never left it this long. I don't understand it. It's so cruel and so very unlike her, you know? But then I do understand how time can slip by sometimes before you realise it."

Having actually verbalised it all he found himself close to tears. He made as if to let his head drop into his hands, but Lucy was there first, and pulled him to her.

"No!" She began firmly. "This is ridiculous sweetheart. Something's not right here. You're not being told the whole story. This reeks of intrigue."

Duncan looked up at her as he pulled out his handkerchief. Lucy stared at him intently, her hands on her hips.

"Well. Can't you smell it Duncan? It stinks. Matilda would never do anything like this to anyone, never mind to you!"

"She hasn't spoken to you has she?" He asked her, but Lucy shook her head. Her rich psychic instinct was on full alert, although she scarcely needed it. To her it was obvious that this was all something to do with Anne. Maybe the time was coming for their inevitable confrontation, because she wasn't going to see either of the two people she loved most in the world hurt and upset the way that Duncan was at this moment. She turned back to him. He was attempting to eat the rest of the cobbler. She sat down and laid her hand on his shoulder as she said.

"Are you working tomorrow?"

His mouth full, Duncan shook his head, swallowed and said. "No darling, you know it's my day off!"

"Right. Come on." She said. She had pushed her chair back and was already picking up her bag. Duncan placed the spoon once more on his plate. "What are you talking about? Come on, where?"

"Enough of all this mystery Duncan. London, we're going to see her."

JOURNAL

The car was a write off. My Mother…No, she's not my Mother so she told me, wants me home. The Opera house have given me immediate leave, and as it's so near the summer break, have said that I should not return until September for the new season. I can't think … I can't feel. The lorry didn't stop…The lorry should have stopped…But it didn't, and the world will never be the same again. My lovely Father, to whom I didn't have the chance to speak, and Lucy……She was my Mother somebody told me…Who told me? Anne…I suppose I must call her that now…Anne told me. My Mother and Father are dead and gone, finished.

Dear God. I shall not speak to you again!"

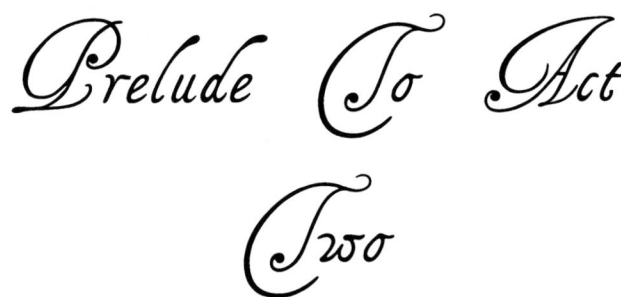

Prelude To Act Two

Giorgio disappeared for the summer. He told his Mother that he had to attend and speak at a conference for the 'Training and Care of the Human voice.' in Zurich. Signora Smith, being his Mother, believed him. There being no one else to whom he had to answer, and having made sure of 'Mamma's 'financial well being for the next few weeks, Giorgio left for Tibet.

Recently the 'vision' had plagued him more and more. It had also expanded. He let his dark head lean back against the head rest and turned his thoughts inwards until the sound of the plane's engines and the quiet conversation of his fellow first class companions hovered in a place that prevented him from sleeping, but allowed him enough relaxation to penetrate his deepest mind.

He saw two young men, one laughing, chasing each other along a golden corridor. Then there was a market place in what was quite clearly a very prosperous town, but where the people looked worried and afraid. What could be threatening them? War? An invading army? Some terrible plague sweeping the land? No, Giorgio didn't 'feel' so. Then he saw thousands of people leaving the town. Some were sailing from the port, others setting off for the hills that rose behind the place. He knew that the other side of the hills was a vast plain on which stood huge, golden pyramids, but he didn't know how he knew such a thing. Wherever this country was, it was breath taking. Then, as if he journeyed with them, he saw the dusty ground beneath the feet of travellers who now tramped across lands, some of which were occupied and some of which were not, and some of which were welcoming and some of which were not. He was aware that smaller groups were splitting off from the main body, and quite suddenly became certain that he had been one of those travellers and that with a few companions he had been heading for a similar destination to the one where this plane was now flying. But when he looked up to where the sky should be, he saw only a pair of eyes. Eyes that registered pain and defiance and that burnt with a bright emerald green colour.

"Carlo!" He whispered. "But this is not Venice!"

"I'm sorry sir?" One of the flight attendants stopped the trolley by his seat and hesitated in the act of handing him a complimentary bottle of wine. Giorgio smiled at her, returning effortlessly to the present. She was charmed. And for the rest of the trip there was nothing that was too much trouble for her concerning this particular passenger.

The next day after some rest, Giorgio set off for the mountains with a guide known only to the monastery to which he was travelling, and a very few select visitors, such as himself. Neither man spoke a word apart from a brief greeting on first meeting, and a quick nod of the head as Giorgio was left in the outer courtyard. It was dark by this time and the moon was fast rising through the clear sky to its allotted place. After a short time Giorgio heard the sound of sandals, he closed his eyes and concentrated. There was one person, obviously a monk, and he was slender therefore probably young. A small door within the larger surround of the gate swung open. He stepped into the inner courtyard. He had very little luggage with him, having left most of his belongings at the hotel. The young initiate showed him to a plain and simple cell. This would be where he would sleep later after his interview with one of the Grand Masters.

"And we all know who that will be!" He muttered to himself as he changed into the more appropriate clothing which was laid out for him on the small wooden bed. Giorgio shuddered. He didn't like it here. It was far too quiet for one thing, and also every time he did visit the place he felt a strong oppressive heaviness. And yet it was supposed to be full of people striving for spiritual enlightenment!

He sat on his mattress, a huge pillow stuffed with straw, and waited for a guide to take him to the Refractory for what he knew would be a depressingly frugal meal, which would almost certainly not include any alcohol! He knew the layout of the place, of course. He didn't really need any guide, but one just didn't wander about. It simply wasn't allowed. When he finally found himself in the dinning area, he was alone. The final meal of the day had finished long ago, and all the 'inmates' as Giorgio called them to himself, were at fun things such as constant prayer till midnight, or meditation, and not a piece of skirt in sight! How could anyone live like this? The silence was already getting to him, and he had to pull himself up sharply in the act of a little gentle humming. Almost as he finished the last mouthful of his meal, a shadow appeared at his side, bowed respectfully, and, without uttering a word, made it quite clear that he should follow him.

He was taken to a room in one of the towers. The windows, which were open to the sky gave a wonderful view over the surrounding land, and the moon above the high rocky mountain range, hung so large that it seemed as if all he had to do was stretch up and put out his hand to touch it. Chu-Pen had entered so quietly that even with Giorgio's highly refined senses, he did not hear him.

'That's why I don't like this place.' He thought, swinging around suddenly as the realisation dawned that he was not alone. 'I'm not as good here at all the things I take for granted everywhere else.'

He bowed to the Master, who barely dropped his shaven head in reply and moved to a pile of cushions, inviting Giorgio to sit on a smaller pile which faced him. It was difficult to sit still under this Master's gaze. Giorgio shuddered again, and wondered if he should speak first. Every time he came here (and that wasn't very often) the etiquette seemed to have changed. He didn't like to be made to feel uneasy. Giorgio wasn't used to that. Sitting in this ridiculous position, in front of this expressionless but very much more powerful being, Giorgio made a quick promise to himself. He would not return here EVER! This would be the last time he would seek help from the East. He would deal with it all himself in future. Such a thought was tortured however by the memory that he had promised himself exactly that, many times before. Chu-Pen put him out of his misery by saying.

"You have had a vision. One that you cannot account for, and one which confuses you." It wasn't a question. Simply a statement of fact. Giorgio had long ago stopped wondering how the hell he knew things like this, much less considering asking him. So he nodded.

"You see this vision because the time is approaching."

'Here we go.' Thought Giorgio. 'More bloody riddles. What the fuck was that supposed to mean?' There was a complete silence. They were too far up the mountain for insects, and the only occasional sound was the swoosh of some winged predator as it started down the mountainside in search of warm blood and food.

'I doubt there's any warm blood in this place, apart from me.' Giorgio thought to himself. I'm not convinced this lot are even alive.'

"You do not concentrate Giorgio. You waste my time. Would you rather we spoke tomorrow?"

"No Master. Please excuse me. I have had, as you know, a long journey. I still find it hard to control my thoughts at such times." Giorgio said quickly. He had no desire to hang around for yet another whole day, he wanted out of here, and off to the warm Greek island where the delectable Louise was awaiting him, as soon as possible. Chu-Pen's ice-cold gaze didn't flicker there was an almost imperceptible nod and then he began to hum. It wasn't an ordinary hum. Even opera singers didn't create anything like this. The vibration caused by the relatively quiet sound was accumulative. It seemed to collect in the corners of the room and build back on itself until the sound in Giorgio's head was unbearable. He shook himself, and just as he thought he would have to get up and leave the room, just as the sound began to penetrate beyond something which could be heard, into the very nerves, the Master stopped abruptly. The intoning had shaken up the air and changed its very nature. You could believe it had become tangible.

"Concentrate!" Hissed Chu-Pen. And Giorgio obliged. He felt himself melt into a familiar vortex. He was being drawn down into the floor, turning round and round at ever increasing speed until he found himself alone, and sitting on a couch from which he had a clear view of the long golden corridor of his vision.

Giorgio was an experienced traveller of his own past. He knew that all he had to do was to remain where he was, and some revelation or other, would come to him. After a while, during which he could feel himself soaking up the atmosphere of the place, a strongly built man in priestly robes, who was making his way along the corridor, paused by the alcove where Giorgio was seated. The man scratched his head and then continued on his way, but not before a 'dream-like' replica of himself pulled itself free and approached Giorgio.

"Always you worry me, Thanius. So this time I intend to give you something. You will come to curse me for it. But I will give it to you none the less." And with that the 'body' disappeared and Giorgio head Chu-Pen's voice. "Anthorus and his shepherd boy. Do you remember?" Giorgio frowned. He had been brought here because of some 'gay' relationship? This priest, if that was what he was, and a shepherd boy? What did he care about that? This was a perfect waste of time.

Chu-Pen was becoming angered by Giorgio's lack of concentration, and the pain which he sent to him through the psychic link presently set up at that moment, was exquisite. Giorgio gasped and pulled himself together with some difficulty. Because he couldn't remember this life which he was being shown, he was forced to stretch and focus his mind much more than usual. Most of the time it was so easy! The familiarity of the castrati life had become as real as his daily life in the 21st. Century. He persevered however and felt himself slip way beyond Venice which had always been as far as he had ever felt the need to travel, and he conjured up the waking dream he had had on the plane. 'Thank God for British Airways!' He thought as the dream began to balance him and a little familiarity started to blossom...

Knowledge! He needed something in order to join some prestigious group. This, Anthorus refused to give him, hence the 'gift' in lieu of, perhaps? And there was something else. He had to cut a glorious stone for this man. An emerald, and then make it into an amulet. Was this perhaps payment for the gift? So, hardly a gift then!

Chu-Pen sent another fission of pain to him in response to his careless and modern extravagance of thought. Giorgio pulled back again and sank even deeper into the time that he was witnessing.

Now he stood in a work place. Two guards held a young boy very much against his will on a slab, as Anthorus worked over him with a light. A light which at times penetrated the boys head between his eyes. By the second things were becoming clearer.

He remembered the screams and groans of the victims. He saw their squalid cages beneath the temples and halls of knowledge. He saw them rigid with fear and desperate to break free. This young boy was rather different however. He cursed and swore at everyone in the room. His long tanned legs kicked out at the guards, and anyone else who got too close was likely to be spat at in a fury. While the priestly man worked with great difficulty over his slab, the same thing happened again. A dreamy version of him broke away and floated towards Giorgio.

"We cannot allow this to happen. It seems it has already started. Once released it will spread like a plague. A plague for which there will be no cure, and never can be. It must be stopped, now!" The dreamy figure began to fade. And Giorgio was aware that the heat was subsiding and the noisy laboratory was replaced by an intense silence. The face of Chu-Pen hovered over him as he lay, having slipped sideways from the cushions.

"You must stop her. She has the key. And if she succeeds you will lose everything, all of the meagre power which you now possess. Surrounded as you are most of the time, by idiots, these powers I know seem to you huge. It is only here with me that you realise once more your weakness. But if you save us all from this. If you stop and destroy her, I will make you my equal. And no Giorgio, you will not have to stay here with me. The world will become your playground. Your abilities will become beyond your present imagination."

Giorgio could not reply and the next thing he registered was the sun shining full on his face the next morning. "Shit!" He muttered as he dressed and put his meagre belongings together in preparation for a welcome return to civilisation. He recalled little of the night's happenings, and what he did remember, he didn't understand. "What a thorough bloody waste of time!" He couldn't wait to set down on the shores of the Adriatic and the delicious Louise.

Chu-Pen watched as Giorgio started back down the mountain behind one of the young monks sent to accompany him. He knew that Giorgio didn't think he remembered, also he knew that when the 'time' was right, he would remember, and he wouldn't fail them. No, he wouldn't do that. Giorgio hated far too much to fail.

ACT TWO

More Skeletons

Dante came for the funeral, and used his considerable charm and social grace to help me with the near impossible situation with Anne. When she asked me (as if it had been the neighbour's cat that had died) if I had thought about singing at the funeral, and could I please let her know as soon as possible if I was going to, Dante's eyes flashed with a fury at her insensitivity and total lack of realisation of my grief and shock. But Anne didn't notice. After all when you are the only person on the planet, you expect to be the centre of attention. When he moved her slightly away from me and said softly.

"I dink not Anna, is no good idea." She simpered like a spoilt child. Needless to say her own lack of grief is amazing, although I suppose in the circumstances which have now come to my attention, not altogether surprising. Even so I think I hate her. Dante crept down the passage every night, having learnt very quickly where the creaking boards were, avoiding them and slipping quietly into my room. If Anne guessed she said nothing

217

and I could not sleep without him there. Out of my misery late one such night I asked him if he was in fact married, and why he never spoke of his family.

"No, I ama not cara, and when we will be in Italia my darling, I esplaina all, everything of your worries."

It was high summer by this time, and, there having been no rain for weeks, all around was dry and burnt. "That's how I feel Dante, dry and burnt." I whispered.

"Si, si capisco. I understand. Soon we willa be in Italia. De change she willa be good. You return for de singing and de rest of your living." I drenched yet another of his beautiful Italian shirts.

Dante took me to Italy for several weeks. We spent the time in his apartment in Milan, and gradually the terrible numbness began to ebb away and I began to feel better. One morning I caught myself humming. It was low and sad, but it was something of a sign. The relative balm of distance and the near constant closeness of Dante finally conquered the effects of the terrible shock. Grieving could begin, and I actually found that I was needing to sing. One week before the new season started, and a day before I was due to leave for London, Dante brought up the dreaded subject. Whatever I had imagined that his situation might be, it didn't come close to what I was to hear.

Dante, it seems, is the eldest son of a Count. Il Conte della Vittoria. This very old and proud Italian family can trace their line so far back into the depths of history, as to render some other European aristocratic families pathetically modern.

The Count, however, has all but disowned his son since the lifestyle that he has thus followed, prevents him from doing many of the things that an heir to an earldom should be about on a day to day basis. One of these things is definitely not becoming emotionally involved with an English woman who is not related to her Majesty Queen Elizabeth. In a nut shell, this is why Dante has been quiet about me since I lack the necessary 'blue blood,' However, his family, convinced that he is a healthy male (he is!) are equally convinced that there must be someone in his life, and they finally extracted the truth from him. They, (mainly I think his Father) are now insisting that he spends some time at the family home. 'Sometime' I learnt to my horror, didn't mean a couple of weeks, more like two or three months.

"I 'avea to go Tilly. But I don't 'avea to stay dere."

"And what would happen if you refuse?" I manage to speak in spite of the football lodged in my throat. Dante had been sitting on the edge of his huge bed, holding his hand out to me, and hoping, no doubt that I would skip over there and be more easily mollified. I had ignored him and he let his arm drop onto the soft deep-blue duvet, and pushed himself off the bed. "I willa be…'ow you say? Not inheritance." I looked at him with little compassion in my face. "You mean, you'll be disinherited? For not running home to Mummy and Daddy the instant they say you must. So, would it matter anyway?"

Dante nodded looking so miserable, I had to turn away in order not to throw myself into his arms and promise something perfectly ridiculous in order to stop his torment.

"Cara, ofa course, 'e matter."

Apparently the love of my life, and the owner of a passion that can knock your socks off, is afraid of relying on himself. What's more it seems that without his family behind him, he would presumably roll over and die. This is a little harsh, and I suppose it must have shown on my face because he added quickly. "Oh! 'Es nota de money."

"Oh!" I exclaimed, sarcasm dripping from both canines. "It's NOT the money!" And stormed into the kitchen. Dante was right behind me. He took my hands and said.

"No. no you not understand. I 'avea duties I must continue. I not know at dis momento 'ow we 'appen."

"How we happen? You mean what you're going to do about us?" I felt my heart sink. After the last few terrible weeks, it hadn't as yet climbed back to its normal place, so it didn't have far to go. Dante looked down at our entwined hands, he was having trouble speaking now. "I am in de torture, cara...Non mi guarda cosi." (don't look at me like that!) "Cara, please. We go onea step at de time...Si?"

He raised his head and I looked at him. His beautiful olive skin had paled and seemed taut across his cheekbones. The 'mouth to kill for' was tremulous. What was I supposed to do? I just wanted to stop his pain. I will be O.K. I'll manage. I have broad shoulders. I can take 'it' whatever 'it' transpires to be. I smiled at him.

"One step at a time." He pulled me towards him with a cry of relief.

Tony London

Martin was pleased. To be much more accurate he was quietly over the moon. His natural cynicism prevented him from showing too much pleasure, but he 'glowed' slightly in spite of himself. Martin had got himself an agent. (To be more accurate, it was Giorgio of course who had got Martin the agent, but he didn't know that.) Finally someone with, hopefully, their greedy little fingers on the pulse, had agreed to represent him in the hazardous side of singing opera, where all careers are made, ruined, or sometimes not even allowed to get off the ground.

It was impossible to make any sort of impact at all off one's own bat. And Martin had managed to interest about the most prestigious man in the country, indeed one might say, in Europe. Tony London, who had already offered him an impressive six-month tour of concerts, commencing in three weeks to be presented through his famous 'London Concerts Agency.' Martin lost no time in phoning Giorgio.

"Good, good. What did I tell you Martin? It's simply a matter of time and perseverance, you see? But we need to work very hard now. I shall need to see you at least twice each week between now and the beginning of the tour."

They made a date for the first session, and Martin hung up. For a few moments he stood quietly by the phone. He wasn't brave enough to trace the source of his mental discomfort. To ask himself, at least in the quiet of his own mind if his audition had been what one might refer to, as normal? Martin had auditioned for Tony London, in Giorgio's studio after a singing lesson. On top of which he had felt for the entire time that he was there, like an embarrassed laboratory rat. It was more like a platform for Giorgio to show off his knowledge and understanding of the human voice, than Martin's audition. After he had performed the arias he had prepared, Giorgio, who had played for him, began to dissect every note and harmonic, while Tony sat with his arms folded not betraying a thing with his facial expression, and only nodding almost imperceptibly at Giorgio's inane comments. After a while he began to feel a little like a fourth former being pushed into the Second X1 by the games master (that being Giorgio) against the better judgement of the Captain of the team.

At last it was over and the three stayed together for dinner, which Giorgio with considerable ability, cooked. After his third glass of wine Martin had decided to forget the circumstance of his audition. What did it matter? He actually had an agent! There were enough people out that who only got on because of that, people who really were not that good at all. The combination of Tony London and his talent, well…he thought to himself as Giorgio filled his glass up yet again, the sky, was the limit! But then there was Matilda. It transpired that not only had the little madam also sung to Tony London, but she had had a 'proper' audition in the Wigmore Hall, no less. On top of that apparently, Tony, had not stopped talking about her since, or so he had been told by other singers at the Opera House. The fact that Giorgio had said. "Oh the silly prat probably fancies her!" Did not alleviate the discomfort one little bit. On top of all this, he subsequently discovered that she was to be his singing colleague in two of the concerts. Martin's pleasure became definitely clouded.

Tony London had granted Matilda an audition because Giorgio had asked him to hear her. Tony, after all, had inquired about a soprano who he might use and not have to pay too much money. Giorgio mentioned Matilda because the more she did, the more chance there was of finding opportunities to make in-roads to her destruction. He had little hope of achieving anything while she was protected by the chorus. He could hardly reach his cold hand into the Opera House and do her any damage.

However, Tony London gave her work because he liked what he heard. In fact he liked it very much. Even more importantly he realised that her potential was prodigious. Tony loved opera, but he was impatient to an absurd degree. You see, he also loved money as much as the art form that provided it for him. So when Matilda rang his office after receiving the programmes she was to sing at the concerts, and having quietly considered the implications of one of the items included, he was not pliable, or as helpful as she had hoped. In fact, his irritation was obvious and Matilda (being Matilda) had drawn back as swiftly as if she had happened on a rattle snake. By the time she had replaced the receiver, she had agreed to everything on the programme, and a little more besides.

Bella, Tony's P.A. picked up on his sharpened tone, and asked him.

"Prima Donna?" "Not really. She's new." Tony replied handing the printed paper with Matilda's details across the table to her. Bella laid it on her desk making a mental note to open up a new file for this latest addition to Tony's fast growing pool of singers.

"Is she any good?" She asked him, returning to the computer screen in front of her.

"Very! Opera House chorus at the moment." He replied. Bella was very surprised by this. "But you don't usually touch choristers with a barge pole Tony, whatever their potential." "I made an exception. To sign with a big chorus in this country usually does constitute suicide as far as a soloist career is concerned. Bloody stupid if you ask me. Do you know what one of our sopranos told me the other week when she auditioned at the Opera House for a solo contract?" Bella shook her head. " Very good, most impressive. But I'm afraid we have a policy not to use British singers. I mean can you credit it? Arrogant bastards! Anyway, that's not my concern. But Matilda has something special. You'll hear for yourself when you go to the first of these concerts. She's doing two of the group that hopefully will launch Giorgio's tenor."

"And will it?" Bella asked. "Launch the tenor, I mean."

"Might do. He doesn't have what she has though. You will have to represent us Bella, I'll still be in the States. Anyway, I'll be interested to hear what you think. I can't put my finger on it, there's a fluctuation in the sound, no, it's a colour. I can't explain it. One second it's there and then it's gone. Anyway she definitely has something, apart from the cold feet of course."

Bella had been reading through the contents of the programme, she paused and glanced back at Matilda's C.V. and drew her breath in quickly. Tony heard her, he was checking his personal papers, he was about to leave for Italy. He waited for the explosion which came a few seconds later.

"Tony! She's only 26!" "Hmm...so?" He replied as Bella swung herself around in the chair. "So, why Turandot? 'In Questa Reggia' Tony this is mad, and completely unnecessary." Bella had trained as a singer, only a lack of vocal talent had prevented her from fighting for a place in the operatic field. Privately she still grieved over her lack of vocal dimension, and even secretly prayed for a miracle. But whatever she could, or couldn't do physically, she knew this was wrong. She understood Matilda's position, she did not understand Tony's.

"Whose idea was this?" She continued. Tony frowned becoming impatient again. "Her teacher's...Giorgio. You've met my friend Giorgio haven't you Bella? He's half Italian."

'So am I' thought Bella. And she knew she should really have left it at that, but her Latin blood had risen to the surface, and wasn't about to be ignored.

"What's the wonderful Giorgio playing at Tony? You know this is perfectly ridiculous, and potentially ruinous to a young voice. Some teacher this friend of yours is. Is there no one out there today prepared to take the time and patience to train people properly? This sort of thing makes me so mad! No wonder she has cold feet. If you ask me her 'feet' are very sensible."

Tony was quiet, and Bella knew that she had far exceeded her position. Her job was not to discuss what this or that singer should be performing however strongly she felt about it. Finally he said. "I'm off now. Keep in touch by E mail. I'll phone you if necessary. See you next week." He had reached the door to the office when he suddenly turned back.

"Oh and Bella. If I want your input regarding the management of my artists, I'll ask for it. Alright? And I think you should remember that your own rather feeble attempts at singing do not qualify you to make such dramatic judgements. One aria is hardly going to cause the collapse of a fine and healthy instrument. The whole role at this time in her career, might well be a reason to question."

He took in a deep and noisy breath, and surveyed Bella with the look of an authority-loving Field Marshal. Bella avoided his eyes, and bent her head over her desk. She was afraid he might read an answer if she looked at him. He left, and she breathed a sigh of relief. The main door to the building slammed and she heard the unmistakable idling of the great London taxi. She sat in a dream for a few moments wishing it was she heading for Heathrow airport. Then she picked up the dirty coffee cups and cleared them away giving herself a bit of a talking to. She loved and needed this job. (As much as she could love any job that wasn't truly what she wanted.) The hours were varied, the pay was good. It was full of music, even if it was coming out of someone else's mouth, and she got to see something of the world. After all, her thoughts galloped, Matilda was nothing to her, she hadn't even met the woman yet. She was lucky to be earning a living as a singer. What she wouldn't give to be able to do just that. Jealousy and conscience vied for top place. Jealousy won, but conscience gave her a bumpy ride. Oh well alright! She'd keep an eye out for her…if she could.

The old man was concentrating hard. He had to penetrate Matilda's dream consciousness yet again. There was no problem with illuminating himself now, since he had become established there. But to present a new facet to his little dreamer required considerable energy. Skilfully, in the night of Matilda's inner landscape, he drew together two of his brightest stars, closer and closer, until, in a sudden explosion he tripped an electrical current through her considerable resistance and presented the sleeper with the desired scenario.

Matilda had not dreamt lucidly for quite a while, and she had been missing the wonderful inner calm and physical well-being that such experiences brought to her. On first awakening she had smiled at the resurgence of memory, but quickly she noted that the feelings of tranquillity had not existed at the usual depth. The dream was one of those which she referred to as 'semi-lucid,' and it was of her Father and Mother. Matilda was not aware of the old man in the usual way. She was only aware of an impatient guide behind her, almost propelling her forward. Her Father and Lucy (she still thought of her by that name) were standing near Fairies Ferry. She was having trouble attracting their attention, and was inclined to blame herself. Actually the blame, if that was the right word, was theirs.

Still resting from the shock of the accident, they found concentration hard and had little desire to be pulled back to earthly memory just yet. The old man resorted to shouting. "Lucy, Duncan. It's Matilda!" All he received was a wave of memory capped with a tiny fission of pleasure. Oh dear, they weren't really ready for this! There was little, or no focus, and the reason Matilda couldn't attract their attention was simply that they were too scattered. Their identities as she remembered them, still too closely associated with the tragedy, baulked at any attempt to realign themselves, even for their beloved daughter. The old man paused in his work, and Matilda tossed on her pillow as someone started a car engine...'Damn it. She must not wake up!' Expecting conversation was obviously too much! Lucy began to hum 'Casta Diva.' Even in her dream state Matilda followed the music faithfully note by note and bar by bar. She was moving towards them and they turned as she approached. Neither of them smiled, and they seemed to be gazing past her into the distance. They gave her the absurd idea that they were puppets. Matilda waited, she had the strong impression that somebody wanted to say something, but nothing happened and she could feel her energy slipping. She could no longer hold her surroundings in place. Fairies Ferry was already appearing odd. She had tried to tidy up the landscape to agree with her memory, but of course, that necessitated paying less attention to Lucy and her Father, and then of course they began to fade.

'Oh!' Thought the old man. 'You may as well sleep on Matilda. I must find another way.' Matilda spent the rest of the night, dipping in and out of beautiful landscapes, moving too fast and increasingly frustrated at not being able to 'land' in any of them. They flew beneath her, tantalising, and painted in gorgeous shades and depths of colour that she had grown to expect in her nightly wanderings, but never ceased to be amazed by. Close to daybreak the old man renewed his struggle. Matilda could hear the dawn chorus, at the same time she became aware of the 'mist.' From experience she knew that the only way through the mist to some inner gem, was not to allow the sound of the birds to intrude too much, but also not to fight it. In this precarious state she began to breathe deeply and to ensure that she didn't move a muscle. The next second she was standing by the turquoise water near to the old man. An overwhelming feeling of safety and peace flowed through her. She thought to herself. 'I'd like to be able to just stay here.'

"Well you can't.' Snapped the old man. He was tired and Matilda was oblivious to so much. "You must concentrate Matilda." The last thing that Matilda wanted to do was 'concentrate.' She looked around at the landscape.

"It's so very beautiful here." She said.

"I could change that if you don't listen." Replied the old man. "Oh sorry!." Said Matilda, and sat down. She allowed the heady atmosphere to fill her like a sparkling wine. It was a delicious feeling, as if her mind expanded, and in so doing, released all the pressures.

'This was the real thing.' She told herself and she felt a relaxation beyond all understanding.

"Look into the water." Said the old man. Matilda bent forward and gazed through her reflection into the darker depths where pictures started to form: There was Tony London opening a door and smiling at her. She watched herself enter the room, to find it empty and the door closed behind her…Tony disappeared. Then there was Giorgio. He was sitting in the middle of a large audience, some of whom were on their feet, applauding and smiling at her, but he remained seated his head bent forward, he was shaking it slowly, from side to side. Then he was offering her a strange looking cup, brimming with a golden liquid, and smelling deliciously familiar. She knew it was Giorgio, but it didn't look like Giorgio. The young, tall and slender man holding the cup and kissing her on both cheeks wasn't dressed like Giorgio either. She realised that she was in Venice again, but from a very different perspective. It was as if she were watching a film.

How did Giorgio fit in with Venice and Carlo? The truth unfortunately didn't dawn, but morning did, and with it the alarm clock. As Matilda lifted the cup to her lips and tasted the first of the golden liquid, she was pulled back to earth with a rather strident jolt.

JOURNAL

You should never forget your first lessons, nor the admonishments you receive early on. But my mind was somewhere else completely, and my thoughts, very far away from unwritten Opera House rules. I took hold of the door handle, turned it and went straight in. There were two people in the dressing room, a man and a woman. She was sitting on the very edge of the table, and he was standing as close as he could possibly manage into the space made by two shapely legs which were wrapped skilfully around his waist. But it wasn't the position which alerted me instantly. It was the nakedness of the buttocks squashed on the cold table top and the overriding thought of how uncomfortable she must be!

All through the morning rehearsal, I had been enamoured with the glorious Italian baritone (his singing that is!) Following the rise and fall of the dark authoritative sound with my breath and ear, until a golden disc began to spin in my head and the moments of his singing stretched into timelessness. I remember thinking that with such sounds, it was no wonder that men and women are totally immune to the so-called perfections of Hollywood stars, and fall passionately in love with the masters of this magic. The baritone now turned his head. I was frozen to the spot, my chin down almost to my chest, I must have been a sight! Then I noticed his trousers around his ankles, they looked very much more embarrassed than he did. He looked straight at me, and without losing one iota of his impressive rhythm, or his self composure, he gave me a slow, very sexy wink, and turned back immediately to the object of his lust. After what seemed like a small age, only a few seconds I'm sure, I remembered how to reverse, and moved out into the corridor closing the door as I went. The head of wardrobe was standing there, trying to remain upright. It was difficult since he was laughing so hard, he could barely draw breath.

"Gino…" I gasped. "I was looking for you…I thought you would be in there…I mean…I had no idea…Well obviously… I'm…Oh my God!!"

"Hasn't anyone ever told you the unwritten rules of the Opera house?" He spluttered. "You know, the one about not entering a dressing room on a quiet afternoon…" I was already nodding my head and added…"Without at least making a lot of 'excuse me but there's somebody here' noises first. Yes, I know, I forgot." I finished on a groan. He slipped his arm comfortingly around my waist and said. "Well don't worry about it. And don't imagine for one instant that it hasn't ever happened before. Now, if you'll forgive the question. What can I do for you?"

Our laughter bounced behind us, knocking, I'm sure on the dressing room door. If the busy occupants heard it, my guess is they joined in. I do hope we didn't spoil anything!

Monster

Giorgio was getting impatient. Matilda was proving very resil-ient, and every time he succeeded in pulling her away from her natural vocal base, she snapped right back by the next lesson.

"It must be how I see the music." She had said, at a loss to explain her inability to retain Giorgio's instructions from one phrase to the next. "Rubbish!" He had replied, secretly enjoying the battle. "You sound like an upper class twit with a plum in your mouth. Now, watch me. Open your mouth only as much as you have to. Keep it all very small."

This was hugely misleading, but Giorgio would resort to anything to achieve his aim. Matilda had a natural inclination to sing with a flexible and relaxed jaw, and to hold the sound with her body; not her chin, which was what Giorgio's method would eventually encourage, and indeed force her to do. The way she sang, when left to her own devices, at least provided a partial opening and some depth, which in turn allowed a dark and exciting side to the voice to develop. People, worse, other singers and friends, liked and encouraged this.

"I love listening to your voice…"It's such an individual

sound"…You don't sound like just another soprano Tilly"…etc. etc.   Oh Giorgio knew the sort of things that were being said to Matilda. In different circumstances he would have been saying them himself. Matilda wasn't slow to fight her own corner, either. She studied performers from the side of the stage at one of the greatest Opera Houses nearly every night when she could. And she wasn't stupid. He braced himself for the inevitable question.

"Every soloist I watch at work opens their mouth Giorgio. Sometimes, I admit, I can't work out how they focus the pitch so perfectly through such a wide opening. But they do. I mean how can I express huge emotions with my mouth half closed, especially on this sort of pitch?" She said pointing to the line of music she had just sung." I'm sorry Giorgio, I just don't understand."

Giorgio thought quickly, and smiled at her with, he hoped, some degree of sincerity. "Well you see Matilda, these singers that you are lucky enough to hear in the flesh night and day, are way beyond what I'm teaching you now." Matilda relaxed, the frown fleeing from her forehead leaving no trace of itself in the way that it can in the young.

"Oh, you mean this is just a phase, a necessary part of training?"

"Of course." Giorgio replied looking away from her intense violet gaze as green eyes swam there,. "Now, try again."

This last lesson echoed through his memory as he stood by the window, staring out across the lovely garden. He registered a strange and particular feeling of relaxation, but he didn't pick up on it. He was concentrating on the property still pending the surveyor's report, not far out of town. He had no doubt that it could, with the right handling, eventually rival Glyndebourne, but it seemed a rather daunting prospect now that it all actually lay within his grasp.

When it came to Opera, Giorgio didn't trust the English. Total snobs! He glowered, completely ignoring his own English blood. They seemed incapable of listening for themselves, of making up their own minds about what they heard. They cheered those who were held up for cheering, and refused to recognise, or were afraid to recognise anything good purely from their own senses. They were as people brainwashed! To him, so many singers he heard sounded like glorified choir boys, both men and women! And the full potential of many fine voices was never realised. Of course Matilda had a natural Italian inclination to 'open up.' Now, where could she have brought that from, as if he didn't know! He turned from the window and found his hand straying towards an open wine bottle on the side table. He poured a little into a glass and allowed his thoughts to follow their own path.

Perhaps he should sell up, forget the 'perfect' property he had found in Surrey and move back to Italy and forget all about Carlo, Raimondo, Lucciano, Venice, and his plans for revenge. The whole damn thing. But how did you forget about yourself? A spasm of fear gripped him, he had a horrible realisation that the fascination with the past was the only thing that held him to the earth. Without it, what would he think on, plan, or enjoy? A terrible chasm opened up before him and he could neither look away, nor leap into it. His head was splitting and the base of his spine was suddenly red hot. Damn! He hadn't noticed that creeping up. Quickly he placed his glass on the desk and assumed the position taught him by Chu-Pen, and endeavoured to allow his mind and training to do the battle with the heat. He was afraid that he may have left it too late. He might have to resort to his tranquillisers before his body overrode his higher faculties, and betrayed him again. Well, so much for his recent trip to Tibet!

Chu-Pen had not been helpful. He had been much too concerned that Giorgio should remember some ancient life that couldn't possibly be pertinent to the 21st.century! Giorgio had intended to speak more of this 'problem' and to learn further exercises and maybe receive more knowledge, which would help him to control it better. It still had him at a disadvantage.

He shook his head. Maybe these so called mystics weren't capable of very much at all. Perhaps what knowledge they did possess was only the remaining scatterings of something long gone cold of its true power, and perhaps they were almost as lost and uncertain as the rest of mankind. But no! He mustn't forget that he had met with some truly amazing people during his many visits there over the years. People who easily and consistently defied all the 'natural' or they would say 'man made' laws, which the rest of us are forced to obey. He had met, and known people who claimed to be twice the age that they appeared to be, and who acted as if they had arrived at a youthful maturity and stayed there. He had witnessed men and women levitate, and move objects with their minds, and those were considered 'low' level, those were the things that he was allowed to witness! His spirits rose a little as he remembered that in some particular way at least, he was making quite a name for himself. Oh he had no students in the profession at the moment who were setting the operatic world on fire, but that would come. No, it was in the slightly 'mystical' area of curing abused and sick voices where all medical help had failed, that he was earning himself a reputation. Only last week one of the major companies had rung him with an urgent request. One of their young baritones had, 'rather sung himself into a corner' as the voice on the end of the phone had put it. He had not responded to the usual round of E.N.T. specialists and singing teachers. Would he hear the young man? And might he be able to help? The answer was yes, and probably. If Giorgio had any real talent with other people's voices, it was in this sort of area. An area as mysterious as he was himself. Unfortunately, people who witnessed, one way or another, these types of healing, (and he had definitely done this) assumed that he must also be a brilliant teacher.

The baritone had arrived looking pale, drawn and understandably worried. Who ever had asked Giorgio to 'hear' him, was stupid, since the singer could not utter one note. He could speak of course, and he told Giorgio that he had been assured that the actual vocal chords were in tact, and that there was no sign of nodule or bruising. It was immediately clear that the singer had dislocated something, probably Giorgio explained, one vocal chord from the arytenoids, or maybe even both chords. The young man's face dropped even further but Giorgio didn't waste time with anymore words. He was extremely patient and understanding. And he worked so hard in a concentrated manner that the baritone began to feel as if he were in a trance.

"Copy me!" He commanded. Over and over again the distraught singer opened his mouth and attempted to make a sound. Nothing happened. Giorgio rested his fist gently against the singer's mid section and then pummelled it hard enough to make him gasp.

"Again!" And then..."Once more!" Suddenly out of the breathy silence came something resembling the former glory of his Verdi baritone. It was rough and uncertain, but it was there. The young man was almost in tears.

"Drink!" Giorgio handed him some water. Then back o the first exercise. It was hard on the singer, rather like expecting a race horse to walk slowly. In fact it was torture in every way. "No! Don't try to sustain the tone, not yet!" Said Giorgio. Back again to the first exercise. Just one pitch, just one vowel. The baritone coughed, his eyes streamed, he even retched, but finally it was over. He was exhausted and so was Giorgio

"Ah good. Well done my boy, now we rest." Then Giorgio made a time for another session and sent him home with a list of instructions. All this had naturally pleased him, but in his present mood, nothing really penetrated. He could feel himself being immersed in the energy, almost as if it were separate from him. He could witness himself changing. His central core relaxed and seemed to fold in on itself. The heat refused to move up his spine, and he was having extreme difficulty concentrating on the Tibetan techniques, and came close to panicking. This was proving to be a full-blown attack, something which he had managed to avoid for some time now. And he knew that he could be lost in a sexual jungle for days.

Giorgio hadn't suddenly developed a conscience, he was simply desperate not to be discovered. Secrecy was sometimes difficult to achieve, people would ask questions even when they knew that their asking wasn't appreciated, in fact it made them all the more curious. Giorgio yearned for the lost camaraderie of the days in Venice. That sort of friendship was rare, if not unheard of in this sterile century.

He finally found his tranquillisers in his desk draw. He kept a supply in most rooms since, in the event of an attack, he had discovered, to his cost, that any sensorial stimulation, which, in the normal run of events would pass unnoticed, could cast him into a pit so agonising as to render him unconscious, and at the mercy of anyone who happened to be present. The words he heard in his worst nightmare were......"Call a doctor, someone!" The softness of the carpet drew the exquisitely sensitive souls of his feet into a paroxysm of sensorial extreme. Somewhere the thought tripped through his mind that no one would believe the excessive voluptuousness possible from the simplicity of bare feet on pile. It would be inconceivable to most people, they simply would not give it credence. His body began to mock him, and this he dreaded. He feared he would become mad, because his body appeared to speak to him as if it were a separate intelligence. It was chilling.

"See, Giorgio. I am stronger." "No!" He gasped, grabbing a paper knife from his desk top. Until this sweet agony passed he would resort to another lesson, which he had learned outside the hallowed temples of Tibet. He drew the knife from its scabbard, and pressed the point into his hand. Large areas of his brain were becoming fogged, and his intellect slowly strangled, his will slowly manacled. Then the voices began.

"No, no sweet Jesu. Not that!" And he rolled himself into a ball and began to bang his head rhythmically against the side of his desk.

"Give in Giorgio…It doesn't matter…You can take some time away from the world…All that work?…All those singer!… You don't rate half of them!…Go on, give in…This is who you are…It's a gift…Raises you above the norm after all…Tibet! What the hell do they know?…Come back to me Giorgio and enjoy…You've become very English you know!"

But then worse, so very much worse, undulating and turning the heat into a fierce white fire was Carlo's voice. His pitch was so exquisite, setting off an inner vibration which grew in Giorgio's head, until he felt it would surely explode, even wish that it might. The pitch was beyond that which passed for being 'in tune' today. Many singers sounded positively flat to him. The world seemed to have lost the awareness of the finesse it once had. They had simply stopped listening, but he had not. Giorgio's memory, although gloriously unclouded and pure, served only to torture him. And with the pitch came a soulfulness so profound that most members of modern society would not even face, never mind embrace.

Giorgio was on his knees. If he had believed in God, he would have been imploring him, praying to the creator. But he didn't believe and there was nowhere to focus, except on his agony. At the height of his battle he threw back his dark head and roared like a great bear. Then silence filtered through the house, Giorgio had passed out. His mother, in her private flat, had covered her ears with her hands as she knelt before her altar imploring the Virgin Mary to help her son, from what she didn't know. She wept, and Giorgio dreamt the old, old dream. The glorious sound cut short by his hand, the moment of poisoning forever suspended in his memory in vivid, diabolical detail. Love, hate, jealousy and despair swirled round and round until within sleep he became exhausted and finally there was nothing.

Rehearsal

JOURNAL

Giorgio is coming to our rehearsal for the Tony London concert. He suggested a private get together prior to the session scheduled with the conductor, who, much to my relief is a member of the music staff at the Opera House. Considering the aria I must perform I was dreading a total stranger. We meet with Giorgio tomorrow afternoon, our pianist is a friend of his. I'm very apprehensive.

And I had good reason to be! I arrived a little early and sat in on some of Martin's singing. Between you and me I don't know what to think. I still don't understand Giorgio's method, but feel that I have found a workable compromise. Martin, however, follows every word Giorgio utters to the letter and frankly, it just doesn't work. It doesn't sound right, or at least it doesn't move one at all. It's a series of notes, one following the other impeccably as the composer dictated using the medium of a good, healthy instrument, but it doesn't mean a thing. What is the point of that? It might just as well be played on a computer. I'm certain that it is because of all this that his voice doesn't carry, there is no real potent projection. Even in a relatively small studio with only a piano for accompaniment there is a definite lack of real power. One can't help but translate (within one's mind) to a large operatic space and know immediately that it would be wanting. My head should have been spinning in response to his upper register, it wasn't! Giorgio never stopped complimenting him, and yet I sense his exasperation, that underneath he is perplexed. The pianist nodded enthusiastically with every compliment, it was all such a sham. But Giorgio was in a strange mood anyway. When I first arrived, he put up his hand to me, and because of the layout of the room I was rarely out of his eye line. Then, quite suddenly he turned to me and said. "Oh Matilda cara, I'm so sorry, I had forgotten you were here. Come Martin, we mustn't keep the 'diva' waiting must we? Let's have a look at the duet." His modulated tone of voice stepped carefully over the downright sarcastic.

"Can we have a 'pausa' first Giorgio?" Martin asked, his voice resembling sand paper.

"Of course. Let's all go and have some tea."

I couldn't believe it. We all trotted off to a nearby coffee shop. My request that we buy takeaways was totally ignored. The pianist, I believe, was on the point of agreeing with me, but caught the set of Giorgio's face and turned away. So we drank and gossiped about rubbish, and generally wasted more time than I would have believed was possible considering how much we still had to do. Then after at least forty five minutes, we all trooped back. There seemed to be a deliberate resolve in Giorgio's every move. However, as I know I have a tendency to become a little paranoid when stressed or frustrated, I ignored that thought. As we descended on to the studio like a small pack of birds, Giorgio said to me. "I'm so sorry Matilda, but I don't think we'll have time for your aria today." I was relieved. I had not relished the idea of singing that particular piece of music in such a small room in front of the assembled company. It is such a huge undertaking for me at the moment, that I know too much tinkering with it could throw me completely, so I was quite happy.

"That's O.K. Giorgio. I've arranged a call with the conductor, tomorrow on fact." At this Giorgio grunted and turned back to the piano and a score. Martin however, his voice sounding normal again, thank goodness, said.

"Oh bloody big deal Tilly. Private call with the conductor hey? I suppose that's how all the big shots do it?"

"Well!" I retorted. "You should know, you work with the 'big shots' too. Isn't it the obvious thing to do? Anyway, he approached me!"

"Did he now? Right little princess, aren't we?" "Martin…" I began, but Giorgio interrupted chuckling. "Now you two, this is a love duet remember? You sound as if you are about to kill each other! Come let's begin."

I would very much like to stop writing now. Ignore the rest of the proceedings and press fast forward to a more pleasant time. But I feel compelled to express it if I can. Coming from the country I have often witnessed the hunt. When I say 'witnessed' I mean I've seen them collecting outside the pub, or heard the mournful horn sounding through the countryside, and seen riders return home on sweating, heaving mounts still moving at a fast trot so as not to take cold in the Autumn air. It's so difficult to be clear about where you actually stand with the moral issues surrounding this highly emotive subject. The farmer's rights versus the fox's. Suffice to say I love the fox but in spite of never being able to bring myself to join the junior riders at the back of the pack, even as an observer, I never really thought deeply about what it would be like to be hunted.

Then one day while I was still at school, I came up on a cornered vixen quite by chance. She turned and looked at me with such a desperation in her eyes that I had started towards her before I realised what I was doing. Quite suddenly the hunt was upon us, no more than 100 yards away with the hounds baying and the horn making that terrible flat sound, The Master stood up in his stirrups and screamed at me across what was left of the distance between us. There was no way that he could stop them, they had the smell of blood in their nostrils, they would have listened to no one. Needless to say this was a potentially dangerous situation for me that cold Autumn afternoon with the light failing by the second. The vixen had run into Baby Devil's Wood in a bid for cover. By virtue of our position I was standing parallel to her, and for those few strange seconds we faced the hunt together. I had the strongest feeling that we were communicating at some mysterious level. That she was aware of me in the same way as I was of her, and that she understood that I wanted to help her, at the same time knowing that there was nothing I could do. She put her lovely intelligent head on one side in the winning way that dogs often do. Then she turned quite suddenly and ran away from me, further into the woods. The hounds darted forward as I leapt for the safety of a tree, and with one quick cry she was dead. I felt as if I had lost a friend, so deep had been our connection.

And this afternoon I felt as if I were in her position. I did not, of course, die! I was ripped to pieces, but I didn't die. And it proves quite difficult to explain how it was accomplished.

First, Giorgio fussed over the place in the opera from where we would be starting. He wasted at least ten minutes muttering and discussing with the 'Oh-so-willing-to-please-him' pianist, various musical points which for the purpose of that rehearsal were not pertinent. Finally, after I had been hanging around altogether for over an hour, we started. In spite of the traumatic lesson some time ago, concerning this role, I will be performing Madama Butterfly with Pixie in November, so the music is already in good shape, in that I already know it very well. So, in spite of the atmosphere, I felt quite relaxed and had convinced myself that whatever it was I sensed had nothing to do with me. My voice was responding well, considering the long wait. I had begun to enjoy myself. Suddenly I realised that the accompaniment had stopped and Giorgio was raising his voice to me.

"What are you doing Matilda?" I assumed that I had made a musical mistake although I was a little puzzled as to what exactly that was. Martin lowered his eyes to sudden close inspection of his score, but not before I caught surprise on his face. I made towards the pianist saying. "I'm sorry, Ian. What..?" I got no further. Giorgio interrupted me.

"I'm not speaking musically Matilda. I meant, what are you doing with your voice?"

"Nothing…" I began. "Yes, well that's painfully obvious." He cut in again, his voice was like ice. Instinctively I glanced across at Martin, but you can't imagine how full of interest his score was! I was at a loss as to what to say next, Giorgio however, was not.

"You're shouting your silly head off. This, my dear young lady…" He held the score towards me…"In case you've forgotten is Cio Cio San, not Brunhilde. Any Pinkerton worth his salt would run a mile. Didn't you feel you'd be on the next ship back to the U.S. Martin?"

Martin looked up and nodded, but I was unable to discern his true feelings on the point, since my own were in too much of a turmoil. My heart was doing its heavy flamenco, but underneath there was something else, something I was a little afraid of, because I knew that it would be heard at the right moment, and that there was nothing I could do to prevent it. Giorgio continued. "Really Matilda. You know how I hate to waste my time like this. When are you going to learn to do what I tell you?"

"I really didn't feel as if I was over singing, Giorgio…" Giorgio slammed his open hand down on top of the grand piano. The pianist jumped and Martin straightened up.

"I'm so sorry gentlemen, our little soprano seems bent on causing us unnecessary problems. As we have all been working for so much longer than she has, I think we will leave her to the tender mercies of our Maestro. Do you think you'll have time in your 'call' tomorrow to work through this duet with er…What's his name? Because I don't intend to work with you any longer in this frame of mind." He paused, then added in a half whisper, full of venom. "Your voice Matilda, is abysmal."

He moved closer and leant towards me. I had done nothing to justify such an outburst. I glanced at the pianist who was staring straight ahead at the music. Suddenly I knew he was perplexed. It is easier to pretend that something is great when it's mediocre, than to deride it when it's going well. A real musician would have much more trouble with such a denial, and it showed in every line and curve of his profile. I was quite certain that my singing had not been that bad, and that made me very, very angry. I glanced down at the floor, and then stared straight at Giorgio, right between the eyes. All my inner strength flew to my centre where it consolidated itself into silver steel. I seemed to hear my voice as if it was coming from some calm distance.

"I'm sorry Giorgio but that is simply not true!" I picked up my possessions and prepared to make a fairly dignified exit. Giorgio, however, had no intention of letting me have the last word. As I reached for the door handle he said, equally calmly. "Then why are you running away?" I turned to face him, all of them in fact feeling as if I were standing back and watching the whole scene.

"I'm not running away Giorgio. You have made it perfectly clear that I am wasting everyone's time and that you no longer wish to work with me." Giorgio's reply was so unexpected. He dropped his head and looked at me from under his dark eyebrows. "I have no wish to work with you anymore today Matilda. But I would, presuming that you have time of course, very much like to speak to you. Are you working this evening?"

Martin was talking quietly to the pianist about some point of music, and the atmosphere had relaxed slightly. I shook my head. We were not involved in the performance that night. Giorgio made a slight bow with his head. "Good! Please wait for me in the café where we were before. I have just a few things to clear up here. I'll join you shortly."

I stood still for several seconds after the studio door had closed behind me. It was the sudden trio of laughter which sent me on.

I hurried to the café and ordered some tea while I was waiting. I sat there trying very hard to make sense of what had just happened. Also, what was I going to do about Giorgio? Why do I find it so hard to make a move, to find another singing teacher from the dozens that there must be in London alone? I was trying to catch exactly what the 'feeling' was which seemed to make me incapable of making a break from him, and identify the reason behind it, when the café door opened with a shrill burst of the bell attached to it, and Giorgio stood there.

"Come. I'll take you to dinner. We can talk then." I was taken aback, but maybe it wasn't such a bad idea. Maybe I could get through to him, understand a little more of his teaching methods and arrive at a new level of understanding, and even explain my confusion. I stood up and joined him at the door. His car, he assured me, was quite close. I was glad since I suddenly felt very tired. Standing up to a man like Giorgio isn't easy, I've discovered. It had taken me quite a few moments to stop shaking when I had first sat down in the café.

Giorgio chatted relentlessly as we drove, even cracking the occasional joke, and pulling a smile from me. "We'll go to Knightsbridge. I have a most favourite Italian restaurant there. Do you like Italian? Of course you do. I haven't booked, but we're too early to need to worry about that, I'm sure."

Martin, in one of his friendly periods, had once mentioned that this particular restaurant was Giorgio's second home. He loved it apparently. "How will that suit?" "That's fine Giorgio" I replied.

The restaurant, as you may well imagine, was, at that early hour all but deserted. Giorgio ordered wine and some mineral water. Then he leaned back in his chair and surveyed me with his terrifying eyes. His body stance reminded me of Martin as he had been in the restaurant in Milan. Those eyes, of something else entirely. Something that I could not put my finger on, try as I might. He continued to look at me intently, and soon it became slightly embarrassing. He said not a word, simply sipped the very good red wine without taking his gaze from me for a second. Then he did say something, but so softly that I couldn't catch it although, I'm sure he spoke in Italian.

"Sorry?" I said. "Niente, nothing cara. Now, do tell me about yourself. You know we've been working together for quite a while, and I know so little."

I was genuinely taken aback. I had not expected that. Giorgio never shows that much interest in anyone, or so it seems to me. I played for some time. "Well…Where shall I start? You don't want my life story, I hope!" He smiled then and shook his head very slightly, as if a fly was bothering him. "That won't be necessary cara. Let's not talk about mundane things, and we need a little rest from opera. Indulge me Matilda. I have many great passions. We won't go into some of them." He laughed. "But… the unknown, the hidden. What do they call it? The occult! That is hard to rival, every aspect of it enchants me, and particularly dreaming."

I all but jumped in my seat. I also felt strongly that this was not a subject which had leapt into his mind at the last moment. No, I was sure that Giorgio had been wanting to engage me in this sort of conversation for some time. But why?

"Don't look so startled. Did you know that at one time, dreaming 'true' as it is sometimes called was considered quite an art form? I believe that there is great untapped potential in dreaming, for everyone, if they are prepared to work at it a little."

I studied Giorgio closer than I have ever done before. He sat forward in his seat with his elbows resting on the table. He was, as always, impeccably dressed. But having not been so close to him before, at least not in as relaxed a state as this was, I never realised just how much so. Even to my eye the material of his jacket was superb. I found my attention drawn to the buttons on his blazer. They held an unusual design.

"Ah!" He laughed. "You've noticed my buttons. They were designed especially for me in Italy. You won't see anything quite like them anywhere else. Look closer if you wish!" He held his arm up and extended it across the table. It was an awkward position for him, and quite without thinking, I supported him. Immediately a strange quiver went through me. No, don't misunderstand me. It was not an attraction of any sort, rather, it felt like the extreme peripheral of something physical, but without desire. As if my mind remembered something which my body wanted nothing to do with. As nonchalantly as I was able, I studied the buttons. In tiny relief, and leaning against some unidentified vegetation, was a slender young man in Venetian dress of times past. Before I could stop myself I had spoken. "Oh! Castrato!"

I don't know why I said such a thing, after all it could have been any young man. But something very familiar had leapt out and struck me like a snake's hot tongue. I cursed myself. I felt as if I had unwittingly opened a door for Giorgio, a door which I would not have opened had I had my wits more about me. For a brief moment my thoughts turned to the Italian baritone and the ballet girl. My upper front teeth pulled on my lower lip. That ridiculous body response we all tend to, when we've blurted out something that was best left unsaid. Giorgio smiled at me.

"Yes Matilda, castrato. But now back to those other worlds I mentioned. Do you dream Matilda? I mean some people can't remember what transpired in their dream world by the time they've drunk their tea at breakfast. My first wife always used to say that she had dreamt about something, but she couldn't recall anything at all about it, except maybe the feeling attached to it."

"I'd rather not go into that, if you don't mind Giorgio. I feel it's rather private. Will you excuse me?" Giorgio placed his glass on the table and poured some more wine into it.

"Of course my dear." Then after a pause he looked at me unsmiling and added. "But you see that does, in fact, tell me that you most certainly do dream and quite spectacularly." Had I betrayed myself so easily? He placed the bottle down and picked up his glass, saying as he did so. "I dream." He sipped at the wine without saying more. And in that moment his Italian blood was suddenly so obvious in his hair and his eyes, that one could forget that half of him was English. A few people had taken refuge in the restaurant. It was raining outside, and they laughed and glistened their way to a table. One of their party, a very lovely woman, her looks not distracted from at all by the devastating effect of the heavy rain on her hair, now plastered to her superbly shaped head, caught Giorgio's attention. He watched her unashamedly, leaning back in his chair, twirling his wine glass from side to side. He reminded me again of Martin, but this memory seemed endless. The party sat down, the woman out of Giorgio's vision. "Let's order." He said.

I already knew what I wanted, but I scanned the menu anyway in order to ponder a little. I had scarcely paid any attention to the gossip I had inevitably heard regarding Giorgio. He was, according to many people an old fashioned 'wolf' and totally unpredictable. He had, they said, no regard for anyone else, and lived entirely for his own pleasure. He also had strange moods from time to time, and would sometimes, on such occasions, disappear for days at a time. I gave all this very little thought because frankly I'm not interested in Giorgio's private life, and anyway it's not my business. But observing him as he watched what he obviously fancied as potential 'prey' had a disturbing effect on me. It triggered something deep and familiar, and also filled me with a strong need to protect any female who looks as if she might be vulnerable to his attention. This of course was quite ridiculous, but there it was. I looked up from the menu. "Fettuccini Alfredo, please Giorgio." "Good! Then I'll have the same. And green salad? The dressing here is exquisite."

He flipped so easily from necessary (if trite) conversation to things which some people don't even realise exist, and I have to admit, I thoroughly enjoyed it. The only other person I have ever done that with was Lucy, and we had such a short time to explore the things which had come to light the night we had gone to Fairies Ferry. Suddenly the old man boomed in my head.

"Whatever else you tell him, do not repeat any of that!" It was almost a growl. I would have liked to keep the old man close to my mind, to help me. But he was gone as suddenly as he had appeared. Giorgio excused himself and moved gracefully through the restaurant, passing close (deliberately I'm sure) to the table where the 'delectable' one was laughing with her friends and poring over the menu. She glanced up as he passed, and he must have held her eyes because she didn't look away. I found all of this fascinating. It was a side of Giorgio I have never seen before, and despite my misgivings, it was still something of an entertainment. A few minutes later he returned in a swirl of masculine eau de toilette. He sat down and let out a long sigh.

"So, dreams discussion is out. What about reincarnation? Do you believe in that?"

"Do you Giorgio?" I replied. He laughed, a seductively attractive sound which caused the woman to lean across her companion to ascertain if in fact Giorgio were the owner.

"Well of course I do Matilda. I'm certain we've all been here before, many times, aren't you?" I was unable to answer for a moment or two. I did not want to place myself in an awkward position, or to say anything that I would regret either now or later. But Giorgio did not seem offended by my silence. He stared at me and said. "The buttons, you noticed are a reminder to me of one such incarnation."

I felt my stomach contract. Giorgio continued looking intently at me as he said. "It was in fact, an incarnation as a castrato."

I had great difficulty in keeping any emotion from etching itself across my face. By now my stomach was churning violently, and the heat of the fear of being discovered threatened to divest itself in my cheeks. I had a terrible premonition, and suddenly

Giorgio seemed to tower above me like an immense shadow. His smile which always seems to hold more than friendly warmth, positively screamed mystery. I decided to take the bull by the horns.

"How much do you think you remember?" I asked. He looked down at the table. Out of the corner of my eye I could see the waiter bearing down on us with our steaming pasta. "Oh I don't 'think' sweetie, I know. For example I know what my name was. It was Carlo." My heart leapt into my throat. "To be exact." Giorgio went on. "Carlo Ferrucci. And I was extremely talented and famous. Perhaps that is why this time I must teach."

'NO!' I thought. 'NO. I was Carlo!' He must mean some-one else. A different time, another city. I managed to control my thoughts and ask as nonchalantly as possible. "Where was this Giorgio?" "In Italy Matilda. To be precise, in Venice." I could keep silent no longer. "Only I've had two or three very lucid dream experiences involving Carlo, and I'm quite sure that..." He interrupted me. "Ah well there you are then, that's our con-nection. That's where we've met before."

The pasta steamed up from the table. A wonderful smell of garlic and cream tickled my appetite. In spite of myself, I would say nothing. I was not about to allow him to discover anymore about my 'other' side. He was still talking, romancing about what he used to do in that existence. I nodded politely, I would no be drawn. His descriptions were general, he did not go into any real detail. nor was he explicit regarding the emotional side of life for this group of singers. No, quite simply Giorgio was mistaken. I don't know who he had been in that group of friends, but he had not been Carlo!

Having spoken a little around the subject he seemed happy to let it drop. I felt torn because I suddenly found it important to know as much as possible about Giorgio's capabilities in other realms, since they were obviously connected to me in Venice. But it was impossible to lead him away from that city and keep him on the general subject. I was on dangerous ground. So I decided to withdraw lest I inadvertently betrayed myself. I had to clear my mind before tackling Giorgio again, and at the moment, with the concert looming, I simply could not do that. I would not be able, I knew, to think deeply about anything else until it was over. So the conversation turned to singing.

"For now Matilda, I have decided that we will 'coast.' You have enough voice and natural ability to work with. I will be gentle with you." He paused and laughed softly, not totally pleasantly I should add. "However, soon we must look at it again, this voice of yours. This stubborn little refusal to abandon itself to my teaching. We will face the dragon in her lair, yes? Ultimately, although of course we need our health, we sing with our brain. And by brain I mean every facet. Ideally with both sides of the mind balanced. Now that's an artist! Anyway cara, for now enjoy. Just don't go mad with Turandot!"

A weight lifted from me and my whole body relaxed at his words. Only one tiny corner of my mind remained on red alert, a rhythmically flashing beacon which seemed light years away.

The conversation lightened. We discovered that we can make each other laugh quite easily, and there is even a rudimentary form of telepathy between us, although I will always view that with suspicion. Just before coffee I went to the ladies. I also passed the table of the 'chosen one.' It was with some surprise that I registered her eyes on my back like two poised knives. I smiled to myself. 'Surely she doesn't imagine that?..' Well of course she does Matilda. She's not to know the relationship, is she? 'But how?' I wondered, my hands under the dryer by this time. 'How can she be so possessive of a man she, quite clearly, had never met?' It seemed ludicrous. Did he really have this power over women? What a fascinating man Giorgio is! No wonder people find him magnetically compelling, or did not trust him one little bit. One thing was sure though. The lady in question (whoever she was) did not need any protection from me. Feeling rather foolish I headed back to the table only to find my seat occupied. As I got nearer Giorgio stood up…

"And this is my prize soprano, Matilda Gasgoine. Matilda, let me introduce you to Verity Baines." We shook hands. The gracious one smiled at me, now aware of the fact that I was no threat, she excused herself for sitting in my seat. She then presented her hand to Giorgio who kissed it lingeringly, and on a wave of triumph went back to her agog and expectant friends. I sat down as coffee and desert arrived, finding it hard not to smile.

"Now cara, don't laugh at me and don't be surprised. I'm not that old you know!" He grinned. I was only surprised that he felt the need to explain himself to me, but of course that was not the reason for such a comment and he continued.

"You see, little one. A man in my position cannot afford to allow such a chance to slip through his fingers, and since you are not going to grace me with your presence later, and since the lady is so lovely…" He shrugged his shoulders and smiled at me.

"That she most certainly is Giorgio!" My reply covered some confusion. It has never occurred to me that Giorgio had any interest in me in that way. I'm quite sure he doesn't really and that that was the sort of statement men often make in such a situation. A modern form of Knighthood. But there was something else, something that I do have a facility to sense. Anything to do with jealousy I usually see in big green letters, and I am as certain as I can be that Giorgio was using the unexpected turn of events to test the ground to see if I showed any sign of the little green god over what transpired. Further, unless I am very much mistaken, he was a little miffed that I didn't.

Nevertheless, the whole situation with Verity continued to fascinate me. Female curiosity propelled me to wonder just what Giorgio would be like as a lover, and he surveyed me from across the table as if he knew my thoughts. However, clearly in my mind shimmered a picture of Dante as I remember him in his Milan apartment. He was lying in bed, his head propped up on his arm. The white shades behind him were drawn against the afternoon heat, and with the deep olive of his skin against the white sheets, and the wonderful seductive smile on his to-kill-for mouth, he reminded me of a gentle satyr. He reached towards me with his free arm. I closed my eyes, realising with a pang how terribly I missed him since his enforced exile.

'No way Giorgio.' I thought. 'No contest, if you thought there might be.'

I opened my eyes and his face had changed. He looked slightly dangerous again. But as soon as he realised my attention was on him once more, he smiled with concern.

"You must be tired Matilda. Look I'm going to put you in a

taxi…I insist." He added as I started to protest. I gave in easily I'm afraid. He was right, I was suddenly very tired and the idea of public transport simply didn't appeal. Giorgio I realised had other 'fish to fry' as it were and had no intention of losing out on a night of passion in order to drive me home.

"You must come and see my new property one day soon. I don't know if Martin mentioned…" "Yes." I interrupted. "Yes Giorgio, he did." "Good. Well. Maybe after the concert?" And he caught a waiter's attention. The willing man went to the door of the restaurant and hailed a taxi from a rank not far down the road. I was impatient to go. I could sense Verity's eyes on me again. 'Let me out of here!' I thought. Giorgio as always was taking his time. It occurred to me that he never allows himself to be hurried, and he appeared, at that moment, to be deliberately baiting this lady. Such confidence he must have! Just when most people would be falling over themselves to make the right impression. Maybe it's part of his seduction technique. Maybe he was using me to spice things up for later? Charming! My tiredness increased, I'd had enough for one evening. I desperately needed to go home. He kissed my hand in the same manner as he had kissed Verity's, and I heard her indrawn breath.

"Goodnight Giorgio." "Goodnight cara, I'll see you very soon."

The taxi pulled away and I let out a breath of relief in a long sigh. I can't say how I felt then or now, as I write about it. I'm not going to think about it. I'm going to sleep. Tomorrow I have to face Turandot.

Andrew Saunders drained his cup and slid the music across his desk towards him. He pushed back his chair, put the music under his arm and made for the studio and Matilda. He had come to know her quite well during her time with the company, although he had never worked with her as a soloist. He knew that most people in the Opera House were fond of her. He had heard good reports of her voice and musical talent, but personally had always got the impression that she was rather shy. Not the best quality for the operatic world!

This all led him to be quite sure that she had been pushed, one way or another, into agreeing to sing the aria listed in the programme. Tony London could be an arsehole sometimes, but Andrew doubted that even he would suggest this particular piece of music off his own bat. Somebody else was responsible. Well he'd have to help her as much as possible. He was sure that she would be amenable to advice. He turned the corner and there she was, her face pale, and the violet eyes reminding him of a doe peeping out of the undergrowth. He would have to be very patient. In all truth, it irritated him that he should have to play 'baby sitter' on this particular job. It was fairly prestigious and a definite step in the right direction, and he itched to be doing rather more than 'prompting' the stage, and rehearsing for absentee maestri. He had, of course, learnt much from all this, but at 38 he needed to begin to make something of a mark for himself if there was to be any chance of any real success at all. Still, bulldozing the soprano wouldn't help and could reflect on him. He longed for mature, experienced artists to work with, but it seemed it was not to be this time. So he smiled at her and ushered her into the studio. He watched her glance around uncertainly and nervously return is smile. God! He didn't see how she could sing it at all.

Matilda was nervous, this was true. All that was written before the first declamatory phrase was a single, and rather bland chord which, in fact, sounded more familiar on the piano than when played by the orchestra. She gathered herself mentally, while keeping her body relaxed. With strong determination she pushed all thoughts of yesterday's rehearsal to one side, and breathed from the very depths of her being. She couldn't expect her voice to rival the glorious, steely clarion sound of the dramatic soprano, and she wasn't stupid enough to try. She searched for the beauty in the phrase, and the vulnerability of the princess and her most latent feminine characteristics. Andrew was very pleasantly surprised. Anyone hearing this rendition would instantly feel an intense compassion for the character, a sympathy usually reserved for the second soprano part, the slave girl Liu.

This girl was really talented, not simply a lovely voice, but true musical intelligence. Not once had she rolled up her sleeves and given it some 'Wally!' When the last high ringing phrase had cleared the acoustic of the room, he was silent for a few moments. Matilda was instantly dismayed, convinced he hated it, and she felt her heart pounding, partly from the nervous energy coursing through her, and partly from the fear of Andrew's scorn. He looked up at her, and for a moment still said nothing, searching for the right words to explain himself without interfering with what she had done.

"Is there anything that you are musically unsure of, that you would like to go through again?" He asked finally. Matilda assured him not. Andrew turned back to the score in front of him and laid his hand across the printed page.

"Then let's leave it for today. There's no sense in going over and over it for the sake of it. That will simply tire you, and I admire the way you are handling something which we both know is an absolute bastard to sing, and something which you shouldn't even be looking at for the next 15 years at least. Good work Tilly! I'll see you at the orchestral rehearsal!"

Matilda sighed out a grateful breath. "Thank you Andrew." She whispered. Andrew was suddenly aware that she had weathered this considerable musical storm by herself. He had the distinct impression that she had had no support to back her instinctive approach. He watched her leave the studio. This profession never ceased to amaze him. 'She should get on.' He thought, but she probably wouldn't. First of all she was British, that was enough to stop many people. But it wasn't just that, because in this case she just might have leapt over that nasty little political hurdle with the right backing and help. No, it was more that she seemed to belong to another place. He shook himself out of his reverie. Well, that was the shortest 'call' he'd ever experienced, but he felt he'd done absolutely the right thing. And he returned to the main building a very much happier man than when he had left it.

Divorce

Martin had been on edge since about 10:30 that evening. Where was she? He hadn't even eaten dinner, instead he'd snacked on bits and pieces and had drunk far too much. The concerts, or at least the first of them was looming and Martin was not at all sure of how he felt. He had three arias to perform, all of which he knew so well musically, that he could sing them in his sleep. And then the one long duet with 'La Tilly' (as he had begun to call her) which finished the first half, was something he had performed many times before. His first 'spot' straight after the orchestra's prelude to 'La Traviata,' which opened the concert, was the very well known 'La Donna e mobile.' He should be able to sing that falling off a log...Well shouldn't he?

Martin was assailed by self doubts and he suspected that there was very likely a good reason for this. That being, that he wasn't singing the way he really wanted to. He couldn't make the music his own. Whereas Matilda, damn her, God he hated her, just stood there and spun it all out like golden light. Why Giorgio stopped her in the rehearsal the other day, he couldn't imagine! And what happened afterwards when he took her off to 'talk ' to her, what was all that about? Maybe Connie was right, maybe he did fancy her, and all that talk over drinks a few weeks ago, was to clear the runway for his own take off. Giorgio didn't care about him, he just didn't want any competition. Was that it? He declined to give it the energy to even think about it.

Mind you, Matilda was bound to fall arse over tit in the Turandot. This was music usually reserved for mature singers with flexible steel where their intercostals and abdominal muscles should be, and vocal chords which have attained the resilience of an Olympic athlete. You don't have that at 26, especially when the timbre of the voice is not by nature truly 'steely,' the little green devil on his shoulder assured him, promising him a firework display on the night.

That still left Connie. Where the hell was she? Martin switched on the T.V. and promptly fell asleep. Somewhere in a dream he heard a phone ringing, but he was too far into an alcoholic maze, to register it enough for him to swim to the surface of his consciousness and rouse himself. He finally came to at 2:00 a.m. in the morning. He got up from the settee, hardly able to co-ordinate walking from his deep sleep, and made for the bedroom. Gently he opened the door and put his head round it.

"Connie?" He whispered. He could see by the light from the street that the bed was unoccupied. He turned back into the hall and said, more loudly this time. "Connie you here?" Then his eye was caught by the flashing red light of the answer machine, and in that moment he remembered the phone ringing in his dream.

"Shit!" He said imagining suddenly some serious problem. He pressed the 'play' button. After a few seconds, Connie's voice came on.

"I suppose you're asleep Martin. I…er…I've got a bit of a problem not the least of it being some signal failure with the trains up here. Instead of fighting my way back, I'm going to stay with Dawn. See you tomorrow!"

Dawn? Who the hell was Dawn? Rather a terse message too. This was not like Connie, he'd never known her stay with her friends before, not without him anyway. Something wasn't right here, there was something in her tone, something almost defiant. And suddenly he could hear his own voice in his mind…"Con! Look, sorry but I can't get back from here tonight. We're out in the bloody sticks! The last trains was 9.00 this evening, can you believe it? See you tomorrow."

Last trains, cancelled trains, signal failures…all the easiest excuses in the book! That was it, a lie. She was bloody lying to him. The scheming dirty little bitch! He wasn't going to put up with any of that rubbish. But who was she with? He laid down on top of the bed, fully clothed. The drink was still working, and before he came up with the name of a likely candidate, he was asleep again. The next thing he knew, Connie was prodding him.

"You're still dressed Martin. Do you want some coffee? I've made some."

Martin rolled off the bed. His mouth tasted vile, and his head was living its own life, dedicated to his destruction. At least he had until the evening to pull himself together. And there was some thing else…What was it now? Through the mist it flew towards him…Connie!

"Connie!" He shouted, making his way to the kitchen. "Where the hell were you?"

"Didn't you get my message, Martin?" Connie paused, pouring out the coffee and looked briefly at him. 'She's as nervous as a cat.' He thought, but she does look different. He'd seen women have a look about them like that before sometimes after he'd…He blotted the rest of his thoughts out. Blooming! That was it, she was positively blooming. He pulled out a chair and sat down. "Who's Dawn anyway?" Connie placed some coffee in front of him on the kitchen table. "You don't know her Martin." She replied, looking at him over the rim of her cup.

"Well I wouldn't would I? Are you sure she doesn't have hairy legs, and isn't full back for the local rugby team?"

Connie gave him a twisted smile. "And if she were, are you in any position to make a fuss Martin?"

Ouch! This wasn't the time for words. Connie had never been able to resist him when he really tried. (Which of course he didn't very often.) He slunk across the room suddenly nervous of her. A man in the process of seducing his own wife. 'Hmm… Quite erotic.' He thought. Connie stood very still, It was suddenly almost eerie how still and focused she seemed. Maybe she was baiting him with all this, trying to make him jealous, after all he could be rather a naughty boy, rather often too!

"I'm not really a naughty boy." He said, attempting to look exactly like one. She moved away from him, her eyes making full contact with his own.

"No Martin, I don't think that you are. You're not a naughty boy at all. What you are is a deceitful and selfish man who likes to pretend that all he is, is a 'naughty boy.' And I would be very pleased if you would grant me a divorce."

"What…" He half laughed. "You're…You're kidding!" Connie didn't reply, she simply continued to look at him. She most definitely was not kidding.

"Oh great Con! This is all I need just before a bloody concert."

"And that is all you ever think about isn't it? Well not quite, we have all your little trollops, don't we? At least, you have them, I have to put up with them!" Martin was so taken aback that he forgot to 'deny'. He parried feebly. And finally came out with. "Con, can't we talk about this after next Friday? I really do need to put everything on the back boiler until then." Then, as she turned impatiently away." Come on. I married you didn't I?"

"And I'm supposed to be eternally grateful for that, am I? We'll leave the discussion until after next Friday, since that is when you will be giving birth to your grand and glorious career. Until them I'm going to Dawn's. I only came back to pick up some things. Do not try to contact me. I mean it Martin! When I come back, you can get out. I don't care where you go, just get out! Oh and by the way, you need to make an appointment!"

"An appointment? Now what the hell are you talking about Connie? You're going bonkers!"

"No Martin. I'm not going bonkers. In fact I haven't felt this sane since before I met you. Like someone has wiped a cold flannel over my face. And there's nothing like a trip to the V.D. Clinic to make you feel like that." That said, she picked up her coffee cup, and headed to the bedroom where she began packing a small bag. Martin slouched over the table staring into space. His mind was working furiously and he wasn't altogether sure that he believed her. He got up suddenly and followed her into the bedroom.

"How do you know it was me?" He asked her. Connie froze mid packing. "What?" She spat. "Well if we do have something, there's more than me could have brought it home." "You have a cheek Martin Roberts. An unmitigated nerve. You regularly lay half of London, and you dare to accuse me? You have the reputation of an alley cat, and I'm the one who's infected you? Do you know what really sickens me Martin? You could so easily have left me alone. You usually do, you bastard! God I hate you." Finally her control broke, and the brittle front which he had mistaken for something else, splintered into little pieces, and bordering on hysteria she threw the rest of her clothes into the bag. He made a move towards her, thinking her vulnerability would let him pass her anger.

"Don't!" She shrieked. "If you touch me, I swear I'll kill you. Anyway you stink. Get away from, go on...Piss off!"

Martin had never seen such passion from her. If the situation weren't so serious it would be quite a turn on. By now the tears were pouring down her cheeks, and uncontrollable sobs tore up from her chest. Finally she picked up her bag and stalked to the front door. She opened it and turned back one last time.

"You know something Martin? You don't deserve to live. You're a bloody waste of space." The front door slammed and Martin was alone. He sat down on the edge of the bed. Everything had happened so fast that he couldn't quite grasp it yet. He knew he was a bastard, but he had always been so sure that he was clever enough for any woman, and his tracks had always been perfectly hidden. Why had she become suspicious? And as for the other unfortunate state of affairs, well he was sure that is wasn't anything serious. A course of antibiotics, a few weeks abstinence, and it would all be back to normal again. He couldn't think why he hadn't noticed anything. He had always understood that women were the last to know. As he took a shower, his mind flicked back over the last few weeks. Now, which little slut had presented him with this basket of jollies? It wasn't long however, before another thought struck him, in his opinion, a much more worrying one. Connie was the main bread winner. His money had improved in its regularity over the last season, and of course signing with Tony London was going to be a big help, but it was all peanuts compared to what she brought home each month.

Connie had opened all the pension, savings, stocks and shares accounts, and she was the one who supported them with regular payments. They had so many he wasn't even aware of all of them. And if it came to divorce, there was no way he could sustain even half of the monthly bills. Connie's job as a financial advisor in a City bank, brought him a security and luxury (he looked around the spacious flat) that he had long since taken for granted. How many times had his friends pointed out to him how lucky he was? And he had never thought beyond just that, luck!

Yes, this was much more serious. Quite suddenly he felt very depressed. Over fresh coffee he made two phone calls. One to a clinic, and one to Giorgio.

Concert

The morning of the concert had arrived. Matilda awoke with the sun in her heart. Martin with rain. Giorgio gave in, and promised Verity she could come to the performance as long as she would behave herself. Many things converged on to that day, they seemed to hover over the characters, waiting for their cue to descend and settle on to the stage of life.

Matilda had an added excitement since Dante had promised to do his best to make it to the performance. The singers were called for rehearsal at 12:00 noon. At 11:45 a.m. Matilda pushed open the door to her dressing room, hurried in, and hung up her evening dress. She took her music, and found her way to the auditorium. Martin she was very surprised to note, was already there, looking a little as if he were about to face the Inquisition.

"Hi!" She said, unsure as always of his mood. But he had decided that today was presentation-of-the- olive branch day.

"Hi Tilly. How are you?" She smiled with relief, after all they were performing together. It would make it so much easier if he would be reasonably pleasant. "O.K. Thanks. I think. I'm not sure!"

"Yes." He laughed. "I know what you mean."

The orchestra, having been working since 10:30a.m.took a break and Andrew came over to speak to them. The acoustic, he assured them, was good. The orchestra in excellent form. The two singers were all too aware that they alone remained to prove themselves. It didn't really help their nerves. Twenty minutes later, Martin stood up to sing his first aria looking a little like a soul possessed. His singing was correct musically, but it passed without inflaming anyone. The duet followed. Members of the orchestra reacted instantly to Matilda's first entrance, and the whole energy lifted. She was not aware of it, already engrossed in the music, but Martin noticed. He felt his confidence slip. This was all bloody Connie's fault. How was he supposed to concentrate properly with all that rubbish going round in his head?.. And what the hell was Matilda doing over there? He had to move nearer to her for his next line. Oh bugger this!

"Excuse me Andrew, I'm sorry to stop. Where are you going Matilda… For a walk?" The orchestra fiddled with their instruments and quietly retuned. Matilda had blushed scarlet.

"I'm so sorry, it's just that, well since we have a stage I thought…" She stammered. Andrew interrupted. "I have to insist that we move on. Sort this out afterwards please. Matilda stand still!"

Matilda did exactly that, in fact she felt rooted to the spot, and there she stayed until the duet was finished. Andrew looked up at them, resting the point of his baton on the thick score. "Good…Fine…Speed O.K?" They both nodded and the rehearsal continued. Matilda launched into her big aria. "Mark it!" Barked Andrew. "I don't want to hear it now." It wasn't that easy to sing this demanding music 'down.' Matilda felt she'd rather risk using a little too much energy than try, after all she was perfectly well, but as usual she did as she was bid. 'I'll have to practise marking.' She thought to herself as Andrew put his hand up with the palm facing her yet again. She took the high declamatory phrases down an octave, and promptly got completely lost as far as the pitch was concerned. She was mortified. 'I ought to be able to do that.' She thought, but Andrew didn't appear to notice, he just said. "Good…Fine… On please…Martin."

Nessun Dorma passed in much the same way as the Rigoletto. Bland, unexciting, but at least correct. Andrew made no comment. After Martin had finished he laid down his baton, thanked everyone, and wished them an enjoyable concert, and that was that. Matilda found herself wishing that they could go through everything just one more time. They had some lunch instead.

She found Martin exhausting. He tried to cover his nerves by acting out a blasé bluff. He talked almost continuously about Giorgio, who apparently had assured him many times over the past few months just how brilliant he was, and that most tenors around would never be able to sing the way he just had. He even found a tiny piece of encouragement for Matilda,

"It's not bad Tilly, not bad at all. But there are still some things that you haven't quite got the hang of you know? Maybe after all this is over, we can do some work together. I could keep an eye on you between sessions with Giorgio. Oh, and don't worry about this bloody big aria you've got to sing darling. Hardly anyone can make themselves heard over the racket from the orchestra. Everyone will understand, I'm sure."

This was all said from a position of leaning back in his chair and screwing up his face an absurd amount, trying very hard to put across to Matilda the validity of his superiority. The last thing she needed at that moment was an argument of any sort. Of course she didn't need insinuations that she couldn't be heard in places either, but it seemed she had little choice other than to listen to the ridiculous diatribe. Considering the amazing gall of the man, and considering his performance was nowhere near that which he imagined it to be, Matilda couldn't help but feel a little sorry for him. He must be desperate. He must know deep down that something is lacking. The problem was, as with many people in this profession, one had to be very careful not to allow their insecurities to 'rub off' on to oneself. It was surprisingly easy for that to happen, and it was not on. After all everyone had their own problems to deal with. She had to get away from him, soon. She glanced at the clock on the café wall, she'd give him another half an hour. There was a couch in her dressing room and she was looking forward to relaxing on it for a while. However, in his present state, Martin was sensitive in the extreme (at least to his own feelings and needs) and as soon as she glanced at the time, he interrupted his flow and said.

"We've got ages yet Tilly. Christ! You don't need to be bloody running back there yet!" So Matilda had to wait for another slight slowing of the one-sided conversation before she could leap in. "Excuse me for just a moment Martin. I'll be right back." And she escaped to the Ladies, thankful that the relatively small café had one. Once there she sank on to the only available chair and letting her head drop into her hands, forced herself to relax. A hot, heavy wave drained from her forehead and she felt marginally better. But she couldn't stay where she was for very long, this was all becoming a bit of a problem. She didn't know how to deal with Martin when he was like this, she wondered vaguely how his wife coped. Part of her wanted to tell him to shut up! But she was uncertain as to his response, so with a sigh she returned to the café where she was quietly delighted to see Giorgio sitting at their table. As she came up to them, he was cracking one of his easy jokes with Martin who began to laugh like a maniac, at least releasing some of his hyper-energy in the process. It was not too long before she could excuse herself and return to her dressing room for a couple of hours of total relaxation.

JOURNAL

In a room by the side of the stage I was waiting for what seemed like an interminable orchestral piece to finish. I was to sing my aria next and I was beyond nerves and found it impossible to sit quietly. I paced up and down, a habit I've noticed is creeping into my pre-performance preparation, and one that I'm not sure is such a good thing. For the third time I forgot the words to the second phrase of the aria. "Shit!" I exclaimed, assuming that I was alone.

"That's the worse thing that you can do just before you sing my dear. We always forget the words when we do that." A voice from the corner made me jump.

"I'm sorry. I didn't realise anyone was here." I said, not very pleased that there was to be honest. I didn't feel like having a conversation at that moment, and anyway what was she doing here?

"My name is Irena Popovitch. I am a friend of Bella Richmond's. You of course know Bella?" She informed me, as if she had read my thoughts. I could hear the orchestra dipping deeply into the Wagner that they were playing as they approached the last few pages.

"I enjoyed your singing in the duet. "She told me. I thanked her, although I sensed a 'but' lingering somewhere. I felt compelled to speak to her and came up with the easiest thing I could think of. "Are you a singer?" I asked her, not really expecting her to be.

"Yes, I am a professional singer. Although now I do a lot of coaching. I am a vocal coach in the old-fashioned sense of the word."

"Oh?" I replied, not able to keep the interest out of my voice. The orchestra was approaching the final bars, I glanced involuntarily over my shoulder.

"Toi, toi Matilda" The lady said. "How do you say in this country? Go get 'em!" She had only a slight accent, so slight in fact, that it was almost impossible to place, although I guessed Russian. She had an amazing face, and a perfectly fabulous smile. The sort of smile that could disarm a cruise missile at 20 paces, That of a wise cherubic child, such was Irena's smile. It was the last thing I registered before hearing the first chord. Almost without discernable pitch it seems (Especially when you're nervous) so bland and unassuming giving no inclination of what was to follow. One of the most unnerving things about performing, is the dichotomy between the inner and outer worlds. The nervous energy in a performer belied by the calm professional profile. Inside rages a waterfall of unbelievable magnitude, waiting to pour forth sparkling energy over its audience. To lift them up into a vortex and suspend them for a short while in a far better world. But it is the music which does that of course. The performer can so easily ruin the whole thing. It's not easy to keep the ego at bay at such times. To insure that it sits like a well trained dog, not to allow it to leap up and start barking.

I had told myself firmly all afternoon that it was much preferable to occasionally sink into the overwhelming sound and be lost for a second or two, than to try to fight it all with one brave little pair of vocal chords. But I was afraid that I might not have the strength to resist. That I wouldn't dare to remove everything but the breath and the support, place the sound firmly on top of the orchestra, and trust it. But I did. I managed to stay calm, in fact there wasn't really anything else to do once you're in it! Martin joined me at the appropriate places near to the end, and it was over. I know that Andrew was pleased. He smiled at me and gave me a 'thumbs up' sign carefully hidden from the audience of course. They however, were altogether another thing. Some of them even stood up. It was overwhelming and most gratifying, (Oh alright I was beside myself, never thought it would happen to me, never even imagined it) I felt a huge rush of gratitude and exhilaration. Then I caught sight of Martin's face and I dearly wished he had received the same reception. He looked like a child who watches his favourite toy being taken from him, but who isn't allowed to cry about it. And there was something else, so insidious, that as he held my gaze for a couple of seconds between bows, those seconds and the space between us seemed to stretch into a pause in time. His eyes bore into me across the space, the applause roared in my ears, and I had the absurd feeling that we could have stood there for ever, and that somewhere we had stood like that many times before. I refuse to dwell on it, fascinating though it may well prove to be.

A few people found their way back stage, Giorgio and Verity among them. She was quite sincere, and I realised something. She genuinely loves music. It softens her slightly, you see a different Verity. Giorgio had already spoken to Martin, I could hear laughter and raised voices clearly as I was changing. He knocked on my door soon after and came in smiling, with his arms outstretched towards me.

"Well done cara. I'm very pleased with you both." His eyes lingered for a moment on mine, and I felt, as always, that there is so much more going on beneath the surface. Then in bowled Verity full of…Well Verity! But she was pleasant to me. She seemed genuinely delighted. After they had left I put all my things together and was about to leave myself, when there was another knock on the door. I opened it, Bella stood there, her tall form resplendent in a turquoise evening coat, setting off her dark blue eyes, shining brown hair and creamy skin. She looked quite superb and I found myself thinking. 'I wonder what Giorgio makes of her?'

"Matilda, congratulations! I'm furious with Tony, he should have been here, but he's off abroad again. I shall give him a good report. I have to tell you, I was knocked for six! I had no idea that you have a voice like that. You should have heard what some people around me were saying! Now, are you coming to eat with us? Of course you are, you must!"

"Well, I…" I was unaware of any after performance meal, but Bella was not ready to hear any excuse. "Yes, of course you're coming. You must eat, and anyway Irena wants to meet you.

She's quite impressed and she's some talent herself. You can consider yourself highly complimented."

"Where do you know her from?" I asked as I picked up my bags, suddenly realising that I was starving. "Oh I used to study with her. She coaches of course, but she does also teach. She's sung all over the world and she sounds as if she still could! A fabulous soprano, and as solid as a rock! I know many a young singer who would give their eye teeth for her breathing alone. Oh sorry Matilda! It's such bad manners to talk about another artist when you're still sweating from your performance."

I grinned and ran my free hand over my still damp forehead. "I didn't realise that you sing Bella" We had reached the stage door by this time and wished goodnight and thanks to the patient man there waiting to lock up.

"Oh I only studied for a short while." Bella replied quickly and rather quietly. "But it didn't…Well work out, you know? After three years of working really hard it was obvious that… Anyway we've stayed good friends. And I have to be honest Irena saved me from long years of anguish." Bella paused to hail a cab. She named Giorgio's favourite restaurant and we piled in.

"Long years of anguish, what do you mean Bella?" Bella turned her deep blue gaze on me and I could sense her great disappointment as she explained. "Well, I could have carried on. But it's one thing to be talented, out of work and struggling, and quite another to be in that position with no real talent to justify the suffering." And she laughed a little hollowly. "But Irena was very gentle. It's not an easy thing to say, or to hear."

She paused, and I realised just how hard it was for her even now to have to face the truth. "Irena was sensitive without leaving any room for misunderstanding. Quite a lady is our Irena, I mean most people with her talent and experience would devastate someone like me without another thought, unless they needed the money for some reason of course! Oh! We're here. You know this restaurant? We have a booking."

"Yes." I said softly. I know this restaurant."

There was an area prepared for the expected party, which ended up not being overly big. The soloists and some close friends mainly. Most of the orchestra had headed straight for the nearest pub, as is their wont, and Andrew, although he made an appearance at the restaurant, pleaded an early call, had a glass of wine, and left.

Before she sat down, Matilda found a phone. She rang her flat hoping that Dante was there, and secretly bitterly disappointed that he hadn't made it to the concert, especially since it had gone so well for her. She felt she needed to prove herself to him, and was never sure of what he truly thought. There was no reply from her phone and she slipped back into the restaurant and seated herself next to Bella.

Across the table, she noted Martin still looking grim. He was making a concentrated effort to drink a lot of wine very quickly, in order to cover up the fact. His voice was getting louder and Matilda's thoughts wandered to the time she had discovered his pending marriage. She remembered how she had tried to phone him only to discover that he wasn't there. "I'm just renting for a few months." Said the foreign voice on the phone. "All I know is, he left to get married and I don't think he and his new wife will be returning here." She didn't remember much else, but she did recall the swirl of icy emotion that had gripped her, drawing out her first reaction. "It's not true!" She had whispered into the phone that she still held to her ear. What she would have given in that moment of shattered romance, to have been in Connie's place...The bride...The chosen one. And how supremely thankful was she now that it had not happened that way. She was embarrassed for Martin when he had been drinking. He was an intelligent man, but after a few drinks, he would shout his thoughts and feelings to the assembled company. Above the gentle murmurings of conversation, his voice rose again.

"I thought the 'Nessun Dorma' went rather well Giorgio. Plenty of ping, eh?" His half smile became a sneer. "I'll show those bloody Italians how to sing it!"

Matilda cringed. 'Giorgio, please shut him up.' She thought. 'He's not doing himself any good at all.' Bella had cast a discerning eye in his direction more than once. Death-wish tenor continued, but Giorgio only smiled and nodded, kept his own voice subdued, and appeared to be much more interested in Bella, than in keeping a rein on his turbulent tenor.

"I think you've got an admirer." Matilda whispered to her. "Oh don't Matilda! He gives me the creeps." Matilda, feeling the most ridiculous need to protect him said. "Some women go nuts for him, so they say."

"Well not this one. He's a friend of Tony's so I've met him briefly before. Those eyes! I'll bet he's into every perversion known to man, not to mention a few no one else has thought of yet. I like my sex straight forward. He looks like every deviant rolled into one." And Bella turned her attention to Irena who was sitting the other side of her.

Matilda leant back in her chair and quietly surveyed him. She gazed in his direction as if she were dreaming, miles away, and the sounds around her became louder but so unfocused as to cease to pull on her awareness. She couldn't have repeated a single word from the many conversations going on, but the familiarity of it all relaxed her in warm light, and Giorgio suddenly stood out in remarkable clarity. Matilda felt herself sinking. Giorgio's hair darkened a further shade, his body lengthened and slimmed…Then they were all in the sea, splashing, swimming and laughing. It was wonderfully warm, they divested themselves of their clothes and played like healthy young animals, oblivious to everything except themselves…Now she saw them striding through Venice. It was cooler, maybe spring time, and they were heading for their favourite inn. Lucciano was sulking. They teased him mercilessly until he began to relent and Carlo gave chase across a small bridge off the main walk way. Raimondo followed them and as they entered a passageway, he caught them up. "Hey, Carlo!" He called. In the distance Matilda could see Lucciano still running, unaware that his pursuer had paused. Carlo turned to face Raimondo. His young girlish face wreathed in a devilish grin. Matilda's heart contracted, he was so innocent, so full of life and joy.

He was talking to Raimondo, but she couldn't make out what they were saying. He threw back his head and laughed. Raimondo drew closer and Lucciano, aware now that Carlo had stopped, started back towards them. These scenes were fleeting and unconnected. Matilda had no idea where they fitted into what she already knew about Carlo. His green eyes glowed as he turned to greet Lucciano and grasped him around the shoulders.

"Lucci, I'm ravenous, come!" The three of them linked arms and joined the rest of their friends. Matilda watched them as they hurried into a warm candle-lit tavern. But which one had Giorgio been? Why had he insisted that he had been Carlo? It disturbed her, and now that the concert was over. It all came rushing back like a tide kept too long at bay. It tumbled into every crevice of her mind. It wasn't something which she could argue with Giorgio about, but she felt as if he were taking something from her with his insistence. Something very precious that she was sure belonged to her. Someone laid their hand on Carlo's arm…No! It was her arm, and now, not then…

"Matilda, are you alright?" Irena had reached behind Bella, they were both looking at her with some concern. Matilda quickly pulled herself back. "Oh I'm sorry. I was miles away. What were you saying?"

Her question went unanswered. Verity, beside herself having watched Giorgio's unashamed leering at Bella or Matilda (she couldn't be sure which) exploded. Even Martin was quiet, while Giorgio, stayed exactly where he was still gazing at Bella and ignoring Verity, who had jumped to her feet and begun to hurl verbal abuse at him, ending with a suggestion that he do something to himself which was physically quite impossible. No one knew what to do, ignoring her was out of the question, although Giorgio was doing a pretty good job as he continued to cause Bella to feel extremely uncomfortable. Finally Verity homed in on the precise object of Giorgio's interest and started round the table towards her. Giorgio, moving as a man half his age was between them in a flash, even Verity was thrown for a moment, and gasped audibly.

"Come my dear, I must speak with you." And he escorted her with considerable force to the back of the restaurant, where Mario held open the office door as if it all been planned in advance. Gradually everyone began to continue their meals and conversations.

"Not too gentle when he's angry is he?" Remarked Bella. "Mind you, serves her right for getting involved with such a plonker." Matilda glanced at Irena, sensing a subtle change in the atmosphere. Irena looked away quickly and said quietly. "Bella, there may be many names we feel that we can label Giorgio with. However, I don't think that 'plonker' is one of them."

Bella shrugged and attacked her half eaten pasta. By the time Giorgio had returned, without Verity, they were all eating with gusto. Matilda watched him out of the corner of her eye. As he sat down he whispered something to Martin who guffawed loudly. 'Still in 'hyper' mood' Matilda thought glancing behind her at the office door. If Verity didn't appear in the next few minutes, there must be a back entrance through there! Giorgio cut into her thoughts. "Verity will not be joining us for the rest of the evening Matilda. She's er...indisposed, I think is the word." He grinned at her and added jokingly. "We have enough Prima Donnas here tonight do we not?" And he bowed his head without taking his eye from hers. Matilda smiled at him and he held her eyes while the strangest expression crossed his face. Most people, glad that the difficult moment had passed, didn't notice, even Martin had turned to the woman sitting the other side of him. But Irena noticed, she watched unobserved as Giorgio's handsome face registered a potent mixture of irritation and deep regret, etched with a cruelty which made the older lady shudder.

She was afraid, or at least concerned for Matilda who sat smiling at him He held her gaze one moment longer and Matilda moved uncomfortably, rather like a child who becomes suddenly aware that the pretty long snake just might be dangerous.

'Oh Matilda! Wake up.' She thought and on impulse she leant behind Bella and said. "I believe I live in your part of town. Why don't we share a taxi? When you're ready of course." "Actually." Replied Matilda. "I was just thinking I need to get home. Would now be too soon for you?"

"Not at all. You must be tired, these sort of days are exhausting. Shouldn't be allowed really!" She added laughing. Matilda nodded in agreement. There followed the usual round of: "Goodnight-well-done-darling- you -were-super-etc.etc.etc." Inevitable at such times. Matilda didn't really like it but there was some sincerity there somewhere, and anyway how else could it all be rounded up? By the time they finally left, her cheek muscles were aching from overly long-held smiles. They found a taxi almost immediately.

"So." Irena said as they recovered form the taxi driver's 180' turn in order to be facing the right way. "Do you have to be at rehearsal in the morning?"

"No, as it happens we aren't called during the day tomorrow. We have 'Aida' in the evening. But I wouldn't mind if we had a morning rehearsal. It's my job after all, and I'm so lucky that it isn't some other job that has nothing to do with music, which I'm forced to do in order to support myself, like so many of my college friends."

Irena nodded gently watching Matilda with a thoughtful expression on her face. There was a long silence, Matilda found it hard to concentrate on conversation, she was suddenly experiencing an uncomfortable premonition about Dante, and noting Irena's expression she said. "I'm so sorry Irena. I was just thinking…A friend of mine from Italy was supposed to come to the concert. He didn't, and I'm a little concerned about what has happened to him."

"Ah I see!" Irena smiled and leaned back into the soft seat. "Amore! Very important my dear, very important!" She added giving Matilda the distinct impression that she hadn't paid that part of her life nearly enough attention. Matilda felt a stab of regret for her. She liked Irena and realised that she was one of those people who you meet, and within a very little time you feel as if you've always known them. Suddenly she realised that she would like to work with Irena, for coaching of course. After all everyone did it. Most singers didn't wait until they had 'something coming up' before they worked with a coach, it was part of their weekly schedule. She took a deep breath, turned to her and said. "I wonder Irena…I mean, would you consider working with me? At the moment I don't work with anyone outside singing lessons. Would that be possible?"

"Of course, I'd love to work with you. Here's my card. Do phone me darling." The taxi turned into Cross Street. The two women said goodnight, and Matilda was about to close the taxi door when Irena, laying her hand on the handle said. "You really did well tonight you know. You should be very pleased. Sleep well Matilda."

"Thank you Irena, goodnight." Matilda had managed to smile but it was hard because she had already noticed that there was no light shining from her flat. Irena sat back in her seat. She didn't know how she was going to say what she needed to say. But when the time came she'd find the words, somehow.

Blue Blood

Dante felt like a man on the rack. At every turn of the screw he was quite sure that he would expire. Not from physical injury, but from the emotional turmoil which threatened to engulf him, and from which there seemed to be no escape. He could have easily caught the afternoon flight. He could have made it in time for Matilda's concert, and been there to support her, to face the monstrous Giorgio and see what the bastard had to say for himself to a fellow Italian. He wished Matilda would find herself another teacher, and had from time to time considered using a little pressure to ensure that she would. But what right did he have to insist anyway? It wasn't as if he were paying for the lessons. Matilda was very independent, and he admired that in her, especially since she now knew considerably more about his family and circumstances than she once did.

He was sitting in the same café in which he had met her, and was whiling away some time until he would leave for the airport, and a flight which would land him in London much later. In time (in fact) for bed. He couldn't bear not to be with her one more time before having to explain what was going on, and what he had to do. How would she react? He knew how most women would react, but Matilda wasn't most women! The rack turned another notch and he found some release in anger, by spitting his beautiful language at the waiter for forgetting a small snack which he had ordered with his fourth cup of coffee. Earlier he had walked up to the Opera House, his mind weaving its way back to the first time he had seen Matilda. There had been several times before he finally approached her in the café. It wasn't his habit to pick up beautiful foreign ladies in rather obvious places.

Dante's family had close friends connected with opera, and particularly La Scala, and he had been chatting to one of them, when members of the prestigious British company had appeared on stage. This was the first time he saw Matilda, and she had reminded him of a curious kitten, completely oblivious of both him and the fact that her exhilaration at being there was obvious. He found it refreshing, and captivatingly sincere. The others moved off into the wings and for a few moments she was left still standing there, gazing at the beautiful auditorium, of which every Italian opera lover is so rightly proud.

His breath had caught in his throat, and he didn't really know why. He found his eyes drawn to her and scarcely could acknowledge the conversation he was having with the opera manager. Matilda was lovely to him, but at that distance on a stage, most people are somewhat enhanced, and that was not enough to explain the shock that had exploded as he had continued to look at her. He could have sworn he knew her, that they had met before, and the feeling remained with him, even as he knew very well that he most certainly had never laid eyes on her until that day. He was aware of an excitement, not that flippant thrill of sexual attraction, although he didn't deny that. But an excitement, as if some deep cavern full of mystery had opened up, and he would never be quite the same again. She ignited something in him, and whatever happened from now until the day he died, he would not forget the initial moment he had laid eyes on Matilda. In spite of all this, he had begun to believe that they were not destined to meet, until that morning he came upon the café, and there she was, sitting alone and staring into space, obviously miles away, in her own world. It never occurred to him to question the strong familiarity that accompanied everything, and there was something else. He registered a fission of relief as soon as he saw her. Some invisible worry slipped quietly away. Dante had far too much on his mind to question any of these things, even if he had been interested in strange phenomena, which he wasn't. His parents were becoming impatient over his marital status, or at least the lack of it, and he suffered large amounts of guilt as he and Matilda fell deeply in love. He knew that if he wished to remain within his family, he would never be able to marry her, or even take her to his extensive and beautiful home to meet his family. His mother would be sympathetic, he knew that. She had triumphed over the fact that she did not possess the credentials which would have allowed her entry to the family, by marrying into it anyway.

Dante's Grandfather had relented in the end, and decided to allow Catrina to be the exception. Of course it must never be allowed to happen again! He had not lived to regret his decision. He had been won over, to a degree, by the lovely graceful woman who his son had so proudly introduced to him, but she possessed something else that had intrigued the Conte and calmed his fears. She had a rare gift. Wherever Catrina went, people smiled. After she had been there for a while, they felt better, lighter, and happier about life. There was no way that Dante's Grandfather could ascertain whether she were entirely innocent of her own soft spirit which suffused the atmosphere with love, or if she knew her own power and deliberately engaged it. To the hardened old man, it made little difference, he needed to be around her. He wanted to breathe in the precious uplifting air that followed her everywhere, And so he eventually agreed to the marriage, much to his son's great joy, and to the immense chagrin of the old Contessa. Dante's Grandmother had never let her husband forget what she considered to be his big mistake, even on his death bed. As the old man thankfully exhaled his last earthly breath, she was still criticising that decision made so many years before. Dante had always felt sorry that, as his Grandfather beheld whatever it is that we behold at such profound times, his last impression of earth was that of the tongue of a nagging wife. Despite her barely veiled contempt for Catrina, the old Contessa knew her family duty, and immediately took over some of Dante's training. It was she who instilled into him the terrible gruelling duty to family that was to blight his life, as it now did.

She never ceased to remind him that they could trace their family connections back to the Knight's Templar, and beyond, and that their extensive library (which he knew Matilda would adore, he would probably never be able to prise her away from it) contained more secret knowledge than the books stored in the Vatican, which, according to her were more often or not deliberately distorted truths anyway. Cardinals, and even occasionally The Holy Father of the time, had visited the estate with the express purpose of spending time in the cool quiet room, that was lined from the floor to the ceiling with books, some of which were the only copies in the world. He must, he was regularly reminded, do his part to preserve all of this and continue the family line.

"Is there no other way? Can I not allow just a little of modern life, and a more expanded understanding into all this, without destroying the family history?"

At such an innocent question, the depth of his Grandmother's fury, made it quite clear to him that there was no other way, and the rules laid down and adhered to for centuries was the only possible tenet for an eldest son of the Vittoria family to live by.

But in spite of his acceptance at the time, a certain rebellious spirit had been born in Dante, and he never paid homage completely to everything that was expected of him, not in his heart, anyway. And now was the moment that his heart was to be challenged. Now he had to hold up the rebellion and discover just how water-tight it was. And he was afraid. The lessons of duty, and the daily imprinting of his young mind, he was discovering, were very deeply etched. Too much so for him to simply ignore. It had been absolutely the truth when he had said to Matilda that it 'wasn't the money.' It really was something much more. To cut ties with any family would always be difficult, of course. To cut them with such as his, was unthinkable. Even now that his Father was insisting that he stop seeing Matilda, he could not deny the great love he felt for the Conte and Contessa, that only made it harder, and the rack tighter.

But there was worse, much worse. Dante must marry someone already chosen by his Father. Someone with the 'correct' background, someone whose family were flattered by any attention from the Vittorias. She would, no doubt, be sweet, young and attractive, with the ability to produce a healthy brood of children, to make the family feel a little more secure in these changing times, She would most certainly not be Matilda!

And with that thought he had felt so depressed that he had to force himself out of the taxi, and push the key into the door of Matilda's flat, hearing as he did so, her lovely soft voice in his head. "This is our flat Dante, not just mine. Think of it as ours."

From any other young woman, he would have been suspicious that not far from this statement would be lurking the question. "So where's the rent my lovely rich Italian Count?" But he knew Matilda had not even harboured such a thought. After the explanation of his family situation, he had wondered a little, and found himself watching her, and misunderstanding some of the things she said, he realised that his whole focus for a while, when he was with her, was on suspicious alert. Eventually her obvious innocence shamed him, and he never doubted her again. He removed the key from the lock and stared for a moment at the ground. Only after a few deep breaths was he able to glance up at the top floor where he noted the darkness behind the windows.

Duty

Perhaps he was asleep? Matilda closed the door quietly and stood still, listening. The flat seemed to welcome her like a silent pet, and she could almost feel the air descending in a caressive spiral from the stairwell above the front door. She crept up the stairs and carefully pushed open the sitting room door, and tip-toed through to the bedroom. The bed was flat, there was no one there. When she was quite sure of that, she flipped the light on, dropped her bags and coat, and hurried into the kitchen. Hopefully she placed her hands around the body of the kettle. It was stone cold. No one had made any coffee that evening, and Dante invariably drank it until quite late at night, It amazed her how he could sleep at all. So where was he? She flew to the phone, one message. With a shaky hand she pressed the button. It was Dante.

"Hi darling. I see you tomorrow. I will esplaina den. We meet for a lunch. I ring in der morning. Sleepa well."

"You're joking of course!" Matilda spoke aloud. She wasn't pleased. If Dante was in London, where the hell was he? And why wasn't he with her? Matilda was not easily given to jealousy and had always considered herself a little blessed when she witnessed just what it did to people. But as the first stirrings of suspicion took root, all sorts of green-tinged pictures began to develop. She ran a bath and made some herbal tea trying to put Dante out of her mind. After all he had done exactly that as far as she was concerned, it seemed. By 12:30, she was in bed and beginning to drift off, when the phone rang. It rang and rang. First in her dreams, and finally, when she had imagined that she had answered it, only to find herself still in bed, she stumbled across the room, squinting at the clock and picked up the receiver for real.

"Hello?.." "Matilda isa Dante…"

"Dante! Where are you? Are you alright? What's happening?"

"I am O.K. I am in a 'otel."

"A hotel? Why? Why are you in a hotel Dante, what's going on?" Matilda was incredulous.

"I am…I am … Der coward"

"Yes." Said Matilda. "But what's going on?"

"Please cara, to listen. I 'ave something I musta tella to you." Matilda's heart sank and her body filled with apprehension. "I come to de flat…No please listen…" As Matilda spoke again. "I can not stay to tell you dere. You 'ave de big concert, is a big ting for a you. An' so I leave, I come to 'otel."

"Which hotel? Where are you? I'll come…"

"No, no Matilda you musta be exhausted. Go anda sleep. I ring in de morning." Matilda couldn't see that she had much option but to agree.

"You won't run off to Italy in the night, will you?" She asked tearfully, hating herself for her weakness.

"No cara, I not run off. An' Matilda…" There was a silence as Matilda tried to fight her tears enough to reply, when she couldn't, Dante continued gently. "Io t'amo and I am alone." Matilda replaced the handset. She believed him, but her heart was pounding at the question in her mind. What did he have to tell her for God's sake? Somewhere of course, she knew. She saw an imposing aristocratic family, exquisite palazzos and a whole life so far away from her own as to be frightening. It seemed alien, a breathless place, and it was Dante's. It didn't help as she realised that it was not a life she could want.

"I'll never sleep tonight!" She whispered to herself as she made her way back to the bedroom. But she did. She slept and she dreamt. She dreamt of a lavish funeral. A funeral in Venice. The church was filled with music lovers mourning the loss of their favourite young castrato. If the music lovers were deeply saddened, then the opera lovers wept openly and their sobbing was so loud it was scarcely covered by the music. She saw Lucciano, his head bent over, his shoulders shaking, and when he did glance across at his friends, desperate, it seemed for consolation that they could not give, there was a look in his beautiful eyes which she would never wish to see again. Partly roused from her sleep she heard her own voice cry out in horror at the pain on Lucciano's face. She sat up in bed with tears wet on her cheeks. Even so far removed from that time, she desperately wanted to take the pain away from him. For a while she sat rocking backwards and forwards, until the coldness of the room drove her back under the duvet, where in spite of herself the dream continued.

She saw Lucciano desperate with grief and beyond help from the others, although they tried.

"It was one of those things Lucci. He wouldn't want you to grieve like this. Come, you must sing. You have work to do, music to learn. They have been very understanding, but they will not be patient for ever. Always there is someone to take our place. We must fight to stay in one spot. Come to rehearsal, Angelo will be there and you can talk to him afterwards. He will calm you…Please Lucci… Vienni, vienni…"

"No, never!…Giammi! I will not sing again."

"But what will you do? How will you live?"

Then Matilda saw that Lucciano did not live. She saw the knife in his hand, and the terrible cut across the lovely throat which had emitted such a grave beauty of sound. She saw Angelo fighting for a decent burial for the young man. The church, of course, was outraged by this heinous crime.

"But he was mad! Mad with grief. God will forgive surely, He will see the terrible weight which Lucciano could not carry, and He will forgive him." The church, however, did not agree. Neither did they have Angelo's faith regarding God's forgiveness. They exerted cold political authority which would accept no argument, closed ranks and disposed of the young man's body in a way they saw fit, refusing to divulge the resting place even to his beloved friends. It made them feel ever so much better.

Just before she awoke, Matilda saw a tall slim figure kneeling beside Carlo's grave. He was alone, and his face resembled granite, his eyes iced-diamonds.

"Do you see what you've done?" He hissed. "Do you? Wherever you are Carlo Ferruci. I curse you. So sing little brother, sing while you can, sing with the angels, who no doubt have welcomed you into their shining midst. God may listen to your voice, but I Raimondo will never, never forgive you!"

JOURNAL

I met Dante in a small restaurant on the edge of Covent Garden. We have often eaten there, and refer to it as 'our' restaurant. Dante had already drunk half a bottle of red wine. He had ordered mineral water for me, knowing that I won't drink before a performance. He stood up to embrace me, holding me for several minutes, his face buried into my neck, much to the delight of the waiters.

"You shouldn't go off an' leave 'er for a so long Dante!" One of them laughed. I was too preoccupied to remember his name now. Dante held my eyes with his and I realised how truly haggard he looked, I raised my hand to his face. "Did you sleep at all?" "A little." His voice sounded husky. We sat down.

"I 'ave order, is O.K?" He asked me. "Of course. Dante. But now, what are we going to do? Do we have a choice? I assume this is to do with your family?" For a moment he didn't answer. Then he said gently. "There is always a choice, my love." At this I relaxed slightly. After all he could simply have disappeared had he not wanted to see me. I would have no way of contacting him.

"I 'avea been selfish, I know dis day, she musta come. Why I tink…We could escape?" I was listening of course but suddenly I felt the full effect of the last 24 hours, and the dream had left its sombre mood with me. I didn't yet feel myself. Tears were not far off, but I tried to ignore them. I forced myself to speak . "Has your family discovered that we are still seeing each other?" Dante avoided my gaze, and grabbed his wine glass.

"Isa much more worse dan dat Matilda." I went cold. 'Worse?' My mind flew to every possibility, except the right one. After all, who would expect arranged marriages now, in this century? The pasta arrived and went, for the moment, untouched. Dante was speaking again.

"You see, cara…I 'ave to…I musta…" He began. "Gran Dio non posso…I cannot!" I began to panic. What was this? Was he ill? Was he going to die? He took a deep breath, and stuck his pasta with great force.

"I musta marry Matilda. I 'ave toa marry." He spoke quietly, the words mingling with the rising steam. I found it a little hard to assimilate everything. So what was the problem?

"Well." I said gently, feeling the waves of apprehension subside like the tide. "I'll marry you Dante. Did you think I wouldn't?"

But Dante didn't look up. He kept his head down and his eyes averted. And the full impact struck me with the force of a ten ton truck. The restaurant swung around me, I grabbed the table. I became, I'm sure, a terrible shade of white.

"Oh!. I whispered. "How stupid of me. I'm sorry Dante. You mean that you must marry an Italian, and one with the correct background." I was amazed by the calmness and coolness of my voice. He bent his head lower.

"Donta mock me darling. I don'ta want to marry 'er."

"Then don't Dante. You're not being held at gunpoint are you?" I said, sharper than I intended. The 'HER' struck me like a king cobra. And the poison of realisation was seeping through my mental workshop, showing me things I didn't want to see, rather like a boring friend with family snap shots. But much,

much worse was the familiarity he already had with his bride-to-be. He obviously knew her. They had met, no doubt, discussed the wedding, probably even…I slammed the door shut. But pictures of Dante, passionate and charming, in the early stages of wooing were too much. I felt sick, and a huge scream pressed inside my head and against my chest. I stumbled to the Ladies and leaned against the cold wall. Was I never to have peace and career hand in hand. Would it always be like this? The scream, having found no outlet, turned in on itself, and drained every bit of energy from my body as if someone had turned a tap on.

"Signora, are you alright? Dante, 'e worry, please to come out." I came out, feeling as weak as a kitten. "May I have some coffee please?" "Si Signora, of a course." I sat down. Dante did not appear to me, to be very worried. He hadn't moved. Suddenly I was very angry. Driving a bulldozer over my finer feelings, I said lightly. "You must appreciate Dante, that it is very difficult for me to understand completely. I'm just an English country girl, after all. I know you are to be married. Congratulations by the way. But what I'm confused about is, does that change anything? I mean the mark of an aristocrat is having a mistress or two, isn't it?"

Dante drew in a long shuddering breath, and looked at me. I no longer cared that he looked drawn, I could cheerfully have thrown half the restaurant at him. My hand itched to at least slap him, but I stayed it. He looked at me across the table over his still untouched pasta.

"I 'ave toa marry…" He began miserably." I know, you said!" I picked up my fork, it was an act of defiance, I wasn't hungry.

Dante put his hand against my own and I placed the fork back on to my plate.

"I wonta let you go, Matilda I cannot!" He said softly. "I don't want to be in that position Dante." I whispered. "This is the 21st. Century for God's sake. How can you allow yourself to be forced into marriage this way? How long does it take you aristos to catch up with intelligent society?"

"I donta especta you toa understand." "Too right. I don't!" I snapped. He ignored me and continued. "But, I want dat youa listen to me. Whatever is my family problems for us. 'Owever is 'ard for us. Der isa something else."

"Yes, well it won't be so hard for you, will it? At least two women to keep you happy. And the added luxury, of them not even being in the same country. Talk about the privileged classes!"

Dante stood up quickly. I have never seen him so angry. His fist crashed on to the table and pasta flew everywhere. His dark eyes, usually so full of Mediterranean warmth, had turned to unfathomable ice. Their focus was awesome, but as impressed as I was by his bearing, I could not climb down. What right did he have to be angry with me? One of the waiters ran up.

"Please Signor. Dante, Signor Vittoria. I musta ask you to calma. Please calma…" I stood up quickly and said. "Don't worry I'm going." And the next thing I knew, I was outside walking quickly fuelled by my anger and hurt. I had no thought of where I was going, but within seconds Dante was beside me, holding my arm, and preventing me from continuing. He turned me to face him. He didn't apologise for his anger, he simply looked deeply into my face and said. "We musta stay together. Stay close, keep in contact. Beyond all the love and sex cara, der isa something else. Something importante."

"What are you talking about Dante? What can be so important? There isn't anything more important than the way two people feel, especially when they feel the way we do."

"Si. Si, so you musta trusta me. Don'ta allow anything to destroy dis. Please cara!"

"But what is this important other thing?" I asked. Dante moved away frowning. He turned back and looked intently at me and replied. "I donta know cara. I jus' know isa dere!"

I felt frustrated, but I needed to understand him, I moved closer, and standing in front of him, looking deeply into his face. "You mean like my dreams?" He smiled and relaxed slightly. "Si. Ifa you like. Something misterioso, likea your dreams cara."

"But you still have to marry this woman?" He was silent. "Well?" My throat had begun to ache.

"Look cara, I was angry ata home. I leave in big, 'ow you say? Temper. So now I go back, I speaka to dem. Dis I promise, but not you getting' up too mucha 'ope, please cara." I nodded, I wouldn't risk the luxury of any hope at all, I promised myself. "When must you leave?" I asked him. He looked disconsolate and very on edge. "I stay for a few days…wida you?" It was a question. I hesitated for a few moments, turning away and staring unseeing across the street at the crowds of people. But somewhere inside me I trusted him even in a situation such as this. I felt that he really did believe that there was something 'importante.' Then I said. "Go to the flat, please Dante. No more hotels. I won't be very late. The ladies chorus are only in the first scene. I will see you soon."

I kissed him, and he held me almost cruelly tight. I was still angry, but it was dissipating fast. I could feel him trembling, and like my dream, I had such a desire to stop his pain, just take it away. I left him and hurried in the direction of the Opera House. The whole world looked white-washed to me, and the only colour I could focus on was the image of the glorious royal-blue costume which I wear in the first scene of Rigoletto. I held on to it firmly as it gave rise to Verdi's unrivalled music in my mind. I believe these two things alone, prevented me from becoming victim to the wheels of a number 9 bus, as I made my way along the Strand, depression and exhaustion swirling around me.

"Heard the latest?" It was an hour before the curtain went up, and the canteen was buzzing. Pixie was bursting with some secret that she could hardly wait to tell. And I was only too pleased to have my mind involved with something. "No, what?" I said.

"We're having a new Chorus Master." She replied. "We all have to troop in and sing to him in the New Year, and he takes over next season."

"Why do we have to audition?" Alan said with a grin. "We should be auditioning him!"

"Fat chance." Laughed another of our basses, then pausing for a few seconds added. "Nice thought though!"

"What's he like?" I asked Pixie. "Well…" She settled herself in tittle-tattle mood. "Not very suitable, in my opinion anyway. From what I've heard, he's very much more interested in thigh muscles than larynxes, if you understand me."

I groaned inwardly. Lust with talent was one thing. Lust,

in a position of power without talent was potentially disastrous. A sudden wave of worry for the company which I had come to regard as my family, lapped against the edges of my mind. Change for change's sake was of no value at all. By this time everyone around three or four tables were vying for attention with the gossip they had heard on the man in question. I heard snippets of all of them. Too tired to become overly involved I let it all wash over me. Eventually they were cut short:

"THIS IS YOUR HALF AN HOUR CALL LADIES AND GENTLEMEN. HALF AN HOUR PLEASE. THANK YOU:"

Pixie turned to me as we made our way upstairs to get changed. "So how did it go?" "How did what go?" Pixie burst into laughter. "Oh come on Tilly, you can't have forgotten already. A certain little something you did last night, which none of us could attend because we were working?"

I grinned at her. "Oh that!" "Yes! THAT" She replied. "How was old misery guts?" I Raised my eyebrows. "Martin sang very well..." "Which of course could mean anything short of total catastrophe." Pixie interrupted..."Bugger Martin, how about you? How did you feel about your singing?"

I hesitated for a moment then I said. "Good, it felt good." "Which means..." My incorrigible friend continued. "That you were probably fantastic."

"What's his name?" The sudden change of subject threw her for a moment. "The new Chorus Master." I asked. She stopped for a moment, thinking. "Um...Jonathan something. Warrener. Yes, Jonathan Warrener. You know him?"

"After the last half-an-hour I feel that I do. And I don't like him very much." I muttered, and Pixie laughed as she pulled me out of the path of our illustrious conductor. He smiled at us. I turned for a second and watched him.

"You know Pixie? That's a really sexy man." Pixie stared at me as if I had sprouted horns. "Matilda Gasgoine." She spluttered. "I never thought I'd live to see the day."

"Well, have you never thought what you might be missing?" I said. "These are very powerful people, I bet…"

"Enough!" She laughed. Then warming to the subject she added wickedly. "You mean so many international conductors, and so little time? Matilda what's happening to you?"

The first wave of exhilaration had already passed. In my mind's eye, I saw Dante, and quietly cursed myself for not seeming to be capable of disentangling sex from total devotion, just once in a while! I turned away hurrying to my dressing room.

"Life!" I muttered.

Verity Baines

The beautiful body of Verity Baines encased in its perfect skin and topped by glorious hair, and neat, if cat-like features, also housed an uncomfortable spirit. In simple terms Verity was something of a psychopath, although she hadn't felt the need to stick a 9inch knife blade into her best friend, at least not since she was at school. But she did so dislike being thwarted in anyway whatsoever. For example men never left Verity, she was the one who performed the: Goodbye-nice-to-have-known-you-don't bother-me- again, ceremony. And to perform it exactly when she felt like it, and with no more care or thought than a roaming rouge animal might have.

In spite of her Father's considerable fortune, she had whored her way around most of Europe and select parts of the United States. Choosing, always and only, very rich men. Men who she privately referred to as the 'clients.' She could sense the power emanating from real money. It was, to her, a rich and heavy perfume and it always led her straight to the owners of the sort of financial excess, that allowed her to glean considerable amounts, using her unquestionable if diabolical charms. Once in the bedroom she behaved as if possessed by demons, driving her 'victims' nuts, and the rest was easy. Or at least that was the way it had always been until now. Now, Verity was having to learn a lesson. It was a very hard lesson since, given her considerable experience with the male sex, she never dreamt that such a situation would ever confront her, that such a lesson would ever be necessary. But since she had met Giorgio, she had to admit that he was different…very different! Exciting, charismatic, and every bit as selfish as she was. It didn't matter what she did, or how hard she tried, everything remained on his terms. There was no lea way. She had searched and searched for what she considered must be the inevitable 'chink' in his armour, but she had found none, neither in, or out of bed.

She had to admit that he was quite remarkable, and finding him so, she stupidly (she soon realised) relaxed her own power game just a fraction, and before she knew it, he was in control and immovable.

Verity couldn't remember ever feeling like a little girl. From her earliest memory she had viewed most other people in the world as 'stupid, gullible and hopelessly naïve.' It was as if she left out childhood altogether, so by the time she was 13 she was ready to try out more recent developments and she had seduced her father's gardener Julio. Well the poor little bugger didn't stand a chance she had boasted to her friend. But Verity was highly intelligent, this was no hormone driven incident. It was on this experience that she based her blue print for later life. But now she was not in control and she didn't like the feeling one little bit. This was what was exciting. This allowed the energy to rise, allowed her to act like a sexual maniac, and therefore give her the power. It was a beautiful wheel that once in motion became automatically perpetual. And the day that Verity discovered that most very rich men were especially vulnerable to her type of frenzy, was her passport to success. She could remember only two occasions when she had made a mistake, until now that is. But this was a very different type of mistake. She couldn't have seen this coming, she assured herself.

Giorgio was that rare and dangerous male whose appetite was enormous, but whose control was even, and to date, always, greater. A woman like Verity was helpless, smitten, and beside herself as to how to handle him. She was capable of so much, she thought in frustration. Giorgio was not playing fair, he refused to give her a free hand. However, there was another great passion which Giorgio provided an outlet for, and that was Opera. Verity adored Opera. She also loved pop, Latin dance music, ethnic music, anything really, but she had a particular weakness for Opera. It swept her imagination off to some pin-point of light where it opened up into another world.

The really bizarre thing about her on-going love affair with this art form, was how she came to be introduced to it. After the debacle of Eileen's death…Had she done that?…No! She didn't think so…She dreamt about the shining knife blade so many times since…It must have been just that, a dream. Of course, if she had done it, then Eileen must have asked for it. She could remember feeling fury, and such a fury. And the fact that it wasn't as easy to drive a knife blade into healthy muscled flesh as you might imagine, and even harder to pull it out. The flesh seemed to embrace it, as if it were aware that once the intruder departs, very much more of its precious life blood will be more easily lost.

Once out, however, the kitchen floor became a sea of blood. She kept slipping on it…in her dream of course. Oh! What the hell! It never had been a dream, she had done it. It was the right thing to have done, she had performed a good deed for the world. Eileen was a pain A silly whingeing little mouse, who had no thoughts of her own, and who had dared to tell Verity that she was not behaving in a very nice way. Also, more to the point, she smiled and simpered at Julio, who smiled and simpered back!

In the end there seemed to be as much blood on her as on Eileen. More maybe! When that disgusting spurting had stopped, and with it the pulse, she watched fascinated, as Eileen's face had gone from pale to ashen. It had occurred to her that had she been a vampire, she would have been able to dispatch the silly girl so much more simply, and in rather better taste! She was about to get herself outside, as the smell of still-warm blood had begun to affect her, when Manuela, the maid entered the kitchen, dropped the tray she was carrying, and let out a piercing scream, all in a single second. Everything then became a blur.

Verity was 13, and Eileen her best friend 14, and very horrid she had been to Verity that day, too. Verity couldn't remember exactly what she had said and done, except that it had started with the same argument as usual, but this time harboured some sort of threat, but she still remembered the rage. So, Eileen must have deserved it. It was all her fault, but other people wouldn't understand that, so she had to invent the 'man.' When, from a sweet 13 year old (Verity was also a good actress) came the obscenities that he was supposed to have uttered. Who would question? Add to that the terrible scene confronting them, and an excellent description from poor little Verity and well, she was home and dry. Everybody handled her with velvet gloves, told her how brave she was, and that she mustn't worry, and attributed her questionable lack of grief, to shock. After a few days they packed her off to a counsellor. This was Verity's first big challenge. The woman was attractive, and very clever. She saw through Verity's lies almost instantly. Verity hated her. However, she too was clever, and knew that she must be careful around Amanda. And it was this creature (whom Verity inevitably regarded as a rival) It was this woman who opened the door to her one day when the overture to 'Don Giovanni' was playing, Verity had, most unusually, walked slowly in to the room, with her eyes wide and incredulous, staring at the stereo equipment as if it were suddenly alive. Her rather high whiney voice had dropped to a sincere pitch as she said.

"Oh please, please don't turn it off. I want to listen." The rest of the session was given over to exhausting Amanda's limited knowledge of Opera. She let it go down that path because it gave her a brief insight to a possible redeemable section of the girl's personality. She had no doubt that Verity had killed Eileen, but no way of proving it. The fact that the 'man' had never been traced, meant nothing. She did ask her out right towards the end of their time together. The girl barely hesitated.

"Look Mandy, you know, and I know!" "Know what Verity?" "The answer Amanda!" Amanda felt a ray of hope, convinced that she had Verity cornered, she expected her to say or do something which would at least give her the opportunity to extend the therapy. She kept her voice low and gentle and said. "What answer Verity?" Instead of dissolving into tears or some temper tantrum Verity replied as cool as you like.

"Amanda, do you feel quite well today? You seem to be going round in circles. Do you have your period or something? Maybe we should stop today until you're feeling more yourself?"

Even from this precocious 13year old with unfathomable psychotic depths, Amanda had not been prepared for that. She gasped, but Verity laughed and said. "Shall we play some more Opera?"

"Aren't you afraid I will tell them?" So now it was out in the open, no more games and pretence. Verity's face didn't change, there was not even a flicker. Just her ever-ready smile as she replied. "Tell them what Amanda? If there was anything to tell, we wouldn't be sitting here now. Except, I suppose we might, since no one would be any the wiser, not if there was anything to tell about me anyway."

Amanda made a mental note to write a paper on this case based on the last sentence alone, that this little terror had uttered. Her almost genius level brains appeared to have nothing anchored in emotion or compassion, because when Amanda asked her.

"What about Eileen's parents?" Verity looked at her with sincere incomprehension and replied. "Why would I think about Eileen's parents Amanda? I scarcely think of my own."

A cold chill had crept up Amanda's legs. There was nothing she could do. Briefly she wondered if the D.N.A. of such a creature would reveal potential alien strands. She made one last attempt. At the open door she said to her.

"Verity you are a brilliant girl, but one day you may need a friend. Remember me if you do." She took hold of Verity's hands, and looked deeply into her dark eyes. Then she took a deep breath and added. "In so far as I am able, I understand."

Verity had chewed her lower lip for a few seconds, almost, she seemed, uncertain. Amanda held her breath, then Verity's mother appeared around the corner, and the monstrous child threw her arms around Amanda's neck, and burst into tears. "Goodbye Amanda, and thank you so much for all your help. I feel so much better about it all now, and I really think that I can put it all behind me, and get on with my life, just as you said I must."

And now there was Matilda! Verity grimaced as an unwelcome picture floated into her mind. Those damn eyes! I mean who the hell has violet eyes for God's sake? Verity hated that type of beauty. The woman had exactly the opposite of her own undeniable looks. Verity wasn't exactly jealous (Verity would never believe that she had need to doubt herself) But what did disturb her was something else. She couldn't put her finger on it, but with Matilda, there was always an extra 'buzz.' She didn't like it, it wasn't something which she could control. And as for Giorgio saying that he wasn't interested in her except as a singer, well that was totally ridiculous. She knew she was right. She sensed the link between them, and what else could it be? God, what did he see in her? The woman was…well she was.. Oh! To hell with it. She didn't care anyway. She just wasn't giving up on Giorgio, not yet.

JOURNAL

You know how some people get hooked on soaps? I actually hear other members of the chorus making statements such as: "I hope he.." (That being their husbands usually).. "remembers to record such and such this evening."

I admit I find it hard to understand this, since I have no interest in this kind of entertainment, and anyway, quite honestly the 'soap' facet of back stage life, is very much more interesting. For a start it's real!

When I had been here only a short time, about half way through my first season, a very beautiful and sexy dancer joined the company. Not the ballet company, but the opera ballet. She had not been here long before she set about engaging the attention of an international baritone, (This was yet another highly tosteronic singer, not the one I was unfortunate to burst in on!)

He is well known for his love of the ladies, and also, for his inability to remain constant to them for more than about 5 minutes! He and his wife both like to drink deeply of life's pleasures as it were, or so I have been told. And the lady is often described as being a thousand times worse than her errant husband.

At the moment it is this story that is most often bandied across the canteen tables, and in the relative privacy of the green room. A place where they both often sit entwined around each other, leaving very little to our fertile imaginations! I know it sounds pathetic to listen to gossip in this way, but frankly, with all the rather distressing things which are occurring in my private life at the moment, it is almost therapeutic. I mean the last thing I want to do, is to get into a discussion about my problems, and this delightful gossip gives one somewhere to go, should the conversation start to 'lag,' and one's friends begin to look too closely, and notice the strain around the eyes, and the tension reflected everywhere else!

Well, Rachel, that's our heroine's name, has been pushed rather suddenly and unkindly to one side. She has not taken this too well. One can't blame her. It seems that the baritone in question was remiss enough to invite her for a drink at his local pub. His wife, (also a singer) who was neither on tour, nor at work at the time, took it into her head to go to the pub and meet him. She walked through the door, only to discover the couple snuggled up to each other, in an inglenook. And apparently, the only thing which will mollify her is a holiday in the Caribbean. And of course it goes without saying, that Rachel is out of his life. Poor Rachel! I have just witnessed what I feel was a rather distressing scene in the canteen, although some people found it amusing. Maybe I'm just being silly, and old fashioned, I don't know. But when you approach a man with whom you have been sleeping for some time, as Rachel did today, and he turns to you and says loudly enough for anyone within ear shot to easily hear. "Yes, now what can I do for you?" With a look on his face of studied boredom, I don't think that 'fashion' has a say. I could cheerfully strangle him frankly, not that Rachel is a particular friend of mine, but she's pleasant enough, and certainly doesn't deserve treatment like that! However, when I expressed this to my friend Maria she said. "Well. He is married you know." "Pity he didn't remember that." I replied, a little angry at the apparent lack of understanding on her part. But before I could say more, Flower, who happened to be sitting with us, added.

"She knew what she was getting into."

"His reputation proceeds him." Said Maria. "I mean everyone knows the score. She can't be that ignorant of the situation."

"But maybe she fell for him. It does happen you know, even to people like him. And since when can a 'reputation' of that sort become that person's defence?" I replied. This was followed by a silence, and I wished I hadn't said quite so much, or anything at all really. I'm not so stupid that I don't realise some of my own frustrations re' Dante were driving me on. Then Flower said quietly.

"Maybe you joined the wrong company Tilly?" "Hmm.. ?" I asked. I was watching the last few seconds of the scene before us.

"Maybe…" She paused for effect. "You should have joined the cloisters!"

I joined in their laughter, I had not meant to appear so stuffy. Anyway there was some truth in what they were saying, and it wasn't my business. AND, much more to the point, they had not seen Rachel's face as she turned away from said baritone. I had, and I know that this little drama is by no means over. Not by a long way! I'll keep you posted.

Prelude To Act Three

Chu-Pen had guided Giorgio for many years. He had helped and strengthened him for one reason only. So that when and if the time came, he, Giorgio would close the Western Gate.

In fact it was Matilda, unknown and unknowing, who was this gate. And it was because of her voice, and the latent potential hidden there. A sacred gift that had begun to blossom in Lothus and was fed by Carlo's great humanity and innocent compassion for his fellow creatures. Music, using the medium of the human voice, was prepared for expansion, not so much of itself in the writing, but through the sound which expressed that writing. There were hidden keys everywhere. The great masters had left them without even knowing themselves what they did. But as these great works were performed the 'keys' locked into place and waited. Only for the moment to pass with no one the wiser. Performers and audience skated over the surface, below which was waiting a release of one of the most exciting steps that the race as a whole has ever taken.

Cu-Pen, however, argued that the race was neither ready, nor deserving of such a fabulous step into new and exciting adventure. An adventure heralded by opera generally, and specifically by an enhancement of natural acoustic. He had held the Eastern Gate for many years. The honour having been bestowed on him by the last Grand Master in Tibet. He had promised Giorgio many more powers if he agreed to help, and to be sure, he was more than capable of giving them to him. Also of considerable concern to him, was what would happen to his kind, should the 'plague' be released? Where would they then stand, in the spiritual power stakes?

If the time came, and left without anything happening. Chu-Pen knew another 100,000 years would pass before the opportunity could present itself again. Before there would be another Atlantis and Lothus. 'No!' He assured himself. 'It is not likely that they will succeed. The 'plague' will be contained, and everything will roll over and repeat itself once more, in ignorance of what has been lost.'

Just to be sure, he kept a watch on Giorgio, he would penetrate into his dreams to speak to him. He needed to ensure that the power remained in the hands of the right people. People like himself, who understood it, and who knew where best to bestow just a little of it, in order to preserve it in its present form.

One of the girls from the village, who helped out at the large villa, belonging to the Vittoria family, stood uncertainly outside the large double doors which opened into the library. She had been sent to clean in this room before, and she didn't like it one bit. When you first entered it seemed quite pleasant, the sun poured in through the long windows for a large part of the day, and even in the winter evenings, with the fire crackling in the grate it was, at first, quite restful. No, it was after you been there for a while. Especially, or maybe only, if you were alone, that the atmosphere of the place made itself known to you. All those books for a start! Of course, she had been admonished several times never under any circumstances to touch them.

"Who would want to?" She had snapped at a friend of hers who also worked in the big house.

"You'd be surprised! They're priceless, some of them." She was quickly informed. Franca was not impressed. As far as she was concerned the books seemed to stare at her from every wall, in a malignant silence. Then, and much more to the point, there was the hum! Oh, everyone laughed at her of course. Told her she was imagining things, that no one else ever heard it. Well maybe they didn't, but she did! And lately it was getting louder. It came from behind the fireplace, as far as she could tell. What could it possibly be? Some electric wiring junction? She sighed and pushed open the door. Soon she would be off to college, she told herself. Soon she wouldn't have to come here anymore. Just a few more months.

If only Dante were around more, it would probably be possible to approach him with her concerns she thought, carefully giving the fireplace a wide berth and heading for the big desk the other side of the room. She moved some of the books and writing materials to one side, and squirted the vanilla-scented polish on to the already shining surface. She had raised the duster to begin to clean, when her breath caught in her throat. The hairs on the back of her neck stood up as she swung round so quickly, that she lost her balance and sat down abruptly on the chair beside her. It was louder than ever! In spite of her racing pulse and dry throat, she stood up, placed the polish and duster on the table, and as if drawn by some magnetic force, walked towards the fireplace. It was the wiring, surely the Count should be informed? Not by her of course, but through the correct household hierarchy. It could be dangerous, and if it caused a fire here with all these books? It didn't bear thinking about! It was her good Italian common sense which encouraged her to place her hand against the wall in the alcove next to the fireplace. She must, she felt discover what it was.

The hum translated into a vibration. It was so strong! It followed a path up her arm, to her shoulder, her neck and…A wooden panel in the wall swung slowly open. Franca's heart was racing so fast that she found herself pressing her clasped hands against her chest, and her whole body was vibrating. She could feel it coming up from her legs and shaking her very core. She took a step toward the dark opening, intensely aware of the squeak of her trainers on the library floor, and the beat of the rain on the windows, which was almost deafening. 'There can't be anyone there.' She told herself, and realised that she must close the panel. She took a deep breath, and pushed the air out through her closed lips, moved quickly forward, and without looking too closely inside the small alcove, she pulled the panel towards her. Just before it clicked back into place she noticed, on a dilapidated, dusty table, piled high with even older looking books, a long thin box.

Her curiosity got the better of her, and any way now that she could see what was actually behind the panel, it didn't bother her half as much. So she stepped over the threshold and with a shaking hand, lifted the lid of the box. She expected it to be locked, or so old that it was too stiff to open. But it was surprisingly easy to lift the lid. She looked inside. How odd! What a strange place to keep part of the family jewels. At least she assumed that is what this was. The Contessa's jewels were famous. Jewels of the House of Vittoria had sparkled from generations of beautiful throats, but she had never heard this piece mentioned. As she stood staring at it she realised two things. That there was something rather masculine about it, and, that it was the source of the 'hum' she had heard whenever she came into this room. Somewhere deep in the emerald green amulet in front of her, there appeared to be some kind of energy field. A force which existed independent of life around it. There was something defiant about it, and Franca couldn't decide in that moment whether it exuded good or evil.

"What are you doing in her girl?" Franca almost left the floor, she was so much taken by surprise. She tried to explain about the 'hum' and the panel opening by itself, but in the cold light of the conversation which followed with the House Keeper, it all sounded very lame. Franca was told that she would be paid to the end of the month, but not to return. She should have felt depressed, demoralised, and maybe even a little worried, she told herself as walked back to her family's home. But she didn't! In fact she felt energised. There were other places where she could get part time work, until the much longed for day when she would be able to set off for Milan to train her considerable operatic soprano at the Conservatoire there.

When she got home, her small brother was suffering from one of his asthmatic attacks. Not overly bad, but Franca felt the tears in her eyes. She adored her little brother. Why should he suffer like this? She felt angry, and scarcely noticed a strange 'buzz' in the palms of her hands. Without thinking she placed them on the little boy's head..

"You don't need this sweetheart, do you?" She spoke gently to him. He shook his head slowly, his dark eyes serious. Their Mother paused in the doorway. There was such a love between these two, that her heart seemed to swell and stretch into the room as she witnessed it. Franca took the little boy on her lap, and gently rocked him back and forth while softly singing one of his favourite pieces of music. He had heard her practise it so often, that even at his young age, he could recognise instantly the haunting Puccini, as the phrases rose and fell.

'O mio bambino caro.' Whispered Franca. 'Mi piace bello, bello.' Lisped her brother with difficulty through the asthma. Then he closed his eyes, and resting against his big sister fell mercifully asleep. The Italian evening wore on. By bedtime the little boy was breathing much more easily. By morning, he was completely recovered. He never suffered an attack again.

Irena was also ill. It wasn't anything that you would notice, not yet anyway. The doctors had given her two or three years, unless she agreed to a course of treatment that would begin immediately. Even then, there was no guarantee of a total recovery. Irena had no intention of putting herself through the gruesome treatment. She didn't know exactly what she was going to do, but it wasn't going to entail destruction of every fighting ability residing in the natural resources of her body.

"I don't mean to be rude. But do you people really agree with this sort of procedure?" She had asked her consultant.

"I'm afraid that at the moment, it's all we have. Go home and think about what I have said. Please think very deeply."

Remembering this conversation of just a short while ago, Irena poured herself another glass of sherry, knowing that she shouldn't do so. It was, after all, barely 11:00o'clcok in the morning. She would break the habit soon, very soon. The sweet liquid was comforting, and she was angry. Was this where her life had led her? Apart from the illness there was the solitude, she hated the alienation, loathed sitting in her quiet house waiting for the phone or the door bell to explode into the silence. At the same time that her incredible ear, musical intelligence and enviable experience were acknowledged by the highest strata of the profession, she was no longer allowed to be part of a company. She had been in opera houses all her working life, and to be separated from the day to day working in a company now for no good reason, (except that she was 70) was rather like being imprisoned. What a narrow age this was! And they all thought they were so sophisticated! 70 was nothing for a musician. Indeed for any artist, maybe anyone at all, if they were ever allowed to prove it. One continued to expand and grow. What she had had to concentrate on in her 40's and 50's, had recently become so much second nature, that she could almost tell by the way a singer inhaled before the first phrase what the problem would be, she was rarely wrong. She often asked God why he hadn't removed her talent, since he deemed it just fine to remove everything else, including now, it seemed, her health! The only light on the horizon, the only definite link to her deeper and more sensible beliefs about who was really responsible for her future, was the possibility of working with the young singer she had heard at the concert a while ago. Giorgio's student, Matilda Gasgoine. Something happened when that young woman opened her mouth and sang, in spite of the things that were not yet corrected in her technique, something definitely happened! And it was different enough, this 'something' to help Irena forget her own worries for long enough to relax a little.

Irena knew Giorgio from many years before. She had recognised him instantly as he sat in the auditorium. His handsome profile was turned away from her as he faced the stage, seemingly completely absorbed with the performance. She remembered the way his dark wavy hair always sat just over the top of his collar as it did that evening. And his relaxed cat-like manner, breathed a sensual power over any unsuspecting female. None of that had changed with the years, none of that had changed one little bit. It brought yesterday so close suddenly, that it made her shudder. She wasn't surprised that he had amassed both fortune and reputation, considering his charisma, and his very real ability to help heal vocal problems which had denied medical counselling and normal teaching practice.

She had coached the baritone after Giorgio had worked his magic on him and she was delighted to find his voice completely recovered. She had to admit, and was indeed glad to do so that the young man could now fly through Verdi (as indeed he was born to do) when only a short time before he was unable to utter a singing sound.

Thankfully, Giorgio had not recognised her either at the concert or at the restaurant afterwards, and she passed as one of Bella's friends. Being quite a bit older than Giorgio, she had no doubt, changed physically more than he had, and anyway their association in the past had always been fraught. A younger Irena had not yet learnt to rein in her considerable temperament at that time. But her exquisite ear had picked up on many bad habits in the young Giorgio's singing. It had certainly not been her place as a colleague to say anything to him at all. And he had not taken kindly to the advice she offered.

"Mind your own business. " He snarled. And many such incidents had flared into artistic fights of the kind most dreaded by the managements that they worked for. Ironically, in performance it often drew out sublime singing from Irena, intent on proving her point to Giorgio. And indeed forced the young errant tenor to his best work. Even their acting in the inevitable and many love scenes translated from hate to grand passion. Many people believed them embroiled in a highly-charged affair, the audiences especially. However this was far from the case, and when vocal damage rendered the sound, if still authoritative, too wayward for professional companies, there was no one for Giorgio to turn to. It was too late. He had disappeared from the German Opera House where they had both been working at the time, and she had heard nothing of him until the concert. This brought her back to Matilda. Had she heard what she thought she'd heard? Or had it been her imagination? She tutted impatiently.

"They're getting to you Irena. " She spoke aloud to herself. If she were an international conductor, she wouldn't question herself like this, and neither would anyone else! It was just that it was something she had not encountered before. And she wasn't quite sure what she would do with it, even if she were given the chance. All she knew was that it was a breath of fresh air, and that there was something hauntingly familiar about it. The familiarity hovered like a soft cloud, and inside the cloud, as she looked deeper, with the help of the sherry, she saw terror, destruction, and a vast golden hope.

ACT THREE

Villa Giorgio

Villa Giorgio, which will soon house Giorgio's dream is absolutely fantastic. I was not prepared for it I have to admit, although both Martin and Giorgio have mentioned it many times in the course of conversation. But never did they go into any real detail or intimate the size and staggering potential of the building and grounds. And properly managed, I even begin to believe that it might one day rival Glyndebourne. It had at one time been a farm, quite modest but large enough to be identified as a 'home farm.' All the land has been reclaimed by nature and the only domestic animals there now are 2 or3 horses, (Giorgio adores horses) numerous cats, and 4 rather fierce guard dogs. They seem to be something of a mixture, but I imagine that they have some Doberman Pincer running happily through their veins. Once properly introduced however, they never forget you and will protect and guard you (should the need arise) with their lives.

"Do you ride?" Asked Giorgio. He had driven me down from London. To travel by car was one thing. To try the same journey with tight Opera House schedule, on public transport, quite another, the changes alone could have taken all afternoon.

"Well not for ages, but I used to love it." I replied, remembering the excitement on Saturdays, when I set out for the local stables.

"You must come prepared sometime soon. Then we can take in the estate. It's really very beautiful, especially my amphitheatre!" I nodded. I could well believe it and the idea of an amphitheatre was indeed magical. "All this makes me home sick. Not for home exactly, I haven't been for ages, but for the country. You know what I miss the most?"

"What?" Asked Giorgio.

"Being outside after dark. Does that sound crazy? There's nothing quite like it, it's wonderful."

"I agree. I often go out at night myself. We sound like a couple of vampires." Said Giorgio.

"Oh! Didn't you know?" I joked. Giorgio laughed and the sound reminded me of the evening he took me to dinner at the restaurant, when he first met Verity. I glanced around wondering where she was. My scalp prickled just a little when Giorgio, in an exaggerated gesture, leaned closer to me and whispered a little disloyally, I felt.

"The witch has flown." "Giorgio!" I admonished him lightly, wondering as I did so if I went too far, but he smiled and replied.

"Oh, I don't mean that quite as it sounds, cara. Just enjoying a few days peace and quiet." And I fully understood that Verity might well not know the meaning of personal space, except her own of course! He changed the subject.

"Come, lunch is ready. We mustn't dawdle, you have a show tonight I believe?"

"Yes." I answered "I shall have to be back by 6:300ish."

"No problem, cara. I shall run you right to the stage door."

I must describe a little of Villa Giorgio. I am full of admiration for anyone who has the mental energy to conceive such an ambitious plan, as I am gob smacked by the number of noughts on various bank accounts that it would undoubtedly take to engineer it. The whole project is basically ready for the (no doubt) 'grand opening,' although no date has as yet, been set. Certainly no more construction or remodelling can be necessary. The kitchens are fully equipped to deal with the restaurant, where we had our lunch, to 'christen' it as Giorgio put it. There will be chefs, indoor staff, outdoor staff, a housekeeper, and that's before the music even begins, My head was spinning and Giorgio smiled back at me over very fine pasta.

"You worry for me Matilda? Don't. The restaurant itself will soon pay back much of the outlay. I intend it to earn it's own name, and quite separate from the Opera company. You must own me to know good food and wine."

Of course I did! Giorgio is, as they say, the owner of a fine palate. He continued, explaining that the music, and the company's reputation would develop very much more slowly. This was to be expected. He wanted orchestral participation he told me. "Opera just isn't the same without it, is it cara? But then of course, you are spoilt, since you sing regularly with arguably the best operatic orchestra in the world" And he smiled at me with that smile he uses when he wishes to convey something other than what he is saying, Although I can't work out why, nor what his real feelings are regarding my career position. It is quite ridiculous actually. I mean anyone would think I am a famous soloist! But it is a smile which says I am in charge, don't even think about gainsaying me.

"It adds considerably to the financial out lay of course, there are so many of them to pay." He laughed, "But I shall not worry about that, just take one day at a time." The feeling from that smile hadn't completely dissipated, and as usual I felt the need to say something, anything. I pulled my mind into 180 degree turn from what I was thinking and said.

"This is a huge project Giorgio, what if…"

"If it fails, it fails. I would be sad, but it wouldn't be the end of the world. The trick is not to become overawed by anything. You have to be able to shrug your shoulders and move on, should that prove necessary. Let's hope that doesn't happen." And he raised his glass to mine. I had broken my no drinking before a performance rule at his special request to drink the future of this venture. And why not? I do after all wish him well with it. He placed his glass down and continued.

"Don't worry cara. I shall, of course, soon do all my teaching here, when I have sold my house in town. I know it's a difficult journey without a car, but you don't need me too much at the moment anyway."

'I don't?' I thought. I was slightly suspicious of such a statement. He'd said we would 'coast' not give up altogether. Giorgio caught my eye, then, (as so often happens) he looked quickly away as if I reminded him of something he didn't like, or something he didn't care to remember. He appeared momentarily, almost afraid of something. Considering his devil-may-care attitude concerning what must run into millions of pounds, I find this most strange. I changed the subject.

"All this has happened very quickly." He was immediately normal again and assured me.

"There wasn't a huge amount to do actually, which was why I was attracted in the first place. The theatre was already here. Many of the ensuite bathrooms. I needed to redecorate, but the really big job was the grounds. Bringing in trees to make instant wooded areas, to compliment the amphitheatre which is where I intend to give birth, as it were, to the company. Luckily much of the land had already run back to Mother Nature. But if you've finished your lunch Matilda, we'll look over the house."

Where can I start with the house? The first 2 floors are given over entirely to the theatre, dressing rooms, a green room, rehearsal areas, the restaurant, and bars. The house was originally the country seat of some long-forgotten aristocrat in the 18th. Century, and the inside theatre which is by no means as small as I assumed it would be, had a lovely acoustic for singing. The orchestra pit is deep and it will be easy for the conductor to accommodate the singers.

"It's perfect." I breathed. "I think so." Giorgio agreed as he placed his arm round my shoulders. Why did I feel so uncomfortable? In the operatic world, touchy, touchy and any excuse for a kiss was commonplace. Anybody complaining was soon told not to be so precious or consider themselves so wonderful. But this felt different. Why did I automatically assume that an affectionate gesture on Giorgio's part, covered a dark and even sinister motive?

"I would so like you to be part of all this Matilda." His voice was low and gave you the impression that he was speaking in your mind. Many people found his eyes hypnotic, and while I believe them, I have to admit that I never experience this. But his voice, especially as it was now, 'cupo' in Italian, was having a strange effect. It echoed of Carlo. He drew closer and my stomach turned over. What had I done? I was virtually alone here in this huge place and with a man who at the least possessed startling self confidence, and at the most, strange powers, and to boot, a man I do not really trust.

"Does Verity like it?" I asked intending lightness. My voice refused to play ball and it sounded exactly as I felt. I could feel the heat from his body. Even through my tenseness it occurred to me that his energy must be vast to put out an acknowledgeable heat such as this.

"Why should I give a damn for what Verity thinks. I don't you know…" He added staring into the auditorium as he began to stroke my shoulder with his fingers…"Give a damn what she thinks about anything. That is not how I am. I don't become subservient to any terms or conditions placed on me by other people. And most of you try you know. Oh yes you do."

'Move' Screamed an inner voice. 'Give me a reason.' I screamed back. I knew without any doubt that it was not his intention to push things any further. He was enjoying the precipice we were on. It had a timelessness which he didn't want to interfere with. It suddenly occurred to me that he was torturing himself, but that the torture was exquisite and far in preference to any redemption, whatever that might be. Briefly the old man came towards me. Turning round and round like a ballet dancer. Giorgio sensed my tension, it would have been hard not to have done.

"Don't you think that you've done your 'bit' as a chorister?"

"I don't think of it like that Giorgio. It's the music…I can't explain it…It's a wonderful place to be. If other things happen, they'll happen and I'll know that's the time to move."

"Will you Matilda? It's not always so easy to walk away from regular money when you've become used to it you know."

"Giorgio, I'm not ambitious … I never have been… I just love the music."

"Well." Said Giorgio, continuing to rub my shoulder so gently that I had to concentrate to be aware if he were actually doing so, but at the same time making the muscles in my arm jump involuntarily. God I pity Verity, I bet he's a handful. He stopped, almost as if he read my thoughts, but he remained extremely close to me. He said.

"That is a terrible waste, Matilda. You saw for yourself what happened at the concert. Martin was very much put into the shade, and he's a tenor."

"And I'm just a common Soprano, is that it? If people spent less time making stupid comparisons, and did away with ridiculous 'tenor scenario' and the theories given ludicrous birth by it all, singers like Martin (since you bring him up) might well receive much more the kind of response which they crave. At the moment he's singing for the wrong reason isn't he? Hello world I'm a tenor so I'm bound to knock your socks off!"

There was a pause. I was afraid I had said too much, after all Giorgio is also a tenor, and I do appreciate the sound of that voice. I waited. Giorgio sighed in his breath, the theatre seemed warm, almost drowsily so. Finally he answered.

"Ah Matilda, you are very wise." He was laughing at me,

I'm quite sure of that. "But don't you see? The reason it's a waste is not about the voice. You're sincere love of music means that you don't sing for effect. You put yourself second to the music, unconsciously and completely. Thus your pure love shines through and it affects people. And this time…" In spite of his closeness I turned towards him and looked hard at him as he continued…"This time it's your turn, as it were. You mustn't waste it. In fact it would be very wrong of you to do so. There are things that you need to put right from before. Things which can only be put right this way."

"Are you talking about Venice, and Carlo?" 'My Carlo.' I added to myself. Turning back to the auditorium I stared purposefully at the stage. I was furious with Giorgio. That sound, that wonderful sound which I don't, in my wildest dreams even assume I could ever now approach, had been mine! I'm not jealous of the fact. How can one be jealous of oneself? Carlo is for me an inspiration. All the more so because no one can recreate that type of voice anymore. Castrated or not, the knowledge has gone for ever. Giorgio has no right to impose on all of this. I felt very close to tears, as if someone were threatening my identity… Then he was there, A very young Carlo came to me. A young and freshly mutilated boy, crying and sobbing uncontrollably, in terrible shock and some pain.

"They've taken me away." He sobbed as Angelo held him on the blood stained bed and rocked him gently, as if he were a baby.

"Capisco, capisco tutto! I understand it all. They haven't taken you away my Carlo. You will never be hurt again."

"No." Gasped Carlo. It was said with fury. "No I will not,

never again!" He began to moan, a deep guttural sound which rose from his depths until it tore into his throat with such a fury, that even Angelo with all his experience was disturbed. Carlo raised his head and stared at the ceiling. The cry went on and on. Angelo had never witnessed such agony, or such breath control. They always cried, of course they did, just as he had done. But he had never seen such rage. One felt that the very earth might quake with fear. At last Carlo stopped, but his eyes were glazed, and stared unseeing from his lovely head. Angelo took him by the shoulders.

"You are angry? You hate them? Then repay them Carlo. Sing, sing until they beg you for mercy. Put their hearts and minds on the velvet rack of music and torture them, and when they beg you to stop, when they writhe on the floor in their agony, take them away from themselves and leave them amongst the stars. BE Carlo, Kill them with your voice."

And at last the lad had relaxed, and quietly wept himself to sleep. Angelo called for ointments and clean sheets. He washed him, and did what he could for the pain. Then he sat with him all night and the next day, while Carlo lay drugged with potions to help him forget his agony. Gradually he healed. Gradually he became stronger. One evening not too long after he presented himself at Angelo's door, and on it being opened said to his compassionate friend and teacher.

"Maestro, I am ready…." "Are you ready Matilda?" I was so confused I replied without thinking. "Si Maestro…I'm ready."

"For some tea Matilda. Then I'll get you back to the Opera House. Will that be O.K?" He kissed me briefly on the cheek. I barely noticed it. His eyes searched deeply into my face, and I pulled myself forward with difficulty.

"Tea would be lovely Giorgio, thank you." "Good, well come on then. I bet you can't find the way back!"

"Bet I can." I laughed. He waved me ahead with a smile. As I turned our journey on its head, I found myself thinking. 'Why can't he be like this all the time?'

Enter Jonathan

Giorgio backed the car by the side of the Opera house and prepared to drive home. He was sitting quietly for a few moments, musing on Matilda's 'dream sequence,' some people would have thought she was day-dreaming, Giorgio knew better, when his attention was caught by a familiar figure leaving the stage door. He opened the car door and leaning out he shouted.

"Hey, Jonathan, over here it's me, Giorgio!"

The man stopped, and recognition lifted his rather sour face into a delighted smile. In a few strides he was by the side of Giorgio's beautiful deep-green Porsche. Grabbing the hand extended out of its door he whistled low and long, his eyes roving over the lines of the car as if it were a woman.

"What a beauty!" He breathed. Giorgio grinned and said. "Haven't seen you for ages Jonathan. How are you? Here get in."

He leaned across and opened the passenger door. Jonathan lowered himself into the car and leant back in the seat. What he wouldn't give to own a car like this. Giorgio noted the open envy with amusement.

"What are you doing in this part of town? And at 'Mecca' no less!" He grinned. Jonathan brought himself back to planet earth.

"Actually I'm going to be working there."

Oh?" Giorgio felt a prickle of interest. He needed to keep company with Jonathan for longer than polite, long-time-no-see-how-are-you?

"Well, I was about to go and eat. Care to join me? We can catch up on what's been happening since we last spoke, which was, when? Oh ages, yes?"

"Why not, that's a great idea Giorgio, thanks!"

Giorgio smiled to himself. Ask someone out for a meal, it never failed. "Well this is a pleasant coincidence." He continued as Jonathan pulled on his seat belt. In actual fact Giorgio didn't believe in coincidences, and every instinct was on alert. "Do you still live in Surrey? We'll go to a place I know down there, and I'll drive you home afterwards, how's that?"

"That sounds great." Replied Jonathan, and he allowed himself to blend into the power of the car as Giorgio pressed his foot down and they left the centre of town with the energy of a baby jet. After a while, without prompting Jonathan began to explain.

"It's all still a bit hush-hush at the moment. It's certainly not general knowledge that the Opera House is in the process of engaging a new chorus-master. But you know how these things get out."

Giorgio nodded slowly, but he smiled to himself. Everyone knew, of course! Martin had mentioned the fact to him only a few days ago, although he hadn't divulged the name, indeed that piece of information he obviously hadn't known, since Giorgio had asked him. Jonathan sighed deeply and continued. "This was the final interview, just to dot the I's cross the T's as it were. It'll be a great job! Just when I need it too! Although I'm a little nervous about facing that chorus. I've heard they can be tough on chorus masters. Teaching and coaching the music is one thing. But all those egos at one time and every day? God help me."

Giorgio laughed but said nothing. Jonathan looked at him. "What?" He asked. Giorgio changed gears, and the car purred out into the beginning of the green belt, passing everything in it's path with the ease and grace of a cheetah.

"I'm quite sure you don't have too much to worry about my friend. Remember most of them have been there for years, they love what they do or they'd have left. Most of them know the entire rep' backwards, they must do…"

"But?" Jonathan pushed him, hearing the word on the air as clearly as if it had been spoken. Giorgio quickly assured him.

"Oh nothing to concern you. It's just that I have a student in the chorus at the moment, a right little madam."

"Really? Who is she?" Jonathan continued to play straight into Giorgio's hands. Giorgio sighed and appeared to consider, finally replying.

"I don't know if I should name names, but then you'll get to know her soon enough, and Jonathan you must keep positive you know! You'll make a great chorus master."

"Lets' hope…But who is she Giorgio?" And Giorgio played his little game. "Who?"

"The singer in the chorus, the madam?" Jonathan was sounding frustrated, just as Giorgio wanted him. "Ah!" He appeared to remember. "Matilda, Matilda Gasgoine, generally known as Tilly I believe."

Jonathan frowned and after a silence he said. "Now where have I heard that name? I believe they are quite impressed with that young lady."

"Well of course they are." Beamed Giorgio. "I told you she's my student. I didn't say she wasn't talented, she is, very. But it'll be wasted. Bound to be, she'll never leave the chorus, of that I'm quite sure."

"Matilda, Matilda…Ah of course, Richard! A friend of mine, he was playing for some…reauditions, last season not long before they went off to Milan, I think it was. Well, he said that they were discussing the possibility of doing something about her, whatever that may mean. He said they talked about it for at least 10 minutes."

Giorgio was irritated. "Oh? She didn't tell me."

"Well to be fair, she wouldn't have known. I don't think the pianist is supposed to broadcast what he hears, good or bad."

"Hmm!" Was all Giorgio said as he turned off the dark country road and headed towards the restaurant. He had had no idea about any of this, and although it didn't exactly surprise him, it did however jolt him a little. He felt vulnerable, not Giorgio's style! A stroke of luck like that for Matilda, and she may well elude him. Then there would be no choice in the matter, he would have to resort to… "Ouch!"

"What's up Giorgio, you O.K?"

"Just hungry." Giorgio replied as icy-green eyes stared at him from the dash-board. "Let's go!"

The restaurant was situated several yards from the main road.

Jonathan looked around him. It was nothing if not sumptuous. It was quiet and efficient, quite perfect in fact.

"How do you find these places Giorgio?"

"I have to admit that I haven't been here for a while, so let's hope that the food is still as good as it used to be. You know it's very stupid of me. I could have shown you Villa Giorgio on the way here. You must come down soon, before you become too busy with your new job."

On the drive down Giorgio had mentioned the outline of his project, and now Jonathan cursed under his breath. He had not really paid too much attention. It sounded too fantastic, and he had switched off, half wondering if his old friend had 'lost it.'

"Actually…" Giorgio continued, quite aware of Jonathan's discomfort…"It was Matilda I dropped off at the theatre just before you came out. She had been down to see the property. Surely you must have passed her at the stage door?"

Jonathan was glad the difficult moment had disappeared in the thread of another topic. He thought back. "Hmm…Tallish, dark hair, unusual violet eyes and very pale skin?"

"Yes that'd be her." Giorgio nodded, nonchalantly viewing the menu. He knew that Jonathan's preference was for short skirted blondes, natural or not, he didn't really care, as far as Giorgio remembered. "Beautiful girl." He continued. "Stands out a bit on stage though."

(Giorgio had never seen Matilda on stage at the Opera house, or any other operatic stage come to that.)

"Does she?" Jonathan said.

"Actually, yes…just that bit too tall, you know? I think for the chorus, the smaller the better. What do you think?"

Jonathan immediately became animated. "If you really want to know. I think it looks a bloody mess most of the time, and if you want my opinion…"

"Oh I do Jonathan, I am, after all, about to form my own company, remember?"

"Well." The other man continued, getting into his stride. "They seem to have these crazy ideas. For instance, that a good 'mix' is best…" At which Giorgio tut-tutted and shook his head.

"I have ideas and I intend, if I get the chance, to instigate a few changes, for example…" Jonathan was off now like an intercity express…"Both vocal and visual I…"

Giorgio faded in and out of his guest's diatribe. The wine had arrived, but Jonathan barely noticed. Giorgio quietly poured it and sipped gratefully on the richness. He had to endure this twaddle (as he believed it to be.) He made all the right outer signs of understanding, but inwardly he groaned. This man was about to strike at the very foundation of a superb chorus, of whom it had been said, in his hearing, by a very famous Italian baritone, that they were the best in the world. His attention had wandered even further, when he suddenly realised that Jonathan had changed track. He was looking into his glass, having at last picked it up.

"I need to be successful with this job, very successful actually. I've…er…I've been a bit stupid."

"How so Jonathan?" Giorgio was totally focused once more on the other man.

"Well it's the tax man really!" He sounded so sombre suddenly after his enthusiastic outburst, that Giorgio laughed.

"Oh you mean he's been stupid!" He said.

"Not really. More like mean. Well I guess it's all my fault. But the fact is I'm into the tune of £20,000 in some form of horrendous, monthly payments of...Oh god. I haven't dared to register how much...Until, well it feels like until I die. Which I mustn't do too soon, or on my next visit to this planet of ours, I'll probably have a tax demand printed on my bloody forehead."

Giorgio smiled to himself, and for two reasons. One: £20,000 was peanuts to him, and Two: This fact just might make it possible to use Jonathan. He grinned across the table saying. "You sound as if you could do with a, shall we say, more experienced accountant?" Jonathan nodded slowly, and Giorgio added. "Also a good friend?"

The tax evader looked non-plussed, then he smiled. "Oh you mean a rich friend?"

"Well, surely you'd rather repay an understanding pal and have the tax department off your back?"

Jonathan looked thoughtful, he wasn't quite sure where this was going. "£20,00 is a lot of money Giorgio." Who the hell did he think was going to lend him that?

There was a short silence. Then Giorgio drew in a deep breath and focused on his dinner guest with a formidable concentration.

"I don't want to boast dear boy, but that really is nothing for me." He replied quietly. He felt the thickening of the energy in the air, and he probed Jonathan's aura.

"I could write you a cheque for a full amount right now. Pay the bastards off, get all that off your back, start your new job with a clean slate. Then..." And he paused in his usual rather cruel manner. It was all Jonathan could do to remain quiet.

"Then you can either pay me as and when you can manage it, or do me a really big favour."

Jonathan could feel his pulse suddenly slow and heavy in his throat. Short of killing someone, any alternative would be like a miracle. He was literally at a loss for words. Unfortunately, like most people finding themselves in such a situation, he was also at a loss to hear the tiny voice in his mind questioning why? It was like a continuous hum until, not being given any attention, it stopped.

Later, after a superb meal, long discussion of the 'good old days' and the depositing in Jonathan's pocket, of a cheque written for more money than he ever thought that he would see in one place, they were in the car again and speeding towards a small village not far away. Giorgio dropped him off, they promised to be in touch soon, and then he headed towards the motorway, Heathrow, and the errant Verity, this moment on a return flight from Switzerland. Giorgio let the Porsche roar and purr with arrogant ease. He could feel the resentment from the driver of almost every car he sailed passed. At the moment he felt good, very good.

At last Carlo was in his sights…Shit! He really must not confuse the two, one though they may be (in his mind anyway.) He had felt a great love for Carlo at one time. He was not so careless as to imagine that the effect of that love had totally died. He did not need it rising up like a shining angel at just the wrong time. No, what he should have thought was…Matilda was in his sights.

He had not suffered from his 'condition' recently, and he always hoped that one day it would be vanquished for ever, while leaving him with the benefits of course! And finally there was

Verity. There was something about Verity which made him want to hold on to her, for the moment anyway. In some ways they were kindred spirits. Indeed, if he were honest, he felt as if his life had opened up since he met her. So long as he could continue to easily hold her off from taking over parts of his life style that were sacred, he found himself quite excited regarding the immediate future. Especially since the main stumbling block, i.e. The Opera House, looked as if for a mere £20,000 would be removed, and Matilda would be so much easier to destroy without that large impressive company behind her. There was a slight ripple of regret, but it was not conscience. The fact was that Verity had been right. Her cat-like instinct laser-beamed to the truth of the matter. Giorgio did fancy Matilda. In fact it was more than that, he often suffered overwhelming desire when he was around her. A certain movement of her head, the way she responded to music, even, occasionally her phrasing when she was singing, it could become almost painful. But even had she been willing, such a consummation would never be able to be part of the plan. He needed to keep his energy on edge where she was concerned. It was delicious and it motivated him perfectly.

When the pain became too much, he simply took it by the hand, and allowed himself to sink deeply into its realness. He took each point of agony to its further-most reaches and fought it by quietly allowing it to overwhelm him. Eventually, it stopped. Then he could return to the world, shriven of its power and strengthened by the awareness that he could vanquish that under which most people would stumble and fall.

Irena

And what of Dante and me? I have not as yet fully assimilated my position with Dante. I am grateful that my busy lifestyle is protecting me from agonising over the situation. I don't dare look it in the face. I don't dare sound the words in my head. Somewhere in my mind there is a black hole, which at the moment contains all the history of the last few days, the tears, and the heavy hopeless emotion. For now I have to keep it all in darkness. And so I have confided in on one. I am too numb to cry and it is easier not to talk. Anyway, I am not ready to release any of this agony. And, I'm trying very hard to hold on to the faith Dante asked me to remember, and cherish it in the fore front of my mind.

Tomorrow I see Irena for the first time, and I'm really looking forward to it. I have much work to do. My recital is beginning to loom on the horizon. There will be another Tony London concert, and my performance of 'Butterfly' with Pixie…So much to do. And I've been dreaming every night recently, and always of Raimondo.

"No darling you can't breath there!"

"Oh. O.K. where then?"

Irena reflected. Matilda was too pliable! It helped her musical side of course, but it did tend to dampen the temperament which Irena was sure lurked in there somewhere. But there was time to allow that to blossom later, when the technique was conquered. She brought her attention back to the moment.

"You don't breath during that phrase at all." She answered.

"But I must have at least a 'snatch' breath. I don't think I can do it without" Matilda said.

"Yes you can, and yes you will. Listen!" Irena stood up. In some ways she denied her age to the eye. To the ear it was denied completely. She breathed almost without visible movement, and proceeded to fill the room with glorious sound, executing the high, difficult phrase in one, single, easy breath. Her voice was as fresh as a young woman's. It was beautiful. Perfectly focused and the pitch never wavered for an instant. Matilda's mouth dropped in disbelief and when Irena had finished, she could not contain herself.

"Please show me how to do that, Irena!" Irena sighed and said gently. "Musically I can, but I can't get into vocal technique. It isn't ethical my dear."

"But I really need this Irena. I feel, I have always felt, that I'm on a wing and a prayer. That if I hadn't been blessed with a resilient instrument, I would already be in big trouble."

'And still could be!' Thought Irena. Resilient instrument or not, a voice would only take so much abuse. In the ensuing silence, Irena stroked the piano keys, her eyes cast down. Then she bathed Matilda in the full force of her amazing smile.

"What I can do is give you my honest opinion as to what I hear in your singing. In the sound itself, and what I feel that you need to do about it."

Matilda nodded and braced herself. She both wanted and dreaded this.

"O.K Sit down Matilda. Now this is what I hear. Your throat is not open. I know you think it must be, but believe me it isn't, not completely anyway. And most especially not, in the back here." And she laid her hand across the lower part of Matilda's head.

"But, surely that can't open up can it? It's my head, it's solid bone." She exclaimed.

"It's the back of your throat, and it must open up. It's soft tissue, which will become very flexible if you work at opening it."

"Well I suppose I have, very occasionally, been aware of some sensation there. But not all the time." Matilda replied. To which, Irena nodded, sniffed, and carried on.

"You don't support enough, actually those two things are linked, believe it or not. Then there's your breathing. You sometimes gasp for your breath, especially when you feel stretched. It's all much too laboured. You look as if you're trying to empty the room of oxygen. Try taking in as much as you would to appreciate the perfume of a flower. Also, you consistently push the sound up from a lower register to the higher ones. That must stop as soon as possible!"

By this time Matilda was staring at her in horror, and she added more gently.

"But you do possess, in my opinion, a fine and very beautiful instrument, with fabulous potential. What you do with it is up to you."

There was a long silence. The clock ticking in the hall, sounded suddenly louder, and children passing outside on the road, cut into the room like the sound of a television with the volume up too loud. Irena moved on the stool and waited. Matilda knew that she had to have this knowledge, there was no way she was going to pass it up. But Giorgio, as always was there, ominous, in the background. She felt trapped and the only way out was to be honest with Irena.

"You must think me very silly, having just asked you for advice, and then seem to be hesitating, but…"

"Giorgio?" Inquired Irena.

"I don't know why I find it so hard to state out loud certain facts that have worried me about his teaching. I've admitted it to myself a hundred times." Matilda said. Irena nodded as if she understood exactly what Matilda was trying to say.

"All I can say is that in this business you have to watch the 'loyalty trap.' Sometimes people go into that, and never find their way out. This is your life, and your career, it is not Giorgio's. I suggest you go away and think about it. We can continue work today, if you'd like to. But, try to be brave enough to discuss it with him, you never know, he might be relieved. Men don't always know what to do with female voices you know. They don't really understand them enough. But you won't catch many of them admitting it!" She added with a wicked grin. Matilda smiled back, then said.

"Do you know Giorgio, Irena?"

"From long ago, yes. I understand the difficulty which you

may feel you have with him, believe me. And Matilda, I am going to say something now. I shall never refer to it again, nor will I repeat it. In my opinion, Giorgio is dangerous."

Matilda felt a shiver, while her intellect questioned the sanity of the woman seated in front of her.

"You may think me mad, and I could easily be wrong. But I feel that I must say this to you, So, whatever you decide, please be careful. And please don't forget one thing. Because you don't need anyone to teach you that. SUPPORT! Not one note without it, you understand? In the bath. In the chorus, when you think it doesn't matter because no one can hear you and you can coast that day, because you're tired. It does matter, and you can't coast, ever. Standing at the bust stop, on the tube whenever there is music running through your head, support it, pull it on to your body, and imagine the highest harmonic you possibly can at the same time, and SUPPORT IT! Now, shall we work?

Matilda nodded and they returned to the music.

Pixie slumped down on to the empty seat opposite Maria. "God, I'm exhausted. All this and Butterfly too!"

Inwardly Maria groaned. Pixie was not her most favourite colleague at the Opera House, and she too was tired. Actually they all were. The ballet was away on tour, and this always put more strain on the chorus. Where the two girls found the time or the energy to rehearse Butterfly as well, Maria couldn't begin to fathom. She had realised that Matilda had seemed a little odd lately, almost secretive. This was so unlike her, that Maria's curiosity, not to say concern was aroused. Reluctantly she decided to open up a little to Pixie. She leaned across the canteen table.

"Pixie, is Matilda O.K.? I mean, I don't want to pry, but is everything alright?"

"You too, eh?" Pixie grinned. "I was about to ask you the same question. I don't know. Has she mentioned Dante to you lately?"

"No, not especially. Oh yes! I asked after him, and she said he was fine." Replied Maria. "Hmm." Pixie mused. "Look, I'll try and have a word with her, if there's ever time for one which isn't sung!"

Maria laughed. "Too right. Come back the ballet, all is forgiven!"

"I'm fine, really I am. Bless you both but…Oh shit! O.K. Dante and I have reached something of an impasse. A rather difficult situation with his family…And this new coach I've started to work with, who is fabulous by the way, thinks I need major surgery to pull my voice into line. Apart from that everything's just dandy!"

Pixie looked so amazed, and at a loss for words that Matilda burst into laughter. Her shoulders shook with it and continued to do so, until with her head in her hands, everything melted into sobs. Pixie pulled her into a quiet bar near to the tube station where they were headed after the performance. She spoke to her firmly.

"Alright Miss Hold-it-all-in-till-you-bust. I can take on the world and not notice. GIVE! After I've got some drinks."

Pixie had her own ideas about the 'Italian situation' as she had begun to call it. She seemed to think it was terribly romantic to be the mistress of a Count.

"Anyway with this job Tilly we're all so busy. I mean, it's

your whole life isn't it? So this arrangement with the Italian aristocracy is perfect as far as I can see. Think about it! Don't you imagine that it'd be very hard having someone around all the time? I don't know how the married women do it. Then very often kids on top of that! I mean you're not hankering after all that are you?"

Matilda thought for a moment. Then she said. "I don't know Pixie. Maybe that's part of my problem. If I'm honest I don't really know what I imagine the future to be. I've never thought about anything but music, and being part of this world. I can't even work out how I feel about Dante's bride-to-be. After all, it doesn't necessarily affect him and me does it? Oh I suppose I shall hate having it all pointed out to me in 'Hello', or whichever high society magazine gets rights to the wedding pictures. Because, lovely as most people are, there's bound to be someone who won't be able to resist from pointing it out to me, just in case I don't know!"

"And?" Pixie raised her eyebrows.

"Well. Where's all the blood curdling jealousy? It seems to elude me. I'll never sing Tosca! What's wrong with me Pixie, am I abnormal or something?"

"Yes." Grinned Pixie, in an effort to lighten Matilda's sudden serious mood. "Haven't you realised that yet?"

Matilda looked so stricken that she regretted it instantly.

"Joke! Remember those? A few words, followed by laughter, either sincere or faked out of good manners. Lighten up Till! You may not be ready to kill with jealousy, but all this has plunged you into a dark and serious place, just one minute." And she swept up the empty glasses and made for the bar. Matilda watched the admiring glances that followed her there and back. Pixie was tall and very athletic. She wasn't the type of beauty which stared at you from most magazines, but she possessed a fabulous ivory skin and a fascinating confidence which screamed at you, 'I don't give a fat rat if you like the way I look or not,' with every step she took, and she had the sort of background that had taught her how to dress.

"Stronger this time." She grinned placing the fresh drinks down. Then she picked up the conversation as if there hadn't been a pause.

"So, let's leave Dante for a moment, what about this new coach, what's her name again?"

"Irena. Irena Popovitch." Matilda muttered over her raised glass.

"Yea, so what exactly did she say? I mean, I assume that you are exaggerating about the major surgery?"

"Yes of course. But she listed things that she hears in my voice. Negative things I mean, and one after the other…" Matilda trailed off as her mind went back to the session.

"Well you don't have to listen to her you know. You don't have to go back to be crucified again! What makes you so sure that she's right?"

"Oh she's right." Replied Matilda quickly. "It was too much of a revelation for there to be any other explanation. It's also something of a relief to hear problems set out like that, by someone who knows what they're talking about."

"But does she know? You know what it's like out there. The world and his wife think they can teach singing. It all seems so easy to them. And in they go and start tinkering, really mess-ing people up, while it turns out that most of them have never even stood up in public and performed.! Look, I did a 'Messiah' last Christmas time, out in the wilds of Wiltshire somewhere. And afterwards, over very nice hospitality, this lady came up to me and started to give me 'notes' on my singing. You may well look horrified…" She added as Matilda's jaw dropped. "When I asked her where she studied, to shut her up, I knew she couldn't have studied anywhere, unless it was for a Ph.D. in 'flannel,' she looked at me as if I had sworn at her Mother or something. She hadn't got a clue, Tilly. But she was up for putting her oar in, so how can you be sure?"

"I don't know. But I know she's been a professional singer, for all I know she may still perform. And I sense that she's totally sincere."

At which Pixie sighed and looked thoughtful, and then said. "So! What's the problem? Let her help you!"

"Well, it's not quite that simple." Matilda said quietly guessing the reaction that that would bring forth. Sure enough Pixie raised her eyes and pulled a face. "Oh do tell. why not?" "Well there's Giorgio. He is still officially my teacher and…"

"Leave him. I know he's gorgeous, but your voice is much more important."

"It's not that easy." Replied Matilda, and Pixie was silent for a moment before she said quietly. "Obviously not!"

And now Matilda was more tempted than she had ever been. It was so strong it was almost like a pain in her chest. She folded her arms, pressing them against the weight which seemed to be resting behind her sternum. The release in explaining everything to someone, promised to be so sweet, it made her light headed.

Her enforced silence had the effect of alienating her, and an unpleasant sensation of loneliness engulfed her. She missed Dante badly and would have given anything to see him pop his head round the pub door. So when she glanced in that direction and saw Martin, the familiarity momentarily confused her, and she actually registered Dante there. Her heart leapt in her chest and forced its way through the weight, which promptly dissipated. She rose to her feet, then, embarrassed, she sat down again and looked at Pixie.

"I'm going nuts! I thought that was Dante."

"Where?" Pixie twisted round in her chair. Matilda studied the back of her head. Martin was with a couple of friends from the Opera House. A baritone, not Matilda's favourite person by a long way, and Mike. They did not see them, and Pixie swivelled back.

"Shit! That's all I need." She hissed. "What do you mean?" Said Matilda trying to feel inconspicuous. "Well surely you've heard? Mike and I split up."

"Actually yes, I have. I'm so sorry Pixie, I haven't said anything because I wasn't sure if you were ready to talk about it."

This was quite true, but Matilda felt a stab of guilt, considering Pixie's concern for her. Her mind was swiftly put at rest. "Oh I don't need to talk about it. It was all my idea. I got fed up with being an appendage to a marriage. Mike was a little taken aback at first, but I don't see him weeping, do you?" She smiled ironically, then continued. "I need to concentrate on my career much more if I'm ever going to do more than chorus. I was beginning to feel really blocked. He was actually starting to complain about my other work. Our 'Butterfly', for example. What a nerve these men have! You know it didn't even become clear to his 'thickness' when I explained. He turned into the heavy-handed Victorian, and, if you please, started quoting his wife at me. Can you believe it? Anita, he declared was always 'there' for him. She wouldn't fly off all over the country to sing for a few old fogeys."

Matilda laughed in amazement and said. "What did you say?" Pixie took a sip of her drink, then she replied. "Well, first I asked him if his precious wife is so bloody marvellous, what's he doing with me? And could it possibly be that the reason she doesn't fly off all over the country to sing to anyone was because no one ever asks her. No doubt they'd rather be boiled in oil. This did not please his 'stupidness,' he actually thinks she's talented. She's auditioned so many times for the chorus that Pamela, in the office told me, she recognises her handwriting, and keeps putting her application to the bottom of the pile as long as she possibly can."

"That bad?" Asked Matilda. Pixie nodded. "Uh, uh. Something resembling a stuck pig, I believe."

"Pixie! You mustn't say things like that!"

"No? O.K. She's bloody awful and not likely to improve enough in this life time to join our illustrious ranks. Anyway I'd had enough, so there's no beating of breast and wailing for me. I just don't feel like speaking to him yet."

Matilda watched from under her lowered eyes, as if full normal focus might possibly magnetise the three men, and cause then to look over in their direction. She breathed a sigh of relief. "They're making for the other bar."

"Good!" Said Pixie. "Now, where were we?"

The discussion continued until the two friends had rather

talked themselves into a corner. Matilda offered to drop Pixie off, she had decided to grab a taxi. It was a suggestion Pixie welcomed. On the way home Matilda reflected. She would love to take Pixie into her confidence, but sanity prevailed. How could she explain about Carlo, or expect anyone to understand the 'realness' of that dimension, that world, and the closeness she felt for the castrati? They'd have her sectioned! And anyway Pixie, bless her, did have a rather one track mind when it came to attractive men. Her comment regarding Giorgio had stayed in Matilda's mind. Surely Pixie did not suspect that she found it hard to leave him because he was attractive? That would be too absurd. But all this aside, Matilda was really looking forward to singing with her. Pixie possessed a superb dramatic mezzo voice, and Matilda knew that there was a good 'feeling' when you sang with Pixie. It sort of lifted you up, you felt good, bursting with energy. Funny that, because once, when they were both still at college, Matilda had said as much, and Pixie had turned to her, serious for once, and replied. "That's funny. That's what I always notice when I sing with you Till!"

Matilda was working hard at what Irena had talked to her about. Time was slipping by, and the phone call from Giorgio caught her by surprise. The conversation with Martin at the Opera House the same evening, equally so. She sensed a tiny conspiracy.

"I told Giorgio, Martin. I've been busy."

"All the more reason for lessons." He pointed out with his usual smiley sneer.

"Well. I'm having plenty of coaching."

"Oh bugger that! You're not the grandioso finished product

you know who gets by on a few coaching sessions. Get your arse to Giorgio!"

"As charming as ever I see!" Said Matilda, feeling irritated and forced into a conversation she did not wish to have. Martin pulled a face, "You women are all the same." He spat.

"Where did that come from?" Matilda said, taken aback by the sudden dart-like delivery.

"Forget it. A little trouble on the home front, that's all. Anyway, I'm coming to Butterfly, so you'd better be good!" Now, the idea of Martin being at the performance was disturbing. He watched Matilda closely as he continued. "Giorgio asked me to go as he is otherwise engaged, and can't make it."

"Taking notes are we?" Matilda answered tersely. She was tense. It arose, she knew, from the realisation that the difference in her voice would be obvious to Martin, who would (no doubt) joyfully recount every detail and dotted quaver to the 'Maestro.' The intercom burst into life requesting their presence for the final scene of Verdi's 'Ballo in Maschera.' Thankfully, Matilda escaped. But Martin fell into step with her on the way to the tube. To stop any continuation of the earlier conversation, Matilda said.

"How are things at home Martin?"

"Connie's been going through a bad patch. But I've got it under control." Matilda was not impressed.

"A bad patch? Why was that Martin?" Martin looked away as if to check the completely traffic-free street and muttered. "God only knows!"

"Wouldn't have anything to do with your er…life style, would it?" Matilda said. Martin feigned outrage and stopped in the lighted doorway of the famous pub. He stood to one side in invitation as he said. "What do you mean darling?"

"Martin, for God's sake why don't you grow up? Real life isn't so bad you know. You might even find it an improvement." Martin placed himself square to the doorway again, removing the invitation. Not that Matilda had had any intention of accepting. He looked down his nose at her and said sharply.

"Well Matilda. I think you know very well that the likelihood of my changing is about as, what can I say now? About as likely as you becoming the next Contessa della Vittoria!"

And he disappeared into the pub.

JOURNAL

There was a stranger sitting in rehearsal today. "Who is he?" I asked Maria. Before the rehearsal began.

"Jonathan Warrener, our soon-to-be, Chorus Master. Getting our drift as it were. Looks a bit anxious, don't you think?" "I do." I replied.

One of the second basses, Paulo (about as Italian as I am, but who cares!) lent forward in his seat and whispered.

"Don't worry ladies, we'll soon pull him into shape. We've done it before!"

"What if he pulls us into shape?" I said, feeling for no accountable reason, suddenly insecure. Paulo laughed.

"Are you kidding luv? 68 to 1...No contest. He'll never know what hit him." I grinned back at him knowing without doubt that it couldn't be that easy, and that many of the older choristers' unspoken tenet of 'The Chorus Rules.. O.K?' Was largely wishful thinking. But worse than this I had felt Jonathan's eyes on me many times, and it made me feel uncomfortable. What's more other people noticed. Martin bounded up to me in the break. Apparently all hostility-free.

"So Tilly, still charming the birds out of the veritable? I congratulate you. That's good politics, I didn't know you had it in you!"

I chose not to be provoked. "Do you know him? He makes me feel uneasy. I'm sure I'm not his type, so why the apparent interest?"

"Obviously your pristine reputation proceeded you. Even if you're not a short-skirted blonde, he's intent on going where others have found it impossible to go. A moral, upright operatic soprano. Just about unheard of I'd say."

"Don't be ridiculous. No! It almost looks as if he's deciding things about us before he even hears us. Surely he should at least hear us first, I mean the voice has to be the most important consideration."

Martin adopted an ultra serious pose and tone of voice, which I couldn't help but smile at. "Tilly, this business is changing. Vital statistics will now be taken as a mater of course at all, and every audition, and may, in the future remove the need for female members to be 'heard' at all. I predict..."

"Shut up Martin. And do you KNOW him?"

"Never heard of him, and don't know anyone who has."

I asked Irena the same question, but drew a blank. I rang Giorgio and booked a lesson, for after Butterfly. (I don't want him to disturb what Irena's doing.) He sounded fine, so no conspiracy then? Maybe it's my paranoia again?

Butterfly

The night before Butterfly, Matilda dreamt lucidly for the first time in a while. There was no sign of the old man, and as she set off across the room, she paused to look back at her body lying peacefully asleep in bed. There was nothing there! A crumbled duvet, but nothing else. The shock almost woke her, but her experience in the dream dimension saved her from that, and she refused to give the thought any energy. 'I'll think about it tomorrow.' She decided, and continued straight through the wall.

Carlo was there, sitting on a long bridge which spanned a deep ravine. Somewhere in the depths of which, Matilda could hear water running. He was banging his heels rhythmically against the white stone, his arms folded, and he watched her through slightly narrowed eyes. So this was the owner of the sweet voice. He had only the softest memory of her dipping in and out of his life. Almost like a beautiful shadow watching over him. It often drove him into deep and happy contemplation. Did God intend that we dream of our own future? And if so, why?

"Carlo?" She said, feeling suddenly just a little shy." Si Signorina!"

"What are you doing here?"

"And what's wrong with here?"

"Nothing. It's just that it isn't Venice. That's where I usually see you, in Venice."

"I'm afraid, dearest of ladies that I understand very little of all this.". Matilda felt a jolt of pleasure at his sweet tone.

"Oh this is fascinating. Don't you think it's fascinating Carlo?" Carlo laughed, even that was like a charming cadence. "It is, I suppose as you say, fascinating." He agreed. Matilda beamed and looked around. Beautiful Italian countryside was blossoming and they seemed to be at the centre of some rich renaissance painting. And by an artist whose pallet had been lent him by the gods, since no man ever mixed such colours surely? Carlo smiled and pointed to it.

"You see cara. It's not so much where e'er you walk, more like where e'er you smile."

She began to speak again, but Carlo raised his hand, a theatrical gesture, but one full of sincere expression. He really was beautiful. His green eyes smouldered, and she felt herself being drawn into their vortex.

"Please lady. I'm not as experienced at this as you are. I find it hard to concentrate, and I come here with a purpose, it is very important. But my mind keeps forgetting. Please stop thinking about my, our friends, and Venice, and particularly of Opera and singing."

There was so much that Matilda wanted to ask Carlo, that to honour his request was quite an effort, but she grappled with the temptation, turning her mind instead to the complexity of the fact that he was meeting her in a dream as if they were meeting

"Sure! Of course you can have it Pixie, but I haven't actually got it on me at the moment. Monday O.K? And thank you, It's nice to know what Irena is doing is working!"

"Working? You'll go right to the top if you keep singing the way you are."

Matilda stopped and stared at her friend. "Oh come on Pixie…" But Pixie interrupted.

"I mean it Matilda! You must realise just how good you sound, for your own confidence."

Matilda was a little taken aback. She had only been aware of the comparative ease she was now experiencing, and had not realised the total effect. At first she was simply delighted, but a nagging worry soon began, that Martin would be bound to notice the difference. As they piled back into the car however, he said nothing. He began holding court again, and she dearly wished he would shut up. They all were tired, and she for one, was very hungry. Pixie, she noticed, was staring out of the window. Matilda leant across towards her behind Martin.

"Do you fancy a curry, Pixie?" "Do I? I'm ravenous Till."

They arranged to be dropped off near an 'Indian.' No one else seemed to be interested. Neil Palmer who had sung Pinkerton with them and their baritone, Pietro Silveri Obviously from an Italian background, but as 'South London' as anyone can be) both had to 'get home.' Martin hadn't made any comment at all. But when the car pulled up in Holborn, he muttered something to the two men, and leapt out.

"Don't mind if I join you girls, do you!" It wasn't really a question, more like an assumption. A forgone conclusion. Matilda noticed Pixie barely hiding a sigh, she had obviously hoped to discuss Irena further, and Matilda bit back a grin. The warmth of the restaurant embraced them. It had started to rain outside, and the air was cold. Martin took over as the young Indian waiter approached them. He asked for a table for three, no smoking. He then chose from the choice offered and strode ahead like an Arab out with two of his wives.

"Does this mean he's paying?" Muttered Pixie. "Don't be wicked, and don't be daft!" Giggled Matilda. Pixie drew closer to her and continued. "I don't think he intended to join us you know. I think we were so crushed in the back, that when we took the pressure off, he sort of jumped out like an uncoiled spring, and was too embarrassed to jump back!"

The picture which flew to Matilda's mind was so ludicrous, that she laughed out loud, unable to control herself.

"Now girls, no secrets." Said Martin as they settled themselves down, pulling off coats, and placing bags, bulging with scores and theatrical paraphernalia out of the way of innocent legs.

"So, are you happy? You should be, you both did very well."

"Martin." Snapped Pixie. "We're not amateur school girls, don't be so patronising. You'll be patting us on the head next. I mean, what exactly does 'very well' mean. What? In spite of…Or considering…in then circumstances? If you think that Tilly did 'very well' rather than bloody great, top level singing, you my dear sir, are deaf!"

Matilda looked uncomfortable, and Martin assumed his drawl loud enough so that everyone within earshot received the benefit of his Operatic knowledge. Matilda quietly prayed that he wouldn't drink too much.

"Well…" He began, leaning back in his chair. "Butterfly is a very special work. Of course, poor old Neil was struggling a bit. I bet you wish I'd been singing, don't you girls?" At this last remark, Pixie flared her nostrils, a fair sign that she was hugely irritated.

"Neil is not so old Martin. And anyway he sings with so much commitment, plenty of passion. I bet the audience didn't even register the fact that he just happens not to be 25. What do you think?" She ended with an exaggeratedly innocent smile. Martin looked daggers across the table, but Pixie didn't flinch. The popadoms arrived, and Matilda heaved a sigh of relief. The waiter assured them that he would return soon to take their order, reminding them that they hadn't yet decided. All this gave enough of a pause, and Matilda hoped that it would diffuse the tension building between Pixie and Martin. But he was not about to back off. Finding the performance to be a dead end, he decided on another tack.

"What's the matter Pixie, missing your boyfriend?"

"Now why would I do that? The break up was my idea Martin." Martin raised his eyebrows. "Oh? That's not what he says!"

"Then he's more pathetic that I thought he was." Pixie was obviously furious.

"Children, children…" Matilda said, feeling she must do something to avert disaster. "Come on let's enjoy our meal." But Pixie snatched up her bag and made for the Ladies. Over her shoulder she growled.

"Order for me Tilly, I don't care what I have." And she marched off.

"Temperamental little thing, isn't she?" Martin said, staring after her.

"You're stirring it Martin. And you're deliberately annoying her. Just leave it O.K? Enjoy the rest of the evening. 'Chill out' as they say!"

"Now how can I do that after what I've just had to sit through? What's this bloody woman telling you for Christ's sake." Martin glared at her looking mutinous. 'Here we go!' Thought Matilda. She broke off a piece of one of the popadoms, and dipped it into the chutney in the centre of the table.

"First of all Martin, if it was that bad why didn't you leave? You could have popped across the road to the pub, drunk the evening away, and still got a lift back. I'm sure Giorgio would have understood. But as to Irena…" She went on quickly because Martin looked as if he was about to say something. "She's a very experienced singer and coach Martin. And, she's from the old school. She knows her music, and she knows what she's talking about, you should consider working with her!"

"Bollocks!" Martin's voice was becoming louder again. An Oriental couple at the next table turned briefly in their direction. Matilda dearly wished that Martin would forget about his beer until the food arrived. At least the rice would soak some of it up. Unfortunately, there was no sign of the waiter, and she gritted her teeth as Martin took another large gulp of the liquid. .

"You're going to make a fool of yourself Matilda."

"What?" She exclaimed, scarcely able to believe what she was hearing. " You can't be serious Martin, do you know how many people made a point of finding me to congratulate me afterwards."

"Oh bloody hell Matilda. That was just because you happened to be singing the title role. They probably thought they had to. Anyway what do they know about it? The man in the street…" He was about to get into his stride, but Matilda cut in… "May not understand the finer points of technique, or music. But they know what they like. Their ears are not contaminated by their own ambitions, or egotistical ideas about what they would like to prove to the world."

"And mine are, I suppose?" Martin spat. Matilda sighed deeply. "I didn't say that Martin. But forget them, Pixie seems anxious enough to get her hands on Irena's phone number. She says she's really impressed with the change in my voice." Matilda finished, being to feel a nagging doubt in spite of herself, and her exhilaration, began to fade. The waiter arrived and they ordered. Matilda wished Pixie would hurry back. Martin had ordered a second beer and was staring into it as he said smoothly.

"Well I hate to think what Giorgio will say. He'll probably throw you out!"

"Don't be ridiculous!" Matilda tried to parry with confidence, although she felt far from it. "O.K. Martin, tell me. Be specific, what exactly is bothering you?"

"It's the bloody sound Tilly. You know, you were beginning to get somewhere. You're just going to mess it all up. Still have it your own way. I'm not discussing it anymore. I shall leave it to Giorgio." He ended on a flourish and looked up as Pixie rejoined them. The much-needed food arrived and Matilda watched Martin begin to weave his considerable charm. Was it all deliberate, or had it become so much of a habit that he wasn't aware that he was doing it anymore? She said very little, allowing the two to keep up the conversation, and increasingly amused by Pixie's response. Gradually, in spite of her recent fury, she began to warm to him and was soon laughing and joking.

"You O.K. Till?" She asked at one point, and Matilda nodded. "Fine Pixie, just a bit sleepy now. It's the food I expect. I think I'll slip off soon, if you don't mind."

"What no dessert?" Put in Martin, addressing her for the first time since his last scathing remark. "Come on Tilly, you can't say no to Indian ice cream. It's absolutely delicious." Pixie joined in. "Yes Tilly you deserve it. It's Sunday tomorrow you know. You can stay in bed all day if you want to."

Resistance was futile. "Oh O.K!"

Pixie and Martin continued their bantering, which gradually and subtly gave way to flirting. Matilda switched off. She was fantasising about a long hot bath and bed, and had leant back in her chair. The light in the restaurant was suffused and strange, and the noises around her, melted into it. The Indian music, which she rather liked, acted as a buffer to her questions and frustrations. She watched her two friends with a slight smile behind her eyes, if not actually on her mouth.

There was a waiter behind Martin busily serving a party who had arrived late. He was irritated, he calculated that he wouldn't be out of the restaurant until at least 12:30. And he'd promised his wife especially that he'd be early tonight. But they were short staffed, and now this late arrival. He was hurrying as much as he could, he might still make it! He turned quickly, too quickly. His sharp elbow crashed into Martin's skull. Before anger registered, Matilda saw another expression there, and without warning she was plunged back into the Cathedral, Carlo was dead and his grieving friends had gathered to bury him. She saw Lucciano turn with the look of agony as he lifted his hand towards his face.

There was that same pain which now disappeared to be quickly replaced by anger. But then, in the Cathedral it had found its peak of anguish and crescendoed through Matilda's heart. She gasped in shocked realisation, and her eyes filled with tears. Lucciano! Martin was Lucciano!

Pride

Long before Martin next arrived in Surrey, bursting with 'tit-tle-tattle' regarding Matilda's performance, Giorgio had heard through the ever present grapevine, all about her working with Irena. Contrary to that lady's belief, he had most certainly recognised her. He had trained himself over many lifetimes to retain memories and conscious awareness, and it would hardly be likely that he would forget someone in this life who had been as important in his early singing career as Irena had been. Important because after he had stormed away from every confrontation in an arrogant fury, he had secreted himself away and tried his best to apply what she had said.

Exactly why he sensed that Irena was right he didn't stop to discover. Nothing of his far past had come to him at that time. Nothing of the past where he had been so ready to offer himself to Anthorus in order to study with Osiria. The Osiria who died along the way during the escape. Who had written with such insight of the 'Unknown Opera singer,' The Western gate, or at least the most important part of it. The same stream of consciousness who had had no part in their lives in Venice, but who appeared in Europe with vocal guns blazing, and temperament to match. He had listened for the mistakes in vocal production which she pointed out, and attempted to eradicate the imbalance, which, in actual fact he had been to some extent aware of.

But, as they say a little knowledge is a dangerous thing. His pride would not allow him to accept her help face to face. To his horror however, the more he tried to follow one instruction, the more other problems he uncovered. The sound was too 'spread' she had pointed out. When Giorgio had stormed away from that little battle and started to practice with it in mind, he found that he ended up with a stiff jaw and an edge to the sound.

"What are you doing?" His coach had exclaimed at his next private call at the Opera House. "You sound terrible! For goodness sake, leave it alone Giorgio. It may not have been perfect before, but it sounded much better than this. I'm well aware that a certain soprano says more than she should, but I think she should teach you openly and properly, or keep her mouth shut. Except when she sings that is, what a sound eh? If you want to follow her advice, go and work with her properly. You could do a lot worse than letting her help you know! But whatever you do, don't fiddle around on your own. You know as well as I do that singers need a pair of ears on the outside, especially when there are changes going on."

Giorgio had said nothing, but he had been furious. For a short time he had suspected that Irena had been Carlo, but that had not lasted long. Carlo had been in his power when he had killed him, and he believed that the emotional web would still be in tact when next they met. And this situation was not right. Once he realised that, the idea evaporated as quickly as his next breath. He couldn't accept that a woman could train any man to sing, particularly if that man was a tenor. On some dark and rigid level vocal suicide was preferable, so vocal suicide it was. Which was a very great pity, because Irena could not only have helped him, he may well have developed into a world class performer under her formidable tutelage.

Irena had gleaned secrets in Russia, knowledge which seemed to be unheard of even in Italy. It had been guarded and adhered to for centuries. No deviation was acceptable, and as with their prodigious ballet dancers, this had developed phenomenal artists.

"So Martin, in what way did the performance bother you?" Said Giorgio looking across the piano at the young tenor. Martin had to pull himself up, he didn't want to get off track here, and there was very much more than Matilda that bothered him. The tenor for example. There was enough material there for the entire lesson, but he concentrated on Matilda.

"I don't know where to start Giorgio. It's not easy to put into words. She sounds different. I mean, I suppose one must admit that it's bigger, it would certainly carry anyway. But something bothers me." And he screwed up his face into something resembling a concerned football thug. It left Giorgio in no doubt that what 'bothered' him was his own inability to accept the fabulous potential which Matilda had, that would, under Irena's guidance inevitably begin to blossom. Of course it sounded different, but the change was positive. He wished that Martin would control his dark brooding, at least until Matilda was in a more vulnerable position. It was only a matter of time, after all. Martin was talking again.

"She's not going to be easily dissuaded from continuing coaching with this woman though, Giorgio."

'Of course she isn't!' Thought Giorgio. Martin continued. "She's bloody convinced the woman's brilliant. I mean who the hell is she? Do you know her Giorgio? She was at the concert the other week if you remember."

"Yes she was, and as a matter of fact I do know her. Between you and me I'm afraid she was responsible for my early vocal demise, and in my humble belief, the real reason that I never really 'made' it. I sang with her in Opera houses all over the place, especially in Europe, and many years ago now. Although she was quite a lot older than me, I liked her. She was a very beautiful woman with an unbelievable smile, I remember. And could she sing? What a soprano, absolutely glorious. Oh yes she had most definitely been very well trained. However, when it came to passing on that knowledge she had (God knows where it came from) She was hopeless, didn't have a clue! This often happens, you know? Well the long and short of it is, she tried to help me. I was young and still needed guiding. After all I was singing big emotional roles in big opera houses, and therefore against full sized orchestras. I wasn't stupid, I knew the potential dangers, but in spite of my awareness, and of my willingness to follow her to the letter, I was ruined."

"Ruined?" Martin felt an odd combination of emotions. Somewhere in there was a dark gleam of joy. He ignored it, but to his shame it was there. Giorgio sensed it of course and said. "Don't worry about Matilda, Martin. I'm due to see her…Let me see, when was it now?" He drew his diary across the top of the grand piano, and studied it for a few moments. "Ah yes, there we are. The day after tomorrow. I'm free afterwards, I'll keep it that way and have a word with her, tell her my story. We'll see if she's quite as sure of the lady after that. Now, let's work my boy."

Martin began to sing, following the familiar exercises. Giorgio appeared to be in deep concentration with what he was doing, but in fact he had switched off from the very first note. He found Martin's singing dry, and deader than ever, and besides which, he had other things to think over. He was a master at teaching on automatic. He changed the key chords and uttered instructions. Martin, although an overly sensitive soul in some ways, was not aware of Giorgio's lack of attention. He moved to the next exercise, an Italian sentence sung out on a single pitch to achieve... Martin was not sure what, but he was sure that it was helping. And he became absorbed in dreams of his own success. Giorgio, on the other hand was trying to decide what would be the best way to deal with Matilda. He could simply ignore it, after all he had the best reason to believe that everything would soon be taken of. The fact being, that there was no one more yielding than someone who could see themselves easily out of debt. He was sure that Jonathan would streak through the Opera House naked, if it would remove the horrors of the Inland Revenue. And even given Matilda's voice and her quickness in learning, Irena would not be able to turn everything around quite that fast. Muscles and brain pathways took their own sweet time. He smiled, and Martin believed he was suddenly sounding like something between Caruso and Bjorling. But Giorgio's smile was because he suddenly realised that all this could work in his favour. He had learnt a long time ago that when one is plotting and planning, and fate drops an opportunity into one's lap, you accept it gratefully, and any time that things go in the desired direction all by themselves, you certainly don't hinder them. This was a time for quiet rejoicing.

He would encourage Matilda to continue with Irena. Further, he would suggest she save her money and leave his studio, for at least the time being. He took a big sigh and leaned back in his chair. Martin grinned at him. "It feels good Giorgio." To which the monster replied, smilingly assuring. "Sounds good my boy. Sounds very good!"

When Matilda opened her mouth a couple of days later, he knew of course exactly what was happening. She already sounded much more true Soprano. The sound was finer but more exciting. The focus was beginning to take the listener beyond the sound to an emotional response that would, given some more time, become almost physical to the audience. He also thought he heard something else, or the ghost of something, but he pushed it to one side, and although it kept worrying at him for a while, he could make no sense of it, and soon forgot all about it.

He was concentrating on his next move, and he set the trap and watched Matilda, so relieved that there had been no dreaded confrontation, walk straight into it with a smile.

"Well, I must congratulate you on your choice of coach Matilda. I don't think you could have done better." (That at least was true.) "Sometimes being told things by a different person, can make all the difference. We both want the same results of course. But the human mind is such a complicated place, that it is able to translate perfectly from one person, while another, who is saying exactly the same thing, cannot get through. Please send Irena my warmest regards."

Needless to say, Giorgio made no mention of his relationship with Irena, neither the actual truth, nor the tissue of lies he had intimated to Martin, he didn't deem it necessary. But while Matilda was relaxed and happy, he quickly shifted gears.

"By the way, my dear. What are you doing for Christmas?"

JOURNAL

Giorgio asked me what I am doing for Christmas today. I couldn't really tell him since I haven't given it any thought at all. So much has been happening and it is still happening that I've had no time to ponder the immediate future. The first thought I had on my way to the Opera house for this evening's show was that I suppose I should really phone Anne. I have had no contact with her at all for months. But in retrospect the idea of struggling on the train at this time of the year, in order to spend the season of 'Goodwill' with someone for whom I feel so little, seems hypocritical. I don't suppose her attitude towards me has altered. And how would I deal with our 'Very Reverent' after the diabolical scene with him back just before the accident? After all, Anne was sure to invite him to one of her many pre-and -after Christmas entertainments. And she would be fussing over at the church, no doubt playing 'Lady of the manor' not very well. There would not be a single relaxed moment. And now that I consider that, I realise that I feel as if I have been on a roller coaster for months. Suddenly the idea of enjoying the time to myself, quiet and relaxed, is very appealing. Also I remembered that we will be working Christmas eve' so that puts it all into place, I can forget Anne.

There are Christmas decorations everywhere, but it is impossible to find time to shop. Although my recital programme is finally decided and memorised so I can not have to worry about it until the New Year. I still have to find a pianist, hopefully from the Opera House. It will be so much easier to arrange rehearsal times, and also I don't want to use someone who I don't know at all, and then spend precious time going through a 'getting-to-know-you' prelude.

Dante is, of course, on my mind much of the time. He had promised me that we will spend a little time together before Christmas. I'm sure he will do his best, but I mustn't look forward to it too much. It's very difficult for him. It has just occurred to me, however, that regarding all the misunderstanding regarding his marital status earlier, it might be rather amusing to allow Anne to discover that I am officially the mistress of an Italian count. I wonder if the aristocratic connection would alter her self righteous opinion in any way? My guess is that it would. I'm not going to mention it though, if I ever do come across her again. I don't want to get back at her. I simply want to stay away from her...

Matilda found a pianist, a member of the Opera House staff.

"Oh! Exclaimed Pixie when she heard who it was. "You are the honoured one. Damien Willis, willing to play for a member of the chorus, and for a solo recital no less!"

"I don't think he's like that is he Pixie? He thinks of us as singers in our own right I'm sure. He doesn't strike me as a musical snob."

"That's not what I heard. Anyway, he's a brilliant pianist,

so go for it! He's no doubt been swept away by your talent and your gorgeous violet eyes." Teased Pixie. Matilda ignored the last remark, but smiled at her friend and asked.

"Have you rung Irena yet?" There was no reply. "Pixie?" Matilda followed her friends gaze. A group of extra chorus singers converged onto the stage where they were standing waiting for the second half of a rehearsal to begin.

"What?.. Oh not yet. But I'm definitely going to. I meant what I said about your singing you know. There's Christmas holidays looming, well for most people anyway, I though I'd wait for New Year."

Pixie replied still staring across the stage, until one of the singers in the group they had watched taking their places, put up his hand to her. Matilda smiled and then exclaimed, a little embarrassed.

"Oh sorry, I though he was waving at me." "Hmm…?" Pixie turned back to her. "Tilly, you're great, but sometimes you can be just a little naïve you know?"

Her attention had wandered again. Now looking at Matilda she continued.

"But maybe that's your saving…Excuse me…Se you later!"

Christmas shopping did get done in spite of the seeming impossibility. Matilda felt that she had reached a plateau of peace. She even accepted Giorgio's invitation to spend Christmas at Villa Giorgio.

"I'll pick you up after the show on Christmas Eve cara. Otherwise you'd never get to us. Do come it will do you good. I want to hear what Irena's been doing with you, you must keep me up to date you know. It wasn't easy for me to part with my prize pupil even though I know we'll work together again. There will be other guests as well. New people for you to meet. What do you say?"

Giorgio could be very seductive, and not just sexually. He had arrived at the stage door one evening before the 'half,' looking extremely sophisticated and handsome, with the express purpose of inviting her. As she looked at him Matilda couldn't help but wonder how many Christmases Carlo and Raimondo had spent together in Venice. And whatever their personal relationship had been, she imagined truly wonderful times must have ensued. The memories surged on a non verbal wave, and it was as much for that as anything that Matilda found herself saying 'yes.'

Anne was forgotten. Swiftly the year was drawing to its close. Matilda found she was looking forward to the holiday, she was happy. The old man however, was not.

Christmas

"We've left the others behind." Said Giorgio. He had turned round in his saddle, his hand on the raised back. Matilda pulled up the grey mare beside him and looked at him questioningly. The sky behind her was full of snow, everywhere quiet with anticipation of the release of it. Matilda's violet eyes above the pale grey of the mare and in front of the slate of the horizon, caught Giorgio unawares, causing his stomach to lurch with a longing for Carlo that was so strong he felt certain he must have paled.

"Are you alright Giorgio? Maybe we should go back. It's about to start snowing any minute, let's rejoin the others."

She was expecting to see Verity and Giorgio's friends from the village farm appearing through the thick growth of trees veiled heavily with holly, and winter greenery. Giorgio's powerful bay shook his head and snorted as a small breeze danced across his dark mane. Giorgio was staring beyond her, his hands gripping the reins, He nodded dumbly. Tiredness suddenly invaded him. Depression settled like a heavy rock behind his ribs. The young woman's open energy shamed him. His head filled with sound. It expanded as if it were physical. Tiny specks of energy danced in the air. He could see them clearly as he supposed Matilda could. She found comfort in them. He did not.

"I do not feel too well cara. We will go back with or without them. I cannot face searching for them, you understand?" He didn't wait for an answer, but turned the magnificent bay, and set off at a pace which totally belied his last statement. Matilda followed him easily. Both horses were glad to be moving in the cold afternoon, and they needed no extra bidding as they sensed their warm stable and food. Matilda had not ridden for some time, and she seriously doubted her ability to remain on the grey's back, as Giorgio moved faster and faster away from her into the gathering gloom. The breath was tearing in her throat as they pulled up in the yard. Giorgio threw himself off his horse and, still holding the reins, grasped the fence which ran along the side of the yard. He was bent over.

"I'll see to them Giorgio, you need to get inside. I'll be as quick as I can. Will you be alright?" Giorgio nodded, he seemed to be dealing with some great pain, but it was hard to guess its whereabouts. 'He shouldn't be alone.' She thought. But he was already setting off for the house, determined to make his own way there. Matilda unsaddled and rubbed down both horses. They whinnied softly, and despite still feeling unsettled about Giorgio, she started to find a great comfort and healing with them. It was growing dark, the stable lights were soft and the horses muzzles even softer as she offered them some apple she had brought with her. She stretched up and straightened the bay's forelock.

"I shall be seriously stiff tomorrow." She said aloud. The grey mare moved closer, demanding her share of attention, and if at all possible, more apple. She smelt so sweet that Matilda buried her head into the strong dappled neck. It was utterly quiet, and then the snow began. Thick and fast it tumbled into the yard and began to pile up with audacious abandon at every available space.

Matilda experienced such a oneness with the animals that it began to blossom into one of her most favourite states. Expanded moments which gave birth to a most wonderful connection to everything and everyone. A beautiful awareness of ultimate balance and harmony in a golden light soaked through her whole being. Time expanded, and she saw herself singing at the Opera House, and in Venice as Carlo, in the Tony London concerts, in Butterfly, and there was no difference. The 'oneness' cut through all practical concerns, all so called 'scientific facts.' Quite gently it turned everything on its head. Everything became possible. She was smiling with pure pleasure.

"I'll feed 'em Miss!"

Matilda jumped, as they say a mile. "Oh Albert, I didn't know that you would be around today. Merry Christmas. Feeding is all that's left to do. I don't think I've forgotten anything."

"I can see that Miss. Now off you go and have a nice evening."

The horses had already turned their attention to Albert, no doubt their first love. Matilda perceived herself as quite forgotten. She smiled, then suddenly remembered Giorgio. She wondered, as she hurried towards the house, what could be amiss? A sudden 'flu virus maybe? There was enough of it around. Whatever it was it had struck like snake bite, because Giorgio had been in his usual top form until they had stopped to ponder where the others were. She stepped into his living room. A vagrant band of cigar smoke hovered in the air as if unsure of what to do in the absence of that which had given it birth. Partially filled glasses were strewn around the room. A large one, still containing brandy, near to Giorgio's chair. She placed her hand on the cushion and fancied that she felt warmth there. She left the room calling as she did so. "Giorgio, are you alright? Where are you?"

There was no reply, and still no sign of anyone else. She was unsure as to what to do. Should she wait for someone to arrive before she attempted to find Giorgio's bedroom? What if he simply needed to sleep? He wouldn't appreciate her barging in on him. He might even get the wrong idea. And if he didn't, Verity most certainly would. She gave herself a shake. This was no time for coyness. Giorgio might really need her help. Determined, she made for the stairs and the upper rooms, when she noticed that there was a light coming from the area leading to the theatre. Without pausing to question, she started off towards the auditorium calling his name again.

A muffled sound caught her attention, and suddenly Matilda panicked. She ran into the auditorium shouting at the top of her very healthy lungs.

"Giorgio answer me. Where are you? What's wrong?" She stopped in full flight, and was forced to grab the back of a theatre seat to keep her balance. Giorgio was in the middle of the stage. He was huddled over and moaning as if in the utmost agony. Matilda was shaking and in tears by the time she reached him. She placed her hands on his back, completely at a loss as to how to handle the situation. Her wishes turned to prayers regarding the arrival at that moment of just about anyone. Even one of the house pets would have been welcome. But there was not a cat in sight, and the dogs were off in the grounds somewhere with the errant members of their riding party. She bent forward over Giorgio and spoke to him again, when suddenly he straightened up, narrowly missing knocking her out. He pulled back from her, and his voice was a hiss.

"This…This is what you have done. This is your accomplishment."

Matilda was horrified by his appearance and his words. His face was a powered-grey, and he suddenly looked 20 years older. His body jerked in uncontrollable spasm, as if electric shocks were being administered. But it was his voice which horrified her the most. It was harsh, raspy, and vicious. Uncertain, she pulled away from him, but not quickly enough. He grabbed her wrist in a painful grip and pulled her towards him with surprising strength. Quite suddenly she was very frightened. Normally she would, finding herself in such a situation, have no compunction about fighting back. She was tall and strong enough to deter all but the most determined attacker. But Giorgio's state prevented her. He looked so ill that she couldn't bring herself to fight him. She'd never seen anyone like this before, it seemed a contradiction. His colour and general condition spoke loudly of serious weakness, while the energy, which she could sense coursing through him, was vast, huge in fact. It was like being close to a thundering herd of animals. She spoke clearly, trying to keep calm.

"Giorgio, let me go, you're hurting me."

"Oh, I'm hurting you am I? And you deserve so much more Madam!" But he let her go. Matilda flinched at the hate in his words. He pulled something from his pocket, something which rattled with familiarity. Pills! Ah, medicine, so he was ill! He poured two or three of them into his palm, clamped it over his mouth, swallowing them instantly. The bottle rolled across the stage, and he swiped at it sending it skimming over the covered orchestra pit, into the comparative darkness of the auditorium. Giorgio placed his hands on the wooden boards, and with his head bent over, he breathed heavily and quickly as if he had just finished a marathon. Sweat poured from his still-grey face, and the dark green silk shirt stuck to his back and chest. Matilda watched him in horror. He was still more animal than human, and the animal was angry. Her knees felt too weak to support her and she slid across the stage to the proscenium arch and huddled against the wooden column, unsure whether to run and leave him to his own devices, but still not convinced that he wasn't about to collapse into unconsciousness. Gradually his breathing slowed, and the colour of his native Italy swirled uncertainly back into his face.

"I have spent much time in Tibet, Matilda." He said finally. He had sat back on his heels and sighed deeply. Then, after a moment's pause he pulled himself to his feet. Matilda said nothing. She was uncertain if an answer was expected. Giorgio slid from the stage across the covered pit, and sat down in the first row of the stalls, uncomfortably close to Matilda, who had relaxed not one bit.

"I learnt much there. I put into control what you seem to play with like a spoilt child, as and when you will...No?"

"Not as and when I will Giorgio. I don't have conscious ability to instigate these things. The dreams come when they will,

I can't force them." Matilda spoke as quietly as a lake after a storm, but she watched Giorgio warily. He seemed determined to deliberately avoid direct eye contact with her. A fact she didn't mind at all. He continued with a sneer.

"I have worked and studied with Masters. And do you imagine they would enter into conversation with such as you? You would be as nothing to them!"

"No." Said Matilda. She didn't really care what 'Tibet' might think of her. But she was careful not to let Giorgio notice her indifference, since it seemed to matter very much to him. He moved in the seat and Matilda jumped, completely unable to control the reflex action. Giorgio smiled, or at least, he showed his teeth.

"You do well to fear me cara. When this rage is on me, I could quite easily kill you."

Matilda found some courage. She stood up, still pressing herself against the proscenium arch, and said. "Kill me? Why Giorgio, what have I done to you?"

"You imagine, if my memory serves me right, over our cosy little dinner some time ago, that in our Venetian experience together, you were the beloved and brilliant Carlo Ferrucci?"

"That's how it seems to me Giorgio. It's not my intention to make any wild claims. It was a huge surprise to me. But you see Giorgio, it's just…"

"Crap! That's what it is Matilda. Utter rubbish. Like many dabblers in ancient knowledge and the noble art of 'dreaming true,' you make enormous assumptions while casting your precocious self in the title role, like the greedy little Prima Donna you are in the process of becoming."

Matilda's stomach flipped, and heat rose from its disconcerted centre. Somewhere she could hear Christmas carols being sung by an untrained, but energetic soprano. Giorgio got up and started towards her. He appeared to have recovered and moved with the grace of a panther. Matilda's fear returned, she was to all intents and purposes, trapped. To leave the stage and plunge into the total darkness which engulfed the sides, would have been madness. She had no idea what was back there, and an accident of some sort was inevitable. She could only watch as Giorgio moved closer and closer.

There was a strange feeling to it all, as if this were a performance, and within its happening, she tasted the memory of rehearsal. Upon her at last, he placed one hand firmly against the wood close to her head, and allowed his weight to lean into the muscles of his arm. This brought him very much closer than she would have liked. His other hand grabbed her chin, even in his violence, registering the satin of her skin. The singing was coming closer, but Matilda could not have cried out, Giorgio's grip was iron.

"I was Carlo…" His dark eyes followed the subtle path of reaction across her face. "Oh yes I was. And you, you jealous baggage, were Raimondo. You killed me, poisoned me. Unable to bear the huge success that I enjoyed both in, and out of bed. You were driven to the most disgusting act of all. Do you see in your 'dreams,' the stirrup cup? Do you remember it? The beautiful Venetian glass which you so sweetly offered me after my last performance, just before I was due to leave for London. Do you remember the golden liquid into which you slipped the vile poison…. DO YOU?"

He shouted in her face. Matilda nodded, tears stood out in her eyes, but she still held on to her belief.

"I remember…But…I… I drank it. You…It was you who gave it to me!" And she gasped in sudden realisation. At this Giorgio's eyes narrowed dangerously and Matilda's mouth went so dry it felt as if the sides of her throat were stuck together. Her heart pounded, and the muscles of her legs shook in anticipation of flight. Giorgio's face throbbed with a strange sensuality which was almost beautiful, the full mouth slightly open and he moved even closer to her as he said.

"How can I explain it to you Matilda, so that you might at last understand? I have been regressed by Masters. These men and women are capable of things that here in the West, our Oh-so-clever scientists would laugh and decry as dreams of the mad. But they are not mad Matilda. And they are indeed capable of many wondrous and magical things. I know what I speak is the truth because it came from them. You deceive yourself, stupid bitch! Face up to facts and know yourself for what you are."

She could not look him in the face so close to her own it was, and angled in fury. She had lowered her head in an effort to avoid his eyes at the last onslaught. Her mind whirled in anguish and uncertainty. She could feel Giorgio's breath on her hair, parting it every few seconds.

"Giorgio, let me go!" She cried. He moved his hand from her chin to her forehead, the palm flat against it. There was some force in the quick action, and her head slammed into the wood with a sharpness so that she barely noticed the contemptuous kiss he planted full on her mouth. However, someone else did.

Verity broke off her rendition of 'God Rest You Merry Gentlemen.' in mid-note and stormed towards them.

"Giorgio, you utter bastard."

"Yes, yes Verity. But then you already know that, don't you?" He replied in a tone of utter boredom, his eyes not leaving Matilda's face. He did not even bother to turn in Verity's direction. He recognised that his 'extra' strength was failing and that he would soon be 'normal' again. His nervous system, devoid of its awakened power, would have no option but to return to unadulterated humanity, Although he knew that he was never quite the same as other people, too many journeys into inner power had seen to that. It had never occurred to Giorgio just what he might accomplish with his ability had he set it on a positive track.

Verity screamed something totally unrecognisable, and bore down on him with nails flaying at the ready. He let go of Matilda in order to stop her, laughing all the time. Verity was light-boned, and shorter than Matilda by a good few inches. She was furious, but to Giorgio it was merely an extension of a game which they often played. He had no deep-seated vindictiveness against her.

"You're just jealous it wasn't you, that's your trouble my girl!" He was laughing so hard that for a moment she almost got the better of him, and he firmed his hold on her with one hand, saying. "Oh, I see m'lady." While he tore at the fasteners of her dark-brown jodhpurs, with the other.

Matilda had fled the theatre at the first possible opportunity. Her mind swirled in a vast mist, in which no coherent thought process was possible. She made for her room.

'Why had she come here?'…'What the hell was she going to

do?'…'Who could she talk to?'…'The police!'…'Don't be stupid…STUPID BITCH…'Was she?..' Had she killed?'…

Her hand was on the door of her room. So desperate was
she to get inside, that she turned the handle with too much
force and the door wouldn't open. Blind panic engulfed her,
she fancied that she could hear Giorgio on the stairs behind
her, fancied he was almost there, that this time he would kill
her. If she had known what Giorgio and Verity were up to at
that moment in the theatre, with no thought for a possible
straying guest's considerable embarrassment, things might have
remained in a little more prospective. But she didn't know,
and she was in no state to guess. Finally the door opened, she
burst into her room, slammed it shut and locked it. Unable to
sit down she paced, almost violently, up and down, until her
mind folded in and everything became a blur. Then she sat on
the bed and found to her horror that all she had to focus on,
were the feelings that the last half an hour had given rise to,
there was no one to talk to, and no release from the fear she was
experiencing. After a little while she went to her case, opened
up the zip pocket and pulled out her journal. Maybe writing
about it would calm her down.

JOURNAL

I write here about the last two days. Christmas night I was too
exhausted to put pen to paper, although I tried. I fell asleep over
my writing which was actually a blessing. So I must start again.
Almost equal in disbelief to what happened in the theatre, was
my reception at breakfast the next morning. It seems that everyone believes that I had been ill, and that I took early to bed not

wanting any part of the evening's revelries. Well, that much was true, I certainly didn't, but not for the reasons they assumed.

More disturbing is Giorgio himself. He is acting as if nothing has happened. I tried to broach the subject with him this afternoon when we were at enough of a distance from anyone else (but still within full view. No! I'm not stupid!) He doesn't so much deny, as act totally perplexed.

"Cara…I remember leaving the horses with you, Bert tells me you looked after them superbly, very sweet of you darling, you must have been exhausted, we'd been out riding for hours after all…" He began, I felt I was in danger of losing the plot, but Giorgio didn't give me a chance to say anything…"But I don't remember the rest. Matilda, it could be very possible that you are entering a certain stage in your personal, inner development when you are finding it hard to differentiate between dreaming, and this reality. We've all been there, and believe me I know that it can be very confusing."

He smiled at me and pulled at the collar of his silk shirt, dark crimson in colour today. He continued…"These 'real' dreams are, of course, glimpses into other very real dimensions. You must keep a clear head, and your dimensions straight. It's quite possible to keep a monitor in your mind all the time. Keep a rein on your personality, because any preconceived ideas about anyone will surface as real as this conversation we're having. There must be a part of you, cool and centred, which always remains unaffected by where you are or what you are doing. What you should be asking yourself, is why you should be drawn to such a violent possibility regarding me. I can't begin to imagine why, can you?" Whatever line I take with him he always manages to end up forcing me to face the question he has placed in my mind. Was I his murderer, or he mine? I find myself haunted day and night by Lucciano's face at Carlo's funeral. Was I the cause of what followed? I will find it hard to live with, if it is the case. I have to know and I have decided that as soon as I feel calmer and more rested, I will challenge my inner self. I will demand an answer, call on the old man. Failing that I intend to instigate something that will be a sign, anything which points me to the truth. Oh dear! I'd better get myself down to dinner and some human contact, I'm beginning to sound like the worst type of so-called psychic. The sort of person who has rather more confidence than talent, and who advertises in suspect pamphlets!

I miss my flat, and the Opera House, and good hard work. I feel as if I have been off for weeks instead of barely 2 days. I know if I could have a good sing my perspective on all this would become much clearer. On top of all this, I still have to face Verity. She was not at breakfast, and I did not see her all day. Of course, Verity! She is in fact my proof! At least of the part of the scene in the theatre which she witnessed. She was mad enough not to forget that in a hurry. I hardly expected an answer so soon. Suddenly I feel better...

When Matilda put her head around the door of the main sitting room. Verity was there by herself. She was curled up on the settee, with her head bent over a magazine. She was (almost) wearing a short black dress with a scarlet woollen shawl wrapped around her shoulders. A black-widow spider came somewhat easily to mind. Matilda closed the door quietly, and stood there for what seemed like several minutes, uncertain what to say or how to begin. Verity didn't look up. She certainly knew how to make things difficult. Matilda wondered if she did it on purpose, or if in fact she even realised. Finally she said.

"Verity. Could I have a quick word with you before the others come down?"

Verity looked up and seethed inside, while she stared at Matilda, her face completely expressionless. Matilda was distinctly 'under' dressed. Add to that the fact that she had not, by all accounts, been well, that she wore very little, if any, makeup. And all this, instead of distracting from her looks, seemed to be exactly what was required to enhance her tragic type of beauty, and especially accentuated those damn eyes!

"Sure!" She said as lightly as possible, uncurling her legs from under her, and slipping her feet into a pair of impossible shoes. Matilda swallowed.

"It's about yesterday afternoon…" Verity interrupted…"Yes, Giorgio told me, he explained."

For a moment Matilda felt her mind go blank. But having launched herself into the 'lioness's' den, she was too energised in that one direction and she continued…"I don't really know where to start Verity. Maybe, you know when we lost you all when we were riding…" Verity sighed impatiently…"Don't bother. I just told you, Giorgio explained."

"Explained what Verity?" Matilda probed as gently as possible. She needed to hear this! "Explained about the rehearsal! Hmm…Othello wasn't it?"

Matilda felt as if she had been slapped very hard around the face. She could do nothing except stare in silence at Verity, who was becoming more and more impatient. She began to speak slowly and loudly, as if Matilda had lost all her cognitive abilities.

"He told me that he was explaining some part of Act Three to you. Some possible staging for the big duet, or some such thing. I just love the music. I don't really care what any of you get up to on stage." The last said with an emphasis which left no doubt that off-stage would, however, be met with no such understanding. As Matilda still stared at her blankly she added…"Surely you remember, Matilda?"

Matilda's head had begun to ache, and her energy drained quickly downwards, as if into the earth itself. For a fleeting moment she was afraid that she might faint. Verity was still talking away. If Matilda hadn't been so preoccupied, she would have realised that Verity had a sneaking respect for her. She didn't like her, of course. Verity didn't really like anyone, except Verity, but she almost admired Matilda's honesty, and was finally convinced that any attraction between the singer and Giorgio was firmly emanating from Giorgio alone, and that Matilda was not interested. Verity's strange mind did possess remarkable instinct. Undisciplined and psychopathic as it was, but remarkable none-the-less. It was some seconds before Matilda gathered her thoughts, and picked up on Verity's flow again…"So, it's just a few of us this evening. Giorgio's invited that tenor. You know the one from the concert, what's his name? Martin isn't it? And the little woman of course! It'll be quite cosy, won't it?"

She had moved to the door, her heels clicking on the wooden floor. The dress clinging to her as if its life depended on it. Matilda was rooted to the spot. The door closed behind Verity in a swirl of expensive perfume. Matilda heard her call to Giorgio as she set off towards the kitchen where he was preparing the meal.

Cooking was, as with many singers, a hobby of his. Apparently he was very good! And for this Matilda was grateful. 'So.' She thought. 'All this, and Martin too!'

Boxing Day

"………..And this is Martin's lovely wife, Connie."

Giorgio was introducing her. Matilda put out her hand, not too quickly, she hoped. She was faced by a very intelligent looking lady, some ten years older than herself. She was extremely well dressed, but she was nothing like that phantom from the dim and distant past who Matilda had imagined the mate of He-who-had-deceived-her, would be like. Connie was blonde with a trim pert figure, and an unusual face. Not exactly beautiful, but certainly she was someone you would not easily ignore. Verity was purring over Matilda's shoulder in the sure and certain realisation that she was 'still the fairest of them all.' She didn't count Matilda, who was desperately hoping that she wasn't going to blush. Every time Connie met a female friend or colleague of Martin's, she must surely (given her husband's reputation) assume that at least an attempt at seduction had taken place. Well this time she would be right. Matilda tried to raise a strong feeling of vindication, by reminding herself that she had known nothing of Martin's engagement. It was not as easy as one might imagine. However, if Connie was questioning the possibility in her mind, nothing of it registered in the clean, neat features, and her handshake was warm and friendly. Giorgio disappeared into the kitchen, and Matilda felt certain that she noticed a look of relief cross Connie's face.

"So how's my personal soprano?" Martin said rather too loudly, he had passed Giorgio in the doorway, and was making his way straight towards them. He gave Matilda a quick hug, and she reacted in the way that she supposed she must, in the way everyone would expect. She giggled witlessly, hating the sound of it while she attempted to draw Connie into the conversation by asking if they had had a good Christmas day, and hoping they wouldn't inquire about her own. She supposed she could always use the 'under-the-weather-ploy' she thought as Connie smiled and made a bee-line for Giorgio's book shelves as if drawn by a magnet. She stood with Martin alone, noticing that he looked more morose than ever under his hearty greeting, and not a little drawn and tired.

'Lucciano…Lucciano…' She thought, looking at him. This wasn't something that she had ever done before. A direct conscious thought linking one life with another. The result was amazing. Martin stopped in mid-sentence.

"What did you say Tilly?"

"N…nothing." She stammered, completely taken aback by his response.

"I heard you say something." He laughed. Matilda shook her head. "Too much Christmas cheer Martin!" She said.

"Oh bollocks!" He replied. "First today!" And he raised his glass, adding. "I know you said something, you just didn't move your lips." He grinned at her.

"Oh shut up Martin. I didn't say anything!"

"O.K. So, I must be reading your mind." He continued with ridiculous Halloween effects. Matilda wished he'd drop it and she swallowed uncomfortably. "I didn't think you believed in that sort of thing?" She said.

"Oh, I don't." He assured her. "Although I have been having some really crazy dreams lately!"

'Be very careful.' Thought Matilda. Martin leaned closer to her. "Wouldn't you like to hear them?" He leered.

"No thank you Martin. I'm sure they're hugely indecent."

He laughed again, rather too loudly. Instinctively Matilda glanced over to where Connie was immersed in one of Giorgio's old books. But she was in a world of her own.

"Talking of indecent…" He lowered his voice considerably. "Don't suppose your sexy friend is with you?"

Matilda sighed. "Which one Martin?" He looked at her oddly for a second or two, made as if to say something serious, but then (to Matilda's intense relief) seemed to think better of it, and said.

"Pixie! I though you might have brought her with you."

'Why?' Thought Matilda as she replied. "No, the invitation was just for me."

"What a shame!" Sighed Martin. And looking under his eyebrows at her intent on her reaction. He continued. "We've been getting on rather well lately!"

Matilda couldn't believe her ears. Pixie and Martin? He seemed overly eager for her to know. She could be forgiven for believing that he wanted to make her jealous, although she couldn't imagine why. But she was suddenly mad at him.

"Martin, how can you? Pixie is a lovely person." Martin interrupted. "Oh believe me darling this I know to be true, Lovely all over she is."

"You cannot go around hurting people like this all the time." Matilda hissed as she suddenly remembered Pixie's behaviour at the stage rehearsal just before Christmas and the references to her 'naiveté.' Martin made a face as if the most diabolical smell had suddenly wafted under his nose.

"Don't be ridiculous Tilly. Pixie can look after herself, she knows the score. She's not a child."

"Who's not a child?" Verity, who had been stalking them for the last few moments, cut in. Martin smiled at her and replied, as he looked her up and down. "You for one darling." And he turned his back on Matilda with a rudeness, that even for him, she found hard to believe. Suddenly axed from the conversation, she felt stupid and was relieved to see Giorgio. He looked at Martin and Verity with scarcely disguised amusement and said.

"Martin, don't monopolise the ladies." He then walked straight up to Connie and offered her his arm saying. "Martin, your wife looks wonderful. Come on, my masterpiece awaits, we'll eat in the small dinning room. There's a log fire in there, and we won't rattle around so much as we would in the Restaurant... Matilda you still look a little pale, are you sure you're recovered?...Verity, tear yourself away there's a good girl...."

And he led them along the oak panelled hall which ran parallel to the restaurant, to the small private dinning room at the end.

In spite of herself. Matilda relaxed on entering the room. Soft lights and candles burned everywhere. The round table in the middle was laid for a feast and the long table along the side wall, gave evidence of Giorgio's industrious day. The smell was so delicious that Matilda found her mouth watering for the first time in ages.

"Wow!" Smiled Verity, and Giorgio beamed making an expansive gesture with his arm. "Prego amici miei,'elpa youraselves!" He said with a flourish. Dante flashed into Matilda's mind, followed quickly by a concerned question mark. But he had promised that the New Year would be theirs. Maybe he'd ring tomorrow? Perhaps there was already a message waiting for her, at the flat?

"Matilda, please…" Giorgio was placing a beautiful dinner plate into her hands. He pushed her gently towards the others who were already loading their plates as if expecting famine to descend. She gazed at the spread noting that Verity had left Martin's side, and he was actually being charming to his wife, 'Good!' She thought. Giorgio certainly knew how to pull out all the stops when he wanted. All of this must have taken hours, and he surely must have risen at dawn to accomplish it. He had prepared Goose, Venison and. Duck, beside the more usual Turkey and ham. Each with more than one choice of sauce, which were all his own recipes, he told them proudly. They were so delicious that Connie, in spite of her reservations regarding Giorgio, begged one of the recipes from him, and he smilingly presented her with a copy. He had prepared vegetables in every conceivable way imaginable, some appearing in as many as three different guises. The dessert trolley was no less impressive. Matilda decided that Giorgio must love cooking and preparing meals such as this, she was quite certain that an inspection of the rubbish would not reveal any Supermarket cardboard boxes, still cold from the freezer. Even the ice cream tasted different. There was an appropriate wine with every course, not to mention drinks before and after. Finally, way beyond sated, they all collapsed in front of the huge log fire with brandies, and streggas. It was still quite early and Giorgio clicked on the T.V.

"Let's watch our little Matilda." He said as Matilda frowned. "What?" She muttered. Martin turned to her. "Boheme from the Opera House. It's being shown tonight darling, had you forgotten? You do remember it being recorded don't you?"

"Of course." Matilda yawned. She'd had a lot to drink, (for her anyway) And she watched in quiet amazement as Verity reached for the brandy bottle yet one more time. It didn't appear to even dent the surface of her equilibrium, however much she drank. Sometimes Matilda had to admit, she did feel something of a freak.

The opera had already begun, they were two thirds of the way through the first act. Matilda watched the familiar set through sleepy eyes, experiencing the odd sensation of being in two places at once. Watching the stage from the front, while having a firm memory of what it felt like to stand in that same space. She began to drift in and out of awareness in the very comfortable chair. She did not lose a sense of where she was, but the others' voices floated around her in profusion. It was strange how the volume seemed to have its own rules in this state, and for no apparent reason, a sound would suddenly stand out from all the rest in an absurdly boom-lie manner, as if the owner were shouting. Martin was making rude comments about the tenor who was singing Rodolpho. But what did she expect?

The man had hardly spun out the first page of music of 'Che Gelida Manina' before he cut in with his laboured criticism.

"Christ Giorgio. What's he doing?" He said, his voice slightly impaired by all the alcohol. Verity glared at him from the crook of Giorgio's arm. "We don't need a running crit' I'd like to hear the music." She snapped.

"Yes darling, wouldn't we all?" Martin retorted full of sarcasm. Giorgio said not a word, although he grinned and buried his face into Verity's soft, thick hair. Matilda floated back from some safe, warm place and forced herself fully awake. She felt she must say something. The Opera House had been buzzing about the singing from everyone involved. It was generally considered to be top notch in a world of excellence, and silly though it seemed she felt it was her duty to speak up.

"I think he's great." She said softly. "Oh bloody hell Tilly. Can't you hear it?"

"Hear what Martin? A beautiful tenor voice? And listen to the phrasing see what he does with the next phrase. Hear that?.."

"I'd very much like to." Spat Verity. "Sorry Verity" Matilda muttered, and felt herself blush. The handsome tenor had reached his top 'C' by this time. He held it with the courage of one accustomed to success. It soared out into the Opera House, and Verity cheered as if he had scored a goal. Giorgio laughed and ruffled her hair. Martin sulked deeply into his chair, and Matilda went back to sleep. During the interval, while some non musician from the T.V. broadcasting company, attempted to discuss both the opera and Puccini, Giorgio served coffee, and Verity shouted abuse at the screen, even managing to rouse

Martin to join her in an attack on the presenter who had obviously read everything available on the subject in hand, but who clearly didn't have an operatic bone in his body. Giorgio touched Matilda's hand and said, holding a small cup towards her.

"Here my dear. I don't mind you sleeping, but you must stay awake for the next act. You are featured you know!"

"Along with over 60 others!" Martin was becoming worse for several brandies, and he was in danger of becoming offensive. With determination, Connie drained her cup and said brightly.

"Who's for a walk?"

"What a marvellous idea Connie." Giorgio said nuzzling Verity's neck. But she moved deeper into the settee and said. "I'm going to stay here."

"I'll come" Matilda swigged her coffee hoping it would vanquish this terrible sleepiness. "I'm not desperate to see myself on tele!"

"Really?" Exclaimed Martin. Connie threw him a warning scowl, and he looked quickly away. The air was crisp, and the ground crackled beneath their feet. With the clear, full moon above them, they hardly needed the torches which they had brought. Giorgio strode ahead with Connie and Martin. Verity, true to her word, had stayed with 'Boheme.' and had teased them mercilessly for leaving before the end.

"None of you so-called opera singers staying here?"

"Well I've seen it." Giorgio joked, as if they were talking about a film. Verity had thrown a cushion at him, and made a rude sign.

"Are we going to the stables, Giorgio?" Matilda asked, as Giorgio seemed bent on that direction. "Absolutely." He assured her, adding, as he turned and smiled at her.

"Two minds with but a single thought." Their voices carried on the silvery air and the horses whinnied gently. Giorgio pulled open the top door and rubbed the beautiful noses. He whispered to them in Italian, and they shook their heads as if they understood.

"What a shame, we have nothing for them." He said. Matilda grinned as she joined them and Martin, now more sociable, but with the beginnings of a vicious headache asked her what was funny.

"Oh nothing." She replied, pulling some apples from her pocket. "I just thought we might end up here."

Giorgio's eyes sparkled. "Good girl. You are hereby forgiven for sleeping all evening." Matilda handed him the apples, and for a moment their eyes met. 'He's a different person.' She thought. Then quickly blotted everything out pertaining to the day before, which had begun to feel like weeks away. It was too much to deal with. Anyway the night air had restored her, and she felt much better.

"Want a lift tomorrow?" Martin kicked at the ground with the toe of his shoe. "Giorgio mentioned that you need to get back."

Matilda felt a weight lift from her shoulders. Since yesterday, she had berated herself several times over the fact that she didn't drive. Had she done so she would have made straight for Islington instead of having to lock herself in her room for the rest of the day. She smiled at Martin gratefully. "That would be great Martin, if that's alright with Connie?"

"No problem. We'll have you home by tea time."

Martin pulled away from the curb as Matilda put her key in the door. Connie was gearing up to say something, he could feel it. They turned left at the end of Cross Street, and pulled into the main road. It was deserted. Already the rather 'dead' after Christmas feeling was settling over everything. The decorations looked as if they had been up too long, and in the frosty air the various seasons greetings had lost their Christmas spirit. Martin pulled up at the first set of lights.

"I bet she gave you a run for your money Martin." Connie said suddenly and quietly.

"Before we were married Con." Martin had stopped the 'deny' game some time ago. He knew that what little value it had had at one time, was now faded. He leaned forward and rubbed the windscreen. It was freezing mercilessly, and the glass wasn't clear.

"Thoroughly nice young woman is Matilda. I like her. Did she refuse you poor boy when she discovered we were…What shall I call it…Clapped in irons together?"

"Women don't refuse me Connie, or so you've always told me." Martin turned the wheel to the right and they sat in silence until King's Cross station loomed up at them, and Connie said. "I think we should keep an eye on Matilda, Martin."

"What?" Martin slammed on the brakes as the lights turned against them. It was an excuse to vent his anger. The back wheels skidded slightly sideways, but neither of them even commented on it. "What the hell are you talking about?"

"I've told you before. I don't trust Giorgio. I feel…" "What Connie? What do you feel?" Martin cut in, sarcastic and edgy. He hated this sort of situation, and he hated the fact that Connie had become so au fey with his private life. She stared out of the window and for a moment he thought she wasn't going to answer. They pulled away from the lights, the only car on the road in the middle of London in the 21st. Century. Christmas or not, it was hard to believe.

"I think that somehow, Matilda is in some sort of danger." Connie cut across his thoughts. Martin laughed. "What do you think he's going to do Con? Murder her in the middle of a singing lesson? Don't be so bloody stupid. Are you just trying to punish me a bit more?"

Connie ignored him and continued. "Knowing you, I imagine you caused her some grief." "Well thanks wife of mine." Martin muttered, turning North towards Hampstead. "What exactly are you saying Con? Come on out with it, I know you've got some plan forming in that head of yours."

"What I'm saying is this. It's not likely that anyone else would know anything about Giorgio…" "Neither do we!" Martin interrupted. Connie put up her hand. "I would like to invite her over for a meal in the New Year, and have a talk with her."

"No!" Cried Martin feeling as if the ground beneath him was turning to liquid. "Absolutely not. Giorgio is a perfectly decent person. Look at the great time he's just given us. I mean did any of us have to lift a finger? He's extremely generous Connie, he treats his friends like bloody Kings. I just don't understand your mad ideas about him, never have done."

Connie was silent for a moment then she said. "Well, he's calmer since that little viper has moved in with him Martin. But it's still there."

Martin was becoming extremely impatient, he revved the

car engine and sighed deeply before asking her. "What? Exactly what is still there? What are you talking about?"

"There's something, and it is to do with Tilly. I won't push it if you're adamant. But I'm right I'm sure I am, we'll see." A few moments later she added softly. "Martin, it doesn't involve you, does it?"

Martin reached over and turned on the C.D. player. The Verdi Requiem with all the force of Mount Olympus filled the car with the Dies Irae. He didn't answer his wife, but suddenly he remembered his recent, frequent dreams. They rose up in his mind like dragons breathing fire. He stopped the car suddenly, opened the door and got out. He managed to put some distance between himself and Connie before he leant over, and threw up violently in the road.

The flat was silent, the whole house was silent. Matilda dropped her bag on the floor and stood still for a moment, feeling the inevitable tension of driving in a car with an ex-lover and his wife, gradually leave her. She deliberately blotted out Christmas day and headed for the phone. Her stomach flipped. There were three messages awaiting her. She took off her coat, pulled a frozen meal from the freezer and placed it on the counter for later. Then she flipped on the kettle. With a weak cup of honeyed camomile tea in her hand, she finally pressed the button on the answer machine and held her breath. The first message was a shock.

"Hello Matilda. This is Anne. Thank you for your card. However I'm very disappointed that you did not even contact me over Christmas. I had thought we might see you over the holiday. But, I suppose you may be working at your place. A call would be appreciated."

Matilda felt rather numbed. Then a ray of amusement warmed her. Who the hell was we? The Royal 'we,' or Anne and the very Reverend unpleasant? And her 'place'? She almost laughed out loud. Anne couldn't bring herself to name the Opera House. The little green god must be the busiest in the human psyche…Her mind swirled a little…

"And you, you jealous baggage…" No! She wouldn't go there. Not now, not yet. The second message cut in. It was from the Opera manager. She was ringing round the chorus in order to inform them that Jonathan Warrener would be hearing each singer towards the end of January. Just to acclimatise himself with each of them. Also there would be no other reauditions this season. Hope Christmas was good and see you Monday. There was one message left. As soon as the speaker drew breath Matilda knew it was Dante. It's strange how you can recognise inhalation over a machine.

"Merry Christmas, darling." Matilda's stomach unknotted. "I ama sorry about it all beforea the 'oliday it was a mess. I 'ope you 'ad some gooda time. I am O.K. buta not so 'appy withouta you carissima. Ia ringa you soon."

Matilda was beaming from ear to ear by the time the message had finished. And she whispered. "What a lovely man!" A sardonic voice in her head answered her. "Do you think so? Is it really so wonderful of him to take the time and trouble to leave one message in a week? How long did that take him, 15, maybe 17 seconds? Perhaps while his fiancé was making coffee? Oh no, they have servants to do all that. Come to think of it though, it must be very hard for him to find time by himself to do anything at all, much less ring his mistress!"

"Shut up!" Matilda said aloud. "Just shut up!" She turned on the T.V. and headed back into the kitchen to make some more tea. It was not a pleasant evening. She felt nervous, as if some monster paced the edge of her mind, but she could not name it. The television helped a little. She attempted to relax into the pro-grammes, and being Christmas the range was considerable. She tried to quiet her mind by giving it something else to focus on, but it was a battle. She told herself that all she needed was to get back to work, that the daily routine of the Opera House would calm her and help to place everything into perspective. Finally she went to bed, and found it impossible to sleep. At around 3:00a.m. she muttered to herself. "Old man, where are you?"

The old man had fought hard for some time, and he was some-thing of a warrior when necessary, but he needed Matilda to fight with him. He needed her to name her monster, point a rebellious finger at it, and then destroy it. He also knew that in her present state, she wasn't aware of her own truth. He could not make contact, and there was worse, much worse by far…

To the north of the turquoise lake, lay deep glorious forests. The lush vegetation was as verdant as ever. The myriad of greens blended into the sky-line. But deep amongst the roots of the trees there was movement. Not caused by fresh breezes nor the cooling rain, but by something he dreaded. In the sweet-smelling mist, in the glades and forest landscapes moved the long sinuous black snakes of paranoia and deep mistrust of the self.

New Year

The canteen was buzzing. Dancers and singers jostled each other for Christmas Fare still on show in the plastic cases.

"Haven't you had enough of that?" One of the male corps de ballet teased another, sticking his finger playfully into the muscled mid-drift.

"You could eat like that all the time and it'd never show. Not like us!" Grumbled Pixie, who was standing behind them looking the worst for 'Christmas wear.'

"Don't you believe it!" Laughed the shorter of the dancers, hesitating between a mince pie and a slice of Christmas cake. "It sits like lead does this stuff, tastes good though!" Pixie smiled a smile which clearly stated that she didn't believe him, and firmly replaced two mince pies back into the display cabinet, and picked up a banana. When she finally reached the check out she glanced round hoping to see Martin. He wasn't there of course. Boheme was still running, not due to end until after New Year. There were no extra singers required. The stage was bursting with enough actors to start a small drama company, and non-dancing Opera ballet dancers all over the place to 'pretty up the picture.' Pixie sometimes wondered how much the singing really mattered. There was so much to look at in fact, that she was amazed half the audience had time to register Puccini at all.

She spotted Matilda sitting, miraculously, alone at a small table, and made straight for her as quickly as possible through the crush. She sat down with a sigh and put the banana and a black coffee on to the table in front of her. Matilda was engrossed in her book and she looked up in surprise, not expecting anyone else just yet. She had come in early needing to find a corner full of Opera House buzz where she could let it flow over her, without having to expend too much energy, she still felt drained.

"I feel dreadful!" Exclaimed Pixie. "I ate far too much...Both days...Before meals, during meals, between meals. God! It's a wonder I made it through the night!"

And she attacked the coffee as if it were the elixir of life.. Matilda closed her book and smiled at her.

"Well. I don't see any evidence. Even if there is, you'll soon lose it!"

"Yea, I guess. Hmm by the way, heard the latest on Rachel and Co?"

"No." Matilda replied, taking a sip of her tea. "So what's happened now. I mean I thought that was all done and dusted."

"Well. Apparently his lordship has relented. It seems he can't live without our lovely Rachel, and is braving the furies of hell from 'er indoors to continue the liaison!"

"Presumably 'er indoors doesn't know it's continuing does she? Mind you if half of what I've heard about the lady is true, she doesn't have room to talk!" Said Matilda.

"This is true." Grinned Pixie. "At least he limits himself to one at a time. I've heard the wife has a rostra set up when she's singing somewhere. You know…" As Matilda's eyes widened. "Fred at 2:30, Tom at 3:00. Etc, etc…"

"Oh I can't believe that!" Laughed Matilda.

"Why not? Melba used to have them lined up in the interval. And, what's more the opera couldn't continue until she was um… ready! And as for Chaliaplin.."

"Well if you sing like them, I guess that's different."

"I don't see why." Pixie replied. "I mean God's already given them the cream of his vocal material. Why should they have all the fun as well? Anyway. Having been the cause of a Caribbean holiday for the 'Mrs.' Rachel is now insisting that she be given the same treatment."

"Good for her! It's just as well that he is in such demand in the operatic world, must cost him a packet between the two of them!"

"You haven't heard the juiciest bit. You remember that dishy Italian producer? What did he do now? We weren't in it…"

"Hmm…Fancuilla, wasn't it?"

That's it. Well, it seems that the lovely Rachel has caught his eye, and she spent the holiday in Milan with her new boyfriend. The English camp was not happy about this little piece of news and is demanding a 'replay' as it were."

Matilda was giggling by this time. "Pixie, shame on you. You make it sound like a football match."

"It reminds me of one. England versus Italy. Just as long as no one scores any goals." "Pixie stop it." Admonished Matilda, but her friend, well into her stride now, shrugged her shoulders and continued. "Well I saw her just now and I thought she's putting on a bit of weight, you know?"

"Enough! No more Pixie. We'll be starting a rumour next. You know the walls in this place have ears."

"Well whatever. But watch this space, as they say. Now back to us, so how was Christmas with Giorgio?"

Matilda ached to tell her exactly what had happened on Christmas day, and the bizarre contrast with Boxing day. She looked at Pixie. Here was an old friend she could trust, she knew that, so surely she was also someone in whom she could confide? She took a deep breath and searched in her mind for a starting place, for the right words. It would be impossible to leave anything out and make sense of it all. But then to tell it, would, she realised, be asking for trouble. So all she muttered was. "O.K!" But Pixie barely noticed. "So, what's she like?" She asked. "Who?" Matilda was, for the moment confused.

"Tilly!" Pixie cried in exasperation. She leant across the table as if anyone would hear her in all the noise that was going on. "Martin's wife…What's her name…Connie!"

Matilda was thankful she hadn't commenced on a journey into Giorgio's behaviour, or any other part of the whole complex situation come to that. She smiled at Pixie and replied. "Well, unusual and not what I expected at all. You wouldn't call her beautiful, but then you certainly wouldn't ignore her either. She was generally quiet. Martin was disgusting, drank more than he could handle, so what's new? (Oh sorry!) They gave me a lift back yesterday. By the way, have you phoned Irena yet?"

Matilda hoped that she may have changed the subject and veered Pixie away from the whole charade. She hadn't!

"No. I'm going to wait until the New Year. Did you speak

to La Con? You obviously know about Martin and me. I hope you're not upset?"

"Yes, yes and definitely not! But I hope you know what you're doing. Martin is a perfect bastard when he wants to be. I don't suppose he can help it.. "(As Lucciano floated into inner view).."But that's not the point…"

"It's just a bit of fun Tilly. Relax. I'm having a wonderful time. It's just sex, no strings, and no romantic intrigue, or deep true love. It's a breath of fresh air. You should try it sometime."

Matilda felt a chill, and inexplicably tears rising, their suppression feeling like a dead weight in her throat. She would have said a lot more, but Pixie had turned her attention to her and Dante.

"You're wasting yourself you know?"

'And you're not?' Thought Matilda, raising one eyebrow, a slight movement but Pixie caught it.

"I know, I know. But this is as much on my terms as Martin's. But you and the Italian Count? I mean when did you last even speak to him? I know you haven't seen him for months I think it's unfair, completely unfair to you."

Matilda was rather hurt and frustrated. How could she expect anyone to understand about Dante? "He left me a message over Christmas Pixie, and anyway we are about 'true love' if that's what you want to call it."

"A message hey? That was good of him. As to the 'true love' Tilly, please don't fall for that one. He's got it made the Iti bastard!"

Matilda put Pixie's rudeness down to the effects of her excessive Christmas. But it had upset her. There was no comparison between what she and Dante had, and Pixie and Martin's affair. Was there? No, she knew Martin, Pixie seemed to conveniently forget that. Like so many others she had appeared to make the mistake of assuming that with her it would all be different. Matilda faced the nasty feeling rising up from her chest, and in order to subdue it, she came to a quick and quite sudden decision. She smiled slightly and said. "Well, we'll see. But why are we arguing over men for goodness sake? That's not what we're about Pixie. We've only been out of college a couple of years. All this was our dream. Don't you remember sitting up in the gods, and just longing to be on this stage? The same space which we now tread nearly every day. We can't have become blasé so quickly. All the rest can wait a few years. We're here to sing."

Pixie looked at her seriously for a few moments. Then she said. "No Tilly. We're here to live."

Matilda looked sincerely puzzled, and frowned as she replied. "Same thing, isn't it?"

The delights of Boheme, L'Elisir D'amore, The Nutcracker, and Sleeping Beauty, swept through the Opera House over the next week. As she left the theatre late New Year's Day after their matinee, the operatic contribution for the day, Matilda suddenly realised that the next day was Sunday. She had certain things that must be done, but, after that was all accomplished she decided that she would sit very quietly and think. No interruptions and no more procrastination. She had already made some moves regarding her career, and she had sent off for auditions to smaller companies in the London area.

"You're mad." Pixie had said. "They're terrible to work for, apparently. Rotten conditions, impossible schedule and hardly any money. Also, you have to get N.A's from here. I mean is it worth it?… "

"Good idea!" Said Maria. "Get yourself heard outside a bit. Do something away from here!"

Irena had nodded wisely and agreed with Maria by pointing out to Matilda that she shouldn't wait for Tony London's agencey to do all the work, because chances are, how ever well she sang at the concert, and what ever Bella told him about her, he wouldn't do much, or at least not enough. It was experience she needed. So what did it matter if the money was poor and the circumstances less than what she was used to? After all she had a good, well paid job….

So, three to one, no contest! The auditions wouldn't be for a few weeks yet, she thought pulling up her collar. It was freezing outside. A group of people arriving early, in order to eat before the performance of Sleeping Beauty that evening, spilled out of a taxi right in front of her. Fate! she decided, and stood to one side while one of the party settled with the driver.

"Will you take me to Cross Street please?"

"Sure luv', 'op in!"

God bless the London Taxi. She was home in 20 minutes.

JOURNAL

What a peaceful time New Year's Night and today have been. It should be mandatory for everyone to spend a certain amount of time to themselves regularly in order to keep their lives straight. I mean, how can anyone keep up with the best way forward for them, if they never actually have the peace and quiet to think about it? Just coming to definite decisions is like a week's holiday. All I have to do now is carry it all out. First I'm going to take my courage in both hands, and phone Dante. He has given me his number for emergences, and we have a cover story. I am his English publisher. Well, this is as good a time as any.

It's always unsettling, the way phones in foreign countries ring differently. Matilda's stomach did a few back flips as she listened to the phone buzzing in the palazzo, but she held fast to her decision and didn't hang up. Finally it was answered.

"Prego? Il Conte Vittoria…"

Matilda had expected a servant to answer, she seemed to have got straight through to God! Carefully she composed herself.

"Buona sera Signor, e posso parlare a Dante per favor? Son Signora…" She didn't have to finish the cover explanation. There was a grunt, a "momento" and an impatient call for Dante. Matilda hoped fervently that this phone was in a hall, so there would be a certain amount of privacy. She could pick up no clues at all although she found herself straining against the ear piece trying to do so. The next thing she heard was Dante's voice.

"Prego?"

"Dante, darling. It's me , I'm sorry to phone but I had to speak to you." There was enough of a pause for Matilda to be concerned, and enough of an edge in Dante's voice for her to be devastated. At some point he whispered furiously into the phone.

"What you do Matilda? 'Es nota for dis use. I say emergency, is whata I mean." Then he continued speaking at a normal volume as if he was talking to his English publisher, whose Italian is rather slow. Matilda had gone cold. Never had she heard irritation in Dante's voice. When she could get a word in, she tried to explain.

"Dante, it's not as if I make a habit of this. I just needed to hear your voice it is New Year after all. I don't expect you to talk for long…"

Dante interrupted her . If he hadn't…If only he hadn't said what he then did say. Matilda would have forgiven him anything. But she was at heart, something of a romantic. And this was not what she expected to hear from a passionate lover whom she had not seen for some time and who had asked her at their last meeting to hold tight to the faith of their love, and that they must stay together whatever happened. No this was not what she expected. Dante hissed at her.

"My voice. Donta be ridiculous! Es a stupida ding toa say.!"

"What did you say Dante?"

Through her confusion Matilda felt strength rising like a volcano and as it erupted she watched the part which adored Dante distinctly disengage, saw it stand off to one side as if in exile, shining in its purity, but incapable of much else. She was even more strengthened by its release, and she repeated her question at considerable volume.

"What did you say? Basta! If that's how you feel you can get stuffed. Run back to your wonderful old family, and leave me alone. Bugger off Dante!" And down went the phone.

The young Count replaced the hand set and took a few moments before returning to his guests. He stood staring out of the window into the lighted courtyard below. Friends were still arriving. He watched the shining expensive cars come softly to a halt to allow their shining expensive owners to alight. What a selection of fur coats and designer clothes! He could almost smell the perfumes from here. The aristocratic families of Southern Europe were assembling in his Father's ballroom, where his soon-to-be-fiancé was waiting for him to join her. It was all waiting for him. His glorious golden future. It was nothing more than he had been prepared for, trained for, expected, but not wanted. Only his Mother saw his anguish, but even she didn't know how deeply it ran. How much he longed for freedom, or failing that, death.

He decided to find her before the evening got under way. He needed to speak with her. He had already spoken to his Father, to no avail, but he was very much aware of the pressure to announce his engagement and forthcoming marriage that very evening. After all what better time to do so? Once that happened he would really be in the 'soup' how would a 'Vittoria' back out of such a contract? It would be unthinkable. He made for the library, and sent a message by one of the many extra servants hired for the evening, to ask his Mother to join him there. He sat down and waited.

What was that hum? The wiring? It had to be. He must talk to his Father about it, if he could ever speak about normal things to his Father again. The fire was very warm and the hum seemed louder than ever. He closed his eyes wishing himself far away from where he was. That hum was more vibration than sound!

The next moment he was in a dream. He was sitting in the same room, but there were candles everywhere, the rain was pulsing on to the glass and every now and then smoke puffed into the room.

He was sitting opposite a young, handsome and very slender man. They were in deep conversation about something, but Dante couldn't register what they were saying. However, as he glanced down at himself in the dream, his attention was drawn to something he was wearing around his neck. A deep-green amulet set in a strange and unusual setting. As he looked deep into the stone, the vibration intensified and he awoke with a start to find his mother seated on a chair the other side of the fire place.

Catrina Vittoria drew her silk shawl more closely around her slender shoulders and was gazing at Dante with intense affection.

"So my love, what is all this with your Father?"

"What do you mean Mamma?"

"Dante, you avoid him, and he you. Also he has been roaming around like a mad bear. Please don't shut me out, I'm not an idiot. How can I help you two, if I don't know what's going on? Now tell me!"

Dante dropped his eyes from the still-lovely Contessa's face, and chewed his lip.

"I…I can't marry Leonora, Mamma. I love someone else."

"Ah!…" Breathed Catrina and paused before asking. "Who is she?"

"It doesn't matter who she is, she's not suitable, not to Papa anyway. She's English. You know who she is." He finished with some irritation.

"You haven't stopped seeing her?"

"I haven't stopped loving her. And just now, on the phone…I was stupid…We argued and she told me…"

"Yes?" Catrina raised her dark, arched eyebrows.

"She told me to bugger off…" Dante skilfully translated into Italian an approximation of what Matilda had shouted down the phone. He was never sure which century his parents were living in. And was suddenly afraid that his beautiful and refined Mother might be horrified. To his relief and some surprise she bit down on her lower lip and smiled at him.

"She has spirit then?"

"Mamma, she has…" The library door opened, and his Father stood there.

"How long must our guests wait, Dante? Come my dear." And he offered his arm to the Contessa. She hesitated, then gently said to her husband.

"They can wait a little. We must listen to Dante." At this the Count's eyes grew cold and defiant, but Catrina was at his side, and she added. "Yes, we must…Just as your Father listened to you."

The Count sighed and closed the door. "I wondered when that would come back to haunt me. So what do you have to say for yourself Dante?"

Betrayal

So, we start a New Year. It's hard for me to write, as it's hard to untangle my emotions. Anger and anguish intermingle, and are frozen over with fear. I face the beautiful ghosts by night, and only sleep by crying myself there. By day I'm sure I seem normal (if a little brittle) to my friends. Oh but it is a blessed relief to have such a job. To be so busy and engrossed is by far the best therapy. How long will it take me, I wonder, to lay the shade of Dante's smile, his dark beauty, the sound of his voice?

I catch myself laughing at work and stand back wondering, how can this be? Everything appears normal. My voice, so Irena tells me, continues to improve, and certainly feels so healthy when I sing that it is a joy to open my mouth. It ceases to matter if I have an audience or not. It fast becomes a form of physical meditation which I would not be without. But I see the part of me which adores him, still exiled outside myself. Head bowed and curled in a corner and only creeping back to totality at night when the music finally stops. I no longer see Lucciano's face in the Cathedral for I have no space left for another's misery.

It was a few weeks into the year, and not too long before Matilda's recital. Jonathan was making a phone call to an old friend.

"Giorgio? It's done! Just thought you'd like to know."

"Good. I'm sure you'll live to see the wisdom of all this." Replied Giorgio. Jonathan sincerely hoped so. "She certainly is good Giorgio." This was something of a gross understatement!

"Of course she is! Why do you think I'm taking all this trouble?" Giorgio's reply was somewhat edgy. Jonathan was silent. His conscience was pricking him very hard at the moment. He had yet to meet the music staff and he was sure there would be questions. Not only was he insisting that they pass up on a very good talent, everybody, it seemed liked the bloody girl! His silence irritated Giorgio, who did not need the idiot to go back on his decision. He continued.

"We both know why you agreed to do this Jonathan, don't we?" Jonathan attempted to laugh, but he laughed alone. Giorgio, in typical fashion now felt, in spite of what Jonathan had achieved for him, some contempt, and Jonathan felt it. It hit him like a frozen boxing glove, suddenly and without warning. He felt nauseous, but it was too late, and anyway the relief at being rid of the tax man breathing down his neck was so sweet it was almost intoxicating.. He promised himself two things. Never to get into debt again. And to get into the pert little thing that he had lined up to replace Matilda, as quickly as possible. That made him feel ever so much better.

Martin had had dreams like this before. Dreams that he had mentioned in passing to Matilda, on Boxing day. He had no dreaming skills to help him, and so this meant that usually he soon forgot the facts on awakening, and was left only with the emotion. That would often follow him around for days, dogging his every attempt at normality and a good time.

He was rapidly tiring of Pixie. The lust had worn off, and frankly there wasn't much else, certainly not love, heaven forbid! And he realised, not that much affection. To be honest though, it was not all her fault. In fact very little of it was her fault. He was so bloody tired, and that brought him back to the dreams again. Maybe he should talk to Matilda? The problem with that though was that she was mixed up in them somehow, but he could never quite remember in the morning just how she was involved. Only the feeling remained, and even he was not too proud of that.

He felt as if he could cheerfully throttle her. No…Not exactly throttle, but something to do with the throat. And now this last little gem, He sat on the end of the bed, shaking and in the full knowledge that he would not be able to get back to sleep. At least Connie didn't know. At least she wasn't asking questions, and demanding answers.

The undignified little scene from a few months ago haunted him still, and he hated it although it had procured him financial security.

After the Tony London concert, he hadn't, as his wife had requested, left the luxurious apartment in Hampstead, but had waited until she returned. He then begged her to have lunch with him. Entreated her to 'talk things over.' He had then taken her to Knightsbridge, to the restaurant which Giorgio favoured so much. It was a relaxing atmosphere, and the waiters, as if on cue, treated Connie as if she were a film star, but with the sincerity of the Latin male. It wasn't something which she could ignore, or become suspicious about. He had sat opposite her that Sunday lunchtime and had been as contrite as he knew how to be.

"You must think me a complete prat!" He began, expecting his wife to leap in and deny it for him. She didn't. She remained silent but looked at him with eyes which seemed to bore into him. He was not a little uncomfortable.

"What can I say?.." He began. And then she did interrupt him.

"What can you say? Nothing actually. At least nothing that will make any difference!" Martin had gone cold, believing himself to be almost out on the street. Or at least skulking in some damp little flat somewhere with no hope of ever improving his situation. "Oh come on Con you're not going to throw me out are you? What do I have to do, beg you?"

"I told you, you can't say anything that will make any difference. So keep quiet, and after we've eaten I'll tell you exactly how it's going to be. How it's going to be that is, if you want to stay in our very nice apartment. And keep yourself warm with my money."

Martin squirmed at the last remark. He had a natural need to be the major bread winner. The need was natural to him anyway. Times had changed, he knew that. Most of his friends referred to him as a 'jammy bugger.' He laughed, joked and went along with it all, but it wasn't the way he really wanted it.

Then they had eaten their meal with scarcely a word spoken. From Martin's point of view, this was because Connie was so 'mad' at him. From hers however, it was much more complicated. Because, despite everything, Connie loved Martin. As various rumours had inevitably found their way to her, almost since her marriage began, she was forced to admit to herself, she had tried very hard to stop loving him. He, after all, treated her like 'shit.' A fact her friends never lost the opportunity to point out to her. She had set about working in her mind with a definite 'dismantling' technique for her feelings. This was something her friend Dawn had come up with having successfully used it as her own first marriage hit the rocks.

However in Connie's case it didn't seem to work. Try as she might (and indeed she did try very hard) she couldn't unplug certain aspects of her relationship, and finally she had to admit, to herself and Dawn only, that she was 'stuck' with him.

"Well O.K." Dawn had accepted. "It's no good if you're banging your head against the wall. But don't let him treat you as if you're a second class citizen. Point out to his 'pratship' occasionally, just who is holding everything together financially. I mean singing for a living. Whoever heard of anything so ridiculous?"

Dawn was not sympathetic towards art or artists. But although Connie had never discovered anything of that nature lurking in her own mind or heart, she did possess an innate understanding of artists. Unfortunately! She added to her own thoughts. And apart from all this Connie was not the most secure cookie in the jar. She had never got over the fact that Martin had taken any notice of her in the first place. Yet, despite the huge chasm between them in a professional sense, their affair had escalated quicker that she even dreamt that it might, and when he actually proposed to her that beautiful spring night, she at last allowed herself to believe that he really did love her. She had accepted in what could only be described as a 'heightened' state, and saw their future rolling out in front of them. What could possibly go wrong? Well, plenty actually. She soon discovered that she had married a weak and selfish man. A man who finally turned from her totally after a disastrous miscarriage which had left her deeply distressed in very real need of some kindness. At some point she remembered him accusing her of having an affair.

"The timing was off for me to have been able to be the Father." He had shouted. "You can't get pregnant at such a time!"

She had been much too upset to retort, that you could, in fact, get pregnant at any time, and the depth of her feelings threatened to consume her entirely. After that he rarely approached her sexually, unless he wanted something. She began to realise that he was infuriated by what he considered as her 'failure,' while at the same time being rather relieved that it had happened. The complication of an addition to the family, was not something that he wanted, not deep down anyway. It was the injustice of this memory that laid the basis for her demands. Separate rooms was one of them. She had painted the condition in highly colourful terms, in language which Martin for one had never heard her use, and from that day she had changed a lot. Ironically, because of this and for reasons which he didn't bother to question, Martin found that sometimes he was in danger of falling in love with her all over again.

However, he had rather got used to sleeping alone, and quite liked it. It was condition number one. How had she put it? Oh yes: He could keep that dirty little thing away from her, since she couldn't be sure where it had been. He grinned despite himself. Connie had been so furious! Except for her use of 'little' he found himself on the edge of applauding the perfect rhythm which such anger can sometimes bring to a speech.

Christ! There must be something wrong with him He didn't seem capable of true feeling anywhere in his life except in these damn dreams.

This time he did remember a little more than usual. He was standing in front of a big, rather grandioso-style bed. Beneath the crumpled silk sheets lay a figure. The figure was very beautiful, but here some mist was rising, because one moment it represented Matilda, and the next it appeared to be a young man. A young and rather effeminate man to whom Martin was strongly attracted. No, it was more than that. A bit of sexual arousal in a dream which featured a man would not have bothered him unduly, after all it was only a dream. No, what threw him completely was that he was very aware that he loved this man totally, in fact there was almost adoration for him. He was certain that he would have died for him without a second thought. And this was something which other shadowy people in the room didn't seem to understand. They kept trying to take him away, insisting that he must go and sing somewhere. He leaned forward and shook the sleeping figure. But it wasn't sleeping. He realised that this beautiful enigma, was dead. He opened his mouth to scream, and awoke, aware that he was making an odd moaning noise, as if the dream were too far away for him to match it physically. The only question to resound in his mind for the next 48 hours or so, was why in God's name could he not feel that way about a woman in the waking world?

The alarm penetrated Matilda's final and unremarkable dream of the night. She turned over and hit the knob, then snatched her arm back under the duvet. It was cold, the heating had yet to kick in. She couldn't think why she had set the alarm so early. Clouds scudded fast across the sky passed her window. It had been raining, and was still very dark. Reluctantly she swung her legs over the side of the bed, and pulled on her dressing gown, at that same moment the boiler fired. She decided to make some tea and bring it back to her still warm bed until the flat lost its chill.

She had obviously taken a N.A. for the day from the Opera house, but as it happened the chorus was not required for that evening's performance anyway. She stood the tea by the bed and climbed back in keeping her dressing gown on and drawing her knees up to her chin. Solo recitals, she was in the process of learning, were proving, in her experience anyway, much more nerve racking than Operatic performances. First of all, she mused, you're on your own, except obviously for the pianist. And then…Well, that was enough really.

She much preferred to be part of a cast. It suddenly seemed terribly lonely. The phone rang, and so deep in reverie was she that it caused her to jump. The tea, barely tasted, and still very hot from lack of milk, spilt over her hand, which immediately turned bright red, and stung furiously. She let the phone go onto answer, and moped up the tea. She was to meet Damien at 12:00

o'clock to 'top and tail' and run through one or two other parts. As she thought about it, her mind took over and, starting at the beginning of the programme, began to go through the words. She shut it up quickly before it had a chance to establish the habit of the last few months. One thing she was sure of was that she knew the programme, backwards!

Damien was late. He had not taken a full day's N.A. and he had had calls at the Opera House earlier. Matilda hung up her dress, of which she was quite proud, and used the empty hall to warm up in. She had worked her way through to the upper register by the time Damien popped his head round the door, and she didn't hear him. He pulled back into the passage for a few moments, waiting for the right psychological moment to enter the hall. Finally it came.

"You sound in fine form Tilly. Sorry I'm late, hold up on the tube. Is Irena here?"

Matilda was surprise by the question. "Not until tonight Damien."

He nodded, but secretly he was torn. He had played for many singers who found it impossible to even warm up on their own the morning of a concert. It was normal practice to have one's teacher present, but usually he had never thought it was a very good idea, not healthy. But in this case, while he admired Matilda's independence, he really wanted a private word with Irena. He had, just that morning heard something at the Opera house which both surprised and disturbed him greatly. It concerned Matilda and this was certainly not the time to tell her. But he needed to find an opportunity to speak to Irena this evening. Matilda must be told gently by someone she trusted. She didn't deserve to discover this through the usual channels. By a note at the stage door and a taut and strained interview in the Opera office. However much the powers that be were amazed by it all, they would be forced to stand by this ridiculous decision. They certainly couldn't be seen to thwart the Chorus Master's. He wasn't even due to start the job until next season. It would be ludicrous for them to complain. Anyway they were all far too involved in important Opera house business. It was nothing for them to replace a chorister. They had a list of hopefuls as long as your arm. Anyway, the report on Matilda's singing was in fact, glowing, and his reasons for not wanting to renew her contract after the current season without hearing her again, were, on the face of it, positive. But who, Damien wondered as he began the introduction to the opening number, did he think he was, making such a decision for other people? Maybe she was quite happy to sing her working life away in a chorus?

Matilda's voice soared out into the auditorium. Well, it really was a top quality sound he thought. Maybe he was right this new 'Wunder Kind.' Maybe she should be pushed out of the nest? They stopped, and went to the end and to the last few bars. He, however, knowing just how heartless and selfish the music profession could be, was not so sure.

Journal

So, the winds of change. The force of destiny. It seems that I have lost my job, the very part of my life which I did feel was constant, about which I had few real fears. It doesn't matter how amazed and disgusted my friends and colleagues appear to be, there is nothing to be done. The Opera House is no longer interested in me. Oh it may be that it has all been generated by the new chorus master, but I am a member of that chorus, and I can't turn anywhere else for help in a situation like this.

I could insist on my right to audition again in 6 months, but there would be no one else there except Jonathan, and he (apparently) has made it very clear that he is not interested in hearing me. Frankly I don't see the point anyway, because I know that I sang well. I also know that our new Maestro doesn't like me. It will be hard for the rest of the season, but I'm determined not to let anyone see just how devastated I am. Coming so close to the big argument with Dante (from whom I've heard nothing) I'm beginning to feel more than a little paranoid. That, as I've said before, is my 'nemesis,' but I have been remembering what my Dad told me once when I mentioned what I considered to be my problem.

"Just because you're not paranoid, doesn't mean that they're not out to get you!"

And really I know that it's just one of those things. Jonathan Warrener has no reason to treat me badly, end of story. However I'm glad that there were quite a few members of the chorus at my recital. They were, it seems sincerely impressed and this was before any of them knew about 'dear 'Jonathan's decision, so it wasn't pity. Of course, then we come to Irena. Damien told her after the recital. I wondered what they were closeted up a corner about. When she spoke to me, Irena was gentle, sweet, and absolutely furious. She is prepared to ring the Opera House, and to tell them exactly what she thinks of them, and she is insisting on sending a recording to our esteemed Musical Director. But really, what can he do? He doesn't (as far as I know) have 'absolute power,' I'm just another chorister. Anyway he's far too busy, I feel sure that he won't even listen to it. Irena seemed disappointed when I said we shouldn't bother, but as positive as ever she replied.

"On the other hand darling, you don't need them. And if they are prepared to throw away such talent and a committed hard worker such as yourself, on a whim of an idiot such as this Warrener must be, then they deserve all they get. And if some of the things that I've heard on the grape vine are true, that's exactly what they will get!"

I was too miserable to ask her what she meant, and for once I couldn't care. Noticing my expression, she tailed off. It was impossible for me to engage any energy in thoughts of vengeance. Try as I might I couldn't see myself singing at La Scala or The Met. while rude signs were carried across the Atlantic ocean, or through Europe, on the spiral of deafening applause.

"Let's forget them." Irena continued. "I'm delighted with the recital and so glad that we have a tape. You should be over the moon. It was top class it really was!"

I'm not sure how much of this is true, and how much she exaggerated, in order to cushion my fall from grace. I suppose I can't be sure how anyone genuinely reacted, in the light of the circumstances which now surround me.

Irena had meant it. She questioned her own exuberance for one reason only. Was it coming solely from the way Matilda was singing, or was it being helped by something else?

It seemed strange, but Irena was aware that she was feeling very much better. She still had the 'thing,' (as she called it to

435

herself) she supposed. Well, obviously she did. Illness like that didn't simply disappear, if at all, certainly not in the short period of time since she had seen the Consultant. Since, well yes, since she had been working with Matilda really! Come to think of it, no doubt that's what it was. She needed to work with real talent. There was nothing like it for raising the energy, and therefore the spirits. That'd be what it was, no doubt!

Knife

Martin had gone to the concert. Against his better nature, something had driven him there. That, and the fact that Giorgio had asked him to go, since he was off to Switzerland with the 'lady.' Yes, well if he didn't feel that he needed Giorgio so much, he would have tried very much harder than he already had done with Verity. Giorgio's words filtered through his thoughts.

"Let me have a blow by blow my boy. I have to go I'm afraid. Business you know!"

Martin shifted uneasily in his seat, and hoped that he wouldn't doze off in the warmth of the room. Why did they have to have it so hot for God's sake? He didn't study Matilda too closely when she first entered. He could see at a glance that the dress she wore suited her admirably, and the velvet colour was a near perfect choice, but then he had always loved green velvet. All this he could ignore by simply not looking at it. The sound which she had begun to utter however, that, unless he blocked his ears, which was obviously not an option, that he couldn't do. He could only sit and squirm and curse Giorgio, who he assumed at that moment to be checking the money in his Swiss accounts. Instead of being here, which would have freed Martin from all this irritation.

Within seconds, Matilda was using the acoustic as if she sang in the bloody place every day. How could it be so easy for her? He knew it wasn't something that could be taught, that it wasn't something everyone could do. It was very instinctive. His frustration soared causing him to be incapable of sitting still and his whole body followed a nervous, slow dance, punctuating the music, until a member of the audience, who was sitting behind him, leaned forward between numbers, tapped him on the shoulder, and enquired if it were at all possible for him to keep still.

He decided that after the interval, he would stand at the back, if possible, providing that he stayed for the second half. He turned his attention to the audience. Pixie was around here somewhere. Don't suppose he could persuade her to leave, and have some dinner with him? No, not likely! This was torture, more so because he knew everyone would be impressed, and spend the interval trying to out do each other with adjectives expressing the 'glory' of La Tilly!

His eyes lit on Irena. Hers were closed and her mouth moved gently in time with the music, obviously tracing every phrase in her mind. She wasn't intrusive. In fact you'd have to concentrate very hard if you weren't a singer to realise what she was doing. Bloody female conspiracy! Tilly was one of hundreds, no, thousands of sopranos. She'd always had her own way, his thoughts continued. It's about time she was brought to heel a bit. His head had begun to ache, his sleeping pattern had not improved, and last night was as disturbing as ever.

Matilda returned for the last song group before the interval. The audience were expectant, and Martin mentally rolled his eyes, let's just get it over with. He leaned back, folded his arms, and let his chin sink almost to his chest. Matilda had taken a slightly different position on the small stage. It really was extremely warm in the hall, and he felt his head beginning to nod slightly, caught himself on the verge of napping once, and, in spite of his misgivings at being there at all, felt a pang of embarrassment. Gently he shook his head and focused on the singer in front of him. The figure seemed blurred. It didn't matter how hard he tried to focus, he could not. Her voice was distant, miles, no years away. It took on a strange sound, a sound which he recognised somewhere in his vast unconscious, but which his logical mind denied even before he could try to put a name to it. Images flashed through his mind, bright but fleeting. As soon as he managed to capture one, it was replaced by another.

The green of Matilda's dress reminded him of eyes, of something lost, something that leant into the core of his being that seemed to be tied up with the very reason he now lived.

Strange names rang in his head, snaking in and out of the music. He began to feel even hotter, and quite suddenly a sharp, choking pain grated across the front of his throat. The audience was applauding Matilda and Damien were bowing. Sweat poured from Martin's brow, he stood up and made for the exit. He kept going until the night air hit him. He still did not stop, and he did not return.

It was a few days later that Giorgio phoned Matilda. He had left a discreet space, lest it appear that he knew the bad news rather quickly, but as soon as Martin had left, after his lesson, which did not go well, not to mention the mood he seemed to be in, Giorgio felt it an acceptable time to commiserate with her. When she first answered, her voice sounded devoid of energy, although she tried to inject it with some life as soon as she realised who it was.

"I'm fine Giorgio, really. Thank you so much for phoning. Maybe it's for the best, you know? I probably would have stayed there for ever and missed any opportunity I might have for anything else."

"Exactly, cara. You are absolutely right to look at it this way. Keep your chin up. Everything will be alright. I just know it. You haven't had anymore bad day dreams about me, have you? No more delving into your dark side about your old friend?"

Not exactly the most diplomatic move, slipping straight from one subject to another, and such another! Matilda had not expected anything like that. "Er…No Giorgio!" She managed.

"Good, good. Well I must go, Verity is cracking the whip as usual! I'll speak to you soon Matilda. Bye now."

Matilda replaced the hand set. The usual uncertainties swamped around her. She had blotted out Christmas completely, had not given it any thought, but Giorgio as usual, reminded her of the very thing she most wanted to forget.

JOURNAL: *FEBURARY*

People always want to destroy. This is how it seems to me. Unless they can perceive one's 'other world' as a place of danger and forbidden darkness, they're not prepared to accept it's existence at all. They will take all the light, all this wonder, all the energy which can surge up the spine like the Gatwick express, and spin it into some dark Gothic myth. Make you feel guilty if they can, make you think that you have no right to these experiences. But worse by far is the habit which Giorgio seems to have developed. That what I know for sure happens in this world, has not happened at all. That I am in fact, experiencing some 'dark side' and that what I perceive is nothing more than a violent possibility. My memory of Christmas Day was no possibility. I know that it happened. My head sustained a bump to prove it. But why would Giorgio do this? It brings me back to why he insists that I was not Carlo. I do not wish to think about any of that just now. I am right, I KNOW it all happened, and I'm sure I was Carlo…Wasn't I?

Matilda forced her feeling of desolation to retreat, and turned the corner of the road at express speed. She bowled through the stage door, almost colliding with an international tenor of glorious voice, and dubious reputation.

"Excuse me." She blushed. Her act of 'I'm-just-fine-can't-you-tell?' would have to be pulled more into line. She couldn't afford to end up knocking out the soloists, they'd get rid of her before the end of the season at that rate. This soloist didn't mind at all. He was most gracious. Anyway, she thought as she made her way to the canteen, he's a big lad, he can take care of himself. She only hoped that she could.

A few moments later she sat down opposite Martin as Pixie rose to buy tea, having offered to get hers as well. The energy was still coursing through her, and she found she needed conversation to keep her mind occupied, at least until she had calmed down a little. She said the first thing that came into her head.

"How's Connie, Martin?"

"She's fine Tilly." Martin folded his arms and leaned back in his chair, watching her like a cat watches a mouse. His eyes glittered. It was very quiet in the canteen, lunch was over and there were only a few dancers from the Opera ballet bent over a table in heated discussion.

"What's cooking over there?" Martin said turning back from devouring every sinuous line. Matilda glanced in the direction of the group and replied.

"I could hazard a guess Martin, but you probably wouldn't want to know, too close to home. Anyway, I can't believe that you haven't heard all about it."

Martin sighed and smiled. "Come on Till, give…I love a bit of the latest gossip."

Matilda leaned slightly forward, enjoying the intrigue, it helped her to forget all her problems. "Well, you know Rachel?"

"Certainly!" Replied Martin opening his eyes wide and licking his lips. Matilda raised her eyes to the ceiling, and grinned.

"Yes, alright Martin! Well, apparently she was waylaid yesterday on the corner just outside by Joan Sinclair." Martin's eyebrows jumped a few inches. "Quite!" Matilda interrupted herself. "The lady informed her that she has finished with her errant husband, and that Rachel can have him. And, what did she think she was

doing refusing his offer of marriage? The fact that he is not free will be rectified as soon as possible. As if that's not enough, Rachel still refuses to have anything to do with poor old Stephen, who by the way cannot sing unless she is standing in the prompt corner, where he can see her. The Opera House has asked her to accommodate this need until Aida is over. Which she is doing. The chorus think her refusal is all a sham, that she really wants to marry him and that she's punishing him for making her play 'second trombone' as it were for the last 2 years. But…" Matilda paused and took a breath…"The dancers are convinced that it will probably go down in operatic history. So, enough gossip for you?"

"Little vixen." Martin looked back once more at the group. Then he turned to Matilda.

"But what do you mean too close to home? You don't think I'd leave home for anyone except you, do you Tilly?"

"Shut up Martin. That's not funny!" Matilda glanced anxiously to where Pixie was paying for the teas. "Honestly, do you take anything seriously?"

Martin's grin faded. "Oh!" He said, making patterns on the table top with a stray stirrer until it snapped. "Some things I do. Yes, some things I take very seriously." His tone was slightly disconcerting. Had he worked things out? Matilda wondered. And if he had, what did he make of it all?

"Did you know they've put the prices up?" Pixie placed 3 teas on the table, and there was none of her usual joie de vive, Matilda noted as she glanced up at her.

"Oh darling, did you have to take out a mortgage?" Said Martin. Pixie ignored him and addressed her next comment to Matilda.

"I thought we were subsidised?" "We are Pixie." Giggled Matilda. "Doesn't mean the prices can't ever go up."

Her friend grabbed the sugar and groaned. The three sat in silence for a while, drinking their tea. The ballet girls got up from their deep discussion and left the canteen, Martin's gaze following them our of the door. Noting Pixie's unhappy reaction to this blatant display, Matilda said abruptly.

"Do you know anything about the Castrati Martin?"

"The whatie?" Martin pulled his attention back to the table and grinned at Matilda.

"The Castrati." She repeated. "Why?" He asked. "Do you think I'd get on quicker if I went under the knife.?"

"It's too late for that." Snarled Pixie. Martin took her hand, very much against her will, and stared close to her face. "Do I detect a latent desire to rid me of my manhood?"

"Someone should! "Pixie said quietly.

Matilda realised suddenly that she was not far from tears. She sighed inwardly. She had warned her. Martin stood up and picked up his tea. "I'll see you lovely ladies later." And he disappeared into the Green room. Pixie watched him go, and then glanced at Tilly before picking up her cup.

"Don't say it Tilly. Just don't say it. Please!"

Matilda was silent. She had a rather nasty feeling that her reference to the Castrati had sent Martin on his way as much as Pixie's behaviour.

JOURNAL

I had a singing lesson today. Irena was as always patient, but I felt that I tried that commodity rather more than usual.

"Darling you do yourself no favours when you do that."

"What am I doing?" I asked her.

"You overload the instrument. No doubt you are still upset about everything. But when you arrive anywhere to sing, anywhere at all, you must learn to leave all your problems outside the door, Otherwise, all these little glitches hold on to the sound. They anchor themselves to it, and weigh down the instrument. You are flat my dear, there's not enough overtone. The sound is far too fat it can not pass through the, what singers from the past called: the eye of the needle."

She stood up and began to pace around the room. Moving with the flourish of someone used to the vast operatic stage.

"In this part of the voice, this so-called 'upper passaggio' the sound must be long and fine, otherwise it 'blares' at me. It isn't focused. I know that these days one hears that sound all over the place, from the most unlikely people, occasionally even at the Opera house I suspect. But wherever you hear it, you must mark it in your mind as wrong. We are terribly vulnerable to what we hear Matilda, we copy without realising it. Now, try again."

I tried very hard, too hard. Irena stopped me again. "No, I did not mean that you should sing 'off' the voice. Think from the very depths, but not with weight…better. Now, add some line…Use your breath…Spin it, keep it going…Don't hold on to it…"

And Irena sang along with me until I caught up with what she was doing, and she could let go of the 'leading rein' as it were. When we stopped she leant back and sighed deeply. I was mortified. "I'm wearing you out Irena. I'm so sorry." But she shook her head replying, as she took a sip of water and what appeared to be aspirin. I instantly felt worse.

"No, it's not that. Just a little headache. Now you are at a stage that you must pass through you must keep going for what you want, the best sound you can produce. It is not easy to do so, because I'm sure that it feels quite easy and comfortable just as it is. Am I right?" I nodded, and she continued. "You could stay at this point and sing like this for ever, but it isn't right. Quite apart from potential health hazards in the long run, you will not please any conductor who knows his stuff. And even those who don't know consciously, will much prefer the sound that I am trying to help you find. Also…"

Irena paused and I waited for her to continue. she seemed uncertain as to whether she should say something or not. Then she shook her head and said.

"Sing this phrase for me will you?"

It was the final phrase of the notorious 'Sleepwalking Scene' from Verdi's Macbeth. There are 4 notes in this phrase, the penultimate one being a high exposed D flat. I started with confidence, after all I had had a sneaky try at bits of this opera on my own from time to time, including this final scene! But by the time I was poised for the top note, I knew there was no way in hell that I had prepared my voice in order to be able to reach it. It needed to 'soar' up there. Well, soar it did not, sore would have been closer. My throat felt as if it was pulled in two directions at once. I missed the pitch completely, and burst into tears. Irena waited for me to calm down. She smiled at me, and said one word: "Tea!" This we had sitting in her lovely lounge which is full of photographs of her in various operatic roles. What I found interestingly unusual is that not one of them was a 'posed' picture. In every one she was in full flight, mouth wide

open, and occasionally exhibiting a ferocious facial expression. I found this refreshingly undiva-like. She talked about her career, of how it was in the days when she sang all over the world. From Europe to South America and back it seems, and I wondered how I would stand up to such a life if I were ever given the opportunity.

I longed to talk to her about other things. I had a strong feeling, for some reason, that she would be receptive to my strange and unusual experiences. But every time I thought I might be at a point in the conversation, something would happen, and the moment would pass uncharted. She did say one thing which was a little strange though. Just as I was finishing my tea, she looked at me intently and said.

"You know, you have a very unusual sound Matilda. Sometimes I hear things in it which confuse me, don't get me wrong, it's very exciting! But I was wondering, are you aware that on occasion there is a ghost of something else hovering there, just waiting to make itself heard?"

I had no idea what she was talking about. She made an impatient move with her head and said lightly. "It doesn't matter, probably just an old woman's imagination. If it happens again I'll point it out to you."

I hope I will come through this 'impasse' and manage to find the whole truth the other side. Apart from the obvious artistic reason, I must, for the first time, consider my financial future. After all, it will not be too long before a regular pay cheque will no longer present itself in my bank account automatically. A chill runs through me as I consider this. What will happen if I do not find work easily? I am all too aware of the terrible time

that some of my college friends have had trying to survive. "It's a jungle." This I've heard from some of them more times than I care to remember. If only I had some money behind me. It is all beginning to worry me.

Feburary / March

Giorgio slipped as gently as possible from Verity's sleeping grasp. He pulled on his dressing gown and left the room. Wanting to check through the final plans for his forthcoming 'grand' opening, he made straight for the study. He knew that he had completely exhausted Verity, but he had not managed to have the same effect on himself. Most men, so he had always been told, rolled over and were often asleep almost with their next breath. Well they were lucky!

He sniffed and picked up the thick file containing all the pertinent information. Carefully he checked through from beginning to end, noting every detail and nodding to himself in happy anticipation. He had turned some music on, and without thinking he had started to hum along with the familiar phrases. He stopped abruptly.

Even now he hated to hear the slow, dead vibrato which oscillated both sides of the pitch. He drew in his breath. It didn't bother him when he was teaching, he was too caught up with what the student was doing. But when he was alone, the force of the emotion which arose unbidden, could still spread like cold

449

dismay through him, as if the original awareness of his lost career was only yesterday, and he had just awoken to his first morning of bitter realisation. All this brought him inevitably to Carlo and Matilda.

'Soon.' He thought. 'Soon!' Slowly his gaze rose from the file in front of him. Unfocused and unseeing he sat like a statue, following the seductive line of Verdi's 'Aida.' The 'Invocation scene,' held him in wrapt attention. Pyramid-like shapes formed in his mind. At the back of his head the door was opening, and he could feel the heat of the sun and the sand. He felt his energy enter the pyramid, and it was as if it had just been built. As if the sandy floor had just been swept in some ancient style so that the ground was patterned as if to signal energy and light to meld with its shapes.

Standing on this patterned floor was Chu-Pen. He turned to face Giorgio, and began to speak. At first Giorgio couldn't hear what he was saying, he simply watched the hard mouth moving, forming words. Then, in the middle of a sentence, it was as if the volume had suddenly been turned up as on a television.

"You sleep Giorgio! You think that you remember so much and so well. But you remember little! Everything with you turns around Venice, with music, ambition, sex and jealousy, these little human grievances are trite, a waste of time, and a deplorable waste of energy! This music you all love so much though, that is another thing altogether. It is dangerous, a direct link with God and to the universal energy which surrounds us. The plague is about to be released through this fine frequency. If that happens, it will spread like forest fire leaving destruction in its wake. You must remember more deeply, and more precisely

Giorgio. Remember the emerald fire! It holds part of the key. The woman's lover has it. Find it Giorgio! Find it and destroy it. You made it, it is yours to destroy."

Giorgio was completely immersed in the magic, and pulled down into the golden vortex. The last 'Immenso Phta!' had ended and it was several seconds before Giorgio blinked and came back to the present. Chu-Pen! He had been aware of him so much in the last few months. He had dreamt of him, seen him in altered states of consciousness, such as this one he had just experienced, and had even imagined his stark aesthetic face peering at him from unlikely surfaces, and catching his attention from shop windows. Many times recently he had swung around in the street, unable to prevent the reaction, and only to find, of course, that no-one fitting Chu-Pen's description was there! And what in God's name was this 'Emerald fire?' Why the hell couldn't these people forget their riddles and come outright with what they wanted to say? Although he realised that by dealing with it in this manner, Chu-Pen was endeavouring to raise his energy enough so that he might remember the life which he apparently lived long before Venice. The life in the place with the golden corridors, from which he and many others had, for some reason, been forced to flee. If Chu-Pen simply told him about that experience, it wouldn't have half the impact of his own remembering. And for some reason, no doubt related to this 'plague,' which he kept referring to, Chu-Pen definitely seemed to need Giorgio to remember everything. The emotion, his thoughts and ambitions, as well as the 'facts.'

It was not the best time for time to be using his energy to follow some ancient dream however, not with the grand opening

on the near horizon, and still so much to do. He shook his head to release the vision completely and pulled the papers towards him. Quickly he wrote at the bottom of a list he had been making on a fresh piece of paper in the file. At the top of this list, as a heading, he had written the word EXTRAS: And at the bottom was the name Matilda? He placed the file in his desk and poured himself a brandy. He'd never be able to sleep tonight, of that he was quite certain, and his mood was too impatient to consider meditating, even if his teachers had told him that that was the very time he should do so, as a challenge to his discipline. He knew that Verity would turn the Villa into hell-on-earth, if he woke her at this time of night, and anyway he felt like a change!

He needed something to put all of this out of his mind, at least for a while. He picked up the phone and tapped in a number. 15 minutes later, he was showered, shaved, and dressed, and speeding away from the Villa in his dark-green Porsche.

JOURNAL

We rehearsed Turandot today, all day. I stayed on this evening for a while, in order to do some of my own work, but almost two hours were wasted in the canteen just waiting for a studio to become available. I have had no chance to speak to Pixie, in fact, I barely laid eyes on her, and have a suspicion that she went home early. She must have been feeling unwell. The company is not sympathetic to people who sing around the rest with germ-laden breath, and I've known a request be made to the office that anyone suffering in such a way should be allowed to go home. More often than not the request is granted, and everybody is happy.

Martin wasn't overly friendly today. Moody so-and-so! He blows hot and cold, like an English summer! I don't really care on a personal level, but you never know what you are going to get. I've had various comments from other members of the company re' you-know-what, and ranging from:

"Sorry we're losing you…" To: "Warrener is a prick, we're going to hate working with him. He doesn't know a voice from a hole in the ground."

I don't know what is or isn't the truth anymore. I got home and was much too tired to eat…There was nothing on television…I didn't feel like listening to music…Then the phone rang. There was a silence after I said "Hello?" It was just long enough for my hear to leap. It was Dante! He was sorry, he begged for my forgiveness and promised me the world, or at least a substantial part of it. I didn't want the world I told him. He paused, and then carried on. He had spoken to his Father he told me and he has been given some 'time.' He begged me to hang on just a little longer and then he added something else. If my well-meaning friends had heard him, would cause immediate ridicule and scorn! He said. "Whatever 'appens cara. We musta stay together. Dis, she is very importante. You understand me? Please say you understand me! And when I see you, I 'ave somedin' fora you, is very special."

I assured him that I do understand, although to be honest I can't say that I really do. Mainly because I don't know if I've agreed to understand his need, or something else entirely. The, I presume 'present' which he has for me, is like water off a duck's back. The last thing I want is to be bribed by some bauble or other.

Oh dear! I'm quite sure that I will not sleep easily tonight. Maybe there's a late movie on, that might help...

Matilda fell asleep on the settee, and awoke at 2:00 in the morning, stiff and miserable and with a very dry throat, the coughing from which was responsible for waking her in the first place. As she reached for some water, she realised out of the blue that she hadn't even mentioned to Dante that she had lost her job. Matilda had never taken time off from the Opera House before, except after the accident, and she made a quick decision. She set the alarm clock for 10:00 a.m. and decided to ring in sick. Her bed was cold and pristine after the settee, but gradually she felt sleep creeping upon her with its usual assurances of tomorrow being much better than today had been, and with relief she found herself falling slowly into the dark pit of oblivion. Tonight, what was left of it anyway, she had no wish to dream.

The old man studied the landscape. It had changed. The lovely strong mountain range had grown too high, and its character had altered. No longer did it invite the eye by the whitened slopes which turned to green as they approached the deep valleys. Now the huge shadows were sharp, angled and unapproachable. Unlovely architecture indeed. And the velvet dark-blue canopy of the sky, which usually reflected in the turquoise water, turning it to indigo, was moonless, starless and harsh. The old man surveyed all of this with some concern. What was in front of him could, he knew, change in the blink of an eye. But what was not so easy to change was the heaving floor of the forest, for as Matilda's boundless energy began to fail her, she was becoming incapable of fighting the negative situations. They were quickly taking root, and from their substance the black snakes repro-

duced at will. Adding to the gloom a terrible fog of depression, which had begun to rise from the floor of the forest. The old man knew all this. But he also knew that Matilda, while realising that she didn't feel like her normal self, was as far away from this picture of it as he was from her Opera House.

"Guard your thoughts Matilda." He murmured. "Please guard your thoughts!"

"Where's Tilly?" Maria caught up with one of the second mezzos as they made their way to the stage for the morning rehearsal. She had already asked several people since she first arrived that morning. Jessica shook her head and shrugged. "Haven't seen Pixie either." She replied.

Martin bounced up behind them and offered an unwanted opinion. "Playing truant are they?" He grinned at Maria, running his eye over her in a way that she found offensive. "Don't be ridiculous Martin." Said Jessica. "Neither of them would do anything like that."

"Never can tell Ladies, never can tell." He replied as he overtook them on the stairs. "What is his problem?" Whispered Jessica. They were approaching the stage by now.

"God knows, and only he could sort it out I think. But Martin looks terrible these days, completely washed out, have you noticed?"

Jessica nodded as the stage manager surveyed them suspiciously, and they both became silent and intent on their work.

Matilda was at this precise moment, curled in bed under the duvet, in a classic foetal position. She had no desire whatsoever

to move, and it was only hunger, which much later, at about 4:00o'clock that afternoon, finally drove her from the warmth and protection into the cold light of day.

Pixie hadn't eaten either. Her reasons however were very different. You don't eat or drink for a full 12 hours before a general anaesthetic, and some hours after it, she still had no appetite. She also felt numbed, confused and depressed. She didn't like what she had done, but she didn't see that there had been any option. She loathed herself and she hated Martin. Matilda had been right about him. How come she understood him so well? He wasn't simply an immoral and totally selfish cad. What she had been attracted to, that which appeared to be a freedom of spirit, was gained totally by a manipulation of others, especially when those 'others' were sleeping with him. Yes, there were black depths to Martin, unfathomable and hidden like quicksand.

March / April

JOURNAL

I've begun the audition round. First, of course, for the smaller companies. They are already beginning to hear people for the productions that they intend to put on next season. It's a strange feeling working on these roles. I don't feel anywhere near ready to attempt them, even though Irena has told me not to be so silly, and to stop treating myself as if I'm a baby. It isn't just the actual singing of the roles though, it's the whole scene out there. Take two days ago, I sang for a small company which is based in the London area. The audition room was small, with a low ceiling (horrible to sing in) but it had, by way of glowing compensation, a beautiful grand piano. However the pianist, and I use the word advisedly, chose not to play it, preferring instead it seemed, a keyboard which gave me no support at all, since once I was singing I could hardly hear it. It transpired however that this didn't really matter because the pianist had no intention of accommodating me, and played consistently one-half bar ahead of me throughout the piece. Either he didn't know the music, or

he was bored to death, or he was in dire need of a 'loo' break! I recounted all of this to Martin when he plonked himself down in front of me in the canteen yesterday.

"You're spoilt Tilly. You'll have to get used to the real world you know!"

"REAL world?" I spluttered, "What the hell is all this then, Scotch mist?"

"No, I mean you'll find lots of things as you've just described out there. We all just laugh it off. Anyway how's this brilliant teacher of yours, what's her name again?"

"Irena!" I replied. Thinking that I was quite sure that Martin knows her name, after my 'Butterfly,' it's probably engraved on his heart, how can he be such a fraud? I didn't want to get into any discussion about Irena or my career. Martin has already made a nasty little comment that maybe my dismissal from the Opera House was connected with the singing teacher I was going to, so I added quickly. "She's fine thanks. And Giorgio?.."

"Fast approaching opening date. Hope you're going to be there, cheer us on Tilly?"

I shrugged. Giorgio rang me a few days ago and asked if I would consider going down to help out. No offer of singing I noticed, but then, to be fair I'm not his student anymore. And I'll bet he's very short on general 'dog's bodies.' But he did offer to pay me, this as you know is now quite a consideration, not something that I should easily ignore! I hate to appear the 'Prima Donna,' anyway I don't think I'd mind helping out. But other people have been horrified. When I mentioned it to Maria she suggested I tell him to, and I quote, 'stick it where the sun doesn't shine!' It's not easy contemplating being free-lance. I glanced up at Martin.

"He had invited me down, and I'd love to come of course, but it depends what's happening. I do still work you know."

Martin raised his eyebrows and said. "I hate to be the one to point this out Tilly. But we're talking September you know, Giorgio has some nutty idea that he wants it all to happen around the, what do they call it, Equi…something?"

"Equinox." I put in. "Right!" Said Martin. "But whatever, you won't be here then!"

I suddenly felt hugely uncomfortable, and was aware of a feeling of pressure rising through my body. I keep trying to remember how my mind used to work, the pathways of thoughts which were habitual for me, in the hope of returning to calmer days, and hopefully to lift this heavy feeling inside which is becoming horribly permanent. I glanced at the canteen clock and then down at my watch.

"I must go and get ready Martin, See you later."

Martin watched her leave. It would be supremely satisfying for him to have her running around at the Villa while he was rehearsing and performing. See how much attention she'd get when she wasn't singing! Maybe he'd finally get some of the results he knew that he deserved, even a little adulation wouldn't go amiss. There were still times when the spontaneous reception which Matilda had received at the end of her aria in the first Tony London concert several months ago, would burst unwelcome into his mind. And it still caused him irritation and anger when it did so. He knew that Giorgio had offered to pay her for any help which she might be prepared to give, and that money and the opportunity to earn it, must fast be becoming

a big consideration in view of what her position would be in just a few months.

He was about to go and prepare himself, when Jonathan Warrener came into the canteen with a little blond piece hanging on his arm. Martin threw himself into 'future work' mode, and without looking too obvious he walked quickly up the aisle as if on the way to buy himself another drink. He even pulled the money out of his pocket and studied it intently. Then, with impeccable timing, he looked up as Jonathan, having placed 'Blondie' at an empty table, also began to move towards the queue at the counter.

"Hi Jonathan, how are you? Can I get you something?"

Jonathan groaned inwardly. He had thought that he would have Susie to himself. Time was now of the essence, since she had a boyfriend who, having been on the continent for some weeks was about to return at any moment. He was about to put some pressure on her regarding his 'payment' for next season's contract. Well, he supposed that Martin, involved as he was with the morning's rehearsal, wouldn't be able to hang around the canteen for too much longer, and he decided that discretion was far the better part of valour. So he smiled and said.

"How kind, two coffees please."

Martin hurried off. He'd recognised Susie immediately, and in some ways he knew her very well, although he didn't remember her last name. What he did remember was that she was one of the little sluts he had been forced to contact as a precaution after his little brush with 'marital death' a few months back. He looked forward to seeing her squirm as Jonathan introduced them.

'Of all the blondes in all the world…' He misquoted to himself as he picked up the tray and headed back to the table. At the other end of the canteen, Maria was chatting to Robert Jones, one of the baritones in the company. He had been a member of the chorus, but in a quite unprecedented move, instigated by a Musical Director before Sir Clive's time, he had been promoted to small parts. Very small, usually, but Robert wasn't worried about that, he considered himself very lucky, was very happy, and therefore a thoroughly nice man who had a quiet little 'crush' on Matilda, and was as outraged as the chorus themselves over the treatment meted out to her. Maria glanced over her shoulder to where Martin had sat himself down with the coffees.

"Who's that?" She asked Robert, as she paused in the act of pushing her chair back from the table, and grabbing her bag. As they passed the little trio Robert nodded briefly, and smiled at Maria as they pushed open the door to the green room. Once it had swung slowly closed behind them, he stopped, and raised his eyes to the ceiling.

"Do you know what I think?" "No, what?" Maria asked him. "Well I'm pretty sure that that's who will be taking our Tilly's place next season." Robert replied.

Maria moved out of the way of some fast approaching orchestral players bent on grabbing a quick drink.

"What's she doing here with Warrener? Fancy being ogled by those two, at the same time as well!" Maria fumed.

"If that's who I think it is, it wouldn't bother her one little bit!" Robert laughed ironically. "But what is disconcerting, is that although Mr. Warrener wouldn't agree with me, or anyone else, it's common knowledge that Susie Walton cannot sing her

way out of a paper bag. She has very little voice to start with. She'll be nothing but a passenger here. It's scandalous that she's joining us at all, let alone that one of our best voices is pushed out to make room for her."

"I still don't understand why she's here, backstage now. And with Warrener…Oh dear…" Maria added. "Pardon my na-iveté…Now let's see. Good soprano gets the boot by slimy little chorus master and lo and behold, her place is filled by equally slimy little soprano and it seems that one slime ball knows the other.. er socially…shall we say? Well there's a surprise!"

"Best not mention any of this to Tilly. How is she by the way? I haven't had a chance to speak to her." Robert said.

"She seems fine about it all. Of course, you can't always tell with Tilly, she'd hate to be a burden about it. But then she is young, that always helps. She still has plenty of time, not like some of us." Replied Maria.

"Oh for goodness sake!" Laughed Robert. "Anyone would think you're on your last legs. If half of what I've heard about your voice is true you'll be singing when you're 80, and very well probably!"

Maria moved out of the way of the orchestral players on their way back, and grinned broadly. It was impossible not to be pleased by such a comment.

"I won't of course say a word to Tilly. She doesn't need to know about all that rubbish, and…" She stopped mid-sentence and gasped as two other members of the chorus came into view already dressed for the morning rehearsal…"Oh my God, I for-got. We're in costume!" She exclaimed, and fled in the direction of her dressing room.

Irena closed her front door. She had just finished a consultation lesson with Pixie. Matilda had been right about her friend. She did possess a superb voice. There was a lot to do, a lot of hard work to pull it into the sort of shape which it was ultimately capable of. But Irena was convinced that Pixie wanted, and was prepared to work properly to achieve it.

She had long made it her business never to work with what she called, 'dabblers.' They were a waste of time and energy, and not only to her, but to themselves too. Time wasted that could well be arming them for survival in the world, doing something else which was almost bound to be better paid, unless they were lucky enough to make it to the top of this notoriously fickle profession. She made herself some tea, and wondered what had happened to real hard training such as she had endured. If dancers tried to learn their trade popping in and out of classes as and when they felt like it, while trying to learn the basics of the art, there would be no dance companies in existence. Of course they simply weren't allowed to behave in such a manner, and the basics at least were always there, always recognisable. With both Matilda and Pixie, though, neither of them had ever been shown certain basic rules, and they both covered up the inconsistencies without being aware of it. Good voices responded to being used, so in spite of this sad lacking in their musical education, they had grown and flourished, to some degree. Matilda, of course, was already reaping the rewards from the little work they had done, although at the moment she was at something of a stand still, due, Irena had no doubt to the fiasco at the Opera House. There was more to that than met the eye. But really, thought

Irena, it was a very small glitch in the wider picture. She mustn't let them cause her such personal distress.

She understood about the financial side, of course she did. But despite this, she couldn't help but believe it was somehow for the best. Matilda would never get on if she stayed where she was. So now she must rediscover her spirit. It was just a few months ago that her handling of music in the concert had impressed Irena so much, Just a few months when she had seemed consumed with a glowing energy shot through with a wonderful instinct. Irena had wanted so much to help her to mould all that into true artistic ability. Matilda was a sweet girl, but there was no way that anyone in this business could be spoon fed. She had to find that energy once more, demand its presence, otherwise everything would lose the impulse and the singer would simply be singing notes, and Irena or anyone else would be helpless. She had to shape up. Irena sighed and shook her head and reminded herself that she needed to be honest at least in her own mind. The fact was, that one of the reasons that she wanted Matilda to hurry up and get over losing her job, was that she was impatient to hear again that 'extra something' in the sound which she had noticed before. It fascinated her. It was like being on the verge of some new discovery. If it was lost forever because of this stupid operatic intrigue, (the more she thought about it the more it became obvious that that was what it was) Irena would find herself genuinely disappointed.

Some way away in the living room of a fairly young and ambitious conductor, a deep intense discussion was in progress. The woman who sat opposite him at the round wooden table sipped her coffee and said.

"Next?"

The conductor read quickly through his scribbled notes and replied. "Er…Matilda Gasgoine. What did you think?"

The slight little woman sifted through her notes, and said. "Oh yes! Chorus at the Opera House, that the one? I don't think so!"

The conductor, surprised, replied. "What? I liked her, very much."

"No!" The woman repeated emphatically.

"Why not?"

The woman shook her head slowly, and placed her coffee on the table, turning down the corners of her mouth as she answered.

"Far too traditional for what I want. I don't think she'll be flexible. She's been standing on that stage for two or three years now. I want to go beyond what people expect to see. She has Opera House written all over her."

"That's not really fair. She may well be flexible. She's still very young. Look, I'd like to have her back under the pretence of needing to hear her again, and you can have most of the time with her, see how she comes through your stage work exercises. I intend to offer her concert work anyway. The voice is stunning."

"So?"

"This is opera Sandra!"

"Yes it is. And I'm directing the show. I'm fed up with all this wailing about the voice, and the sound and…I told you when you interviewed me that I wasn't going to go down the old worn out path."

"I know you did Sandra, but this is Opera. However different we want to be, we can't cut away the basic necessities. This girl is a gift. She has all the vocal and musical attributes while not having any preconceived idea about what she wants to do with the role. Which leaves you a blank page to write on. I like her and I want her to be seriously considered."

Sandra shook her head. "No, I don't want her!"

The conductor sighed. Bloody directors! He wished someone would point out to them in language that they could understand, that Opera is not straight theatre with music. Did the woman have no ears at all? He drew a line through Matilda's name and moved on to the next candidate.

JOURNAL

The next time Giorgio rang me about his opening night I tried to get him to be more specific as to what he would want me to do. But by now, you know Giorgio, he doesn't give away anything that he doesn't want to give away, and on top of all that, everything happens at a speed which he alone dictates. So I am none the wiser, but I did sort of agree. ..Well O.K. I agreed! When I mentioned it to Irena she went ballistic. I was completely taken aback at her anger, it seemed rather an over reaction. I tried to explain that I will soon be in a position where I will desperately need to earn money, but she talked right over me, which she is quite capable of doing. I was cornered into silence half way through a sentence. It seems at the moment that I am irritating nearly everyone around me. Everywhere I turn people are starting sentences with…"Oh Matilda…"

I keep hoping Carlo might appear again. I would find his

Venetian manners most welcome. But where is he? Where are they? And where is the old man?

Giorgio patted his horse's neck, breathed in the healthy scent of the animal and sighed with pleasure. He had escaped from the Villa and Verity's nagging. The air was mild and there were proofs of Spring everywhere he turned. He had to admit that on a day such as this, England was a truly beautiful place to be. One's focus turned with ease from the traffic roaring along the motorway, several miles to the West (although Giorgio suspected that there were few people who would be able to pick up that drone as easily as he did) to 'A Lass on Richmond Hill' and to what young men heard 'Early one morning.' Those old English songs placed him in a mental sea of lavender and green broom as surely as if he had flipped back a few centuries.

Two of the dogs had accompanied him to the edge of the parkland, and now became uncertain whether or not to cross into the wilder country with him and Tempest. They trotted back and forth along what they sensed to be the boundary of Giorgio's land, barking from time to time, and stopping with their heads on one side, whimpering. Giorgio looked at them. He did not wish them to go further with him. He raised his arm and shouted. "Go…Go home…Off you go!"

Immediately the dogs set off the way they had come, turning back expecting to see him following them, and slightly concerned when he made no attempt to do so. They stopped and watched him intently for a few seconds before finally speeding off by themselves, towards the Villa, racing each other and disappearing quickly into the shrub land.

Horse and rider set off for the 'mile' a stretch of flat smooth grassland which allowed a fast gallop as free from danger as that can ever be, Giorgio set Tempest up and allowed him to have his head, remembering as he did so once reading in a book many years before that the 'extended gallop' was a fool's paradise. He understood why it was so called, but laughed at the hidden warning. Giorgio had a 'way' with animals, at least that was how people described it. He knew that it was a lot more than that, that it was connected to his questionable 'gift' and heightened sensorial energy. He had no doubt that he could easily align his instinct with Tempest's, and together they had little to fear.

He leaned forward over the big bay's neck, crouching almost in to the classic jockey position. The countryside blurred past in his peripheral vision as if it were moving and horse and rider were still. Giorgio finally pulled the hunter up at the end of the 'mile.' Tempest danced sideways, half reared and generally flirted with his bit as if he could rid himself of it, if only he danced for long enough. Giorgio laughed out loud and stroked the arched muscled neck firmly. Horses were so much easier to deal with than women, no substitute of course, but much easier to manage. Verity, for example was driving him nuts at the moment.

"Where was he?" "Where had he been?" "Why hadn't he taken her with him?" What was he up to?"…And worse of all. "What exactly was his problem, sexually?"

At the last question he had burst out laughing and turned to her saying.

"There is a problem my pet?" When she attempted to leave his bed where they had spent the last 3 hours, and he had grabbed a strong buttock with one hand, to prevent her, he mut-

tered. "You should be grateful." And bit her shoulder just a little too hard, laughing at her response to cover up his concern as she snarled.

"I wish you'd let me in on the secret Giorgio. Because if I can't keep up with you, I'm damn sure no one else can, ever could, or ever will!"

At this, Giorgio was quietly a little dismayed. Verity was intelligent enough to work out the truth. It wasn't likely, but not impossible either. He had no desire for anyone to discover his dark secret, he didn't really know why, it was an instinctive reaction. And Verity was no different from anyone else when it came right down to it.

Tempest, sensing Giorgio's lack of concentration on him pulled hard on the reins and snorted. He rubbed his great nose along his foreleg, then threw his head up suddenly, hoping to have loosened Giorgio's grip on the reins, and imagining that he might find himself free. He was up for the 'mile' again.

"Hey, don't play games with me Tempest." The horse quietened down, he was only testing the waters anyway. He liked Giorgio, and trusted him, there were no problems between them. They turned back towards the park at a more sedate canter. On such a horse, Giorgio reflected, one could imagine oneself a centaur, more part of the fabulous animal than a separate being perched on the strong, pliable back. He would have liked to turn off the trail and to ride deep into the forest. He had sensed such wonderful creatures there, and he wanted to explore further than he had ever done before. He didn't have time today, there was still so much to do, and besides Verity would only start at him if he were too long.

"Oh Giorgio!" He said to himself aloud. "What are you doing allowing a woman to control you?"

He had determined several times to rid himself of Verity, but she always managed to make him change his mind. He had never really asked himself why before. He had come to accept that they were meant for each other. In some ways, of course, she was quite perfect for him. And as far as he was capable of the emotion, Giorgio suddenly realised that he must love her, he supposed anyway, it was hard for him to tell. It was such a surprise to him, his feeling couched in those words, that he pulled Tempest up sharply. Tempest of course, objected.

"Stop being so grumpy young man." Giorgio spoke to him in Italian convinced that his Mother tongue was far more calming than any other language would be. So, where did all this ruminating leave him? Could Verity replace Carlo? This he doubted but had to assume that it was possible. Was he prepared to give up his vendetta against Matilda after all he'd done to achieve what he perceived would be almost total success, given a few more weeks. And what of Martin? At lesson after lesson Giorgio had tried to reach through to the young man's icy centre and ignite it, without breaking the brittle shell which surrounded it. Could he give up on him, consider him a lost cause and walk away forgetting Lucciano's agony, and the curse which he had sworn by Carlo's grave? And did that curse have him in its power as strongly as he had meant it to have Carlo? And what of his own private double edged curse? Was he prepared to allow it to die in the flame of love? Burnt to a crisp by the deeper flame of unconditional surrender?

Too many questions. But one thing was clear, he must not

succumb to a situation which Verity was trying hard to create. He smiled, and turned off the path towards the deep silent wood. He would contemplate the situation without words, find his answers from the creatures who even now stirred as they sensed the approach of a kindred spirit.

JOURNAL

It's the first night of Turandot tonight. We've had to work very hard it seems on this and as it's a new production we have the day off. I found myself staying in bed again. Well, I hate to admit it but I was tired. I'm always tired…I sleep and sleep, but I'm still tired…

April / May

JOURNAL

The season seems to be galloping. Every time I turn around we are into another month. Today, Pauline called me into the office. It was a friendly gesture. She hoped (she said) that she might persuade me to reconsider my right to have a second audition with Jonathan, (first names already then!) I promised that I will think about it. It's impossible for anyone else to understand how I can possibly know that it would be a complete waste of time, and I appreciate that. I know also that they believe I'm afraid, and have lost my nerve. But this isn't so. I feel without any doubt that for some unfathomable reason that nothing would change his mind.

I took some advice from Maria and phoned Tony London's office today, after all he is supposed to be my agent! But I felt awkward and stumbled and muttered, repeating myself absurdly. I must have sounded a total mess. If only Bella had answered the phone, but she didn't. It wasn't that Tony wasn't quite nice, he was, and he apologised for not being around for the concerts that I took part in. He mentioned where he had been, some exotic shore, but I can't remember now where it was. But he then informed me that he knew that I was undergoing some retraining, he didn't see the need for it, but while I was going through it, he had decided it would be better if we left things for a while, until I had a chance to consolidate everything. Therefore, I wasn't officially on his books until at least next season. He finished by saying that I should feel free to ring him then.

I must have stared at the phone for at least 30 seconds after I had hung up. This has added to my troubles for more than one reason. Firstly this is not the time for me to lose my agent, even if it is temporary. I need to sort out some sort of work now, not after the summer. I also feel very used. I mean he was happy enough for me to do the concerts, paid me what my friends referred to as, 'London's pittance,' and then casts me aside just when I could do with some real help. Underneath all this is the question, how does he know about my working with Irena?

I hate the underlying feeling the business side of things in this profession can make one feel, it is so depressing. When I consider my experiences that have shown me Carlo's world, I can't help but think how much easier life was in some ways for all of them. Everything appeared to be so clear cut. I mean you could sing, or you couldn't sing. You made the grade or you didn't. Politics there may have been, but the art itself was so much more important to society, and therefore it was protected, and so were the singers. They were not cast aside on a whim. Neither were artists dressed in silk, when their true garments were sows' ears. Everyone had much more pride in their ability to hear and the courage to say what they knew that they heard.

I know what greeted my friends from Venice at the end of their performances. Towards the end of a night's sleep, in my distant mind, as my consciousness is rising like a cork pulled gently from a bottle, I've heard that spontaneous and unselfconscious cry from the audience, who found themselves transported beyond their normal reality, and who rise to their feet before they know they have done so. It is indeed centuries away from the hollow sounds which greet some of our soloists today, even when they are great enough to enjoy the 'Roar of Venice.'

All this is most depressing, we have alienated ourselves by our intellectuality. We deny our true feelings and choke on the result. This is hard enough to bear when one is surrounded by the best, but very soon I shall be surrounded by nothing at all. It has just occurred to me that I don't even have a piano…

I had closed the book, but as I did so, briefly but vividly Carlo arose from its pages. Well why not? There is certainly enough of him contained in them. He smiled at me and said in his strange but beautiful tone. "Non Piangi little sister."

I am ashamed when I remember how they suffered for their art, that I dare to assume them better off. We know nothing…

Matilda was feeling very much better. The weather was warming by the day and her energy was rising to the extent that she began to feel much more like her old self.

The old man had not been able to contact her, but at least he perceived that the mists had cleared, and the forest floor was not quite as infested with paranoia as it had been. He wouldn't like to say that Matilda had bounced back exactly, but she was much lighter, and he was less concerned than he had been for sometime.

Irena was pleased also. Matilda had entered her studio a few days before with her old energy, having no idea of how physical her presence was, and how well defined her energetic print lay in the air around her. Irena had sighed with relief, the old man set about more productive work, and Matilda and Pixie began to work together, filling their free time with all the wonderful duets they could think of, and discussing the technique and Irena until their heads spun.

"Where do you think she got this knowledge?" Pixie asked Matilda one afternoon over a tea break.

"I don't know for sure, but I'm certain Russia is involved somewhere. There's the slight accent of course, that should give us a clue, I think it could be Russian, don't you?"

"Maybe." Said Pixie. "You could well be right, but it is almost unnoticeable. Did Martin ever mention about Giorgio knowing her in the past, and actually singing with her?"

Matilda couldn't imagine that. To her ear those two voices were as far apart as it was possible to be. She didn't trust herself to speak so she shook her head. What she was pleased about however, was that Pixie at last was managing to mention Martin's name without looking as if the world was about to stop turning.

"We should ask her." Pixie continued. "Yes." Matilda said slowly. "So who's going to do it, you or me?"

Pixie grinned at her. "O.K. You made your point. She is a very private person, isn't she? Anyway you don't really get an opening to enquire where she came by what she teaches, she's too busy teaching it. I have had other singers ask me about various things though. You know like how come I can do this or that, I'm more than happy to explain, but when I do, they're not exactly in a hurry to rush off to a studio and experiment themselves. I find that odd, don't you?"

"Too much like hard work I imagine." Said Matilda. "Or at least too much self discipline needs to be exerted." She paused and looked hard at her friend. "You don't doubt the method she teaches, do you?"

"How can I when I hear the sound you make, and the sound she still makes. The latter should be enough on its own. She sounds like a young woman. I mean there's not a sign of wear and tear, roughness, stiffness or anything like that."

"But?" Matilda could hear that word loud and clear above all that Pixie had just said.

"It's just that Martin mentioned that Giorgio told him, that trying to follow what Irena suggested he needed to do was what ruined him. That's why he has this terrible slow vibrato in his voice, why he can't perform anymore. He is, after all, not old, and a darn sight younger than Irena."

Matilda was quiet for a moment. She didn't really believe that Giorgio had told the truth about this part of his past, but to say so would be the easy way out. So she replied.

"So why didn't singing that way affect her then?"

Pixie took a deep breath and said. "Well, I guess that brings us to the core of any worry I might have." To which Matilda looked blank, and Pixie continued. "It's extremely rare to find a singer who can turn their hand to teaching in a big way. Coaching maybe, but not actual teaching, you know that Tilly. We've both heard it a hundred times!"

"That's a generalisation Pixie, I'm sure it is. At one time it was the other way round. For example, the Castrati… "Are you off on them again?" Pixie leapt in. "They were entirely different, surely! We can't compare ourselves to them!" She had begun to sound impatient and continued. "Martin said you have an unhealthy preoccupation with them." "Martin said? But I've barely mentioned them to him, to anyone except Giorgio." Matilda replied, amazed and slightly uneasy at this revelation.

"Well there you are then, those two obviously spend more time gossiping than working, or so it seemed to me when I was confidant to the dear man."

There was a silence, then Matilda said quietly and with heavy irony which only she recognised. "Well, I suppose only 'time' will tell."

A little of the depression swirled back. She pushed it away firmly, she was not going back there. She would not think of it, would not allow the ridiculous inner chatter to begin again.

This same afternoon, Martin had driven down to 'Villa Giorgio.' He was in a good mood. He hoped to discuss the programme for the opening concert. So far Giorgio had said nothing about the actual content of the music, but the whole level of anticipation for Martin had lifted a notch when he learnt that an orchestra and chorus were being pulled together for the event. (The level of appreciation for Giorgio's bank accounts had also risen at that knowledge. Natural enough really when one considers the numbers of people involved and all needing to be paid.)

He parked his car in the area outside the Villa. Only a few people were still in the restaurant eating lunch, it was already 2:30. As he made for the main staircase, which led up to Giorgio's studio in the back of the house, he had to admit to a feeling of real excitement. The whole place had the ambience of money and realised ambition, it was intoxicating, almost seductive. If this took off, and Giorgio had the sort of mind and experience that could ensure that happening, Martin realised that he would be Principal tenor performing all the main Italian repertoire. He had made his way to the large room at the end of the corridor by now, and he tapped gently on the door and went in.

It was a beautiful room with windows from floor to ceiling and a high timbered roof. In the bay of the window was Giorgio's prize possession, his Steinway piano. Martin was surprised that Giorgio was not yet there. He was usually standing at the window, gazing out over his parkland, or sitting at his piano, but the room was empty.

A table stood to one side of the piano strewn with papers, plans and lists. Some of them had slipped to the floor and Martin knelt down to pick them up and replace them on to the table. It was inevitable that in so doing, his eye was caught by the information written there. He grinned as a strong feeling of success coursed through him. He'd show the bastards who continually doubted him. All those bloody jammy international buggers, he could sing them off the stage and back on again if only he was given the opportunity. His eye sped down the cast list and he turned cold. Opposite his name there was a, C. C. standing, he had no doubt, for Cover. Anger and disappointment swamped him, especially since he could see by the notes that Giorgio was not presenting a concert, and had decided to devote the whole evening to the first two acts of Verdi's Aida, followed by a champagne supper. He couldn't believe what he was reading. He had been so sure, Giorgio…Well in fact Giorgio hadn't actually said anything definite, but it had always been taken as read. He was given to understand that he would be the tenor for the evening. He was still staring at the papers in his hands when the door opened.

"Martin!" Giorgio had entered the room and was standing, watching him. "This is not the way for you to find out. I intended to explain to you properly today."

"They were on the floor Giorgio, I was just picking them up." Martin said quietly and feeling as if someone had ripped through him. Giorgio crossed to the window and closed it. Then he turned back to Martin. He folded his arms and sat down at the piano as if they were about to commence an ordinary lesson.

"Martin, I want you to understand that I'm trying to start a brand new company here. I don't want it to be yet another little 'Operatic group' like so many others in this country at the moment. I want to reach out and really make something startling. There's so much out there that frankly is crap. People are encouraged to go to performances because of the production for God's sake! No one cares about the music or the singing anymore."

He stood up. "Well I do! I care and I want to bring back some of that magic." He looked at Martin and took a deep heavy breath. The younger man was white.

"Just at the moment my boy..." He began quietly. "At this point you're not really ready. It's not the actual instrument." He quickly lifted his hand as if in assurance. "It's more the performance. It takes all of us time to find our feet you know, and you must be patient for a little longer."

"I think I've been patient for quite a long time Giorgio, don't you?"

Giorgio moved to the table and began to sift through the jungle of papers there. He ignored Martin's last comment and said.

"When you see who it is you're covering Martin, I'm quite sure that you won't be so upset." He handed the list to Martin. He tried to focus but found it impossible, so he pretended that he read the name but didn't recognise it. He looked at Giorgio and silently handed back the list to him shrugging as he did so.

"Don't you remember, a few months ago the Opera house lost their tenor in Butterfly? He came down with some virus very suddenly. Well this is the tenor that they brought in for the last couple of performances."

Martin looked disgusted and nodded his head, thinking. 'Why was it always that way in this business. To them that hath let it be given. To them that hath not, well piss on them from a great height.'

Giorgio caught Martin's look and said quickly. "I'm not using him for that reason Martin. I'm using him because he's good and ready, and he has international experience. This is what I want for my company."

Martin didn't answer him He remembered the name Francesco Riffi, a young Italian tenor. He had saved the day, apparently learning the production in the limosene from the airport, and walking on to the big stage, into the Gladiators arena as it was sometimes called, without so much as a music rehearsal. And on top of that, all the bloody stupid women swooning over the little bastard.

"I know it's hard for you Martin." Giorgio continued." But this isn't how it will always be you know. If you keep working your time will come, it must do!"

Giorgio was becoming a little impatient. He really didn't have time for a sulky child, and he needed Martin to consent to the covering contract, because Francesco was not available until some time close to the performance. They must have someone to sing in the tenor role of Radames, so that the company could rehearse properly and be ready for the opening. To chose Martin would have meant that he compromise his position, and Giorgio had no intention of doing that. He believed that he must do his part in trying to reverse the slippery slope which he and many other musicians perceived the art to be sliding down into a mediocre mess. As far as he was concerned there were only a few places in the world where real quality was appreciated to the extent that anything falling short of the result that only years of hard grind could accomplish, was not tolerated. Everywhere else, or so it seemed to him, almost anything went. Well, not in his company. He was starting as he intended to go on. The Italian tenor had cost him an arm and a leg, but he had determined to have him. His voice, although still lacking the depth and breadth of a mature sound, nevertheless reminded him of the so-called 'old singers'. It had an open sound which was so 'natural' in its delivery, that to the ignorant it belied the years of sweat and blood behind every note. Giorgio was aware that a certain young lady had already achieved the basics of this even before her work with dear Irena! But that was another story. And the future of opera would not tremble and topple because of the unfortunate circumstances of one worthy soprano. His own needs were not to be confounded in all this, and he would ensure a parallel running. Anyway there were many things which she did not possess, important and necessary to survival in the 'music jungle.' He knew for example that until people got to know her well, they easily misunderstood her, and that worked very much in his favour. The door opened behind him, and without turning around Giorgio said. "Go away Verity, I'm in the middle of something."

In spite of his ever increasing misery, Martin felt his spine tingle slightly. How the hell did he know that it was Verity, it could have been anyone for Christ's sake!

"It'll only take a moment you insensitive brute!"

Giorgio laughed, muttered an apology to Martin, and moved to the door, pulling it almost closed behind him. Martin could hear them sparring in an inaudible hiss. He felt rooted to the spot and had a strong desire to throw off the entire cloak of ambition and walk happily and freely away. But he knew that he wouldn't be happy, and, what the hell would he do? He was trapped, and as far as he was concerned (whatever lame excuses were given) Giorgio had pulled a fast one on him. He just wanted a 'name' for his bloody opening. Well there was no way he could sing today, he may just as well head back to town and go into work, at least he could still do that.

He drove with little care and considerable speed back to London with one person in mind, Matilda. He couldn't wait to express all this to her. Even the strangeness of that fact didn't penetrate his totally self-absorbed fury.

JOURNAL

Pixie and I had a wonderful time this afternoon, working through the score of 'Aida.' It's so much in our minds at the moment anyway, since it is enjoying its second run of the season. At about 5:00 o'clock we decided we'd better stop for the day, after all we still had a performance that evening which wouldn't finish until nearly 11:00 tonight.

As we made our way to the canteen, Pixie stopped suddenly with an expletive which sounded completely unbelievable as it issued from the same mouth which had been enriching the studio with glorious sound all afternoon.

"Shit. I have to go down to the chemist. I'm out of make up remover. I'll see you later Tilly."

I decided to go and eat early in the canteen (I thought) on my own. I was ravenous. Singing makes you hungry, it's no wonder some Opera singers get so big I thought, aware that there were rapid steps behind me on the stone floor. "Tilly!" I stopped quickly and turned round as Martin nearly fell over me. "Where are you off to?"

"In search of food Martin, I'm starving and it's a 7:00 o'clock start tonight, why?"

"Feel like eating outside somewhere? The Italian at the end of the passage?"

Martin referred to a reasonably cheap and very passable restaurant which many of us went to quite regularly. I looked hard at him, he seemed extremely upset, well I was certainly hungry enough to venture into the outside world, and he definitely had something on his mind that he didn't want the ever flapping ears of the Opera House to pick up on. I agreed and we turned back to the stage door, and headed to the nearly empty restaurant, settling ourselves at a quiet table, well away from the door and the big glass window which would afford no privacy to us, should a passing member of the company walk that way into work. There was a strong possibility that they would bounce in and join us, and Martin was quite obviously in no mood for that, or I suspected, I would not have been there at all!

I have to be honest, I was appalled at what Martin had to tell me. Obviously he wouldn't make up something like that, but it was hard to believe that Giorgio had actually done something like that to one of his own students, and much harder to know what to say to Martin. Everything that I was madly rehearsing in my head sounded trite and insincere.

"Maybe it's just for the first show Martin. " I ventured carefully…"You know what I mean? To get everything off to a flying start…I mean…" As Martin tore into me with a cold lift of one eyebrow…"I mean, a well advertised start. Most projects need something like that to attract the public. This guy's name is still in their minds, because of the Butterfly." I finished, as a picture of the gorgeous and highly talented tenor flashed across my mind.

Martin continued to rave. There was no real logic to it, he was simply venting an unspeakable frustration. He hated Giorgio…Hated the business…It was all jobs for the boys…etc. etc. Thank goodness our meal arrived and he calmed down a little, although I suspect it was the wine which saw to that. Wiping his mouth free from some of the tomato sauce, he paused and looked at me intently. My stomach contracted, not good when you're eating, but I knew that nothing would prevent the dreaded question.

"Tilly, I can trust you, so tell me. What is wrong with my bloody voice?"

"Nothing Martin." I paused realising that such an answer

was not enough, and added. "There's nothing wrong with your voice, you know that!"

"What then?" His voice took on the edge of bitter frustration, and I realised that as hard as it may well be, the truth was the only way to deal with this. So I centred myself carefully and asked him. "Do you really want to know what people say? It isn't what you imagine."

Martin nodded but looked as if all the demons in hell were about to be released on him. I took a deep breath and laid down my fork. "It's not the voice Martin. What most people find is that you are um…"

"What?" He almost shouted. I felt a little uncomfortable, I understood that he was upset, but I was not the enemy here. Why I had been placed in this unenviable position, I had no idea.

"This isn't easy Martin, but what they say is that you're a little too technical maybe, you know? Rather than getting to grips with the emotional side and the character and the music itself, that's all." It was the kindest way that I could think of to put it to him at such short notice. Martin sat back and allowed all I'd said to sink in. Then he said.

"Why didn't Giorgio tell me? What am I paying him for? He just muttered about not being 'ready' for God's sake! That could mean bloody anything."

"I don't know about Giorgio, Martin. I can't get him straight in my head either." This Martin ignored, he leant forward once more and began to attack his pasta again, saying. "Come to that Tilly, why didn't you tell me?"

This was the last thing I expected from him and all I could say was. "Me?"

"Well, we're old friends aren't we? He stared at me, and I admit I had little idea how to reply. Once again I felt that I was being pushed into a corner, and held to ransom for every bad thing that was happening. I thought quickly, he was demanding an answer. "You wouldn't have listened to me Martin, and anyway it's not my place…" He interrupted me there…"Well I was honest with you after your Butterfly Tilly. I told you things weren't right!"

Oh the twisty little paths we have to negotiate, there was no comparison between theses two scenarios, and if you think I'm being superior I'm not! He was using it so that he could justify blaming anybody else to make him feel better. I was angry but I ignored it and continued. "It's not professional to run around trying to tell everyone what's wrong with their singing."

He had pushed his plate to one side. "So you do think there's something wrong?"

Now I was beginning to feel uncomfortable, as if Martin was using me as some sort of punch bag. I tried to shift the load a little.

Martin, maybe what you need to think about, is what you are going to do about it. I mean do you agree that there is something not right? Do you feel something is wrong? Because if the answer to the last two questions is, No! then ignore the whole thing."

Martin was silent he just stared at me without answering. The early evening was moving on, it was all I could do not to glance up at the clock on the wall. Martin lifted his glass towards the waiter and asked for another drink. He must have felt my eyes on him, because he snapped. "Don't preach Tilly. I bloody need it. There's plenty of time befor the performance for it to evaporate." He remained silent until his wine arrived.

"He's a shit. All he thinks about is himself and he doesn't give a toss for anyone else. You were smart to leave him Matilda."

The use of my full name shocked me slightly, he has never, to my knowledge called me Matilda before. It made me realise just how serious for once, Martin was. He continued. "Apart from anything else. If this bloke's so bloody marvellous, who's going to sing with him? Giorgio has no female singer who can balance him, nowhere near. Of course that alone will make him sound pretty wonderful, won't it? Personally I think he's just bloody jealous of me, to the extent that he's prepared to pay a huge sum to 'Charlie boy' rather than let me be heard."

I didn't answer him straight away. Martin's ego was turning back flips just to stay in place. I waited a small 'cooling' period and then ventured.

"If you go down that path Martin, you'll never know the truth. I don't think it matters if Giorgio is jealous of you or not." (Privately I thought and still believe that this is highly unlikely.)…"You must consider your own future and what you perceive that you need to do in order to achieve what you want, presumably some success and recognition."

Martin glared at me, and as if he hadn't heard a word, said.

"He sounds like a bloody old car cranking up with that slow fucking beat in his voice. The sound of healthy instruments must drive him nuts. I don't see how he can bear to teach at all!"

"That's not really fair Martin. And the point is he does teach, and this moment you are taking his teaching. Whether or not you continue to do so could well be part of what you need to consider. Giorgio is a very complicated man, you know that and…"

Martin stood up and leaned towards me. My heart began to thud, I've had enough of violent, frustrated tenors for one life time. He spat at me.

"Not fair? Not fair? I'll tell you what's not bloody fair. This whole ridiculous fiasco. I expected a bit more sympathy from you, considering your approaching situation. How do you think you're going to manage out there? Stupid cow! Think all the Opera companies in England are going to be falling over themselves to employ you do you?"

I tried to push my ever present fears regarding my future away. His need in that moment was greater than mine.

"No Martin, forget me for a moment, look…"

"No stupida no. YOU look. You should go back to darling Giorgio. You deserve each other. In fact I think you were made for each other. I suggest you watch the sweet Verity because she'll have your bloody eyes out. Couldn't make you any blinder though could it?"

He swigged back the last of his wine and slammed the glass down. Then he turned and stormed out of the restaurant. The waiter was all concern as he collected the dirty dishes. I ordered some coffee, having finally felt able to glance at the clock without incurring the wrath of the gods. I realised it wasn't as late as I had feared it might be and there was plenty of time to drink it and to recover before I went back to the Opera house. When it came I spent some time staring into it, remembering Venice. Was I making things worse by keeping Lucciano so clearly in my mind. Maybe it simply served to heighten an already extremely fraught situation. I was to have no answers in my cappuccino this time. I sighed. Martin had left me with a deep sense of foreboding, and a heavy heart. Not to mention the bill!

June

Giorgio's Mother had first been taken ill the afternoon of Martin's unhappy discovery, hence Verity's interruption. She hadn't recovered and had implored Giorgio to let her come home from the expensive private hospital which had done, as they assured him, 'All they could for her.' She wanted, she confessed to him in a whisper, to die at home near to her son. Giorgio agreed. His Mother had asked him for so little in their long time together, and (more important to him) had never intruded into his private life, or asked questions.

She was the only living person aware of his 'condition' in all forms, or at least she had been aware of his agony from some distant part of the house, and yet not once had she questioned him. Sometime after a monstrous attack, she would come to him, and when he returned to the world again, she would often be there, her hand laid gently on his dark head, and looking deep into his eyes she would say. "I love you Giorgio, and I pray for you."

At such times his eyes lost their hypnotic glitter and looked back at her as they had done when he had been a little boy, before he had formulated and began to understand his memories, before he remembered who he was, and what strength he had, from God knew where, and long before he began to use it to shape his life.

So the old lady was ensconced in her own apartment in one wing of the Villa, with two nurses in constant attendance. Giorgio, unknown to anyone else, spent time with her everyday. They spoke little, preferring to make contact with each other through the music, and usually ended up listening to her favourite composer, which was Puccini. Any Puccini. Gradually she would drift into sleep and Giorgio, after planting a gentle kiss on her pale-olive brow, would creep quietly away.

Time for the opening was approaching fast. Giorgio sometimes felt as if he were on a roller coaster, although as always he was in complete control. Surprisingly enough he was finding Verity a big help. She enjoyed all the organisation and her phenomenal brain was never happier than when juggling what to most of us would seem to be an impossible amount of information, with an equally impossible timetable. Giorgio was quietly impressed.

There had been no problem with his guest star and conductor. The rest of his soloists though, were not proving quite as simple. The young Verdi baritone whom he had saved from vocal disaster not so long ago was happy to accept a one-night contract for this opening, especially since, as he lost no time in saying, he owed Giorgio everything. His agent however, who unfortunately Giorgio did not know, was not proving to be very cooperative.

"I'm moving heaven and earth to get him to release me from a rather ridiculous clause in the original contract which I signed with him. I'll let you know as soon as I possibly can."

Giorgio understood of course, but he quietly cursed the naiveté of singers generally. They were always so desperate to get signed up with an agent that they often barely read the written word finally placed in front of them. The words became, he supposed, blurred with gratitude.

He knew without doubt though, that providing all went to plan, he would have a superb balance with his star tenor. No, strangely enough, it was casting the soprano for Aida which caused him the biggest headache. He knew that he did not possess one student who was strong enough in any way to balance even one of the male performers, never mind if he achieved both of their services. He continually pushed the obvious answer to the problem out of his mind. He would not under any circumstance, ask Matilda!

On learning from Martin that Giorgio was stumped for a mezzo-soprano, his own only acceptable member of that voice range having been whisked off to Germany, Matilda had suggested that Martin recommend Pixie. This he had done, and as Giorgio had been so impressed, he had conveniently forgotten to mention that it had been Matilda's idea in the first place. A fact that he also forgot to mention to Pixie.

"Who did you say the tenor was ?" She had asked him with an air of assumed innocence. Reluctantly Martin had named the Italian, quietly afraid that he might well choke over the word. Pixie, lost no time in rubbing huge amounts of salt into the still festering wound.

"Oh I though that you were singing Radames, Mart. What happened? You're not ill are you?" She had exclaimed, deliberately using the shortened, intimate version of his name usually, as she well knew, reserved only for his wife, and on-going lovers. Martin ignored it as best he could. To be honest he supposed that he couldn't really expect any other reaction. He had treated her shamefully, even for someone with his reputation. But then of course he came to this conclusion without being aware of all the facts.

Pixie floated around on cloud nine for the next few days. Irena was naturally delighted for her, although she wished that they had some more time to work on the technique. Pixie had, potentially, exactly the right sound for Amneris, even if some of the older members of the chorus threw up their hands in horror at the idea of someone her age tackling the role.

"You'll be alright." Irena assured her. "They do have a point of course, but the heaviest of Amneris's music comes later on in the opera, as you know, with the big duet with Radames and the scene with the priests. And you're not going to be singing that part. I have thought hard about this Pixie, and I'm quite confident that you'll do yourself only good."

That was enough for Pixie. She ignored the well meaning advice from her Opera house colleagues and applied herself to the task in hand. She was often to be found, glued to the side of the stage as the glorious Italian mezzo, dazzled the Opera house with her singing. Irena had been completely honest with Pixie, and she wished vehemently that Matilda was singing Aida, because it was exactly the sort of experience that would pull her gently onwards. Apart from this, the four of them would make quite a quartet. On the spur of the moment she extracted Giorgio's phone number from Tony London's office and phoned the Villa. After all, what could be more natural? She had a pupil who would be working for him at his grand opening.

"My dear Irena, how delightful to hear from you. I must just say that I had no idea that you had a singer with such a fabulous voice! I congratulate you on your work with her. She's definitely on my books for the future. It's always such a pleasure to work with real voices like that, don't you find? Now what can I do for you?"

Irena listened patiently, hearing glimpses of various emotions glitter through Giorgio's voice like dusty jewels. She noted sincerity. That didn't surprise her, he would have to be an idiot not to hear what Pixie had. As she traced the rise and fall of the familiar tenor tones, darkened and rounded by maturity, she realised that he knew exactly why she had rung, although neither of them was about to admit it.

"Thank you Giorgio. What I'm ringing about is this. I was wondering who your soprano will be? Pixie didn't know but I suggested to her that, providing it meets with your approval of course, they could work on the music together?"

Giorgio was silent for a few seconds, Irena remembered that little ploy only too well, It had often been a prelude to an outburst of varying degrees of verbal abuse. Not this time however. Giorgio was quite calm when he replied.

"I haven't finally decided yet, Irena my dear. But I will let you know as soon as I make up my mind, and we can talk again."

After she hung up, Irena tapped in Matilda's number. She did not expect to find her at home. She left a message, asking her to phone her when she could. Irena wasn't given to premonition, but she was thoughtful as she waited for the doorbell to ring. She waited, her stomach churning, and wishing that the piercing sound would never happen. Inevitably, of course, it did. It was her taxi, and for the moment she forgot all about everything else.

About half-an-hour later, with her stomach churning even more, Irena closed the taxi door and concentrated on paying the young cockney driver who had, and she was grateful, engaged her in fast non stop banter all the way to the hospital. As he pulled away she turned and faced the large, inhuman looking building which rose in front of her. A few moments later she was sitting in the waiting area. There were already half a dozen rather miserable or apprehensive people sitting there, and really who could blame them for that? She wondered how close to the appointed time she would actually see Mr Keats, her consultant. As it happened she entered his room within five minutes of the hour on her appointment card. She settled herself in the chair in front of the desk, as well as she could, to relax would be impossible, and tried very hard not to notice the large brown envelope that lay there. She suspected it held her latest x-rays, those taken two weeks ago, and showing the on-going medical saga of what was happening inside her head.

The consultant, having greeted her when she first entered the room, removed his glasses, and took an inordinate amount of time placing them with great care on the desk. He seemed to be searching for the right words, and Irena's heart contracted a little. Surely things hadn't worsened suddenly? She felt so much better, even entering the palace of doom as she referred to the hospital to herself, hadn't removed that feeling. Her energy levels had risen, and she had dared to hope that she was in remission, as she believed the term to be. If that was possible in his form of the terrible illness. But now, she began to doubt. Maybe this feeling of well being was just a strange euphoria in the wake of fear. Not fear of death, Irena had realised since this dark period had descended on her, forcing her to look at certain aspect of life, that she had done 'death' many times and that in itself it was nothing to be afraid of. Just an old friend who had the habit of turning up at the wrong time. It was no more really than waiting for your flight at the airport. No, it was the manner of death which caused all the worry, especially in cases which held a situation such as she believed hers to be.

Quite suddenly Irena had a picture of a hideous waiter, a demon-like creature, who smilingly presents his clients with a 'menu.'

"Madam would prefer…Hot or cold? We can do quick or lengthy. A road accident maybe? A nasty untreatable infection? How about something exotic? Make life interesting while it lasts?"

She shuddered and Mr Keats seemed to be pulled out of his silence.

"This is not easy for me Irena."

Irena held her breath. Some part of her mind relaxed and sent vibrations of goodwill to the rest of her, which her heart ignored and thumped in heavy anticipation anyway.

"It's good news for you, but very embarrassing for the hospital. The bottom line is…Well we simply can't understand it. Here, let me show you."

He opened the envelope and removing the plates, he fixed them on to the lighted screen behind him. Irena stared at them.

"What am I supposed to be looking for." She asked him. He traced his finger lightly around a small area deep in Irena's brain, saying. "Here is the trouble spot."

"Apart from some obvious information culled over the years from singing and teaching, I have little knowledge of the human body Mr Keats. But I see nothing in this area you have shown me, as far as I can tell it looks perfectly healthy to me!"

"It looks perfectly healthy to me also." The consultant replied, and Irena felt a quick rush of relief and excitement, and a tiny smug little voice in her mind said. "Told you so!"

But she remained calm and almost appeared unmoved from the outside. Mr Keats continued.

"If we've made a mistake, I can't apologise enough for what you must have gone through over the last few months."

"If?" Replied Irena. Mr Keats smiled. "Well I suppose I'm still being cautious. Let's take a blood test, just to make sure. But it looks likely that somewhere along the way, someone has messed up big time. I don't know if it was a mix up with X-rays, or the blood we took, or both. But what can I say?"

He was obviously embarrassed. He had always treated her with kindness and gentleness and Irena shone on him her wonderful smile and said.

"Without wanting to sound even a little bit rude Mr Keats, you can say goodbye!"

He laughed, thankful that the difficulty was over. Not everyone would have been quite as ready to let it all pass so easily, however thankful and relieved they were. He stood up and offered her his hand.

"See the nurse for the blood test, and I'm happy to say good-bye!"

After Irena had left he found himself musing on the beauty of her amazing smile, and thought to himself what an oasis of hope she presented in a desert of difficult work. He didn't really know why, I mean it had all been a mistake, hadn't it?

Irena walked on air down the short corridor, through the waiting area, and straight past the nurses station, through reception and out into the warm afternoon. She had no intention of repeating a test of any sort. How this had all come about she had no idea, all she knew was that she felt wonderfully relieved. She hailed a cab. "Thanks God!" She muttered to herself stepping into the idling black taxi.

JOURNAL

I saw Irena today and she asked me a very odd question. When I have nothing in the pipe line, outside the Opera house that is, what exactly do I work on? I had to think for a moment, but then as I told her it was really whatever comes to mind. Anything that I felt drawn to including duets, trios, and even quartets. She nodded and looked thoughtful, then she asked me if I would mind if she made some suggestions, and would I prepare it as if I were going to perform it? I told her it doesn't matter to me what I work on as long as it's real opera. She smiled at me then, and said that it is certainly that, and that she has her reasons for suggesting it to me. What these are I don't know, but she did seem a little mysterious, not like her at all.

Martin is speaking to me again, just. I do understand how he must feel, but I can't spend all day commiscrating with him.

He is withdrawn into an icy shell. But something rather disturbing! My landlord rang, and informed me that he wants to sell the house. That of course includes my flat. This is not a good time for such a thing to happen, I can scarcely apply for a mortgage just as I'm about to lose my job!

I'm beginning to fantasise about having Warrener at the end of a potentially lethal Judo hold. He is responsible for all my practical problems at the moment. But I mustn't let that interfere with my concentration. I do not want to end up circling my mind around and around a nonentity such as he is, that would be a terrible waste of time and energy. Considering that the fatal day approaches, I am actually feeling good, much more like my old self. But, I would like to be in contact with Carlo, I really miss him.

The old man had been hard at work ever since Matilda had started to improve. The resurgence of energy had cleared the forest floor. He could not have helped with that, it was something she had to do herself. But it had left him free to concentrate on the less obvious aspects of her inner world. The sparkling blue messages encoded with vital information and leaping at unbelievable speed from one nerve ending to another, took some time to decipher. That however was not the problem. Ever since her walk through the 'dark valley' as he referred to it, he had found it more and more difficult to contact her through her dreams, which was their natural meeting ground.

Time and again he had tried to impress on the sleeping woman those aspects of inner information which he perceived that she required to know, and time and time again he knew that she had not registered it in the morning.

Gone was the time when he only needed to breath a thought from the turquoise water side. Gone, in other words, was her innocence. Life had played its part in laying the foundation of despair and failure.

If only she would come through this, meeting the challenges that presented themselves to her, without losing faith, she would be stronger than ever. And that golden future probability which he had caught more than one glimpse of during his work, would be hers. She would step into that eventuality as simply as drawing her next healthy breath.

He set back to work, determined not to shrink one iota from his goal.

JOURNAL

I received a letter from Dante today. I don't know if I'm pleased or not…Oh alright, yes, I'm pleased. But it does ramble rather. I'm not sure what he's talking about most of the time. He still keeps referring to the fact, that as he sees it, we must keep in close contact, must not lose faith in each other, and must ignore the apparent problems and difficulties which face us. He also says that he will be in London soon, and that he is not about to marry. But he gives me no date for his arrival, and no explanation as to the last statement.

He has signed the letter, Yours forever, having added a short sentence which says again that he has something for me. Something which will, apparently, see off all my doubts. I don't know what to think! Given that, although his spoken English is improving, he wrote to me in Italian, and apart from one or two words, and the odd phrase, I'm not even certain if I have understood correctly. But for the moment, I can't check any of it out.

I'm sure that you're not surprised to know that I'm not about to phone him!

Apparently, rehearsals begin soon for Giorgio's opening. I would have gone anyway of course, to support Pixie, but it seems that I shall be there, as general dogs-body. I don't want to sound like a pathetic woos, but I wish so much that I were going to be singing. I hope I can do this. I hope I can be around all the excitement and rehearsing etc, without falling to pieces, that would be too embarrassing.

July

Journal:

At the end of rehearsal this morning, the entire company was called for 'notes' from our esteemed visiting Maestro. Some of the chorus members muttered about his method.

"It's not really on you know." One of the tenors was talking to anyone near enough to hear him, as we made our way to the stage. " Stage notes are one thing, but when it comes to music, each group should receive their notes in the privacy of their individual rehearsal. International soloists don't want to be told their faults in front of the rest of the company!"

"I'm sure they're big enough to handle it." I replied, a little irritated.

"I didn't say that they weren't. It's just not done, that's all!" The tenor continued and sloped to the back part of the stage.

This particular 'Maestro' was known for doing things his own way, with little thought or concern for tradition. In fact Rodney, our grumpy tenor, was quite right. However, sometimes people flaunt tradition because they can, and sometimes they have to answer for it.

Generally he was relatively pleased. We were, apparently, somewhere near to acceptable. But the rhythm was slack here and the energy missing there, and as for the pitch in this particular place…Well. Do something about it was the clear message Maestri, of course, have no concept of being tired. At least they don't seem to have, and at 70+ when many members of society feel that they should slow down a little, they are still chasing the soprano or mezzo around the piano (literally) and being more than capable of doing plenty about it if they catch her! Must be all that upper body exercise. Anyway, to them the music is paramount and must always be treated with a fervour and dedicated love as if it will never be heard on the planet again. Having finished with us, for the moment, he turned his attention to one of the small part soloists. We are rehearsing Carmen, and it was to one of the gypsy girl friends of Carmen that he said.

"My dear, in ze Act 2 ensemble, you are a little flat…"

"I'm sorry Maestro." She interrupted…"But I have diarrhoea."

There was a silence which filled the air with a whistling hum. Then, I could make out the grumpy tenor shaking his head, no doubt he felt vindicated for his earlier comments, while John, one of our Irish baritones could be heard to whisper under his breath. "No, no, no, no, no."

The general feeling was one of acute embarrassment, although Pixie looked fit to burst with giggles, Maria clamped her top teeth down on to her bottom lip, and quite a few people suddenly became intensely interested in the floor of the stage. As for our Maestro? It was quite an experience witnessing a world acclaimed conductor lost for words. After the initial shock of being interrupted. (This is obviously not done!) He studied the score on the stand in front of him, (while the orchestral leader studied him) then looked back at the stage and replied in sharp tones which bit into every part of the auditorium.

"Vell my dear. For your diarrhoea, I don't gife a shit. Just get it in tune please!"

Chu-Pen was meditating. The quiet of the monastery was even deeper than usual since everyone was aware that the Grand Master was involved in something of severe importance.

Actually Chu-Pen was quite capable of achieving a deep trance almost anywhere. But such devoted concentration from those around him, certainly helped him, and unusually he needed a little help. Chu-Pen was nervous.

The time line was narrowing. Soon now it would disappear into space and in that untraceable point, the Western Gate would no longer be in danger of opening. And the best chance yet in the last 38.000 years for man as an entire race to step into the light of his own hidden abilities would be lost for a very long time.

However, in his meditations, Chu-Pen could hear Matilda's voice. And very much clearer than Irena, he could hear the harmonic. He heard its pearly, translucent quality, floating around the fundamental note, both above and below it. And, peering deeper, he could see strands of D.N.A. beginning to wake up. Spasmodically they would sparkle, as if some tiny charge of electricity had ignited them. Then they would sleep again leaving only the 2 strands on duty as they had been for thousands of years, extending to man the barest information required for survival.

Two things were needed to light the virtual strands permanently. The release of the energy from the emerald amulet, the fire that Anthorus had managed to extract from Lothus and conceal there, and the accursed overtone that was fast being allowed to develop in the woman's voice, and in the process of being brought to fruition by Osiria. Whatever she called herself now, that is how he knew her. By forming her beliefs into writings, she had concentrated their power, and had unwittingly catapulted her consciousness into the very lifetime which placed her in a position to experience her own predictions. He knew only too well the words which the wretched woman had written. And to most people in the land where she now dwelt they would, in translation lose much of their original fire, and would not be likely to be understood. But he also knew that it didn't matter what people thought about such words because what they really were, were a warning to him. They were prophesy from someone who had pleased a passing god and from whom she had received a gift. The poetry itself didn't matter. The message within that poetry most certainly did.

"One unknown shall come, and shall fling wide the Western Gate.

Woe to the defender of the past!

The green fire shall burn the disbeliever, and the sound shall be released.

It will dip into its sacred past, and throw itself into the light of the Giant Step."

Chu-Pen shifted on his cushions. It was the last line which bothered him most. If even a few intelligent members of this accursed race put their heads, and worse, their wills together over that, it would cause him a lot of trouble. But he was not beaten yet. Chu-Pen still had Giorgio in the palm of his hand. He was still at the mercy of the 'gift' an impatient Anthorus had 'cursed' him with. Always on edge, in spite of his training, that the ecstatic agony would finally defeat him. Oh yes, he still had him, Chu-Pen had seen to that. Giorgio's training had been less than complete. Never had he realised total power over himself, because it had never been suggested to him that he could have it. Even in his greatest moments of control over other people, the sword of Damocles swung heavily over his own head.

The old man had also calculated the ever-converging time line and was well aware that this summer/autumn equinox was the last possible opportunity for the merging to happen. That which he had once called 'the plague' he now watched with hope and concern as it rushed towards its impending birth at speed.

He sensed Matilda's inner forces gathering themselves, although she, on a conscious level was totally unaware of anything. She knew only that in spite of practical concerns, she was feeling an enormous sense of well-being ,and something was happening to her voice.

"It's weird Pixie." "What is?" Asked her friend.

"Well, I was working the other morning, before the call, and when I was singing, well…certain phrases…"

"Yes?" Pixie interrupted impatient at Matilda's hesitation.

"It's not easy to explain. But it was as if some of the music went into 3D."

Pixie looked at her as if she was deranged. "Right! Stereophonic sound, eh?"

"No, don't laugh at me. It really was bizarre, especially since when it happened, I felt drawn so far into myself, that I didn't feel as if I was singing at all, and the sound became more of a vibration. But then…"

"Yes?" Pixie exaggerated the questioning tone as if she was speaking to someone who was much the worse for drink.

"Well then, it all disappeared, and I was back to normal."

"Just as well! You've heard of the Bermuda triangle? Well here we obviously have the singer's equivalent!" Laughed Pixie. "Oh shut up!" Grinned Matilda.

Maria and Jessica joined them at the table where they were sitting. The canteen was very busy, full of dancers in various forms of rehearsal dress, and singers in various stages of late lunch.

"I'm shattered." Maria declared. "How are you two?"

"Well, I'm fine." Replied Pixie. "But Matilda here is in danger of disappearing."

"Disappearing where?" Maria looked puzzled.

"Apparently up her own enharmonic passage. " Pixie finished with a flourish. To which Maria raised her eyebrows, and Jessica said. "I'm sorry what did you say. Are we missing something?"

Matilda interrupted, giving Pixie a look that would freeze red-hot metal. "Take no notice, it's just end-of-seasonitis." How's our soap going by the way? Make a good show on tele, that would. Sort of operatic 'Coronation Street.' What do you think?"

"Ssh…" Warned Maria. "Rachel's over there." Matilda resisted the temptation to turn round. "Whoops!" Was all she said.

"What's she doing?" Asked Pixie, who was in a better position to scrutinise the table without seeming obvious.

"I suspect that she's showing off her ring. She showed it to me earlier. It's an absolute beauty. God knows what it must have cost!"

"Which brings us neatly to the point." Pixie put in, staring hard at Matilda. "When is this Count of yours, or should I say Il Conte, going to give you an outward sign of his affection?"

Matilda was about to mention Dante's letter and the promise therein, when there was the sound of raised voices across the canteen.

"What in all hell's going on over there?" Jessica half rose from her seat. Semi-silence, which became total, descended over the whole room as the voices became ever louder. A visiting German soprano was standing behind our Musical Director in the queue, as she assured him in broken English. "Really Maestro, it matters not!"

In true British fashion, the rather aggressive woman behind the counter was not about to be intimidated by either of them. "It's too late!" She said to a bristling Sir Clive.

"What do you mean. It's too late? This lady is our guest, and she would like a steak, medium rare."

"Sorry, but no more grilling until 5:30 this evening. Next?"

But Sir Clive was not about to move. "I insist that you prepare a semi-rare steak for my colleague."

"You can insist all you like. It's not happening, not before 5:30 it's not."

"Do you know who I am?!" He said in a voice closely resembling an angry trombone. The canteen worker was silent for a few seconds, and then with perfect dramatic timing she replied. "Yes, and you're still not getting any steak. Not before 5:30. Now, next?" "How very embarrassing." Mumbled Maria as Sir Clive spun around and marched out of the canteen, followed quickly by the soprano.

"Who's that? What's she here for?" Asked Pixie watching the singer as she disappeared into the corridor.

"I can't remember her name." Jessica replied. "She hasn't been here before, I'm sure I'd remember her. She's here for some Wagner concert at the proms which we aren't involved in, and opens next season I believe."

Pixie raised her eyebrows. "She could have done with that steak. She's small for a Wagnerian soprano."

"She's also very pretty." Jessica added, smiling knowingly.

"No! Uncle Clive's not like that, is he?" Exclaimed Pixie. (Uncle, was a term of audacious familiarity often adopted by the younger members of the chorus when referring to the Musical Director) Maria laughed and Jessica replied quickly.

"Darling haven't you learnt yet? They're ALL like THAT!"

The normal buzz of the canteen had resumed, if slightly modified by what had just occurred.

"It seems to be a day for bringing Maestri down to earth." Pixie laughed loudly.

"Yes what about that? I mean who else would have made a comment such as that in front of the entire company?" Said Maria.

"The entire company shouldn't have been there." Jessica pointed out.

"That's what Rod was muttering as we were going up for our notes." Put in Matilda. Jessica nodded and said.

"Well he was right! God, I can't believe we have to start thinking about getting ready for yet another show in a couple of hours. How many extra sessions do we have this week?"

"Three altogether." Said Maria. "Extra money though! Just in time for the holidays too!"

Matilda, involuntarily, glanced away, and there was a slight tense silence.

"Sorry luv." Said Maria to her quietly. "I don't suppose you'll have a holiday, will you?"

"What's happening about next season?" Pixie said with a forthrightness which frankly, Matilda was grateful for.

"Well Dante's coming over sometime soon, and I'll have a talk to him. That'll be a start. But in our position, there being so many singers capable of doing our job, well it's so hard to know what to do in this profession, isn't it?"

There was nothing the others could say. It was a too threatening possibility for all of them. And they all knew that if it came to it they wouldn't know which way to turn either.

"You don't feel inclined to sing to Warrener again, I suppose?" Asked Jessica gently. Maria shook her head as if she still couldn't believe that Matilda had not been granted a contract for the next season. While Pixie said.

"Waste of time. If the silly idiot can't hear what Till's got, he doesn't want to hear for some dumb reason."

"I'm sure things will work out." Maria said.

Matilda smiled at all of them and found herself, in spite of the worrying situation able to genuinely feel that indeed 'things' would.

Prelude to

Act Four

The equinox was approaching. The time line ran faster and faster (or so it seemed) to its converging point of disappearance. Chu-Pen spent most of his time in deep meditation, and the old man did his best to keep Matilda's faith alive.

Everywhere there were small signs that the 'plague' was already beginning to spread, even before the ultimate release. The signs were, in some cases, too inconsequential for anyone to note, and in other cases, even if more of the 'news breaking' type, then seemingly so isolated that no one even guessed that they might be a part of something greater.

Matilda sat opposite Pixie one morning in the canteen before the call began, and knocked on the paper which prevented her from seeing anything except the print in front of her. Pixie pulled the paper across to one side. "Hi Tilly! Sorry, I didn't see you… I won't be long" She said and went straight back to her reading.

"Don't often see you engrossed in the daily news Pixie."

"This is true." Pixie replied and became quiet again.

"Morning Pixie. Grown a brain over night have we?" Teased John in his Irish baritone. He and Pixie indulged in a permanent, and harmless banter.

"If 'we' grew it then at the moment I have it." She said without lifting her eyes from the article that so engrossed her, but she smiled.

Matilda began to wonder just how long she was going to have to wait for Pixie's attention, and she was about to pull her ever-present novel from her bag when Pixie said to her.

"You know that horrible thing that was supposed to have started somewhere in Africa, and was killing people left right and centre?"

"What horrible thing?" Asked Matilda.

"I can't find the name here now…Something like Nervosa term.. something bla, bla. Anyway they couldn't find a cure, and they have been getting really worried about it because it can spread like wild fire, They were talking about refusing to allow people the right to travel from infected countries, never mind just the areas affected, and starting to pull up all sorts of rules and things. Apparently, only a handful of people who contracted it in the very beginning, have survived."

"I heard something about it." Replied Matilda. "Affects the nervous system, doesn't it?"

Pixie nodded and added. "Horrible little sod it is!"

"Hope you're not referring to me!" John remarked as he past their table to buy another coffee.

"Who else?" Pixie threw at his back. "Well?" Prompted

Matilda. "Well, it's gone! Disappeared. No new cases for a month. Everyone infected since the first lot of deaths have recovered, and according to this lot…." She shook the paper. "They're better than ever."

"Gone?" Said Matilda. "How the hell did that happen? And without a cure? But they were referring to it as the worst plague civilisation has ever known, I remember that from the news just last week." And she stretched across the table to look at the article. While Pixie continued.

"They can't make head or tail of it. An Italian specialist went over to Africa to help in the search for a cure, he's about the top man in the world, and…" She continued reading from the paper.

"WITHIN HOURS OF THE ARRIVAL OF SIGNOR PAULO SOFRI. THE VIRUS APPEARED TO LEAVE." "Oh! A racist virus." She giggled.

"You shouldn't laugh Pixie." Chided Matilda. "Why not? It's gone hasn't it?" Pixie replied innocently.

"But, he must have done something. " Insisted Matilda. Pixie shook her head and said. "No, in fact he had barely settled into his hotel room, and had been nowhere near the laboratory set up in the hospital, and the little bugger fled the country, or was stopped in it's tracks anyway."

Matilda sat back, thoughtful. "Well you know what they say Pixie. God moves in mysterious ways."

"Hmm. It would make life a lot easier if he weren't quite so mysterious some of the time." Pixie said, and then, because Matilda was staring in front of her still deep in thought added. "What is it?"

"I think I recognise his name. The Doctor... The specialist... Sofri was it?"

Pixie nodded. "Oh through your Dad maybe?" She asked gently, since Matilda rarely spoke of the accident, or her parents.

"Must be...Matilda replied shrugging. Then she sat up. "No! Dante. His family know him. I think he lives near them, in that part of Italy. He visits them all the time. I get the impression that they're quite close."

"Come on girls, you can't sit there all day you know. Work, work, work!"

John, with reinforcements from Wales and Scotland (two tenors in fact) Were making their way determinedly to the exit of the canteen, all carrying the remains of coffee or tea in styrene cups. At the same moment the studio door opened, and the morning class of ballet dancers released from the bar, made a beeline for the counter to buy drinks and sticky buns.

"It's not fair, you know." Remarked Pixie, as she watched a tiny female dancer hesitate between a chocolate éclair and an apricot Danish pastry. "They can do that every day. We can't do it once a week!"

"No" sighed Matilda as they hurried along the cool corridor. "But we do!"

The girls laughter spiralled up and out into the air above the Opera House. Long after they had forgotten it, it still lived. There was something in the frequency you see, something that the great big tired world, rather liked.

Irena had been aware of a change in herself since she had been given the 'all clear,' or the Sorry-our-mistake-you -couldn't-have-had-it-in-the first-place. Whatever it was it had given her a fantastic lift in energy. No, it was more than that. Energy tends to rise and fall. This was more a state which, having pulled her to itself, never faltered. It gave her a new confidence. Suddenly she had no intention of sitting in her house and waiting. Whatever her age, it suddenly didn't matter. She simply didn't care. She just wanted to continue feeling the way that she now felt. It had a breathless dimension about it.

She could feel strength rising in her like a particularly graceful animal. Of course, there were the dreams, and she could do without them. But she sensed that the two things were connected. Anyway it wasn't that they were so bad, not what you would call 'Nightmares.' They were just so infuriatingly insistent and regular. She picked up the hand set and pushed in a number.

"Simon!" She said when it was answered.

"Hello Irena. How are you?" Simon was a young conductor, struggling in the impossible world of music, who Irena often used to play the piano for her, when she wanted to give all her attention to a student. She heard the hope in his voice, work was precious. Well, she was about to make his day.

"I wonder if you have two full days free next week that you could give me, Simon? 10:30a.m. through to about 5:00 in the afternoon, maybe going on into the evening if we feel we can? Lunch and dinner on me, of course!"

Simon was more than pleased. Irena was always very generous with her hourly rate, out of interest he asked.

"What would you like me to prepare? "

"Aida." Replied Irena, after all it was in the air at the moment. The music had been following her around for days now.

"O.K. And who's singing?"

"Me!" And she hung up before Simon could make any comment.

"When will you go Dante?"

"Soon Mamma"

"And you will give her the necklace?"

"I must do something practical Mamma. I can't lose her."

"Then do what you feel you must, Dante. Your Father and I understand better than anyone else what it is to be in such a position. But..."

"But?" Dante encouraged.

"It's just that I've never actually seen this piece before. And, well, isn't there something just a little more feminine that you can give her."

Dante had discovered the amulet in the musty old alcove, having traced the 'hum' there intent on checking the wiring. As soon as he saw it, he knew that that was what he must give to Matilda. For some reason it was perfect. He had shown his parents and of course asked their permission. His Father had said with a rather strange expression on his face. "And this is what you wish to give to your little English lady, is it?"

"Is there a problem?" Dante had asked him. The Count was uncertain as to why his son's choice had the effect on him that it had. He couldn't say that he really liked the piece. And yet there was something of great importance shimmering in its green depths, and part of him didn't want to let it go. But, he had agreed to allow Dante to give Matilda something from the family, and he had said no more. Now however, Dante felt his Mother was questioning his choice also.

"Do you think that she won't like it?" He asked the Countess.

"No, it's not that. I can't really say what it is. It's rather a strange piece, don't you think? How about my ruby ring? It was the first piece of the family jewels which your Father gave to me?"

"Mamma, you are very kind. But, if you don't mind it must be the emerald. I feel it so strongly."

"Very well Dante. If that's what you wish. Give her the emerald, with our love."

ACT FOUR

One Door Closes

I know I don't usually bother you with dates, but today is rather important. This evening will be the last performance of the season. The last time I shall be on the most wonderful stage in the world. I can't pretend that I'm not very sad, but I do still have this underlying feeling that everything will work out. Maybe I'm just the rather silly eternal optimist?

Tonight, understandably, I'm looking back over the last few years. How can such a small space of time seem to have gone on for ever, and equally seem to have raced by? The inconsistency of time I suppose.

I received a lovely present from the chorus. I'm afraid I muttered my thanks rather. I knew it would be happening, but when it came to it I was so touched that I was more than a little worried that I might just burst into tears, or flames, or something. Anyway I have it around my neck, and the inscription on the back states 'with love' and gives the date. Quite a few people said things like.

"Warrener won't last long, he's the wrong type…You can always come back."

"Come in and see us, regularly. It'll keep your face in with the powers that be."

"Don't let the bastards get you!"

And many other statements, designed to send me on my way with positive energy. I realise with something of a rush that I have become very fond of them, and I feel like Carlo as he watched his friends letting the old Night Watchman win all that gold in Venice after he had seen the Cardinal. And I thought.

'Oh they deserve so much better than Warrener.'

We had a couple of rehearsals with him over the last few weeks. It was a form of introduction I suppose, and he worked on music for next season, so obviously I was not required to attend.

"Of course you can go if you like Matilda. I'm sure Jonathan won't mind" Said Pauline after she had explained the situation to me.

"He probably won't even notice." I pointed out to Maria, when I told her.

"I wouldn't like to say anything about that 'gentleman'" She snarled the last word. "I don't trust him. I bet he'll gradually clear out as many of us as he can. I suspect he has a whole army of friends just desperate to get in here. Using friendships sometimes, when you can come up with the goods, is one thing, we all understand that. But it's quite obvious that he can't keep his brains out of his trousers, and they're certainly not in his ears."

After the first session with him, she took me off for lunch to the 'Italian' at the end of the passage. But we talked of other things. The only reference she made to the rehearsal was as we actually stepped out of the stage door. Whereupon she looked at me and said.

"What did I tell you? All musical brawn, and no musical heart. The Opera House are nuts! What's wrong with them? Oh let's forget it!"

I will turn my mind to the opening. Irena has calmed down about my helping out. It seems I'm not really going to be a 'dog's body' but stage manager, no less. This goes with a very nice fee by the way. She only wants me to insist on a couple of things.

1. That I have enough time off to keep up my daily practise.

2. That I have a day off every week so that I can have a lesson with her.

Giorgio is fine with both requests. He won't be around at the first rehearsals. He and Verity are off somewhere on holiday before Francesco, the tenor, and Riccardo Biagioni, our conductor, arrive. And we, the responsibility being mainly mine, I add with a shudder, we must have the production ready for Francesco to be slotted into. And the music thoroughly learnt, with the singers completely 'out of the book' for the Maestro.

Martin is going to rehearse Radames for us until Francesco arrives, yes he finally signed the 'cover contract' which Giorgio had offered him. Gareth Evans, the baritone, has a relatively small part as Amonasro, since we are only presenting the first two acts of Aida for the opening. So I suppose he might not appear at the Villa until closer to the date, but from the last week in August, at least some of us will be living there, and actually I think it's an idyllic way to spend a few weeks. The surroundings are beautiful, we will be working with the most sublime music, and for the most part (I hope Martin won't ruin it) the company will be friendly and entertaining. If only I were singing with them, then it would be perfect!

But what will be perfect is the three weeks that Dante and I are spending together in Spain first. It was a lovely surprise when he rang me just the other day. I hardly needed any persuading! Apart from anything else we need time to talk. I would like his advice on a few things. But mainly we need to be alone together, without me having to rush off to work, or him having to leave for Italy.

SPAIN. *JULY/AUGUST 2012*

Matilda and Dante landed in Malaga one Friday afternoon, and were met by a friend of Dante's. Giuseppe Mengozzi drove a white dusty car and whisked them off into the hills to the beautiful village of Mijas. Dante, Matilda reflected as they left the busy Malaga town, seemed to have friends everywhere.

They were spending the first week in a villa on the far edge of the village, where they would have plenty of time to relax and talk. The next two weeks they would spend further along the coast in a 5 star hotel in the highly exclusive area of Marbella.

"It's like being on Honeymoon." Matilda giggled with delight when Dante explained what he had arranged for them.

"Si. Anda promisea me cara, we never losea dis. Promisea me we stay…Come si dice?…Interested in!"

"I hope we stay more than interested in." Matilda laughed as the car spun upwards towards Mijas. She assumed that Giuseppe did not understand English. He had only spoken a few phrases in Italian when he greeted his friend, and when he was introduced to her. As they turned into the village, she could see his profile easily, and it did not betray even slightly, the idea that he may have understood the deeper content of their conversation. The car stopped suddenly. Four goats slowly turned their heads and looked at them as if they were assessing whether or not to allow these strangers into their village.

"Welcoming committee." Matilda whispered. "Si!" Grinned Giuseppe.

Dante winked at her and squeezed her hand. She felt herself blush, but then decided it really was too silly, what did it matter if he had understood?

A small boy came running up just as Dante made to open the car door. He carried a short thick stick and he ran into the middle of the goats shouting in Spanish. This was obviously something that he did whenever necessary, and no doubt it earned him his pocket money. The goats, trying to look as if all this fuss was nothing to do with them, moved to one side of the pathless road, with only a minimum loss of dignity.

The car carried on through the streets of white houses, so clean in the sun that they looked as if they had been scrubbed. More goats, and large trestle tables full of Mijas honey met them as Giuseppe drove on through the lovely village. And on more than one corner they passed groups of children, practising flamenco, watched by older women dressed entirely in black, some of them holding tiny siblings.

"Now there's something I've always wanted to do. And I suppose that next season I'll have the time…" Matilda tailed off quickly, not wanting to spoil the happiness she was feeling. A wonderful sense of relaxation was already embracing her, and she felt a weight descend from her head, and begin to dissipate throughout her body.

That evening, after Giuseppe had left, gallantly refusing their offer of dinner with them, they ate outside on the veranda above the villa's garden. You could just see the ocean, a tiny triangle of water right beneath the skyline where the moonlight caught it.

"Per'apsa Sunday we ridea in de evening up to a little bar further in de 'ills?"

"Dante, I'd love to. I've never ridden at night!"

"Isa beautiful. Isa like you my Matilda."

They didn't finish their meal.

JOURNAL: *SATURDAY*

What a luxury to be able to jump into a pool before breakfast! I'm not really a very good swimmer, but I can see myself improving here quite easily. Dante was nowhere to be seen when I first got up and I fancied that I had heard the front door click just as I was becoming conscious. Still dripping from my swim, I went into the kitchen to make some tea and clear up from our 'interrupted' meal from the night before and found a note in Italian on the kitchen table.

'Gone for breakfast and something else very important. Back soon.'

And he was back soon. I had barely washed the last of the dishes when he burst in through the door, and placed a bag of hot rolls, butter, honey and fruit on the table. He also laid some keys down. He had hired a car in the village. It isn't white and dusty, although it wouldn't have mattered! It is, in fact, rather sleek, and to my particular pleasure, it's a convertible. I've always loved the idea of swaning around in a car with the roof down, especially in a hot country such as this. And it is hot! We attacked breakfast. Both of us were ravenous, well we hadn't eaten much the day before one way and another.

"'ave another." Dante pushed the bread basket across the table towards me.

"I don't think I should Dante. I don't want you going off me." I replied.

"A little fat never she 'urt anyone, cara. Anyway you got skinny, you know? You 'ad a very 'ard year."

He grinned at me, I had already opened another roll and begun to butter and honey it. After breakfast we set off for Malaga to find a Supermarket. I paused at the entrance, revelling in the air conditioning for a few moments. But Dante strode off pushing the trolley, and filling it up as if we have an army to feed. As I caught up with him he said.

"We buy now fora de week. Plenty everyting." I watched as the mound of food grew by the minute, and finally said. "Dante, we'll never eat all this."

"Is O.K. We leave some for Giuseppe. 'E stay nexta week at the Villa wid 'isa girlfriends."

"Girlfriends?" I repeated as a picture of Giuseppe's pleasant but not exactly handsome face, and his rather roly-poly form came into my mind. I glanced at Dante's muscled body and my eyes quickly coursed his beautiful face as he leaned over the deep freeze. If he really tried, with all his attributes, what could he accomplish? I shuddered.

"Giuseppe, 'e likea, come si dice? 'Ow you say, Seraglio?."

"Harem?" I spluttered. "Si. Harem." Dante made a great effort to pronounce the 'H' and looked at my astonished face, as he pulled a third chicken from the freezer to join the other two already lying in the trolley.

"Donta estimate under Giuseppe, cara. My good friend, is a very clever man!"

I was too much at a loss for words to correct him, and I added quickly. "I didn't mean to be rude of course but…"

I trailed off as Dante stared at me still holding the chicken and raised one eyebrow, his smile however disappeared quickly as the coldness stuck to his fingers.

"Dio!" He muttered, putting the offended digits in to his mouth in turn. We took the groceries home, and I was prepared to begin some lunch, but Dante insisted we go out. "But all this food!" I exclaimed. "Is O.K. Come." And he took my hand and pulled me behind him back to the car. We drove through the village and turned away from the coast. The road wound further up into the hills. It was very hot, and we were both sweating by the time Dante pulled up under a large tree beside a wall. Over the wall we could look down into a valley where a small village nestled under the heat haze. Opposite us stood an air conditioned Taverna. To walk into it was blissful. We drank sangrias and ate freshly made paella with green salad.

"Tonight I cooka you Italian." Said Dante. "We eat at 'ome. Is O.K?"

"Is O.K." I smiled. I was so happy and relaxed that anything would have been 'O.K.'

"Good! And after dinner, cara, we talk a little."

He spoke quite lightly and I hope the cloud which floated across my happiness is purely in my imagination.

Later

Dante is asleep, having made exquisite love to me, and insisting that I did very little in return.

"Jus' leta me spoil you. Pretend is youra birthday." And he pushed me gently back on to the bed, and began to massage me with a lovely concoction of oil. The perfume was delicious, he had brought it with him from Italy. He started with good intentions, I know. But I also knew that it wasn't likely that he would last long as a masseur, and when a few seconds later I heard the bottle being stood firmly down on the table by the bed, I couldn't suppress a quick giggle.

"No, donta laugh ata me." He giggled also. "I doa my best. Is 'ard to resist."

"Isn't that why you don't resist?" I asked him, but it took him a few seconds to realise what I meant. "Er…I donta resist because ?…"

"Because Dante darling, it's h…"

He covered my mouth with his and the next hour spiralled into timelessness that only something like that can offer. Beneath a creamy Spanish moon Dante slept. I propped my head on my hand and watched him. His face was mainly in shadow, the dark hair in boyish disarray. He was so relaxed that I could scarcely make out his breathing, and I certainly couldn't hear anything.

Half-an-hour later, aware that I wasn't going to drop off, not yet anyway. I slipped as carefully as I could from the bed, and picking up this book which I now write in, I have made my way out on to the veranda. It is the other side of the villa and the light from the lounge behind me, will not disturb him.

Well, I suppose you want to know what he had to say? But first there was something else. Remember that he had told me he had something for me? Well he brought it with him and gave it to me before we got into any serious talking. I really didn't know what to say. Oh I know people say that all the time. "I don't know what to say!" But I was so amazed by what lay in the box when I raised the lid, that I really didn't know. I just stared at it. I've not seen anything like it before. It consists of a beautiful emerald, surrounded by a sprinkling of small bright diamonds which lay in what appears to be some sort of deliberate pattern. Dante wanted me to put it on, and with his help I did so. I took it off again, as soon as I felt that I could, without hurting his feelings. Not because I didn't like it, but because it is so strong. That sounds a really odd thing to say about a piece of jewellery, doesn't it? I suppose what I really mean is that I felt I should only wear it for very special occasions. Also, I'm afraid I felt a little dizzy. It's the heat I expect. It was hotter than ever today. But as I stared at it in the mirror, there was a feeling like a vibration from the emerald, and it caused my head to spin. Apart from all those things, it has to be worth a small fortune.

"I hope it will be safe darling." I said having thanked him so many times, that he told me, playfully, to 'shut up.'

"Ita will cara." He replied sounding completely confident. "How can you be so sure?" I fingered the necklace, wondering if we could put it in Dante's bank in Malaga for safety until we leave. I asked him.

"I donta know. Buta I do know ita will be O.K. Believe me, no one will toucha dis."

I didn't ask him to explain that, and he now invited me to sit with him for our discussion. At least he discussed, I found myself only listening. As I've always been aware. Dante has a 'duty.' It seems absolutely absurd to me in this day and age, however, there is the family name and all that!

His family line really does emerge from a dim and very distant past. In spite of the fact that the Count was in a not dissimilar position with his own Father when he wished to marry Dante's Mother, there is, in our case a difference because I have a career, etc.etc.etc.

Well you can imagine I'm sure, how the Count's mind is working and the usual pre-determined ideas and requisites of a man in such a position. I closed my mind to the implication of all that. After all, nothing is set in stone, and I find those sorts of paradigm, those patterns built on centuries of the same sort of life and repeated over and over again, acutely tiring to even contemplate, let alone live with. I would never in a million years fit into the role of Contessa, I know that. And it would be perfectly ludicrous to even consider it.

On the other side of things though, Dante and I have something special. I'm sure you're thinking. 'Well, yes Matilda. But everyone who's in love thinks that. And for everyone who is in that state, it is true. See how you feel in a few years.' Am I right? But whatever you may think, I know there is something else. Something that has a pull which is so strong, that I almost feel as if I wouldn't dare to challenge it. When Dante gave me the emerald necklace this evening, and I felt dizzy, I saw within those few moments of disorientation that same necklace around his neck. Oh but it wasn't him! Since I've been sitting here quietly, in the glorious Spanish night, I've remembered who it was. I remember Carlo knocking on his door, distraught and despairing. I remember the kindness and intelligence which dealt with him. And I remember, that all of this came from Angelo, and finally I remember that Dante, my own adored Dante was that same Angelo. So my decision is already made. Dante and I will remain together. When the family insist on whatever it might be in the future, I will ignore my well-meaning and lovely friends. I will close my mind to scornful words and told-you-so speeches, and I will cope. I WILL.

SUNDAY

Perfectly wonderful day. We rode up into the hills, tethered the horses outside and had a late supper in the bar. We had left the riding stables quite early in the evening. Darkness only just having fallen, and the cricket community in full swing. So we really should have arrived at the bar about an hour before we actually did. Well you see, there was this lovely discreet little olive grove on the way.

MONDAY

Finally I got Dane to agree to go to a Flamenco show. We had gone into Malaga to do some shopping and have some lunch, and the waiter was Italian. So during the inevitable conversation between the two of them, Dante discovered that there is a particularly outstanding Flamenco group called 'El Jaleo' Which

I think means 'The Noise.' They consist mainly of gypsies and they come down from the hills and perform Flamenco for the best part of the year, given that summer lasts much longer here than at home. He assured us that they are exemplary, and more than worth seeing. The show begins at 11:00 o'clock tonight. So, I suppose this afternoon, we'll just have to rest!

TUESDAY

They were fabulous. I know nothing about the art really, but it was obvious that most of the audience were long standing, firm fans. There were, in fact, very few tourists. You know how, if you're not a tourist you can spot them all a mile off, and if you are a tourist you can do the same? Well, there were very few.

The group consisted of two main male dancers, as different in style as they were different in build and appearance. Two main female dancers, and a 'backing' group of mixed sexes and very mixed ages. Most of them were, to my eye anyway, beautiful, and to my ear, amazing. However hard I try to work out the rhythms, they elude me. I promised myself during that evening that after the summer, I will enlist in a class.

WEDNESDAY

We drove to Granada today. In spite of a dinner after the show which had gone on for hours with Giuseppe, we managed to be up and out of the village well before lunch. Dante was in a rather quiet mood, finally I managed to get him to open up.

"What is it Dante?"

"Isa noting cara."

"Don't tell me that sweetheart, it's obviously something." I insisted. He didn't answer straight away. But the car suffered from rather overly aggressive gear changing I thought. "Youa will tink I am stupido." He said quietly, and not sounding like himself at all.

"O.K. But why are you stupido?" I smiled at him, and he laughed then (a little) before replying.

"Well, isa de oder night cara."

"The other night. You mean our discussion?" I said, hoping that there wasn't something he had forgotten to tell me which would require further drumming up of strength and will on my part. But he shook his head.

"Youa enjoy very much de dancing' Si?" I realised what he was referring to.

"Oh you mean the Flamenco show? Well yes I more than enjoyed it. In fact…" I was about to say that I would like to go again before we leave, but something in his expression stopped me. There was another silence and I felt uneasy, so I said.

"Didn't you like it Dante?"

"You likea de dancers?" He asked, without replying to my question. I know I can be very stupid sometimes, but the only thing I could think was that I had misread the performance totally, and that Dante was about to tell me that it was mediocre and I didn't know diddley. A few hundred yards further along the road, he said.

"You musta realise I am Italian!"

"I know you are Italian Dante. But I don't know what you're trying to say." I was a bit concerned by now. This wasn't something which would just go away. Dante took in a deep breath and finally in a dark and slightly dangerous tone he said.

"I not like 'owa you watch dat dancer!" Realisation dawned. But sexual jealousy is not something I know how to deal with. I've never been faced with it before. Of my few boyfriends, if any of them ever felt like this then they were extremely quiet about it, and it never came to a head. I know one is supposed to be flattered and all that, but it really is silly.

"Which dancer Dante. You mean the good looking one?..." This was wicked, and I notice his knuckles whiten, and his jaw set even tenser before I added. "The one who looks more than a little like you?"

I could see that he was slightly mollified, but there was no answer.

"Dante are you jealous?" "Si." He muttered, and was about to expound, so I said quickly.

"Stop the car!" "Che?" He replied, surprised.

"Don't 'che' me. Stop the car!" I repeated. Much to my surprise he did so. I unbuckled my seat belt and slid across him. I placed my bent knee near to his leg. And swung myself across him, straddling his lap. I have no idea what possessed me, it must have been the heat. I sat there, a few inches from his face.

"Matilda, what are youa doin'?" "I want an apology!" I said. "For a what?" Dante sounded as if he wasn't sure how to handle this, and I had a brief, but delicious feeling of power.

"For accusing me of having lustful thoughts about another man."

He looked deeply into my face his dark eyes completely unreadable, as he asked me. "You not 'ave dem?" I shook my head. "Of course I didn't. I've never heard anything so ridiculous!"

An open car full of people sped by. They shouted and whistled at us, which made me laugh. Dante, however, did not. I began to be just a little worried. I couldn't back down, so what was I going to do? I kissed him, but he didn't respond, worse he grunted sulkily. "Geta off me!" I stood my ground, as it were! "No Dante, not until I have an apology." A car had pulled up near to us, but we didn't hear it, at least we were too involved to register.

"Ia getting' a very 'ot Matilda." He said, but he made no attempt to move me, and I had no intention of moving. "Fine, let's take some clothes off!" And I began to undo his beautiful Italian shirt.

"Stop!" He said, but he had begun to smile. Well, I couldn't stop now, and become all English suddenly, could I? Anyway I was beginning to enjoy myself. There was a polite cough. We both turned and froze. Leaning against the side of the car, watching us with an air of unmistakeable authority mixed with a little boredom, was a Spanish policeman.

"Buenos dias." And he nodded at us. "Buenos dias." We managed to reply. A silence followed as the officer watched us intently and I looked at Dante.

"You speak to him." I insisted and added "Please?"

"I donta speaka de Spanish, an' I not sittin' likea you are!"

"No, this is true. If it were you doing the 'sitting' I doubt they would have stopped at all." I muttered, noticing the officer's partner in the car speaking into the car radio. I looked back at Dante.

"Please Dante. Italian is much closer to Spanish than English is."

"Spanish, Italian, or English. I cana make them all." Said the officer proudly, and in spite of his accent, in well enunciated English.

"License." He held out his hand. I slid back into my seat, and Dante found his license. He passed it to the law enforcer with a smile. The smile was not returned. The license was scrutinised, he almost held it up to the light. Then he said.

"And where jou going?"

"Into Granada. We area goin' to de Alhambra." Replied Dante, replacing his license in his pocket. The officer nodded. "Of course jou are!" And he turned and rattled some Spanish off to his partner in the squad car. He then, repeated most of it into the radio, then hung up. I didn't know if that was a good sign or not.

"You knowa why we stop jou?" He looked straight at me.

"I…Well…You see…We…" I stuttered.

"Jou not stopa here. For any reasons. Comprendos?"

We both nodded our heads enthusiastically, and he slapped the side of the car, as if it were a horse. "Buena…Go!"

Dante started the engine, and we pulled back on to the highway as quickly as possible. Neither of us spoke for a while, then without preamble Dante said suddenly in a perfect mimicry of the policeman.

"Spanish, Italian English. I cana make them all!"

Well, it obviously wasn't that funny, but no doubt due to nervous reaction we found ourselves speeding towards Granada, helpless with laughter.

Later, when we were having lunch near the Palace, we were talking about our brush with the law, and I was about to say how much I love the Spanish accent. I thought better of it.

Follow The Path

Journal

After Granada there wasn't too much time left before we packed up our things and made our way to our hotel in Marbella. To tell the truth if at the moment, I had been given a choice of leaving for a Five star hotel, or staying where we were, I would have voted for the Villa. But Giuseppe was all set to move in with his harem. One could scarcely disappoint him, besides which it is his Villa, or at least his Father's

So, having made promises to meet with him for dinner one night somewhere along the coast, we thanked him profusely, threw our bags into the car, and set off for luxury.

I've never actually stayed in a 5star hotel before. Dante winked at me when we registered. I was a little non-plussed when the under manager shook hands with both of us, while beaming a smile which seemed a little beyond the normal call of duty. I only fully realised just what Dante had arranged when, in the midst of this man's speech in Spanish to me he dropped in Signora Della Vittoria, and whisked a trolley with two glasses, ice and a large bottle of champagne in the charge of a young Spanish waiter behind us into the lift.

"Dante, you didn't?" I whispered.

"Si, I dida cara. Ssh…" And his eyes indicated the Spanish waiter.

I amend the above statement. I've never been in a Bridal Suite in a 5star hotel, or any other come to that! As the waiter closed the door behind him I turned to Dante and said.

"Dante! What if someone finds out? " Dante laughed and set about opening the bottle.

"An'a who is goin' to doa dat? It not matter…Forget it, an'a come here cara."

Well, the thing is you see, if you are going to go to all the trouble and expense of booking the Bridal Suite, you may as well use it as it was meant to be used, and not leave it at all for the first 48 hours. Not until, in fact, a very apologetic chamber maid begs you to leave just long enough for her to change the linen.

Tonight…That's er…God I've got to work it out, just a minute, yes Sunday evening, we're due to meet Giuseppe for dinner. Although money doesn't seem to be a factor I can't help wondering how many of his 'harem' Giuseppe will bring to the restaurant. As it's Dante's treat, it could cost him a packet. I don't really like to comment on it to Dante, since it might appear as if being in the Bridal Suite has gone to my head! This afternoon Dante took me out and bought me the dress I'm now wearing. I took a discreet look at the price tag. And nearly fainted.

"Dante you can't spend all this. I won't let you, it's ridiculous!"

"Cara, please to remember youa are supposed to bea my

wife." As we both smiled at the elegant shop keeper. "So…" He continued through his smile. "Do asa you area told. Like a good Italian wife she always does!"

"Oh yea. I bet!" I laughed. In the end I couldn't resist. It's a pale leaf-green chiffon with a very low back, and it's just gorgeous.

"You use fora concerts later cara." Dante assured me as I was still 'yes butting…'

"Yes, I could but I'll have to make sure that I'm singing well enough to live up to it."

"No problemo Matilda!" And he took that as a yes and turned to the manager hovering in the background, delighting her by making it obvious that we would be taking one of her most expensive items off her hands.

We were to meet Giuseppe in the restaurant of a very plush Casino, hence the evening dress. As we walked into the reception area, I couldn't help thinking to myself that surely Giuseppe wouldn't turn up here with all of his harem on his arm. Oh dear! I'm really not used to this sort of sophisticated society, I must be careful not to appear like a complete suburban buffoon. We had reached the entrance to the restaurant and Dante went up to the desk to ask for our table. I had moved slightly away to take in the glamorous scene before me. There was not one guest who was not dressed to the nines. It was like peering into a slice of time from the past, a time when people liked to show off their riches and publicise their affluence. I was wondering what life would be like as the Contessa? Suddenly thinking, in an unusual swirl of negative thought, that maybe I wasn't meant to be a singer… when Dante catapulted me out of my reverie by touching my arm, and saying softly. "Matilda…Something' 'appen to Giuseppe. So sorry but we go!"

"Of course Dante." I replied, looking at his ashen face and aware of his trembling hand as he took mine and we made for the main door. Once outside Dante hailed a cab, He was obviously too distraught to drive.

"We geta de car later. Is better!" He said as we were speeding back to Mijas and the Villa. "What's happened Dante?"

"I not knowa…er… Giuseppe, no one of the girls, she ring an' tell them he cannot make.. I don't know what 'append…"

He was very upset. I remained quiet, he obviously didn't want to talk and knew very little anyway. I squeezed his arm and leant back against the seat. We were already approaching Malaga. It wouldn't be too much longer before we discovered the problem.

Twenty minutes later or so, we pulled up into the familiar drive, quickly got out of the cab and made towards the Villa. Dante rang the door bell and we could hear sharp footsteps on the tiled, Spanish floor. The door opened, and a rather distraught youngish woman stood there. She spoke only a tiny amount of English, and no Italian at all. From the large back room we heard another female voice raised in question, in which I could make out Dante's name. A few moments later we were standing by Giuseppe who was lying on the large settee surrounded by four ladies of varying age and appearance.

Dante knelt close to him and spoke softly in Italian. The arrival of his friend seemed to do a lot to raise his spirits, and Giuseppe was calmed by our, or at least Dante's presence. After a few moments Dante motioned with his head towards the open window, took my arm and led me out on to the balcony.

"Whatever has happened?" I asked him. "He's a terrible colour."

"E geta de bada fish."

"You mean, he has food poisoning?"

"Si, but isa a bada one cara. Dey wanta 'im in de 'ospital. Buta 'e won'ta go. De girls dey try to make 'im, but…Now dey willa wanta me, I toa make 'im go. 'E coulda die, but 'e 'ate so much de medical tings, capisco? Anda 'ospital she isa de worst of all!"

"Has the doctor been here?" I asked him and Dante nodded. Apparently the doctor had told the girls to ring for an ambulance the moment Giuseppe became unconscious, which, according to him, would most certainly be any moment now.

"What if den isa too late? But 'ow I force a sicka man? I nota know what to do." He sounded desperate and for love of him as much as compassion for Giuseppe, I said.

"Let me speak to him." Dante looked a little surprised, and so was I. I mean what did I think that I could say to make a difference? I moved back into the room and went up to Giuseppe. I laid my hand on his arm and was about to speak quite firmly to him, when I realised he couldn't hear me, he was already unconscious.

"Call an ambulance." I spoke to the girl friend who had let us in. Dante had followed me back into the room. "Che?" He said.

"He's unconscious Dante. An ambulance, quickly." Someone was already calling. Giuseppe was a terrible yellowy-grey and his breathing was rapid and shallow, his pulse which I managed to find was flickering at an extraordinary rate. Dante stood staring down at him, he was paler than ever.

"I know 'im for years Matilda. Dis is terribile."

"He'll be alright." I said. Suddenly for no accountable reason, I was convinced that he would be.

"You nota know dat."

"Yes, I do Dante. You'll see he will be alright!" I felt strange as if my feet were not touching the floor, and yet at the same time they seemed to extend down into the earth. While my throat and chest were on fire. I supposed it was the shock.

"Don't worry Dante, the ambulance is on its way. The hospital isn't far, he's going to be alright!"

I had no idea where the hospital was. The girls were no use at all, and in order to make him a little more comfortable, unconscious or not, I picked up the damp cloth on the edge of the arm of the settee, and gently wiped his face, neck, and upper chest with it. The girls were hysterical, and Dante was distraught, there was no one else but me to take any sort of control. I was relieved to hear the ambulance arrive and Dante and I followed it in Giuseppe's car which was driven by Rosario, the girl friend who had answered the door to us when we had first arrived.

The hospital was quite quiet and Giuseppe disappeared into an examination room, there was nothing to do but wait. Dante got us some coffee.

"Per'apsa we eat later." He muttered as he handed me my cup. I didn't really care if I ever ate again at that moment. I wasn't hungry, and I knew that Dante wasn't. Of course we were still dressed to kill, but we couldn't do anything about that.

An hour passed. Dante sat leaning forward with his arms resting on his legs, and his head bowed, staring at the floor. I got up and went to stand next to Lola and Carmen who were standing by the window looking out into the night. Lola was crying and I had no Spanish to comfort her. Carmen put her arm around her shoulders and was clearly having trouble not to end up in tears herself. Mercedes and Rosario were curled up in chairs looking very miserable.

"So!" Said a sudden voice in the bleak scene. "Disa is 'ow you mourn youra friend Eh?"

In the silence which followed, Dante looked up from the floor, and the girls slowly disentangled themselves from their various attitudes of despair, and Giuseppe, as he opened his arms to them, caught my eyes across the space between us and held my gaze for a few seconds, with a strange expression on his face. As soon as the girls would allow, Giuseppe embraced Dante, who was sobbing with relief.

"Grazie a Dio, Grazie Signor. Non e posso…."

And the two began in such fast Italian that I couldn't keep up with them. But delighted as I was, I found myself questioning, how was this possible? Giuseppe had been afflicted by a particularly virulent form of poisoning, his doctor had recognised the symptoms immediately. People often die from it, or were left incapacitated in some way. At the very least, it took weeks to recover, And yet here was our friend, restored to us within one hour of being admitted to hospital, standing on his two feet, and only missing some of his olive colour, and that seemed to be returning by the minute.

"Matilda, Ia need to speaka to you. We all go for a drink, and you amici, you musta eat. I woulda like…But per'apsa I resta de stomach. I eata tomorrow!" And he sent the others ahead taking my hands in his own he asked me.

"Whata 'appen Matilda, what you do?"

"Well everyone was so distraught, not that I wasn't you understand…but well, someone had to take control…"

"No, isa not what I mean. In der ambulance whata you do?"

"But we didn't go in the ambulance Giuseppe. They insisted we all came behind, Nobody was allowed to ride with you, Rosario drove your car, and we all managed to squeeze in somehow,"

He let go of my hands and turned slightly away from me, glanced at the others and then he slowly shook his head and sighed. He put his arm around my shoulders and we followed the others.

"What is it?" I asked him. He smiled at me, and I noted his colour had improved already.

"I woulda swear thata I open my eyes, short time in de ambulance, anda I seea you, you sittin' dere wida me, an' youra face is a very calma but, er… determined. But you nota der you say?"

"No, I really wasn't Giuseppe. But you know you were very sick, a terrible colour, breathing fast, and how you've recovered so quickly is a miracle."

"Si. Isa what de doctore 'e say. Signor, is a miracle!"

"Well there you are then, you must have dreamt it."

"Si. I dream it. So now we drinka to miracles."

We had caught up with the others and walked out into the balmy Spanish night, very much happier than when we came in.

The days roll in and out in a long beautiful blur. In spite of sun block and suntan lotion, all of which Dante teases me mercilessly about, I have turned a dark beige colour. Actually I rather like it. I can't imagine it will last very long once I get home though. Giuseppe has recovered completely, and is enjoying his harem. We have spent quite a lot of time with them all. Although often Giuseppe meets us on his own, and occasionally he and Dante have spent a few hours off together somewhere. After one such time, Dante returned looking thoughtful and that night, before we fell asleep, he looked down at me curled so comfortably in his arms and said.

"Cara, reminda me. Werea you in de ambulance wida Giuseppe?" I shook myself awake, I was very sleepy.

"No of course not Dante. Don't you remember? We were all in the car, Rosario drove us!"

"Si. Buta per'apsa I forget. Giuseppe isa so certain tat you were wid 'im."

"Dante, he was unconscious. He must have been dreaming. Anyway what could I have done? We all need to forget it now. It's no good to keep replaying something like that, is it?"

"No. You are right cara. We saya no more!"

And to my relief he closed his eyes and soon we were both asleep.

We are in our last week. We all went off to the Flamenco again tonight, having eaten a fabulous meal in some small restaurant, which, if you didn't know any better you would pass by without noticing. I had intended that, during these three weeks, I would put in a little work on the 'Aida' and I brought it along with me. But never have I found it so hard to open a score. In fact, I admit that it lays untouched since the day it was packed with such good intentions, in the zipped pocket in the side of my case.

And have I seen my secret and personal friends? I have had glimpses. I look up from my book while sitting on the beach, and there they are. An almost indistinguishable group in the distance, cavorting on the sand, in a veritable praise of life. They seem to be able to enjoy themselves so much more than we do. They have less inhibitions, and a deep camaraderie. You still see that today of course, but everyone appears to have to work so hard at it! Whereas they were masters at it without even knowing they were doing it.

The old man has also taken a holiday I believe. I have neither seen, nor sensed him. It's as if they are all respecting my 'honeymoon' with Dante and are leaving me alone. The only tenuous link to that part of my life was the experience with the necklace, and Giuseppe's illness. I did have a bit of a shock yesterday however, when, in answer to my question, Dante replied.

"De girls are nota sure of you, cara."

"Not sure? Whatever do you mean?" I said. Dante looked at me for a moment and then quickly away as if a little embarrassed.

"Dey frightened." He said finally. First I laughed, then exclaimed. "Of ME? You're joking. What? I've turned into some dragon lady?" I asked him, incredulous that anyone would be frightened of me.

"No cara but…" Dante began. Then he took me gently by the shoulders, and smiling continued. "Dey knowa dat Giuseppe…well you knowa too.. 'e should avea died. Si?" "Should have? What is this? Why can't you all just be pleased that he didn't die. Should have! It makes it sound like a mistake."

And if I sounded impatient it was because I was.

"Myself, I donta know whata I tink. O.K? But dey are, I suppose...er... Si, superstition!" I felt a chill and forgot to correct Dante's grammar. (This isn't me being boring, we have agreed it's a good way to help each other with the languages. By the way Dante is streets ahead of me!)

But then I began to laugh. "I wish I could put such a fear into Warrener!" I giggled, and we spoke no more on the subject.

Well, tomorrow we leave. In spite of having had a wonderful time, it's strange how after a while one does feel the need to return to work, routine, and challenge. I am looking forward to going home

"We will come again cara." Whispered Dante, as we lay on crumpled sheets in a close embrace, until the heat finally pulled us apart for the rest of the night.

"Yes, but will they let me back into the country?" I teased him.

"Only if you donta bring youra broomstick, and nota stop de traffic ona de motorway." Then we slept, and as if heralding the return to my normal life, I dreamt of the old man. But I couldn't hold my consciousness in the dream state very easily.

I was in a beautiful place and was being taken along a grassy track, next to a lake, which led to a castle. The lady who was leading me there, informed me that I had to attend for lessons. When I entered the huge front door, I found myself in a big airy room with sunlight pouring in through the windows. The old man was there looking very serious, and holding, to my surprise, the emerald necklace. (This part of the dream was so vivid that when I awoke, just before dawn, I had to check on the necklace, before I could relax and doze once more.)

What followed, was not an easy conversation with my old friend, I'm afraid. I seem to have missed huge chunks of what he was saying. Anyway I remember some of what he told me. I will keep it in my mind, although it makes little sense as it stands.

"Follow the path…Gate…You are unknown…Keep your faith Matilda…Allow it to guide you…Do not fight it…Have you heard me? Follow the path!"

What path is he referring to? I'm more than happy to comply with his directions, but how can I when I have no idea what he's talking about. It's very odd don't you think? The only thing I can be sure of from the experience, is that when I awoke, I had a feeling of such strength running through me, that I had to sit down on the edge of the bed and 'digest' it.

The Stage Manager

Before Dante went home to Italy, he promised Matilda that he would be with her for the opening.

"Youa tella youra boss…No Dante…No stage Manager… O.K?"

"O.K .Dante. I'll ask him if you can stay with me at Villa Giorgio."

"No cara. Youa not aska 'im. Youa tella 'im. Youa donta 'ave to do dis youa know? I can support you…"

Matilda interrupted him. "We've been there more than once Dante. I must work, especially when it falls into my lap as this did."

"You're mad!" Said Pixie, when they had met down in Surrey the evening before the first rehearsal. "Why don't you let him? I don't know if you realise just how terrible it can be out there. So many people out of work. And I'm talking really talented people here. Theatres closing down left right and centre because their grants have been cut. So even if companies want you they can't use you! I mean how will you manage without some help?

Where are you going to live, or have you forgotten your flat's up for sale? What are you going to do?"

"I haven't a clue Pixie. But I promise you I'll take Dante up on his offer if it looks as if I'm in danger of becoming a 'bag lady.'

"Oh yes!" Grinned Pixie. "I can just see you at King's Cross Station."

"Oh no, Victoria." Returned Matilda. "What?" Said Pixie. Matilda looked at her with a wickedly serious expression on her face and replied.

"Altogether a better class of 'bag lady,' so I've heard!"

"Matilda Gasgoine, shut up. Don't even joke about it!"

As they settled down for dinner in the restaurant, Martin arrived. Matilda wondered just what sort of mood he would be in. He was alone, no Connie.

"Wait for me girls. I'll be down in five minutes."

"Do you think he'll be calling us 'girls' when we're 85?" Whispered Pixie as Martin hurried out of the room.

"When we're 85, we'll be delighted if he does!" Grinned Matilda scanning the menu. Actually, Martin was in a rather good mood. He made no embittered reference to being a 'cover' as they had both rather expected. In fact he was quite charming.

"Has our pianist arrived?" He asked Matilda. "I haven't seen him." She replied.

"Well, if he's not here by tomorrow, you'll have to get your lily-whites round the music Tilly!"

"You're joking of course!" Matilda laughed. "Actually I've

just remembered. Didn't Giorgio say something about him driving down with the soprano early tomorrow." She added.

"Search me. You're the Maestra extraordinaire, pulling everything together. We're just singing the thing."

"Don't rub it in Martin." Pixie growled at him. He looked innocent and then truly embarrassed as he apologised to Matilda. But she was still glowing from constant contact with Dante and the warm Spanish sun, and found it easy to let it go over her head.

"It's O.K." She assured him, and they continued eating, and drinking the very presentable wine which Giorgio had put by for them.

Their absent host and employer was, at that moment, fighting his own demons. Verity, who of course had never witnessed anything like it before, was for once, unsure of herself and of what to do.

"Can I get you a doctor Giorgio?"

"Don't you dare. You'll find my hands around that little throat of yours if you do any such stupid thing." He had snapped at her, doing his best to control his anguish. "Just get me my tablets."

"Tablets?" Verity looked around helplessly. Giorgio gestured impatiently to a small toilet bag, which lay on the bed of the expensive suite in the fantastic hotel where they were staying for a few nights on their way back from the south of France. She found them and handed the plastic bottle to him.

"Now get out and leave me alone. I'll be alright in a couple of hours." Verity still stood there, not moving, still uncertain.

"Go Verity. I'm sure you have some little friend in this city, who will welcome you with open arms. Leave me alone." And he turned away from her. Verity scowled at him.

"You are a pig Giorgio. Sometimes I hate you. Without doubt you're the most selfish man alive! But you're quite right, I have plenty of friends in this city, so I'll just go and find some of them, shall I?"

Giorgio didn't answer. Giorgio couldn't answer. For the first time in a very long time, Giorgio was in tears. Red hot, they coursed down his face, that face that he had turned away from Verity. The door slammed. He was alone, and soon, unconscious. His dream was the same as every dream he had had since his last meeting with Chu-Pen.

He was walking through long, wide golden corridors haunted by the ever-present desire for the knowledge. He remembered how strong it was, how close it had seemed, as if he could easily reach out and take hold of it, but also he remembered how it always eluded him. And then there was Lothus standing in the Great Hall and singing to Anthorus. His golden sound spiralling upward and outwards and containing a pearly shimmer which Giorgio could plainly hear in his sleep. He watched as Lothus was dragged to the work place. And all along the way there, his route was lined with silent, familiar figures. Osiria, Caperus, Laria and the Sacred Singers. He could sense that they were desperate for the torture to be stopped, but they were, or so it seemed, powerless to help the shepherd boy, who fought like a mountain lion. In his dream, Giorgio remembered everything clearly and each time he awoke he retained more of the memory. Atlantis was becoming as real as Venice.

Toward the end of this particular dream, when he had passed all the familiar people and the golden corridor had begun to dim, Chu-Pen spoke to him.

"Murder is justifiable in some cases." His teacher assured him. "Let us not even call it by that vulgar name, since this would not be a vulgar act, but one of compassion. Already it leaks like a stinking sewer into the population. But these small happenings are nothing to what will occur when the frequency is totally released. Then you will see its most virulent form. So, stop her Giorgio, Thanius, Raimondo…Whoever you see yourself as. Stop her!"

As he rose to consciousness, Giorgio saw his lives stretching around him like aborted flowers still waiting to blossom. Always he searched and desired, and always he was denied. At last in the early morning, he dragged himself awake to find that he was flung across the large King size bed, fully clothed and that there was no sign of Verity. After he had showered and dressed, he ordered breakfast. Now fully recovered, and in charge of his phenomenal energy once more, he found that he couldn't wait to get back to England, already he had begun to plan.

The old man also tried to access Giorgio's mind, believing it to be potentially fantastic with its energy and concentrated will. He dearly wanted to help him, to hold out his hand and guide him across the abyss. To pull him to another awareness where his power and ability would be able to blossom positively, where he could add to the potential knowledge which was hopefully going to be released, while still enjoying himself. The old man had no desire to turn his crusade into some repressive religious order.

However, Chu-Pen had Giorgio so firmly in his grasp, that

he did not even hear the slightest of whispers. The old man shrugged and turned his attention to Irena.

Her dreams were painfully predictable until just before Matilda returned home from Spain. The old man at last managed to tip the balance in that lady's mind and Atlantis rolled out in front of her like a carpet, which she trod in her dreams, and brought back, not in her case a visual memory, but feelings. Feelings of great power, of a strong desire to fight for something important. Of a wrong which must be righted, and over all of this, was the need to watch, and if necessary, to protect Matilda.

Giorgio was present at the afternoon rehearsal on the day he arrived back from Europe. He was alone.

"Where's Verity, Giorgio?" Martin asked him. "Haven't lost her, have you?"

"More like mislaid her my boy. Lover's tiff, you know?" He joked.

As far as he knew, Verity was still in Switzerland, most likely 'mislaying' herself all over the place! But he had no doubt that she would soon be back. It wasn't very likely that she would miss the final build up to the opening, and certainly not the opening itself. She had put far too much work into it. And he knew that she was, in fact, quite excited about the whole project.

But for now he needed to concentrate on the show, and Matilda. He would never defy Chu-Pen outright, or argue with him to his 'face' as it were. But he wasn't at all sure about making his destruction of Matilda quite so total. It would take the fun out of it for a start. He wanted her to suffer, not escape into some after realm where she could simply re-group, and plan all over again. He understood the complexities of time, and it wasn't outside the realms of possibility that they could all find themselves right back here repeating all this. Not likely, but not impossible. And anyway, he wanted to see the anguish in her eyes when she would be overcome with defeat and exhaustion. To pretend that he was taken in by the brave face she would undoubtedly wear. Although all of this, was of course, based on 'Venice' he reminded himself with a shake of his head. He must endeavour to pull back the other, it was linked, so it seemed, to the place with the golden corridors. To Osiria and the others. And it was imperative that he stop something from happening. As to what that was exactly, he was finding it hard to be clear about. A plague? But a plague of what? Murder he could, and would, contemplate. He had after all committed it before. But he would need to be much clearer in his mind as to exactly why he must take such a drastic path, before contemplating it again...

His thoughts were interrupted by someone humming. Matilda came into the big studio where they were shortly meeting for the first full soloist musical rehearsal.

Journal

Giorgio came back alone form Europe today. Goodness knows where Verity is!

"Where's Queen Cobra?" Pixie whispered over lunch after we had welcomed Giorgio.

"Pixie! He'll hear you." I warned as she looked at me incredulously. "Haven't you ever noticed what fantastic hearing Giorgio has?"

She had shaken her head, but her mouth fell open and her

bare arms crowded with goose bumps when Giorgio, turned slowly from the buffet some 14 feet away, where he was helping himself to lunch, and with a smile on his face, had shaken a finger at her, and tutted in mock anger.

"Told you." I muttered. Pixie was amazed. "Bloody hell! I must be wired for sound." She exclaimed, speaking even lower.

Later, when I went to check that everything had been set up for the music rehearsal, Giorgio was already there. He was staring in to space and slowly shaking his head.

"Is something wrong Giorgio?" I asked him. "No cara. Just off in my own world." He assured me and said no more about it. But he was very pleasant to me, insisting that I leave immediately and go for my lesson with Irena, which I had arranged for that afternoon, knowing I wouldn't be required for the music call.

"Tomorrow is when we shall need you, as you know we're in the amphi' all day." He said and dismissed me with a kindly wave of his hand, adding as I reached the door, that I was a truly wonderful colour and that Spain must agree with me.

As to my lesson. O.K. Now I know that I had, for the most part, a wonderful and relaxing holiday. But I am amazed at the affect it has had on my voice and singing. It feels as if the sound is cushioned on velvet, and I am beginning to be able to access these strange extra 'feelings' and sounds, almost at will.

"What is that Irena?" I asked her, as a note in the upper passaggio took on something else during the course of my sustaining it.

"Are you aware of that?" She asked me.

"I'm aware of something. But I don't know what it sounds like out there."

Irena looked at me long and gently. She seemed to be searching for the right words. Of course, as is easy for singers to do, I panicked and imagined all sorts of terrible possibilities in the space of a nano second. But Irena laughed.

"Whatever this phenomena is, and wherever it is going, it is certainly nothing to worry about. I can't explain it in terms of technique, but I can tell you that there is nothing wrong darling. I am however, a little uncertain of how to deal with it. What do you feel about it?"

I had so much on my mind, that I turned to the easiest solution. I knew that I wouldn't be performing for weeks anyway, so I replied. "I think we should go with it. Let it find its own level."

Irena smiled her dazzling smile in agreement and I realised as we continued that she looks different. Positively bursting with health, on an impulse I said as much to her.

"Bless you Matilda. I know I do. But then, so do you!"

Final rehearsals began. Giorgio had decided to direct the stage himself. Actually, he was very good at it. He had no 'clever clever' ideas about pointing out the blindingly obvious to the audience. He treated the cast with a respect which presupposed they have intelligence. He left the historical placement of the story where it was written, and he didn't try to score any points by intellectualising it into the 21st. Century.

Overall, his natural inclination to allow the music to speak for itself, without the need for patronising explanation, won him much affection and respect from the Italian conductor who arrived with the tenor, one week after Giorgio returned.

Ricardo Biagioni breathed a quiet sigh of relief as Giorgio outlined his stage plan to him on the evening of his arrival. He had not known what to expect, and had only agreed to accept the contract, because Francesco Riffi was a close friend of his. The tenor had taken great pains to assure him that Giorgio, being half Italian would surely have a proper respect for Verdi.

Biagioni was not yet 'top rank' international conductor, but he was getting there, and he didn't want any professional 'hiccoughs' along the way. No one was that confident of continuing success. However, in spite of his fast-growing appreciation of the whole set up, something quite unexpected and out of the blue, did, in passing, confuse him.

After a morning rehearsal a few days after he had arrived, he chanced to hear Matilda practising. She was finding it more and more difficult to fit any sessions in as the big night drew closer. This was to be expected, and she had known that it would happen as she became busier, and rehearsals progressed. She wasn't worried, she simply grabbed what time she could. It just so happened that this particular 'bite' of time that she had grabbed, set her right in the path of the Maestro, as he hurried back down to lunch, having made a quick sojourn to his room. He had stopped to listen for a few moments. Scales, at first that was all it was really. Then some arpeggios, some notes held swelling from piano to forte and back again. A masterful, seamless join of the vocal registers, that impressed him more than anything else. Then, she spoilt it. Why? He wondered hurrying in the direction of the pasta, did she feel the need to use a microphone, or whatever it was she was using which caused the overtones to behave in strange ways. He had reached the corner, and stopped again.

At least, he supposed it was caused by some sort of electronics. To be honest it didn't really sound as if it were, the sound was too, well beautiful actually. But what else could it be? He carried on his way to lunch, and didn't think about it again, until Matilda rushed into the dinning room 20 minutes later, quickly helped herself from the buffet, and sat down with Pixie and Laura Steeple, who was singing Aida. He turned to Giorgio.

"Tell me my friend." He began in Italian. "How come your stage manager has such a fine voice? And what possess her to shut herself in one of your studios and experiment with some form of electronics? She hardly needs it, after all!"

"Electronics?" Repeated Giorgio. "I don't even possess a microphone. You know my thoughts on electronically enhanced music. It's fine in its place, but its not for opera!"

Biagioni was thoughtful and silent for a moment, then he looked at Giorgio, and, continuing in Italian, so as not to upset any delicate egos.

"She would make a beautiful Aida, even though she is far too young for the role. But as we are both well aware, so are they all!"

Her was waiting for a reply. It had not been intended as a piece of 'rhetoric.' Giorgio gathered his forces, and smiled at this man, who was fast becoming his friend.

"Do you not think that Laura sings well? I have worked very hard with her, and she has the maturity to tackle the role."

"Oh, I'm not challenging your teaching, or your choice, Giorgio. But I know you surely hear that she does not possess much beauty in that voice. She'll sing it, get through it, of that I have no doubt. But, surely you know what I mean? surely you can hear…?"

"Of course." Giorgio smiled again. "And you are right, Matilda possess a fine voice, and has some experience. I know you will doubt this in that fine Italian mind of yours, but believe me she can be very temperamental. I didn't want to risk undue upsets on our first project. She begged to be included, and I thought that working around real professionals, she would learn how to behave. And that she would understand that we don't all have a temperament every half-an-hour, and the experience might calm her down."

Giorgio lied as only he could. Smoothly, and with complete confidence. He believed it himself, emotionally and mentally. That, he had learned was the secret. He was rarely challenged. Biagioni glanced towards the table where the three young women were sitting. Laura and Pixie were having an animated discussion, and Matilda turned briefly in his direction. She smiled and nodded at him, and as he registered the power of the energy from her violet eyes, and the innocence of her smile, he was aware of a question in his mind. Giorgio had noted it and felt the question rising to the surface. He leant forward quickly, and added. "She's also a good actress!" They both laughed and the question, melted.

"What's going on over there?" Pixie said, as Matilda turned back to her and Laura. She shrugged. She had not been aware of Biagioni outside the studio door. There was too much happening the other side of that door, and it was making it very difficult for her to keep in check a huge frustration, and not to allow it to envelope her. The 'something' which was happening to her voice, was growing. She began to feel as if she were becoming secondary to the very act of opening her mouth. She was like a driver who, having turned on the engine of their car, became part of the car itself. Every day she was certain that she would find 'it' gone, and every day 'it' grew. As if at its own instigation, and completely of its own free will, it was springing into life and presenting the 'host' with something new, something fresh and not known of or heard before. It was like waking up one morning and discovering that you could fly. And the need to express all this in the normal way for a performer, was growing with it. Ambition was raising its head. She wanted it to be heard, and recognised for what it was. She didn't like Laura's sound, although the woman herself was nice enough. But she realised that no one else had fallen in love with it either, Pixie had made that very clear.

All this gave her much to digest. She would be glad when Dante arrived. Whoops! She hadn't mentioned that to Giorgio as yet.

The timeline raced. Chu-Pen stoked Giorgio's fire and the old man stoked Matilda's. This tiny corner of the universe, so huge and unfathomable to us, waited. If it had eyes, they would have been trained on the slowly awakening D.N.A. strands. If it had ears they would have been straining to hear the pearly shimmer as it grew and took its place. In some other people the potential was there. In Matilda, the unknown opera singer, it was already beginning to establish itself with consistency.

The final spark waited for only one thing. For the release of part of the frequency from the emerald amulet, where it had been imprisoned so long ago by the great Anthorus with as much passionate determination that he now used to prepare for its release.

And the key was in the music itself. In the great works over the ages, those which favoured using the human voice, it lay there, waiting. Every time these works were performed the digital mantra clicked into place. Once, twice and three times throughout these works of every major composer, and at every single performance, the moment passed unconsummated. Over the long years between Mozart and Verdi the mantra had intensified. How many times had the latter genius soaked up the formations from listening to the classical lines of the former? By the time Verdi was working on the score of 'Aida' his vast musical intelligence had retraced the hidden secrets at a level he could use. This was how the frequency was transported from age to age, and how it grew in intensity.

Beneath the notes that appear in the score of 'Aida' is a deep unconscious link with the past. The mathematical formations are the same as those that the ancient Atlantean had secured in order to build the pyramids, and for those that survived to teach them to the Ancient Egyptians. The 'western gate' was prepared. The old man only hoped that the frail and sensitive nervous system which the race seemed to suffer with, had strengthened sufficiently in Matilda to allow her to survive the final formation of the new electromagnetic grid. He had grown inordinately fond of her.

September 21st, 2012

By 8:00 p.m. the amphitheatre, decked in the red and white roses of Giorgio's pride, was filled with an expectant audience, glittering in the soft lights, and filling the seating area with the familiar low, buzzy hum, occasionally punctuated by more distinct laughing and conversation. Gradually the pit filled with the orchestra and they set about tuning their instruments as the clock ticked relentlessly onwards. Giorgio had decided against an opening speech. But he found it impossible to remain in the V.I.P. area where Verity now sat, dressed to kill and full of almost childlike excitement. The last few months had been extreme hard work, but she had enjoyed herself, and the end result was about to burst into life at any moment. It was a quite extraordinary feeling. This was both an end, and a beginning. She glanced at her watch and felt it impossible to relax while she was expecting Giorgio to slip into the seat beside her at any moment.

Riccardo Biagioni was a man of operatic drama through to his Italian soul, and the pure 'theatre' of the occasion did not elude him for a second. For a short span of time he stood with his head bent, one hand resting over the other which held his baton. It was a silent acknowledgement to the birth of what he also hoped would become a successful venture. He liked Giorgio, in so far as he knew the man. No, what he really liked was his commitment to the art, the rest quite simply didn't matter.

He straightened up and raised his arms. The orchestra was an excellent blend of fine musicians from all over Europe, and since his initial bow to the audience, they had not taken their attention from him. Biagioni commanded considerable respect wherever he went, and it had not taken the orchestra long, at their only rehearsal that morning, to know what he had in terms of technique, musicality and experience. Indeed some of them had worked with him before. They practically breathed with him, and played exquisitely from the first note, Giorgio closed his eyes, a slight smile on his lips, and sank into the prelude.

Pixie was sitting on a stray chair talking softly to Martin, he had declined a seat in the V.I.P. area. He felt he would be able to stand it all a little better if he were back stage, rather than out front with the 'hoi polloi,' as he referred to the guests. Mind you, he was musing, as he listened to Pixie, having noticed Giorgio was back-stage, and almost certain to remain there for the first half, that he had missed an opportunity of being alone with the very sexy Verity!

Francesco traced an invisible path over and over as if he were offering deep meditation to his particular god. He was totally unaware of everything, even, it seemed, the music And Matilda, had her head down and her eyes firmly concentrated on the score in front of her, going over and over the first few cues that she had to instigate as soon as the singing began, and people were making entrances.

The rising pianissimo string chords melted into the pause. The prelude was over and Radames and Ramphis the High Priest, entered the stage area up the ramp from the back as if they had just left the temple of Memphis.

The auditorium was packed. There were even a few brave souls behind the action dotted around the semi circle from which rose a small open topped brick structure, commonly known amongst the company as the chimney. Nobody seemed to know what it was for. No one that is except Giorgio. He had found it early on in his explorations of the grounds. It would prove a valuable asset at certain times, he knew. He wouldn't be able to use it in Aida though.

As Francesco settled into his aria, Giorgio could feel the audience relax. He could sense it as clearly as if they had exuded a communal sigh. He felt sure the singer would not let him down… He didn't. Although not yet mature enough to safely tackle the whole role in an 'International House.' He was more than prepared for this sort of introduction to the piece, and he spun the beautiful rising phrases with a lyricism and intelligence often lacking in approaches to this particular aria. Giorgio gently nodded his head in appreciation. The aria became what in his opinion it was meant to be, a love song. Most tenors seemed to have half their mind, and therefore half their sound already leading the army against the Ethiopians. The applause at the end was well deserved, and at that point Giorgio felt the singer also relax. Now he was in his stride for the rest of the piece.

"Giorgio!" Verity had made her way through the passageways beneath the amphitheatre and hissed at him as she approached the chair on which he sat. He waved his hand at her impatiently, not wanting to miss the commencement of the next scene.

"Giorgio, for Christ's sake!" Verity hissed again. He got up, and his face, even in the dim light, was dangerously set. He came up to her and pushed her further away from the entrance to the stage.

"What the hell is it?"

"We have a problem!" Replied Verity. This was a word which Giorgio did not wish to hear. "What?" He growled. "A problem." Verity reiterated, adding. "No soprano!"

"What are you talking about Verity? I've just seen her, She's over there, waiting for her entrance, which by the way I don't want to miss."

"No voice." Verity replied in a whisper. Giorgio turned his head and stared into the semi darkness. The singer was there ready for her cue, but she certainly seemed set on not looking in his direction. He felt himself go cold.

"She sang at rehearsal this afternoon." He continued.

"She marked at rehearsal this afternoon!" Verity corrected him with maddening accuracy. Giorgio tutted impatiently. "So did everyone else. It's called saving the voice. Only an idiot, or a singer performing a very small part sings out full just before a performance."

"The performance wasn't the reason. Didn't you notice something in the sound?" Verity replied.

Giorgio had, as it happened. Not a lot escaped him, but Laura had assured him it was just a touch of hay fever, and that she had it under control. After that he had been so busy with different things and last minute problems, that the whole thing had gone out of his mind. The soprano he had chosen did not possess a voice of great beauty, in fact it was not a memorable sound in that way at all. But she clearly had the strength and focus to deal with Verdi. The slightly edgy sound, at least allowing her to cut through the orchestra with ease.

"What's her problem?" He asked, quietly cursing the vulnerability of singers.

"Tracheitis." Said Verity. Giorgio's heart sank. Singers, once they have attained at least some technique, can often make their way through performances with all sorts of problems. Alas, 'Tracheitis' is not one of them. For the first time he felt beaten. What the hell was he going to do?

"She said she'll do her best." Verity continued. "Maybe she can sing through it Giorgio. Sounds to me as it she can sing through anything." She added. Verity had already expressed her opinion on the soprano's sound. It wasn't her favourite voice. Giorgio gave her a warning look which she couldn't miss, even in the dimness of their surroundings. Then he pushed her further from the staged area and gave vent to his frustration. The air turned a violent blue. Giorgio was beside himself. Then quite suddenly he calmed a little. With a clenched fist he gently punched the wall and turned back to Verity and said.

"She might be alright once she gets going. But where's Tony London? He has arrived I hope?" Verity nodded. "He's in the V.I.P. area with La Bella, Bella." she said, not able to resist the temptation to be rude about Bella.

"Verity!" Snarled Giorgio and he looked at her from under his eyes. "Stop being a bloody prima Donna, and get him!"

"Get him? How am I supposed to do that?"

"I have no idea sweet little witch, just do it. Get him back here, and fast."

As the last pages of 'Celeste Aida' were entrancing the audience, Pixie stood up and smoothed down the front of her costume. Matilda breathed a gentle deep breath, and held both thumbs up towards her. Pixie smiled across the space between them, and fervently wished that Matilda were singing. She found it hard to blend with Laura. After Matilda's mellifluous tones, she felt as if she were singing against a 'corn-grinder' as she had put it to Matilda, who had not commented.

"What are you thinking now Tilly?" As Matilda still did not reply.

"Oh, nothing." She said quietly. Pixie had looked at her intently. "Come on Till."

"Nothing, honestly. I'm just trying very hard not to be pleased about what you've just said." She finally admitted. Pixie had screamed with laughter.

"You're too much Matilda Gasgoine, you really are. But at least you agree with me!"

Now, she moved towards the ramp, ready to join the tenor, and Martin plonked himself down in the now-vacant chair, wondering why Tony London had suddenly appeared backstage and not sure if he wanted to be seen by him. He sat back out of any light which might have drawn Tony's field of vision to him.

It had taken Verity only a few moments to attract Tony's

attention, and he waited for an appropriate moment to leave his seat. By this time the singers had begun the trio, at least the tenor and the mezzo had, Aida still had to make her entrance. The suppressed tension between Amneris and Radames was establishing itself well, and Pixie was rising to the challenge of singing with an international soloist. In site of her own, almost painful feeling of emptiness at not being up there with the others, Matilda had everything crossed for her friend.

"Go it girl!" She muttered to herself as she prepared to cue the lighting for the soprano's entrance. Hence she was busy, and did not notice Tony London in deep discussion with Giorgio.

"It's not possible Giorgio. I couldn't get anyone down here in time even if I had the right voice available."

"Fuck the 'right' voice. I'm not in a position to be fussy, Tony."

Tony meantime, had suddenly caught sight of Matilda. He held her in his sight for a few moments, then turned back to Giorgio, his face full of question, and some disbelief.

"Don't even go there!" Hissed Giorgio. And Tony, although taken aback, kept quiet. Aida entered to the haunting phrase which is the very first phrase of the prelude, and to some extent follows her throughout the opera. Tony placed his hand on Giorgio's shoulder. "Calma Giorgio. Let's see what she's like." And the two men waited.

The audience had been lulled into that particularly pleasant place which states that everyone has everything under control, and they (the audience) can sit back and enjoy. So, when on her opening phrase the soprano fell very short of their expectations, they at first attributed it to nerves. The soprano, however certainly didn't look nervous, more furious at not being able to achieve what she had been working so hard to do. But it would take another singer to recognise the difference. In spite of her formidable concentration concerning her own performance, Pixie was instantly aware that Laura was in difficulty. Some notes were free, and when the music flowed over the phrase it was not too bad, but when the composer insisted on a sustained tone, especially if anything less than a big 'belty' sound was needed, it became increasingly difficult. The trio ended on a climactic and long held high 'B' for the soprano. That at least was alright. She had plenty of strength, and had managed as it were to 'skid' to the end of the scene in a relatively respectable fashion. The music continued straight into the next scene, and the three took their new places. The audience were still of the opinion that Laura was nervous, Giorgio however, knew better.

"She'll never make it. The sound is in shreds already. You can't bluff your way through music like this with brute force."

Tony was at a loss as to what to suggest. "Giorgio…" He began.

"I told you not to go there." Giorgio's voice was cold as ice, but he glanced involuntarily across at Matilda, who was en-grossed in some manoeuvre or other. Giorgio heard her speak into the intercom telling the lighting crew to stand by and giving the male chorus their final call.

'Had she noticed?' He wondered, then his thoughts scampered off in exasperation. 'If only another of Irena's pupils was there. If only…Of course!' He turned quickly to Tony. "Bella!" He said. The music was rising in volume, and many more bodies graced the stage.

"Bella?" Repeated Tony. "You're mad Giorgio, she hasn't sung for years!"

Giorgio didn't buy that. He had never known anyone who, having been forced to give up the idea of a professional career, didn't keep singing in private, even one might say, 'in secret..' Bella had never completely given up on the possibility of a miracle. That he deduced from her when, in spite of her mistrust of him, he had managed to engage her in conversation at the restaurant after Matilda and Irena had left. He had even offered to help her. Of course she had never contacted him. Bella was one of the few women who saw straight through Giorgio, without understanding why he had the effect on them that he did.

"Get her Tony!"

"But…"

"Just bloody get her!"

"O.K. Giorgio, it's your funeral." Tony replied and disappeared into the darkness as Giorgio whispered to himself. "Not yet it's not!"

A few moments later, Bella, looking as if she were being dragged to torture and execution, hurried into the corridor with Tony at her heels. He had outlined the situation. "Giorgio, I'm so sorry but it's just not possible. Aida's not a role I would ever have sung anyway. The most I could have expected with my weight voice, was light Mozart. Anyway, I don't know it. It's out of the question…" She trailed off noticing Matilda. She turned to Tony and began. "But…" Tony shook his head furiously and the question died in her throat.

"Listen to her!" Giorgio almost shouted. "The bloody voice is going by the bar, Well listen!.."

He was becoming out if control and Tony's head was beginning to ache. He knew how much this opening meant to Giorgio, how much work had gone into it, and he was amazed that he refused to ignore the obvious answer. Matilda had glanced their way more than once. Finally becoming aware that all was not well, and assuming that it was to do with the ailing soprano, whose problem obviously had not escaped her. Quite suddenly she raised her hand, even in the darkness they were all aware that it was someone behind them who had attracted her attention. They turned around. There, in a beautiful evening dress, and appearing at least twenty years younger than she was, stood Irena. Her still dark hair was swept higher than usual, and the simplicity of the green silk dress made Giorgio hesitate, and acknowledge a powerful concoction of emotions. She came straight up to him, and said.

"Is there a problem Giorgio?"

At first he thought she had caused to rise in him, memories of Europe all those years ago, but he knew immediately that she had not. And from time to time, when they were still singing together, and since her re-emergence in his life he had sometimes wondered if she had been Angelo in Venice, but having met Dante, he knew that he was wrong there also. Giorgio was quite suddenly, afraid. The strength of this woman, the energy which swirled from her, was, he realised, huge, positive, and riding on the steed of 'truth' at full gallop and straight towards him. Her eyes missed nothing. She had raised her hand to Matilda and had illuminated the darkness with that damn smile! Giorgio squirmed, then swallowing hard, said.

"My dear Irena. You can see how I'm placed. If Matilda

leaves her post, I am lost in another way. Bella has refused my offer…"

"Very sensible!" Irena put in…

"And so, your timely entrance…Will you…Please, to save my opening Irena. I worked so hard with my singing and I failed. I have worked towards this night for a very long time. I don't want to see that fail also."

Giorgio appeared to be begging. But Irena knew that he was not. He was, as always, using the situation to achieve what he wanted. She didn't answer immediately, then she said softly.

"Let me get this right Giorgio. After all we have been through together. After all we know about each other, you are asking me to sing Aida for this unfortunate lady, who will soon be on her vocal knees by the sound of things. And what will you do if I refuse you as well?"

This was a direct challenge, and Giorgio looked straight into the gentle eyes as he replied. "Why then, I shall be forced to stop the show Irena. There's still the champagne supper, as you know. I shall have to explain the situation and hope that everyone will understand."

He was gambling an awful lot on Irena's sense of professionalism, the old 'the show must go on' adage, and her integrity. But he knew that he had her in his sights, he knew she was incapable of ducking what she would see as her artistic 'duty.' And he smiled to himself as she took a deep breath and said.

"Well it's a good job that I still start my day with a vocal work out. Now, how are we going to do this?"

Timeless Night

So night falls over everything, but through its timeless magic it presented various pictures of parts of itself at other conjunctions in the time-space continuum. Great waves of facts spiked through with their emotional content were presented to a dreamer. It depended on the state of their imagination how they interpreted and acted on it, if at all. And so embracing the old man's abilities even if we can't begin to understand them, we can say that at this point in space, Venice was as it had been.

Carlo moaned and tossed in his sleep. Moonlight flooded through the tiny individual panes of glass which made up the huge window in his room, rendering the still-burning candles almost unnecessary. His eyelids flickered, he was dreaming, a very deep and strange dream. His little Contessa watched him with great love. She was counting the days until they were to leave for London. Adventure called her too, and besides that she felt an unnamed fear for her beloved Carlo. Still, she thought laying her head on his bare chest, they were almost there. Only a few days to his last performance, already sold out, then she would feel that they would all be safe forever. It was odd that she felt these things she reflected as sleep finally owned her. Then she succumbed happily, her dark-red hair laying in silken strands across her lover.

Carlo moved in a strange and alien world. A world which he had sensed before, but which he saw much more of now. There were none of his daily sensorial distractions to keep him rooted in what he expected to see and hear. In such dreams he could accept what he perceived and enjoy exploring it. And now he roamed in a large outside area. Ah! He realised quickly, an amphitheatre! The feel of the air told him he was close to his 'little sister.' It was the way it was 'charged' with those little blue lights he kept seeing everywhere that told him that he had most definitely stumbled once more into the world of the 'sweet voice' who had first spoken to him so comfortingly in the gardens of the palazzo. She had calmed his troubled spirit and that had helped to keep his mind clear and bring him to the decision which he believed would change his life.

He heard music in his dream, and such music! It had a depth and a breadth that he had never experienced. The size of the orchestra alone was breathtaking, add to that the sophistication of the sound they produced, and Carlo was spell-bound. But the voices, even amongst his friends in the 'Great Untrained,' he had not heard the like, This wonderful naturalness had been taken and trained, he even recognised some of that training, or at least an extension of it.

Since his very first encounter with Matilda, Carlo had been aware of, and secretly enjoyed his few experiences in the 'dream realm.' He had mentioned her to no-one, not even to his adored little Contessa, whose superb heart-shape face would most prob-ably have crumpled into jealousy-fuelled terror. Maybe because of his self-imposed silence Carlo never questioned why these things happened. But we well might. What did Carlo have to offer to the 'Western Gate?'

Often, as he grew conscious in his sleep, he heard the Cardi-nal's words in his mind.

"Be careful Carlo, lest men use you for your pity."

But Carlo did not pity. Carlo understood, and had compas-sion. For someone of his time he had a vastly extended con-sciousness. Rather like Irena, he sensed without words his need to be where he now found himself. He knew when the time came, he would know what, if anything, he must do.

In his fluid state he had wandered back stage. Two figures sped towards his awareness with such velocity, that he awoke with a start, the names of Raimondo and Lucciano were on his lips as he pulled himself back to the present. There was a delicate weight on his chest, which moved gracefully onto the pillow as he became completely conscious. Carlo slipped from the bed, pulled a deep lilac wrap around himself and poured some wine into a crystal goblet. Quietly, he sank into a chair. It was not strange that he should dream of his friends, that he should see them in unfamiliar surroundings after what they had all been through over the last few weeks. Jealousy, love, lust and insecu-rity, was there no end to it? And where he had just been in his dream, did they suffer from these things, even with such music?

It had been on a sudden whim, an extra little surge of en-ergy that blotted out the reasoning part of his mind, which had caused him to invite Lucciano into the room which he still kept at the Palazzo that fateful afternoon. And yet he knew that Raimondo had seen them leave the rehearsal together as the heat of the day began to crescendo. He felt his eyes on them, until they disappeared out of the quadrangle into the cool of the darkened passageways. The warning was there, he simply ignored it, and he knew that Raimondo would be on their heels. And yet, when he turned to bid 'addio' to Lucciano, the young man had looked so haunted with desire, and at that precise moment a gentle little breeze had embraced them both, and on a surge of passion he had pulled the moaning Lucciano into the room, and into his arms. When some time later Raimondo had put his head round the door with a familiarity which he was confident that he owned, his broad boyish grin had crumpled into a grotesque mask of cold fury. Carlo and Lucciano were asleep, but there was no mistaking what had taken place.

What a madness! How could he have been so careless as to allow such hurt to his friends? And, as if that wasn't enough, there followed problems with his own singing. Problems which first sprung directly from that one little lapse, and then proceeded to turn the tide of his life, or it would do soon. There was a slight movement from deep within the many pillows in the bed.

"Come back to bed, Carlo mio."

At the sudden sound of her voice, Carlo instinctively pulled the wrap closer around himself and then smiled at his foolishness. It was a reflex that he had never been able to tame. A belated attempt at protecting himself. He raised the glass with the unspoken question, did she want some? A slow seductive smile crossed her lovely tiny heart-shaped face. She deliberately shook her head, and pointed a beautiful finger at him. He laughed with delight, as she made her intention perfectly clear. He returned to bed and allowed her to pull his dark head into her breasts. Between the perfection was her heart, and behind his closed eyes, Carlo saw the glorious emerald-green shining there, full of sparkling energy which opened like a flower with pure, unconditional love. Content and relaxed again in her embrace, he was soon asleep once more, and found himself back in the same dream.

It seemed there was much confusion going on. To start with it made it hard for him to focus, and then he noticed Matilda talking animatedly to a dark haired man, whose energy Carlo recognised, but couldn't place. Giorgio had sent Tony and Bella back to the side entrance, and bad them take their seats once more. Meanwhile, he had taken Irena to a small door which opened into a strange round little room, and above which, the dark night was clearly visible. It was a room directly beneath the unusual chimney like structure which sat in the middle of, at the back of, and immediately above the stage.

"You sing from here Irena. You can see the conductor easily, look!"

As Irena leant forward she could easily make out Biagioni's form through a square, gauzed area, where the stones had been removed. Giorgio had certainly thought of everything.

"Your voice will carry incredibly well from here. It will sound as it you're singing in some cathedral. Toi, toi Irena, and many thanks." And Giorgio planted a quick kiss on each cheek, and turned to go. Irena stopped him.

"Giorgio! What do I do if she keeps singing? I mean, if I'm singing, I won't even know!" "She'll stop." Exclaimed Giorgio.

"She must be desperate for someone to do something! We can sort out any problems in the interval. O.K?"

"O.K. Giorgio!" Irena smiled at him and he left. She sat down on a chair to one side of the gauzed opening. 'Now where?' She thought. 'Was Dante?'

Dante waited until he saw Giorgio rush back from placing Irena, and then emerged from the shadows, and hurried over to Matilda. Irena had arrived the night before at Giorgio's invitation, and after dinner she had asked Dante for a tour of the grounds. He had agreed, but explained to her that he hadn't been there long, knew little of them and maybe he wasn't the best person to ask. She had answered him in perfect Italian, and then had led him out into the dark and just far enough away from the house in order to speak in some privacy to him.

"Funny time to view the grounds." Giorgio observed to Matilda, as they sat in the empty restaurant checking over the last details. She glanced up at the two, as they slipped out into the moonlit night, and grinned at Giorgio.

"Oh two more vampires Giorgio? They'll be a whole of gang of us soon." She joked. Giorgio had not answered, and barely acknowledged her comment. He felt uncomfortable, but didn't know why, and he was far too busy to persue the thought.

Dante listened to Irena's strange diatribe, appreciated her mature beauty, and thought her a little mad at first. But, as he recognised her obvious loyalty to Matilda, and as he looked at her, and registered the gentle eyes and radiant smile, standing there in the moonlight he could also feel what Irena called...'Something in the air.' They had come to an understanding Irena and Dante.

He dropped happily into bed with his beloved Matilda and gave it little more thought, but Irena slept very much sounder knowing that should it become necessary, she would have a strong ally in Dante. The strongest one could have, seeing that he carried the pure flame of a strong and sincere love in his heart, and an equally strong passion, uh… everywhere else really.

That meeting flashed through his mind as he slipped up to Matilda and touched her gently on her arm. Carlo, tossed in his sleep. 'What on earth was going on?'

Matilda glanced up from the score. She was set now until the end of the big ensemble, and could relax a little.

"Dante! What's going on?" She whispered. Then, as Dante gently removed the score from the desk in front of her, she added. "What are you doing?"

"Your job cara. De soprano, she is dead."

"Dead?" Matilda exclaimed.

"Si, well de voice she isa dead! I can do dis. You musta go to Irena, quickly cara."

"Irena? What are you talking about? Where is she?"

"She's in data funny little room data sticka up in de place upastairs. You know it?"

"Yes, I know it." Matilda replied. As stage manager, she had been shown every back stage facility in case of some emergency or need. She looked hard at Dante, but he simply smiled and said with some urgency.

"Go! She 'asa somedin' toa say to you!" Matilda obviously couldn't quite take this in, she hedged a little more. "But…Giorgio?" This was the moment Dante had been dreading, he had to lie to her, there was no time for long discussion, he avoided her violet eyes, pretended to study the score and said. "Giorgio knows what isa 'appened, now go!"

Without another word, Matilda slipped from the stool and hurried away in the direction of the room where Irena was waiting. Dante prayed that Giorgio was well out of sight, and hoped that he could do this job he had so blithely agreed to do. Well, he told himself, he had written enough books about the backstage 'mechanics 'of opera. He had watched enough times as stage managers and their assistants had called singers, and cued lights, fiddling with this switch and that lever, and of course he could follow a score.

"Grazie a Dio that I no write de fiction." He muttered to himself grimly.

Giorgio had taken his place around the corner, out of sight of the audience, but as close as possible to the open stage area. He wanted to hear how Irena sounded. And Carlo followed Matilda.

A warning light on Maestro Biagioni's stand flashed. He hardly needed it to. After all no one was more aware than he was that Laura was in dire straits which worsened by the minute. What was going on back stage, he had no idea, but at least someone was attempting to do something, hence the light to warn him to expect anything!

"Dio!" He thought. "She barely gets there by pushing, poor lady. What happens when we hit the first pianissimo?"

He put his head down and caught the leader's eye. The violinist, a young and talented player on loan from The Netherlands, raised his eyebrows, and Ricardo answered with a shrug of his shoulders.

"Ritorna Vincitor!" Sang Pixie as Amneris.

"Ritorna Vincitor!" Repeated the Chorus.

"Here we go." Muttered Ricardo to himself in Italian. He glanced at the stage. The soprano looked as if she were about to be crucified.

"Gran Dio!" He muttered again.

Matilda opened the door to the small round room.

"Irena what's going on?" She half whispered, only too aware of just how resonant that little stone built place was. Giorgio had demonstrated the effect to her more than once over the last few weeks, as they had tried to use the room to make the effect of the High Priestess and the ladies chorus singing from the depths of the temple. But since they couldn't all squeeze in there, however hard they tried, they had to give up on the idea.

"Our Aida is in big trouble." Said Irena, not without some compassion in her voice.

"Yes...But... I still don't...Where's Giorgio?"

"As far out front as he can get, I imagine. He wants to hear how you come across from here. Now, if needs be he'll make some changes and an announcement in the interval. Well..." She added as Matilda was staring at her..."You do know it, don't you?"

Matilda nodded. To be honest that was the least of her worries.

"But where do I start? Are you sure about this? I mean Giorgio didn't say a word to me. He didn't even come anywhere near me. And what about poor ol' Laura, won't she wonder what's happening if I suddenly start to sing?"

Irena smoothly glazed over all Matilda's questions by replying only to the last one.

"Poor ol' Laura sounds as if she's begging for mercy out there! She'd be delighted if a choir boy took over, never mind you! She's heading straight for total laryngitis, any moment the voice will give up completely. Start at the top of the aria, you can see Biagioni from here." She pointed to the gauze, and Matilda moved towards it.

"Just sing as I've taught you Matilda. You don't have to push, your voice will pour out of here like so much honey. I'll be outside so you have space to breathe. You only have the aria before the interval. You can relax and think about Act 2 during the last scene, I'll get you a score and some water in here."

And Irena gently closed the door behind her believing that she had left Matilda completely alone. Of course she hadn't, for Carlo was there.

The orchestra picked up the tempo and played the final bars of the scene as everyone except Aida left the stage. Biagioni prayed to God, Irena crossed her fingers, and Giorgio, most uncharacteristically took hold of Verity's hand and held it tight, muttering.

"Come on Irena, don't let me down!"

Irena, of course would not have let him down, but then, neither did Matilda. Carlo tossed again in his sleep as she attacked the first phrase of the aria. He loved this music, it was fantastic, huge, and he couldn't imagine what it would feel like to sing and perform it, and his little sister managed to maintain as much sweetness in her sound when she sang as when she had first spoken to him, Carlo was entranced.

Riccardo was deeply thankful, and the on-stage soprano was so relieved that for a couple of bars, she forgot to mime.

Matilda sang exquisitely. The end of the aria was a masterpiece of technical control. The audience was completely engrossed with this sound coming, as it did, from some secret place. There was a gentle roar, entwined with the applause. An unspoken statement of deep approval. The action moved on. Dante managed to cue the correct lights and the glorious Consecration scene began. Somewhere in the middle of the scene there was a section of dance which, given that the female dancers wore very little, cheered Martin up no end as he sat in the same chair the other side of the 'prompt corner' still out of sight, and rather fed up and bored. He knew some of the dancers personally, and therefore was certain of a 'refuge' in the interval, certain that he could pass it well hidden by this flock of exotic birds. He leant forward. There was no sign of Giorgio. And where was Matilda? He could just make out the top of a dark head bent closely over the desk, but he got the strange impression that it wasn't her. And who had been singing? It had come from that odd little place out the back, it had a good acoustic, but it was almost impossible to recognise the voice spiralling out of the depths.

Contact

In the interval, Verity joined Giorgio, and was quick to inform him that whoever was now singing Aida pleased her very much more than Laura whatever-her-name-is.

"Who is it?" She asked, as Giorgio picked up two glasses of wine from a tray held towards him by one of the 'silver service' waiters he had hired for the evening.

"It's Irena." Giorgio confided. "Now, I must decide whether or not to make an announcement before the second half, or at the end. I think I'll wait 'till the end. Don't want to destroy the magic, do we?"

He grabbed Verity and kissed her on her neck. And he was so relieved that the performance had been saved, that he didn't give her next comment a second thought. "Irena?" She said. "That's funny, sounded like Matilda to me!"

"Do you really think that I don't recognise Matilda's voice when I hear it my little vixen?" And laughing, he hurried on ahead of her to greet an old friend.

"No I don't think you do. Not when it's coming out of a chimney anyway." Muttered Verity. "Because that most definitely, was Matilda!"

Carlo had sat entranced throughout Matilda's aria, 'Ritorna Vincitor' and although she was not involved in the Consecration scene which followed, he remained deeply engrossed in the music, finding it fabulously powerful. The full harmony of the male chorus had completely taken him by surprise. Nothing in his own time could have prepared him for such a sound. Never would he have dreamt that such harmonies were possible, and then to add a whole chorus of female voices and a soprano solo in the guise of the High Priestess above them! Why it was sheer genius, and the musical result came so much closer to the God who Carlo revered and loved, than all the bungling priests who ruled their lives.

He found himself humming part of the melody in his mind. In his bed he hummed in his sleep, but his little Contessa, off in her own dream, did not hear him, and Carlo remained in a deep restful sleep which allowed him to continue his adventure.

As he watched his 'little sister' she sipped some water which Irena had brought her, and studied her score, pulling down the pashmina which she had thrown around her shoulders and neck earlier in the cooling evening. Half of it swung to one side, and there, lying across the collar bone and glinting in the carefully concealed light was the emerald amulet which Carlo had last seen around Angelo's neck in his villa that night when they had discussed such strange things. Even in his dream, Carlo felt dizzy. All these points of time and realisation merging into a present which was in the dream dimension? He couldn't really understand it all, but what he did understand suddenly and with great clarity was that he must not wake up until this performance was over.

The audience began to return to their seats still carrying wine glasses and obviously enjoying the evening, especially since the indisposed soprano had been so well replaced. Giorgio had been gratified to hear more than one snippet from a passing member of the public..... "My dear this could become another Glynde-bourne...." "Well actually I think it's better. I mean when the weather permits there's this fabulous amphi' for a start...." And so on. He knew that he really should have a word with Irena, but she was managing beautifully, and he was enjoying the congratulations that people were showering on him, despite the fact that the evening was only half way through. No, he'd leave well alone. In true Giorgio fashion, he was not going to be at all emotional over the fact the he was grateful to Irena for helping him out like this, and at such short notice. It would be difficult to get any shorter in fact. And he avoided the question in his mind as to whether or not he would have pulled the plug on the whole proceedings if Irena had refused to sing. Tony London and Bella came into his eye line.

"Congratulations Giorgio, it's all really flying now." Tony shook his friend enthusiastically by the hand. While Bella said quietly. "Yes, Giorgio. Congratulations." "Why thank you my dear. " Giorgio turned and took her hand, a hand that she had not exactly extended and added.

"Don't I deserve a kiss?" Bella smiled wanly at him, and offered a cheek.

"Come, come darling, so English! Maybe that's what holds you back in your singing. I said a kiss, not a brush of the cheek."

And he took hold of her by the shoulders and planted a kiss firmly on her mouth, just as Verity, unseen by any of them was making her way towards Giorgio, She slipped back into the crowd, which was becoming smaller as more people returned for the second half. She was furious, but decided not to make a scene. Too much of her own work was wrapped up in this project. Hard work, over many weeks. She simply tucked what she had observed into a place in her mind and waited for Giorgio to look around for her, pretending to catch his eye as he did so.

"Verity, do me a favour will you? Pop up to Irena and find out if everything is alright? Tell her I'll make the appropriate announcement at the end of the evening."

And he turned back to Bella and Tony as if Verity was no more than an administrative minion. She fumed inside and strode backstage with the neat speed of anger. Dante, suddenly aware of, as he jokingly put it later, a tiny Gerhilde striding in true Wagnerian fashion to join the rest of the Valkyries, had no time, and wouldn't have dared to try, to warn Irena. Verity, having barely knocked, threw open the door, and found Matilda and Irena engrossed over the score in such a way as to leave no doubt as to who had been doing the singing. Matilda held half a glass of water in her hand and her pashmina lay across the chair near to the gauzed window.

"So it is you!" She said triumphantly. "I told Giorgio it was!" And her eye caught the emerald amulet as it flashed its brilliance from Matilda's throat.

"Verity my dear..." Irena began. But Verity's quick mind had already grasped the whole situation. "Oh don't worry!" She laughed. "He won't hear anything from me, not until afterwards anyway. And then I want to be the one to tell him." She added, not leaving any doubt from her tone of voice that this was part of the price of her silence. Then without bothering to say more, she turned and stormed out again. As she came close to Dante she paused, and with an audacity that only people such as Verity possess, said to him.

"Don't you worry my lord, your secret is safe with me. Giorgio deserves everything he gets. It'll do him good to be taken down a peg or two." And she moved closer to him, too close for Dante's comfort, and he averted his eyes and began shuffling the papers, and studying the score in front of him.

"You know what you are doing, do you darling?" Dante moved slightly away from her.

"Si!" He replied shortly, not offering an opening for any sort of conversation. She turned to go and then stopped and turned back to look at him.

"By the way Dante, do you have any more if those gorgeous little necklaces lying around at home that you don't need? Matilda can hardly wear more than one at a time, now can she?" She smiled at him with the confidence of the effect that her charms usually had. Dante studied her warily, and answered her coolly.

"No Verity. Dey nota lyin' arounda anywhere!" Verity's smile widened as she replied. "Being a good boy are we? Well we'll see. There's not a man alive who can resist a quick fling, whatever they may say. And you my beautiful Italian lord, are absolutely no different."

Dante didn't answer, and she continued, leaning towards him "In my experience….." "Whicha is so vast I ama sure my dear Verity, thata I 'ave no wish to become part of it. Please to excuse I ama very busy. You understand?" And his dark eyes bore into her with full meaning. Verity raised her exquisitely arched eyebrows slightly, pushed herself away from the desk watching Dante all the while, and drew in a slow deep breath. Then she whispered. "Pity" And shrugged. She didn't really care, old violet eyes obviously had this one under her little thumb for the moment. But she had sensed a real animosity between Dante and Giorgio, and given how he had just treated her, there would have been an extra justice in having a quick romp in the hay with his fellow Italian. But the little secret she held was even sweeter that an hour with this man would be, or certainly as sweet, and with one last inviting glance, which Dante ignored, she turned away again. She did like that necklace though!

"What did she mean?" Matilda asked Irena.

"My dear, please don't ask questions, just sing. I will explain afterwards, I promise. The show, as they say, must go on. Yes?"

Dante had slipped into the room to warn them of the five minute call.

"Yes of course…" Matilda began.

"Sing!" Said Irena. "Sing cara!" Dante added, dropping a kiss on her forehead.

"Si, little sister…Canti!" Smiled Carlo from his beautiful dream.

It was almost dark. Riccardo took his place on the podium and as the applause subsided a large owl flew silently across the auditorium towards the open meadows in search of his first meal of the night. There was a strangely expectant air hanging over everything. It joined everyone present together in some magic invisible web. There was a sweet tension in the air, a yearning towards a release as deep and as gentle as a lover's need.

Matilda prepared herself and Dante focused his concentration on the prompt score. Verity sat down next to Giorgio still in his small alcove backstage, but hidden from view.

"What's up with you?" He observed her closely. "You look like the cat..." "That got the cream?" She interrupted." I did, what's more I still have it!"

Giorgio felt a slight quiver of concern in the depth of his gut. But the second act had started and the ladies chorus began their canon-like singing in Amneris's apartments. Pixie, looking suitably sumptuous, lay prone on a couch, observing herself in a mirror. She had the kind of looks and stature which became positively magnificent on stage. In his delight at the way the scene appeared, Giorgio forgot the quiver, and sank into Verdi.

The little Contessa Domenica, had woken up. She ached for Carlo's company. The dream that she had just been jolted out of was not as pleasant as it might have been, and it left her with an unnamed worry in her head. She put out her exquisite little hand towards Carlo, then hesitated. He looked so peaceful, he was barely breathing. In the candle light he could have been mistaken for some stray Greek god from another century, resting before his journey home. No, she wouldn't wake him, and she slipped quietly from the bed, to take some wine, and to ponder whether, if she really begged him, would he forgo his last performance in Venice?

Martin had taken refuge in the ballet girls dressing room during the interval, and he should have been feeling pretty good by now. But for some unaccountable reason he had a strong desire to go home. His head had begun to ache, and he had the strangest impression of a vibration, unheard, but felt very strongly, by him anyway. He glanced around at everybody else, they seemed to be completely oblivious to it.

He rather wished that Connie had come. He actually missed her! She was adamant that she was not going to be around Giorgio, adding: "Especially at the moment!"

"And why especially at the moment?" He had snapped, rather destroying any possibility of her changing her mind. She had not answered immediately, and he paused in the process of fastening his black tie.

He had left Villa Giorgio when Francesco arrived. Gareth, the baritone, had shaken his hand with a gusto that always seems to belong to those born with that type of voice, and thanked him for standing in during the rehearsals.

"Good old Martin." He had said, not without genuine affection, but also with total unawareness of Martin's true state of mind regarding the whole thing. Pixie had been standing nearby and had related to Matilda that… "Good old Martin looked as if he was ready to dismantle Gareth bone by bone as slowly as possible. But the friendly tank," (An affectionate name that the girls had quietly christened him) "hadn't appeared to notice."

So the evening of the 21st, found Martin preparing to drive down for the show. He looked questioningly at his wife. But she only shrugged and moved away from him, into the kitchen. A few minutes later he had called. "Bye Con, see you later." And had left for Surrey.

"Doesn't she look great?" Giorgio whispered to Verity.

"If you say so." She replied coolly.

"Now, now Verity. Can't you cage that little green god of yours, just for a while?"

"Nothing to do with that." Verity hissed back at him. "I told you after the 'dress,' if your Majesty remembers, that she's not wearing enough jewellery."

Giorgio made a sign of impatience and Verity continued rapidly. "She's not! She's supposed to be an Egyptian princess for God's sake! She should have borrowed that thing from Matilda, that would have been perfect. Hey! She can still put it on for the Triumphal scene."

"My beautiful harpy." Giorgio began. "Exactly what 'thing' are you talking about."

"Dante must have given it to her. I can't imagine anyone else having enough money to buy a thing like that. You should see it Giorgio, it's simply gorgeous, fabulous. I bet it's a real emerald, and it's huge…"

Giorgio had suddenly stood up and hurried in the direction of the backstage area. Verity raised her eyebrows and muttered to herself. "Well what do you know? God finally listened." And sat back to enjoy the rest of the performance.

"Where is she?" Giorgio's voice cut across Dante's intense concentration, he was busy with lighting cues, and for a moment didn't reply. Giorgio could see he really was involved and would have waited patiently, but the austere face of Chu-Pen floated in his mind and wouldn't let him rest a moment. "I said where is she?"

"Scusi?" Dante always spoke in Italian to Giorgio unless there were other people present. But for some reason he kept to English now. Somehow he was convinced he could keep calmer if he had to think a bit before he spoke, and it was important that he kept his temper under control. The two men just about managed to tolerate each other. When Dante had arrived and Matilda first introduced them, Giorgio had recognised him instantly, as Angelo. Where he might have fitted into Atlantis, he didn't know. Giorgio was uncomfortable with so much from the past rising up in front of him all at once. There was another presence also, it had haunted the edges of his mind all evening. He felt more than a little threatened.

"Matilda. Where the fuck is she?"

"Please to leta me givea nexta cue Giorgio."

Giorgio placed his hand over Dante's and spat at him. "To hell with the lightening cues. Where is your little mistress, and why hasn't she got her arse on the line here. That's what I'm paying her for."

Dante, with great difficulty, suppressed the violent need to punch Giorgio somewhere on his handsome and at the moment, diabolical face. He looked as innocent as possible and replied.

"She's 'ow you say…. sick! Si she isa sick, she nota feel so good. Donta worry I can do.!"

"I'll bet you can." Giorgio barely concealed his contempt.

The duet had now finished. Pixie left the stage and Aida sang the concluding few bars with different words to the same music which ends the aria. Giorgio froze, he was now in a different position, and the sound which flowed out into the night air from the room at the back of the stage presented itself to him in a more distinct manner. But it was much more than that. Giorgio was back in the Great Hall. There was a young lad, a shepherd boy standing in front of the Great Anthorus. He accompanied himself on a small hand held harp and he was singing. As Giorgio watched, he felt the two singers and the two vastly different pieces of music merge. And spiralling out of that merger was the pearly translucent harmonic. It was almost audible to Giorgio and he realised that the 'plague' was about to be released. "Matilda!" He exclaimed, and he turned on his heel and sped off towards the hidden room.

Dante was frantic, but he couldn't leave the prompt corner. The most dramatic changes in lighting of the evening, were about to happen. He had to concentrate on the complicated cues. "Matilda bea strong!" He muttered as the trumpets sounded the beginning of the Triumphal march, and the chorus began to jostle against each other to get on to the stage.

"Hurry up…" "Don't push me…" "You're on my bloody costume…" "Pick it up then, don't you know anything?…" There's loads of time you know…"

Giorgio ran past them and roughly pushed Irena who stood up as he approached, out of the way, Her…"Giorgio, please!" Was completely lost on him, and he flung open the door. Matilda was standing, watching the conductor through the little gauze window. As he entered, she turned in surprise. Still uncertain of who knew what and who wasn't being told, she smiled at him and opened her mouth to speak. The emerald flashed on her throat, which still showed itself a soft beige from the Spanish sun. Giorgio hesitated, staring at her. Then he moved slowly towards her. Irena had followed him into the room. "Remember that she has to sing Giorgio!" He didn't turn to acknowledge her, but still stared at Matilda as he said.

"And very well she's doing too!" He replied. Matilda relaxed slightly, and in that second, Giorgio's hand flew to her throat, grabbed the emerald and wrenched it from her. She cried out, and put her hand to her neck where blood was already piercing the skin. "Presumably she can sing without the help of this?" He snarled, and turned to leave. Irena blocked his way.

Deep in the Verdian score, the first part of the digital mantra clicked into place. Beneath the risen moon, the stage glowed with vivid golden Egyptian light, and the audience became immersed in an exhilarated relaxation. Around the perimeter of the Amphitheatre, and invisible to everyone there, the creatures of the night, having sensed the vibration as it began to gather strength, huddled together, and surveyed the scene with wild eyes and astonished ears. The singing stopped and the dance began. Giorgio moved towards Irena, visions of Christmas rose into Matilda's mind and she was horrified.

"Be careful Irena!" She whispered. "You think about your singing!" Irena replied, not a little sharply. Then she said. "Give it to me Giorgio." She spoke with a deep authority which echoed, Giorgio knew from another lifetime.

The dance had finished and to the rousing chorus, Radames entered at the head of his triumphal troops with the Ethiopian prisoners behind them. Matilda turned back to the window, she had a cue coming up very soon. As she calmed her breath, very necessary in the light of the atmosphere in the small space, she heard Giorgio snarl at Irena.

"Out of my way you old witch. You're not the grand high Priestess of Aum now you know!"

"Give me the amulet." And she took a step towards him. On the stage, Gareth in the guise of Aida's father, Amonasro, was about to open his mouth for the first time that evening. He moved from out of the crowd of prisoners, and Matilda sang. "Mio Padre!"

Giorgio gasped, the tone echoed around the small brick room, and his head spun. The amulet in his hand began to hum, vibrating as it did so, and he glanced down at it involuntarily. Suddenly it was very warm.

Aida and her people begged the Pharaoh for mercy, and the Priests advised him not to listen. The second part of the digital mantra was in place and the sound rising from Matilda's voice suddenly seemed, to every member of the spell-bound audience as if she were standing right next to them, but as if the singing were reaching them from a great domed distance at the same time. Matilda was aware that something was happening, but her instinct overrode any fears she may have had, and she found herself leaning into the resonance with her whole body, and under the unaccustomed energy surge her legs began to tremble slightly.

On stage, Laura, miming her head off, glanced at Francesco who, she realised was having the hardest time not to turn his head in the direction of Matilda's voice. Pixie found herself turning up stage very slightly, her eyes straining to the side. What the hell was going on? As she registered different faces on stage, she knew that they were all aware of the same thing. Everyone fought to stay centred to the front, but when they did so, they were faced with the perplexed look on Maestro Biagioni's face! The only thing he was certain of was that this sound winding its way from the little structure in front of him, was not even in part, the work of any sort of electronic device.

Carlo, however, was so entranced with the music that he spent no time analysing any individual sound. Unable to stop himself he was pulled to the side of the stage where he closed his eyes and allowed the sound to crash over him like a magnificent ocean.

As he began to recognise the returning tune of the main chorus line he started to hum, quietly at first, then as his confidence grew he began to sing.

The amulet in Giorgio's hand was becoming warmer. The third section clicked into place and waited as it had done numerous times before. Verdi's score pulled everything together for the final expression of triumph. As it did so, the digital mantra deep in the music shuddered, and with a final, relieved sigh, it slipped into its place and now waited only for the release of the part of the frequency from the amulet. The amulet which Giorgio still had grasped in his hand as he pushed Irena once more out of the way.

The finale was coming closer. Eight, heavy and slower chords focused everyone, and the stage breathed as if it were an animal ready to pounce. The chorus launched for the final time into "Gloria del Egito." while the soloists wove their own thoughts and feelings around the central theme and the soprano and the tenor standing at opposite sides of the stage, poured out their passionate duet above it all. Instantly the separated part of the frequency released from the crystal.

At first it affected only Matilda's voice, she having been part way there all ready. But as Chu-Pen had warned, once released it spread like wild fire.

"Things such as this know no time." He had hissed at Giorgio. "Things like this make their own rules. They obey a greater power than you can even imagine."

And so suddenly, as if Matilda was the cue, every voice on the stage, regardless of type, quality or any other consideration, took on the overtone. Defying the laws of accepted physics and apparent laryngeal constraints and limitations, began to sound the octave both above and below of the sung pitch. It was subtle and yet powerfully definite. No one would have denied it, and yet no one would have tried to analyse exactly what it was. As the digital mantra dug deeper and deeper into the consciousness, time exploded, which created an emotional recognition that would normally have taken years to achieve.

Biagioni stared at the stage, he felt as if he were trying to control a thousand wild horses as they flew through the night sky. His first instinct (Even with his Italian blood at boiling point) was to pull back. This was quietly removed, and the incredible freedom which flew through him was unlike anything he had experienced. And he knew without turning his head, that half the audience had risen to their feet, barely aware that they did so.

Martin stood up and made his way to the side of the staged area. Verity was standing there unable to speak, and with tears pouring down her face. On stage Laura's voice suddenly returned and somewhere amongst all this Giorgio had fallen to his knees as the crystal burnt fiery green and bit deep into his hand. He dropped it and clasped the wound, the pain from which had him on the verge of fainting. Irena had followed him and she stood over him.

"Are you coming with us Giorgio?" She asked him, as he held the seared hand towards her, biting back a groan. She knelt down next to him and laid her own hand gently over the terrible burn. Within seconds the pain began to subside and as he sobbed a sigh of relief, she added. "Oh yes, I can see that you probably are."

The Western gate swung open, and unable to do anything else, the Eastern gate slipped from Chu-Pen's grasp and opened also. Deep in the heart of the Surrey countryside, the final chords echoed…

"What IS that?…Oh don't close the window, I want to listen!"

"I wasn't going to. I want to hear it too!"

There were several seconds of total silence in the Amphitheatre. Then a spontaneous 'roar' spread like silken honey, round and round. The performers stood still and faced the audience. Not one soloist felt the inclination to bow singly in the usual manner. Instead, quite without any sign, or whispered instruction, the entire stage, orchestra and Biagioni bowed together in perfect symmetry.

Then the spell was broken. The stage shook themselves, and as

Dante, who had been as mesmerised as everyone else, and haunted by visions of two young men sitting in his Father's library, talking about a 'plague,' finally remembered to 'kill' the lights, the singers quietly made their way back to the dressing rooms.

"Matilda!" Dante called as he hurried towards the room, bursting with excitement and as proud of her as he could be. The audience were by now a little more talkative:

"What a sound! Have you ever heard anything like it?"

"No, I haven't. Remarkable effect…Most Odd…Hmm.. It's no good I can't explain it. Don't really know if I want to."

"How did they do that pyramid effect?"

"Oh it was there then, I though I'd dreamt it?"

"Definitely not I saw it, in the last few bars, and just when you thought nothing else could happen, there it was stretching to every corner of the stage, and across the pit!"

"Must have been a holograph of some sort!"

"I suppose so…"

Out of the corner of his eye Dante noticed Giorgio sitting on a chair as Verity knelt by him. They were both still and silent. 'That's a first then!' He thought as he raced passed calling out to Matilda once more.

Carlo awoke in Venice, the whole experience spun into his spirit like gold, to be dusted through his own last performance in a few nights.

And Matilda? As Dante entered the small room, she was lying in a crumpled heap beneath the little gauze window. He couldn't find a pulse, and she appeared to be dead.

An End –
A Beginning

Matilda lost consciousness for barely a few moments. Where she found herself was instantly familiar emotionally, although the surroundings were new, The old man was there, looking younger than ever. He pulled her into his arms and let her rest against his great bear-like body.

'Why did she feel so tired?' She wondered. She never remembered feeling her dream body so heavy in this way before. The old man spoke most gently to her.

"Do you understand what's happened?" To which Matilda shook her head, then paused.

"Well, I'm not sure. No, not really." She admitted into the massive chest.

"I mean am I dreaming, or..?" She left the question unanswered and stood up, releasing herself from the bear-hug. Her eyes followed the violet mist as it curled itself across the ever-beautiful turquoise lake and wrapped itself around the willow tree. Looking at such beauty she found the strength to finish her question…"Or am I dead? After all that has happened, am I now forced to stay here? Beautiful as it is, I want to see what happens there. I want to be with Dante. I suppose the powers that be, have made up their minds." She added with uncharacteristic bitterness,

The old man swung her round to face him and held her at arms' length. He had lost another decade.

"Matilda, you have done me a great service, and helped me right a terrible wrong. So believe me when I assure you, that it's not quite like that."

His voice pulsed in and out of her awareness, and she leaned towards him again.

"I feel as if I'm going to pass out. How can that happen here?"

"You've had dreams where you've 'passed out' into other dreams, haven't you? These things don't only happen when you're connected to the earth plane, you know. But you need to rest Matilda…Come…"

Matilda looked at him with concentrated gaze and replied.

"Yes, I understand, but just one thing first, because I don't want to forget to ask you. And I feel in real danger of forgetting a lot of things for some reason. Can you tell me, was I Carlo, or did I poison him? I need to know the truth."

The old man smiled at the idea of lying. Then he sighed like someone who finds it necessary to explain a complicated scientific formula to a very young, bright child.

"You were and are Carlo. You did not kill him in Venice. But long before that time, in your reckoning, you were a singer in another life. This was someone who you have not been aware of as you have become aware of Carlo. There is something much more important at stake Matilda. There was something else you had to do."

"And have I done it? So now must I die?" Matilda asked him. He smiled at her.

"Just for the moment, I want you to stop thinking about that, or anything else for that matter. What I will tell you is that Carlo's experience in Venice as the great castrato that he was, was indeed your experience. You lived in that body and went through his life with its feelings, passions, ambitions and fears. You chose that neurological network, and the physicality it gave birth to. Also the time, place, and social expression. All this you chose with the express intention of experiencing. In so far as I can say it, yes, you were Carlo...Now..."

"What is 'appen?" The tears stood out in Dante's eyes. "Pleasa to tell me Signor Dottore." He begged, as the consultant neurologist looked at him gravely.

"I can't say that things look good, Signor Vittoria. But there is a faint pulse. She is in a deep coma. As to exactly what has happened to her, and what is wrong precisely, I'm afraid I can't say. It is never easy in cases such as this. But we will, of course do everything we can, I suggest you go home and get some sleep."

"Non e posso. I stay." Dante replied. The consultant sighed deeply. He didn't think that Matilda had a chance, and he would much rather that this young man, obviously so deeply in love with her, wasn't around for what he was certain was her impending death. But he said simply.

"As you wish. I will be back to see her tomorrow. You can sit with her if you would like to. It certainly can do her no harm."

"Grazie Signor. Mille grazie."

They were in a great hall. It was a huge amphitheatre which stretched for ever in every direction. Matilda could see no end to it. It seemed to be constructed out ot the ground rather than on it. The perfect architecture shone in marble which shimmered with a different colour directly affected by the chanting. There was a single note, from which the overtones of their own accord filled the air like exotic perfume. It was sound in colour, texture and form beyond anything Matilda had ever experienced, and she longed to join it.

"This…This is what I have had glimpses of when I have been singing. Nothing as consistent as this, but not unlike it nevertheless. The sound I was making took on a texture…a colour…And then during the performance…It was stronger, so strong, and then from everyone, it was wonderful…"

And she moved towards the sound of the humming, but the old man stopped her.

"I understand how exciting it all is, but I want you to relax, just for a while."

What he really wanted, was to make the circumstances such that she might heal herself. That her shattered nervous system might yet rearrange itself from the patterns in the newly awoken strands of D.N.A. He moved her away to a fresh water side. The sky in the distance was orange and violet, the two colours as distinct as if a line had been drawn between them with a ruler. Matilda found herself sitting under a tree, facing the bluebell coloured water. She sat cross-legged like a yogi. Suddenly she recognised her surroundings.

"I've dreamt this." She said.

"Yes?" He encouraged her. Matilda frowned with concentration, after a while she found the words.

"Am I forming the dream now?" She asked him. "Yes!" He replied.

"But.. But I've already dreamt it."

"Exactly!" Said the old man. Matilda felt the lovely pearl of wisdom glow in her mind for a second, and then watched it slip away. She chased it, but she had already forgotten the clarity that had shone there just a second ago.

"I can't hold that in my mind." She admitted to him.

"Matilda." He said gently. "Don't go all linear on me again. You've just grasped the rudiments of a wider reality. You must engineer your thoughts in a different way. Don't fall back into old habits just because it slipped from your grasp. And again I say, rest!"

The last few words were whispered, and Matilda realised that he had, for the moment, left her. Somewhere behind her was a sun, and the warmth soaked continually into her back without ever becoming overly hot or uncomfortable. She leant forward and placed her fingers gently on the surface of the water. Immediately a glorious Symphony orchestra began to play. Beneath her hands was the sound of a perfection as if the most talented of the planet's musicians had congregated there.

She began to laugh. It was a tickling energy which rose from her diaphragm to the back of her throat, and rendered her helpless in a paroxysm of a laughter so true and pure, that it became greater than she was. She vibrated with the sound and it shook her free from something. Something that was old and finished. Something that was over, and that everybody else had finished with also.

A picture of a butterfly, still damp and dazed, crawling uncertainly from the remains of its chrysalis, came unbidden to her mind. And underneath it all was the eternal life-sustaining chanting.

Dante had sat all night by the hospital bed. Finally, as dawn began to lift the mantle of darkness, he dozed briefly, his head nodding with exhaustion. All this on top of the last couple of days, especially with his unrehearsed part in the Aida made him feel as if he had lived weeks in just 48hours. He heard Matilda's voice from some distant place.

"I bet you've been there all night, haven't you darling? You should have gone home and got some sleep, you must be exhausted, and I'm quite alright you know."

Dante gasped, and his eyes flew open to see Matilda sitting up in bed, smiling at him, and looking the picture of health.

"Cara pleasea to be careful! I call de Nurses…De Dottore… De Consultant."

Matilda giggled. "Not all at once Dante. Especially at this time of the morning. But what I'd really like is a bar of chocolate."

Dante stared at her in disbelief. Finally he managed to ask. "Che?"

"A chocolate bar, for some reason I'm ravenous." Dante shook his head uncertainly and replied. "You musta 'ave bump de 'ead when you fall si?....you 'avea fever, tha's what 'appen, de fever!"

"I have no fever, and no bump on de 'ead." She replied gently mimicking him. Dante got up and went and found a nurse.

The nurse didn't understand. Neither did the junior doctor, nor the consultant, nor the registrar. They were all delighted of course, but they didn't understand. They had to admit that Matilda was in perfect health, radiant in fact. And insisting on going home, which was something they argued a little about with her. But she was insistent, and 3:00 o'clock that afternoon found the nurses stripping her bed, ready for the next patient, and the registrar saying to his colleague.

"Just one of those things Charles!" As they watched Dante and Matilda leave the hospital.

"Hmm." Replied the Consultant thoughtfully, and then just as he was to carry on with his busy schedule, he stopped and said to the registrar.

"I want a full record of all her stats on my desk as soon as possible. Everything from the moment she arrived. And why didn't the machine register the fact that she had come round?"

"Apparently some power surge."

"What, just as she woke up?"

"Well must have been I suppose. But the records will show all that. What's all this about anyway Charles?"

The Consultant turned from the open door as Matilda and Dante finally disappeared at the end of the long corridor and said.

"Even given her youth and resilience, I didn't expect her to last the night. Do you know how far out of it she was? Her pulse rate was 39. But her nervous system was reacting as if she were about to be executed. I've never seen anything like it. But, given that it sorted itself, miracle number one. The fact that she's just walked out of here, having passed every test we could give her with flying colours, well that's miracle number two…"

"I didn't' think you believed in miracles Charles?"

"I don't. That's why I want everything we have on that young lady on my desk, a.s.a.p." And he strode away.

"Do you know whata you musta do?" Dante asked, not certain where the question came from. Matilda looked at him with such an open tenderness, that he felt his heart turn to liquid.

"I think it's probably done." She replied. "And now, I hope I can get on with my life."

"Wida me cara? Whatever 'appens?"

Dante stopped in front of her and held her at arms length, forcing her to look at him. Matilda had the odd sensation that something which had been hovering, made a sudden decision and sprung into exciting life. Even the dirty London streets looked brighter. The fresh autumn air caught the edge of Dante's dark hair, and she put up her hand to straighten it. Calmness descended, she felt as if they had all stepped sideways into some positive dimension which would have welcomed them ages ago if they had only recognised it. She felt the scales of control that affected everything including the private world she loved so much, dissolve in the light. For a few seconds she saw the 'being.' It swirled in her mind and she remembered the words spoken to her at Fairies Ferry that cold night, with Lucy waiting for her near the old oak, and the excitement of the forthcoming tour to Italy hovering over everything. A night that she could still hold in her hand it was so close, but which at the same time seemed centuries ago.

"You may consider yourself privileged, but not limited. The limits lay outside the music. Do you understand?"

"Yes. " She said quietly. "I really think that I do understand."

"Che, cara?" She pulled herself back to Dante and threw her arms around his neck.

"With you caro. Whatever happens."

The 'plague' rolled on, crossing continents as we might cross the street. The magnificent changes that had cost so much to bring about, were accepted almost as easily as the next breath, and before long the last 38,000 years were completely forgotten. History as we had been taught it was replaced by anther probable line, which fitted more naturally into the new present. And the history we knew so well, swiftly became myth.

END: 2003

Susanna James

ISBN 1-41205560-1

9 781412 055604